John Connolly was born in Dublin in 1968. His debut – *Every Dead Thing* – swiftly launched him right into the front rank of thriller writers, and all his subsequent novels have been *Sunday Times* bestsellers. He is the first non-American writer to win the US Shamus award. To find out more about his novels, visit John's website at www.johnconnollybooks.com

Praise for THE LOVERS:

'This is a tightly plotted, beautifully constructed novel where John Connolly exhibits his considerable skills. Possibly, one might argue, the best yet!' *CrimeSquad*

'As always, Connolly's elegant prose and story-telling gift lifts this addition to the Charlie Parker series way above the norm for this genre.' *Irish Independent*

'Connolly has penned some very fine novels over the last decade or so, but this is arguably his finest to date.' *Belfast Telegraph*

'His latest plot is a clever mixture of quest and chase . . . rarely fails to sing' *Observer*

'He (Connolly) deals in those bleak, mysterious margins of human existence where the reader's spine starts to shiver and you check the door is completely shut.' *Sunday Tribune*

'This is a more restrained and reflective Parker then we are used to, but no less powerful a character.' *The Times*

'Heroic . . . chilling . . . heartbreaking . . . gritty crime novel . . . It's not all crooks and spooks; Connolly is far too skilled a writer to create mere schlock-horror. He's at his best getting inside his characters' heads . . . Connolly's latest novel is unashamedly gothic, but ultimately manages to be believable and moving too.' *Independent*

'A complex novel and one that is deliciously ambitious in its exploration of the meanings behind big small words such as love, family, duty and blood.' *Sunday Independent*

'It's not just the completely plausible American voice of books such as this and *The Reapers* that is so impressive as the fact that he's able to work poetic language into the thriller format . . . You may think at times you are reading a literary novel but then Connolly will remind you he's just as adept at the violent strategies of the thriller. Either way you will be left shaken by the experience.' *Daily Express*

'Connolly has brilliantly created a threshold world of suggestion, fear and sleep-depriving ambiguity. He sure scared the daylights out of me.' *Irish Times*

'The supernatural element [is] the perfect complement to Parker's measured narration.' *Guardian*

'THE LOVERS informs and colours all that we think we know about him (Parker) in a thoroughly spellbinding fashion.' *Evening Herald*, Dublin

'Connolly's use of paranormal is su[illegible] powerful enough to send tingles down your spine.' *Lanc*[illegible]

Also by John Connolly

Every Dead Thing
Dark Hollow
The Killing Kind
The White Road
Bad Men
Nocturnes
The Black Angel
The Book of Lost Things
The Unquiet
The Reapers

JOHN CONNOLLY

THE LOVERS

HODDER

First published in Great Britain in 2009 by Hodder & Stoughton
An Hachette UK company

First published in paperback in 2010
1

A CIP catalogue record for this title is available from the British Library

ISBN 978 0 340 93671 9 (A)
ISBN 978 1 444 70467 9 (B)

Typeset in Sabon MT by Palimpsest Book Production Limited,
Grangemouth, Stirlingshire

Printed in Great Britain by Clays Ltd, St Ives plc

Hodder & Stoughton policy is to use papers that are natural, renewable and recyclable products and made from wood grown in sustainable forests. The logging and manufacturing processes are expected to conform to the environmental regulations of the country of origin.

Hodder & Stoughton Ltd
338 Euston Road
London NW1 3BH

www.hodder.co.uk

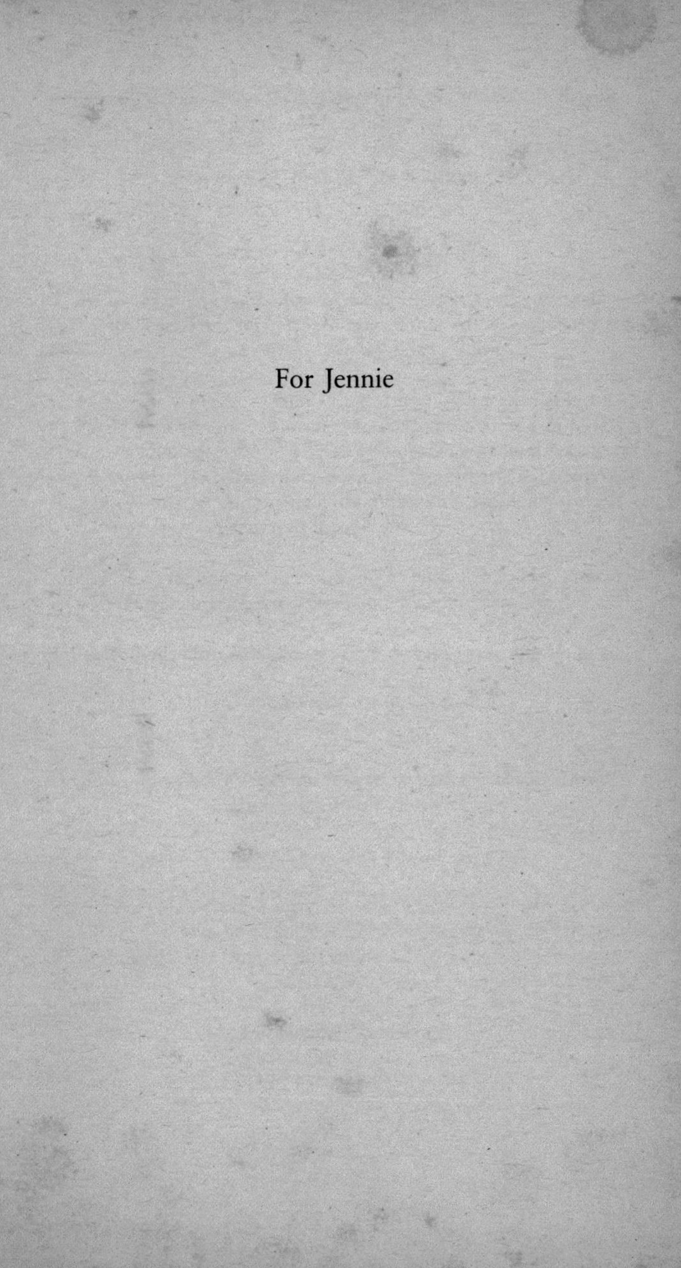

For Jennie

PROLOGUE

The truth is often a terrible weapon of aggression. It is possible to lie, and even to murder, for the truth.

Alfred Adler (1870–1937),
Problems of Neurosis

I tell myself that this is not an investigation. It is for others to be investigated, but not for my family, and not for me. I will delve into the lives of strangers, and I will expose their secrets and their lies, sometimes for money, and sometimes because that is the only way to lay old ghosts to rest, but I do not want to pick and scratch in this manner at what I have always believed of my mother and father. They are gone. Let them sleep.

But there are too many questions left unanswered, too many inconsistencies in the narrative constructed of their lives, a tale told by them and continued by others. I can no longer allow them to remain unexamined.

My father, William Parker, known to his friends as Will, died when I was almost sixteen years old. He was a cop in the Ninth, on the Lower East Side of New York, loved by his wife, and faithful to her, with a son whom he adored and by whom he was adored in return. He chose to remain in uniform, and not to seek promotion, because he was content to serve on the streets as an ordinary patrolman. He had no secrets, at least none so terrible that he, or those close to him, might have been damaged beyond repair had they been revealed. He lived an ordinary, small-town existence, or as ordinary as he could lead when the cycles of his days were determined by duty rosters, by killings, by theft and drug abuse, and by the predations of the strong and ruthless upon the weak and defenseless. His flaws were minor, his sins venial.

Every one of these statements is a lie, except that he loved his son, although his son sometimes forgot to love him back. After all, I was a teenager when he died, and what boy, at that age, is not already knocking heads with his father, attempting to establish his primacy over the old man in the house who no longer understands the nature of the ever-changing world around him? So, did I love him? Of course, but by the end I was refusing to admit it to him, or to myself.

Here, then, is the truth.

My father did not die of natural causes: he took his own life.

His lack of advancement was not a matter of choice, but of punishment.

His wife did not love him or, if she did, she did not love him as she once had, for he had betrayed her and she could not bring herself to forgive that betrayal.

He did not lead an ordinary existence, and people died to keep his secrets.

He had grave weaknesses, and his sins were mortal.

One night, my father killed two unarmed teenagers on a patch of waste ground not far from where we lived in Pearl River. They were not much older than I was. He shot the boy first, and then the girl. He used his off-duty revolver, a .38 Colt with a two-inch barrel, because he was not in uniform at the time. The boy was hit in the face, the girl in the chest. When he was sure that they were dead, my father, as though in a trance, drove back to the city, and showered and changed in the locker room of the Ninth, where they came for him. Less than twenty-four hours later, he shot himself.

For my entire adult life, I have wondered why he acted as he did, but it seemed to me that there were no answers to be found to that question, or perhaps that was the lie I was happier to tell myself.

Until now.

It is time to call this what it is.

This is an investigation into the circumstances of my father's death.

I

I hate and I love. Perhaps you ask why I do so. I do not know, but I feel it happen and I am tormented.

Catullus, *Carmina*, 85

1

The Faraday boy had been missing for three days.

On the first day, nothing was done. After all, he was twenty-one, and young men of that age no longer had to abide by curfews and parental rules. Still, his behavior was out of character. Bobby Faraday was trustworthy. He was a graduate student, although he had taken a year off before deciding on the direction of his graduate studies in engineering, with talk of going abroad for a couple of months, or working for his uncle in San Diego. Instead, he had stayed in his hometown, saving money by living with his parents and banking as much of what he earned as he could, which was a little less than the previous year as he could now drink with impunity, and was maybe indulging that newfound liberty with more enthusiasm than might have been considered entirely wise. He'd had a couple of killer hangovers over New Year's, that was for sure, and his old man had advised him to ease up before his liver started crying out for mercy, but Bobby was young, he was immortal, and he was in love, or had been until recently. Perhaps it would be truer to say that Bobby Faraday was still in love, but the object of his affection had moved on, leaving

Bobby mired in his own emotions. The girl was why he had opted to remain in town instead of seeing a little more of the world, a decision that had been met with mixed feelings by his parents: gratitude on the part of his mother, disappointment on that of his father. There had been some arguments about it at the start, but now, as with two reluctant armies on the verge of an unwanted battle, a truce had been declared between father and son, although each side continued to watch the other warily to see which one might blink first. Meanwhile, Bobby drank, and his father fumed, but remained silent in the hope that the ending of the relationship might lead his son to broaden his horizons until grad school resumed in the fall.

Despite his occasional overindulgences, Bobby was never late for work at the auto shop and gas station, and usually left a little later than he could have, because there was always something to be done, some task that he did not wish to abandon uncompleted, even if it could be finished quickly and easily in the morning. It was one of the reasons his father, whatever their disagreements, didn't worry too much about his son's future prospects: Bobby was too conscientious to leave the beaten track for long. He liked order, and always had. He'd never been one of those messy teenagers, either in appearance or in approach. It just wasn't in his nature.

But he hadn't come home the night before, and he hadn't called to tell his parents where he might be, and that in itself was unusual. Then he didn't make it to work the following morning, which was so out of character that Ron Nevill, who owned the gas station, called the Faraday house to check on the boy and make sure that he wasn't ailing. His mother expressed surprise that her son wasn't already at work. She'd simply assumed that he'd come home late and left early. She checked his bedroom, which lay just off the basement den. His bed had not been slept in, and there was no indication that he'd spent the night on the couch instead.

When there was no word by 3 p.m., she called her husband at work. Together they checked with Bobby's friends, casual acquaintances, and his ex-girlfriend, Emily Kindler. That last call had been delicate, as she and Bobby had broken up only a couple of weeks before. His father suspected that this was the reason his son was drinking more than he should have, but he wouldn't have been the first man who tried to drown love's sorrows in a sea of alcohol. The trouble was that frustrated love was buoyant in booze: the more you tried to force it to the bottom, the more it insisted on bobbing right back up to the top.

Nobody had heard from Bobby, or had seen him, since the previous day. When 7 p.m. came and went, they called the police. The chief was skeptical. He was new in town but familiar with the ways of young people. Nevertheless, he accepted that this was not typical behavior for Bobby Faraday, and that twenty-four hours had now gone by since he left the gas station, for Bobby had not hit any of the local bars after work, and Ron Nevill seemed to be the last person to have seen him. The chief put together a description of the boy at the Faraday house, borrowed a photograph that had been taken the previous summer, and informed local law enforcement and the state police of a possible missing person. None of the other agencies responded with any great urgency, for they were almost as cynical about the behavior of young males as the chief was, and in the case of one who was missing they tended to wait seventy-two hours before assuming that there might be more to the disappearance than a simple case of booze, hormones, or domestic difficulties.

On the second day, his parents, and their friends, began an informal canvass of the town and its environs, with no result. When it began to grow dark, his mother and father returned home, but they did not sleep that night, just as they had not slept the night before. His mother lay in bed, her face turned toward the window, straining to hear the sound of approaching footsteps, the familiar tread of her only son returning to her at last. She stirred slightly when she heard her husband rise and put on his robe.

'What is it?' she asked.

'Nothing. I'm going to make some tea, sit up for a while.' He paused. 'You want some?'

But she knew that he was asking only out of politeness, that he would prefer it if she stayed where she was. He did not want them to sit at the kitchen table in silence, together but apart, the fears of one feeding those of the other. He wanted to be alone. So she let him go, and when the bedroom door closed behind him she began to cry.

On the third day, the formal search began.

The golden host moved as one, countless shapes bending obediently in unison at the gentle touch of the breeze, like a church congregation bowing in accordance with the progress of the service, awaiting the moment of consecration that is to come.

They whispered to themselves, a soft, low susurrus that might have been the crashing of distant waves were such an alien noise not unknown in this land-locked place. The paleness of them was dappled in spots by small flowers of red and orange and blue, a scattering of petals upon an ocean of seed and stem.

The host had been spared the reaping, and had grown tall, too tall, even as the crop decayed. A season's grain had gone to waste, for the old man upon whose land the host was gathered had died the previous summer, and his relatives were fighting over the sale of the property and how the proceeds would be divided. While they fought, the host had stretched skyward, a sea of dull gold in the depths of winter, speaking in hushed tones of what lay, rush-hemmed and undiscovered, nearby.

And yet the host, it seemed, was at peace.

Suddenly, the breeze dropped for an instant and the host stood erect, as though troubled by the change, sensing that all was not as it had been, and then the wind rose again, more tempestuous now, transforming into smaller, dispersed gusts that divided the host with ripples and eddies, their caresses less delicate than before. Unity was replaced by confusion. Scattered fragments were caught by the sunlight before they fell to the ground. The whispering grew louder, drowning the calling of a solitary bird with rumors of approach.

A black shape appeared upon the horizon, like a great insect hovering over the stalks. It grew in stature, becoming the head, shoulders, and body of a man, passing between the rows of wheat while, ahead of him, a smaller form cleaved invisibly through the stalks, sniffing and yelping as it went, the first intruders upon the host's territory since the old man had died.

A second figure came into view, heavier than the first. This one seemed to be struggling with the terrain and with the unaccustomed exercise that his participation in the search had forced upon him. In the distance, but farther to the east, the two men could see other searchers. Somehow, they had drifted away from the main pack, although that itself had diminished as the day wore on. Already the light was fading. Soon it would be time to call a halt, and there would be fewer of them to look in the days that followed.

They had begun that morning, immediately after Sunday services. The searchers had congregated at the Catholic church, St. Jude's, since that had the largest yard and, curiously, the smallest congregation, a contradiction that Peyton Carmichael, the man with the dog, had never quite understood. Perhaps, he figured, they were expecting a mass conversion at some point in the future, which made him wonder if Catholics were just more optimistic than other folks.

The chief of police and his men had divided the township into grids, and the townspeople themselves into groups, and had assigned each group an area to search. Sandwiches, potato chips, and sodas in brown bags had been provided by the various churches, although most people had brought food and water of their own, just in case. In a break with Sunday tradition, none had dressed up in the usual finery. Instead, they wore loose shirts and old pants, and battered boots or comfortable sneakers. Some carried sticks, others garden rakes to search in the undergrowth. There was an air of subdued expectation, a kind of excitement despite the task before them. They shared rides, and drove out to their assigned areas. As each area was searched, and nothing found, another was suggested either by the cops who were coordinating the efforts on the ground, or by contacting the base of operations that had been set up in the hall behind the church.

It had been unseasonably warm when they began, a curious false thaw that would soon end, and the difficulty of coping with soft ground and melting snow had sapped the strength of many before they took a break for lunch at about one-thirty. Some of the older people had returned home at that stage, content to have made some effort for the Faradays, but the rest continued with the search. After all, the next day was Monday. There would be work to do, obligations to be met. This day was the only one that they could spare to look for the boy, and the best would have to be made of it. But as the light had grown dim, so too the day had grown colder, and Peyton was grateful that he had not left his Timberland jacket in the car but had chosen to tie it around his waist until it was needed.

He whistled at his dog, a three-year-old spaniel named Molly, and waited, once again, for his companion to catch up. Artie Hoyt: of all the people he had to end up with. Relations between the two men had been cool for the last year or more, ever since Artie had caught Peyton eyeing his daughter's ass at church. It didn't matter to Artie that he hadn't seen exactly what he thought he'd seen. Yes, Peyton had been looking at his daughter's ass, but not out of any feelings of lust or attraction. Not that he was above such base impulses: at times, the pastor's sermons were so dull that the only thing keeping Peyton awake was the sight of young, lithe female forms draped in their Sunday best. Peyton was long past the age when he might have been troubled by the potential implications for his immortal soul of such carnal thoughts in church. He figured that God had better things to worry about than whether Peyton Carmichael, sixty-four, widower, was paying more attention to objects of female beauty than he was to the old blowhard at the pulpit. As Peyton's doctor liked to tell him, live a life of wine, women, and song, all in moderation but always of the proper vintage. Peyton's wife had died three years earlier, taken by breast cancer, and although there were plenty of women in town of the correct vintage who might have been prepared to offer Peyton some comfort on a winter's evening, he just wasn't interested. He had loved his wife. Occasionally he was still lonely, although less often than before, but those feelings of loneliness were specific, not general: he missed his wife, not female company, and he viewed the occasional pleasure that he took in the sight of a young, good-looking woman merely as a sign that he was not entirely dead below the waist. God, having taken his wife from him, could allow him that small indulgence. If God was going to make a big deal of it, then, well, Peyton would have a few words for Him too, when eventually they met.

The problem with Artie Hoyt's daughter was that, although she was young, she was by no means good-looking. Neither was she lithe. In fact, she was the opposite of lithe and, come to think of it, the opposite of light too. She'd never been what you might call svelte, but then she had left town and gone to live in Baltimore, and by the time she came back she'd piled on the pounds. Now, when she walked into church, Peyton was sure that he felt the floor tremble beneath her feet. If she were any bigger, she'd have to enter sideways; that, or they'd be forced to widen the aisles.

And so, the first Sunday after she'd returned to the parental home, she had entered the chapel with her mom and dad and Peyton had found himself staring in appalled fascination at her ass, jiggling under a red and white floral dress like an earthquake in a rose garden. His jaw might even have been hanging open when he turned to find Artie Hoyt glaring at him, and after that, well, things had never been quite the same between them. They hadn't been close before the incident, but at least they'd been civil when their paths had crossed. Now they rarely exchanged even a nod of greeting, and they hadn't spoken to each other until fate, and the missing Faraday boy, had forced them together. They'd been part of a group of eight that had started out in the morning, quickly falling to six after old Blackwell and his wife seemed set to pass out and had, reluctantly, turned back for home, then five, four, three, until now it was just Artie and him.

Peyton didn't understand why Artie didn't just give up and go home himself. Even the modest pace that Peyton and Molly were setting seemed too much for him, and they had been forced to stop repeatedly to allow Artie to catch his breath and gulp water from the bottle in his rucksack. It had taken Peyton a while to figure out that Artie wasn't going to give him the satisfaction of knowing that he'd kept searching while Artie had faded, even if the other man were to die in the attempt. With that in mind, Peyton had taken a malicious pleasure in forcing the pace for a time, until he acknowledged that his needless cruelty was rendering null and void his earlier efforts at worship and penitence, the occasional glance at young women notwithstanding.

They were nearing the boundary fence between this property and the next, a field of fallow, overgrown land with a small pond at its center sheltered by trees and rushes. Peyton had only a little water left, and Molly was thirsty. He figured he could let her drink at the pond, then call it a day. He couldn't see Artie objecting, just as long as it was Peyton who suggested quitting, and not him.

'Let's head into the field there and check it out,' said Peyton. 'I need to get water for the dog anyway. After that, we can cut back onto the road and take an easy stroll back to the cars. Okay with you?'

Artie nodded. He walked to the fence, rested his hands upon it, and tried to hoist himself up and over. He got one foot off the ground, but the other wouldn't join it. He simply didn't have the strength to continue. Peyton thought he looked like he wanted to lie down and die, but he didn't. There was something admirable about his refusal to give up, even if it had less to do with any concerns about Bobby Faraday than his anger at Peyton Carmichael. Eventually, though, he was forced to admit defeat, and landed back down on the same side on which he'd started.

'Goddammit,' he said.

'Hold up,' said Peyton. 'I'll boost you over.'

'I can do it,' said Artie. 'Just give me a minute to catch my breath.'

'Come on. Neither of us is as young as he was. I'll help you over, and then you can give me a hand up from the other side. No sense in both of us killing ourselves just to prove a point.'

Artie considered the proposal, and nodded his agreement. Peyton tied Molly's leash to the fence, in case she caught a scent and decided to make a break for freedom, then leaned down and cupped his hands so that Artie could put one booted foot into his grip. When the boot was in place, and Artie's hold on the fence seemed secure, Peyton pushed up. Either he was stronger than he thought, or Artie was lighter than he looked but, either way, Peyton ended up almost catapulting Artie over the fence. Only the judicious hooking of his left leg and right arm on the slats saved Artie from an awkward landing on the other side.

'The hell was that?' asked Artie once he had both feet on firm ground once again.

'Sorry,' said Peyton. He was trying not to laugh, and only partially succeeding.

'Yeah, well, I don't know what you're eating, but I could sure do with some of it.'

Peyton began climbing the fence. He was in good condition for a man of his age, a fact that gave him no little pleasure. Artie reached a hand up to steady him and, although Peyton didn't need it, he took it anyway.

'Funny,' said Peyton, as he stepped down from the fence, 'but I don't eat so much anymore. I used to have a hell of an appetite, but now some breakfast and a snack in the evening does me just fine. I even had to make an extra hole in my belt to stop my damn pants from falling down.'

There was an unreadable expression on Artie Hoyt's face as he glanced down at his own belly and reddened slightly. Peyton winced.

'I didn't mean anything by that, Artie,' he said quietly. 'When Rina was alive, I weighed thirty pounds more than I do now. She fed me up like she was going to slaughter me for Christmas. Without her . . .'

He trailed off and looked away.

'Don't talk to me about it,' said Artie, after a moment had passed. He appeared anxious to keep the conversation going, now that the long silence between them had at last been broken. 'My wife doesn't believe it's food unless it's deep fried, or comes in a bun. I think she'd deep fry candy if she could.'

'They actually do that in some places,' Peyton said.

'You don't say? Jesus, don't tell her that. Chocolate's the closest that she gets to health food as it is.'

They began walking toward the pond. Peyton let Molly off the leash. He knew that she had sensed the presence of water, and he didn't want to torment her by forcing her to walk at their pace. The dog raced ahead, a streak of brown and white, and soon was lost from sight in the tall grass.

'Nice dog,' said Artie.

'Thank you,' said Peyton. 'She's a good girl. She's like a child to me, I guess.'

'Yeah,' said Artie. He knew that Peyton and his wife had not been blessed with children.

'Look, Artie,' said Peyton, 'there's something I've been meaning to say for a while.'

He paused as he tried to find the right words, then took a deep breath and plowed right in.

'In church, that time, after Lydia had come home, I . . . Well, I wanted to apologize for staring at her, you know, her . . .'

'Ass,' finished Artie.

'Yeah, that. I'm sorry, is all I wanted to say. It wasn't right. Especially in church. Wasn't Christian. It wasn't what you might think, though.'

Peyton realized that he had wandered onto marshy ground, conversationally speaking. He now faced the possibility of being forced to explain both what he believed Artie might have thought Peyton was thinking, and what, in fact, he, Peyton, *had* been thinking, which was that Artie Hoyt's daughter looked like the *Hindenburg* just before it crashed.

'She's a big girl,' said Artie sadly, saving Peyton from further embarrassment. 'It's not her fault. Her marriage broke up, and the doctors gave her pills for depression, and she suddenly started to put on all this weight. She gets sad, she eats more, she gets sadder, she eats even more. It's a vicious cycle. I don't blame you for staring at her. Hell, she wasn't my daughter, I'd stare at her that way too. In fact, sometimes, it shames me to say, I do stare at her that way.'

'Anyway, I'm sorry,' said Peyton. 'It wasn't . . . kind.'

'Apology accepted,' said Artie. 'Buy me a drink next time we're in Dean's.'

He put his hand out, and the two men shook. Peyton felt his eyes water slightly, and blamed it on his exertions.

'How about I buy you a beer when we're done here? I could do with something to toast the end of a long day.'

'Agreed. Let's water your dog and get the—'

He stopped. They were within sight of the sheltered pond. It had been a popular trysting spot, once upon a time, until the land changed hands and the new owner, the God-fearing man whose estate was now being fought over by his godless relatives, had let it be known that he didn't want any adolescent voyages of sexual discovery being embarked upon in the vicinity of his pond. A large beech tree overhung the water, its branches almost touching the surface. Molly was standing a small distance from it. She had not drunk the water. She had, in fact, stopped several feet from the bank. Now, she was waiting, one paw raised, her tail wagging uncertainly. Through the rushes, something blue was visible to the approaching men.

Bobby Faraday was kneeling by the water's edge, his upper body at a slight angle, as though he were trying to glimpse his reflection in the pool. There was a rope around his neck, attached to the trunk of the tree. He was swollen with gas, his face a reddish-purple, his features almost unrecognizable.

'Ah, hell,' said Peyton.

He wavered slightly, and Artie reached up and put his arm around his companion's shoulder as the sun set behind them, and the wind blew, and the host bowed low in mourning.

2

I took the train to Pearl River from Penn Station. I hadn't driven down to New York from Maine, and I hadn't bothered to rent a car while I was in the city. Whatever I needed to do here, I could do more easily without a vehicle. As the single-car train pulled into the station, still barely altered from its origins as a branch of the Erie Railroad, I saw that any other changes to the heart of the town were also purely cosmetic. I climbed down and walked slowly across Memorial Park where a sign close to the unmanned Town of Orangetown police booth announced that Pearl River was 'Still the Town of Friendly People.'

The park had been created by Julius E. Braunsdorf, the father of Pearl River, who had also laid out the town itself after purchasing the land, as well as building the railroad station, manufacturing the Aetna sewing machine and the America & Liberty printing press, developing an incandescent lightbulb, and inventing the electric arc light that illuminated not just this park but the Capitol area in Washington, D.C. Braunsdorf made most people look kind of sluggish by comparison. Along with Dan Fortmann of the Chicago Bears, he was Pearl River's proudest boast.

The stars and stripes still flew over the memorial at the center of the park, commemorating the young men of the town who had died in combat. Curiously, these included James B. Moore and Siegfried W. Butz, who had died not in combat but in the course of a bank raid in 1929, when Henry J. Fernekes, a notorious bandit of the time, tried to hold up the First National Bank of Pearl River while masquerading as an electrician. Still, at least they were remembered. Murdered bank clerks don't often qualify for a mention on public memorials these days.

Pearl River hadn't shaken off any of its Irish roots since I'd left. The Muddy Brook Café at North Main, on the far side of the park, still offered a Celtic breakfast, and nearby were Gallagher's Irish butcher, the Irish Cottage gift store, and Healy-O'Sullivan Travel. Across East Central Avenue, next door to Handeler's hardware store, was the Ha'penny Irish Shop, which sold Irish tea, candy, potato chips, and replica Gaelic football jerseys, and around the corner from the old Pearl Street Hotel was G. F. Noonan's Irish bar. As my father often remarked, they should just have painted the whole town green and been done with it. The Pearl River movie theater was now closed, though, and there were chi-chi stores selling crafts and expensive gifts alongside the more functional auto shops and furniture stores.

It seems to me now that I spent all of my childhood in Pearl River, but that was not the case. We moved there when I was nearly eight, once my father had begun to tire of the long commute into the city from farther upstate, where he and my mother lived cheaply thanks to a house left to my father when his own mother had died. It was particularly hard for him when he worked his week of 8 to 4 tours, which were, in reality, 7 to 3:30 tours. He would rise at four in the morning, sometimes even earlier, to make his trek in to the Ninth, a violent precinct that occupied less than one square mile on the Lower East Side but accounted for up to seventy-five homicides every year. On those weeks, my mother and I barely saw him. Not that the other tours on each six-week cycle were much better. He was required to do one week of 8 to 4, one week of 4 to 12, another week of 8 to 4, two weeks of 4 to 12 (on those weeks, I only saw him at weekends, for he was sleeping when I left for school in the morning, and gone to work by the time I returned), and one mandatory 12 midnight to 8 tour, which screwed up his body clock so badly he would sometimes be almost delirious with tiredness by the end of it.

The Ninth cops worked what was called a 'nine squad chart,' nine squads of nine men, each with a sergeant, a system that dated back to the fifties and was eventually eliminated in the eighties, taking with it much of the camaraderie that it engendered. My father's sergeant in the 1st Squad was a man named Larry Costello, and it was he who suggested that my father should consider moving down to Pearl River. It was where all the Irish cops lived, a town that claimed the second largest St. Patrick's Day parade in the state after Manhattan. It was comparatively wealthy too, with an average income that was almost twice the national average, and an air of comfortable prosperity. So it had enough off-duty cops to form a police state; it had money; and it had its own identity defined by common bonds of nationality. Even though my father was not himself Irish, he was Catholic, knew many of the men who lived in Pearl River, and was comfortable with them. My mother raised no objections to the move. If it gave her more time with her husband, and relieved him of some of the stress and strain that was, by then, so clearly etched on his face, she would have moved to a hole in the ground covered by a sheet of tarp and made the best of it.

So we went south, and because all that subsequently went wrong in our lives was, for me, tied in with Pearl River, the town came to dominate the memories of my childhood. We bought a house on Franklin Avenue, close to the corner of John Street where the United Methodist Church still stands. It was a fixer-upper, in the peculiar language of Realtors: the old lady who had lived in it for most of her life had recently died, and there was nothing to suggest that she had done much with the house, other than occasionally move a broom across the floors, since 1950. But it was a bigger house than we could otherwise have afforded, and something about the lack of fences, the open yards between properties on the street, appealed to my father. It gave him a sense of space, of community. The notion of good fences making good neighbors was not one that held much currency in Pearl River. Instead, there were those in the town who found the concept of a fence mildly troubling: a sign of disengagement, perhaps, of otherness.

My mother immersed herself in the life of the town. If there was a committee, she joined it. For a woman who, in most of my early memories of her, seemed so self-contained, so distant from her peers, it was an astonishing transformation. My father probably wondered if she was having an affair, but it was nothing more than the reaction of someone who found herself in a better place than she had previously been, with a husband who was more contented than he'd been before, although she still fretted when he left the house each day, and responded with barely concealed relief when he returned home unharmed after each tour.

My mother: now, as I trawled through the details of our life in that place, my relationship with her began to seem less and less normal, if that word can ever truly be used about the interactions of families. If she had sometimes appeared disconnected from her peers, so too was she often at one remove from my father, and from me. It wasn't that she withheld affection, or did not cherish me. She delighted in my triumphs, and consoled me in my defeats. She listened, and counseled, and loved. But for much of my childhood, she acted in response to my promptings. If I came to her, she would do all of those things, yet she did not initiate them. It was as though I were an experiment of sorts, a creature in a cage, something to be monitored and watched, to be fed and watered and given the affection and stimulation to ensure my survival, yet no more than that.

Or perhaps that was just a game memory was playing on me, as I churned up the mud in the reservoir of the past and, when the dirt had settled, picked my way across the bottom to see what had been exposed.

After the killings, and what followed, she fled north to Maine, taking me with her, back to the place in which she had grown up. Until she died, when I was still in college, she refused to discuss in any detail the events that had led up to my father's death. She retreated into herself, and there found only the cancer that would take her life, slowly colonizing the cells of her body like bad memories canceling out the good. I now wonder how long it had been waiting for her, if grave emotional injury might somehow have triggered a physical response, so that she was betrayed on two fronts: by her husband, and by her own body. If that was so, then the cancer began its work in the months before I was born. In my way, I was the stimulus, as much as my father's actions, for one was a consequence of the other.

The house had not changed much, although crumbling paintwork, upper windows streaked with grime, and broken shingles like dark, chipped teeth spoke of a degree of neglect. The color was a paler gray than when I lived there, but the yard was still unfenced, like those of its neighbors. The porch had been screened, and a rocking chair and a rattan couch, both bare of cushions, faced onto the street. The window and door frames were now painted black instead of white, and there was only lawn where once there had been carefully tended flower beds, the grass thin and straggling where it was visible through banked and frozen snow, yet this was still recognizably the place where I had grown up. A drape moved in what used to be the living room, and I saw an old man staring curiously at me. I dipped my chin in acknowledgment of his presence, and he receded into the shadows.

Above the front door was a double window, one pane broken and patched with cardboard, where a boy would sit and gaze out at the small town that was his world. Something of myself had been left in that room after my father died: a degree of innocence, perhaps, or the last remnant of childhood. It had been taken from me in the sound of a gunshot, forcing me to shed it like a reptile skin, or the pupal shell of an insect. I could almost see him, this little ghost: a figure with dark hair and narrow eyes, too introspective for his age, too solitary. He had friends, but he had never overcome the feeling that he was imposing upon them when he called at their houses, and that they did him a favor by playing games with him, or inviting him inside to watch TV. It was easier when they went out as a gang, playing softball in the park in summer, or soccer if Danny Yates, who was the only person he knew who was enthusiastic about the Cosmos and had *Shoot!* magazine sent over to him by an uncle stationed with the air force in England, was back from summer camp, or had yet to leave. Danny was older than the rest of them by a couple of years, and they deferred to him in most things.

I wondered where most of those former friends were now (none of them black, for Pearl River was a lily-white town, and we only encountered black kids at varsity games). I had lost touch with them after we left for Maine, but some were probably still living here. After all, Pearl River – clannish, fiercely protective of its own – was the kind of place that became home to generations. Bobby Gretton had lived two doors down on the other side of the street. His parents drove only Chevys, and kept each car for a maximum of two years before trading it in for a newer model. I looked to my left and saw a brown Chevy Uplander in the drive of what had always been the Gretton house. There was a fading bumper sticker on the rear of the car supporting Obama for president in '08, and beside it a yellow ribbon. The car had veterans' plates. That was Mr. Gretton for sure.

The light changed at my old bedroom window, a cloud scudding overhead giving the impression of movement within, and I felt again the presence of the boy I once was. There he sat, waiting for the first sight of his returning father, or perhaps a glimpse of Carrie Gottlieb, who lived across the street. Carrie was three years older than he, and generally considered to be the most beautiful girl in Pearl River, although there were those who whispered that she knew it too, and that that knowledge made her less attractive and personable than other, more modestly endowed and self-effacing young women. Such mutterings did not concern the boy. It did not concern many of the boys in town. It was Carrie Gottlieb's very separateness, the sense that she walked through life on pedestals erected solely for her own purposes, that made her so desirable. Had she been more down-to-earth and less self-assured, their interest in her would have been considerably reduced.

Carrie went off to the city to become a model. Her mother would tell anyone who stood still for long enough about how Carrie was destined to adorn fashion spreads and television screens, but in the months and years that followed no such images of Carrie appeared, and in time her mother stopped speaking of her daughter in that way. When asked by others (usually with a glint in their eye, sensing blood in the water) how Carrie was getting along, she would reply, 'Fine, just fine,' her smile slightly strained as she moved the conversation on to safer ground or, if the questioner persisted, simply moved herself along instead. In time, I heard that Carrie came back to Pearl River and got a job as the hostess in a local bar and restaurant, eventually becoming the manager after she and the owner got married. She was still beautiful, but the city had taken its toll, and her smile was less certain than it once had been. Nevertheless, she had returned to Pearl River, and she bore the loss of her dreams with a certain grace, and people admired her for it, and maybe liked her a little more because of it. She was one of them, and she was home, and when she visited her parents on Franklin Avenue the ghost of a boy saw her, and smiled.

My father was not a big man compared to some of his fellow officers, barely making the NYPD's height requirement, and slighter in build than they were. To my boyhood self, though, he was an imposing figure, especially when he wore his uniform, with the four-inch Smith & Wesson hanging on his belt, and his buttons gleaming against the deep, dark blue of his clothing.

'What are you gonna be when you grow up?' he would ask me, and I would always reply: 'A cop.'

'And what kind of cop will you be?'

'A New York cop. N! Y! P! D!'

'And what kind of New York cop will you be?'

'A good one. The best.'

And my father would ruffle my hair, the flipside of the light cuff he would dispense whenever I did something that displeased him. Never a slap, never a punch: it was enough to cuff the back of my head with his hard, callused palm, a signal that a line had been overstepped. Further punishments would sometimes follow: grounding, the withholding of my allowance for a week or two, but the cuff was the danger sign. It was the final warning, and it was the only kind of physical violence, however mild, that I associated with my father until the day the two teenagers died.

Some of my friends, rebelling against a town in which they were surrounded by cops, were wary of my father. Frankie Murrow, in particular, used to curl in upon himself like a startled snail whenever my father was around. Frankie's own father was a security guard at a mall, so maybe it was something about uniforms and the men who wore them. Frankie's father was a jerk, and perhaps Frankie just assumed that other men who wore uniforms and protected things were likely to be jerks too. Frankie's father had asked him if he was a fag when, at the age of seven, Frankie had gone to take his father's hand as they prepared to cross the road. Mr. Murrow was a 'royal sonofabitch,' as my father had once put it. Mr. Murrow hated blacks and Jews and Hispanics, and he had a string of derogatory terms on the tip of his tongue for every one of them. He hated most white people too, though, so it wasn't as if he was a racist. He was just good at hating.

At the age of fourteen, Frankie Murrow was put in reform school for arson. He'd burned his own house down while his old man was at work. He'd timed it pretty well, so that Mr. Murrow was turning on to his street just as the fire engines were arriving behind him. Frankie was sitting on the wall of the house opposite, watching the flames rise and laughing and crying at the same time.

My father was not a heavy drinker. He didn't need alcohol to help him relax. He was the calmest man I had ever known, which made the relationship between him and his partner, and closest friend, Jimmy Gallagher, so difficult to understand. Jimmy, who always walked near the head of the town's St. Patrick's Day parade, who bled Irish green and cop blue, was all smiles, and almost-playful punches. He was taller than my father by three or four inches, and broader too. If they stood side by side on those occasions when Jimmy came to the house, my father would look a little embarrassed, as though he felt himself to be somehow wanting when compared to his friend. Jimmy would kiss and hug my mother as soon as he arrived, the only man, apart from her husband, who was permitted such intimacies, and then he would turn to me.

'There he is,' he would say. 'There's the man.'

Jimmy wasn't married. He said that he had never met the right woman, but he'd enjoyed meeting a lot of the wrong ones. It was an old joke, and he used it often, but my mother and father would always laugh, even though they knew it was a lie. Women didn't interest Jimmy Gallagher, although it would be many years before I understood that. I often wondered how difficult it must have been for Jimmy, keeping up a front for all those years, flirting with women in order to fit in. Jimmy Gallagher, who could make the most incredible pizzas from scratch, who could cook a banquet to please a king (or so I had once heard my father tell my mother) but who, when he hosted a poker game at his house, or had his buddies around to watch a ball game (because Jimmy, being single, could always afford the best and most modern TVs), would feed them nachos and beer, potato chips and store-bought TV dinners or, if the weather was good, cook steaks and burgers on the barbecue. And I sensed, even then, that while my father might have spoken to my mother of Jimmy's secret culinary skills, he did not make such references carelessly among his brother cops.

Jimmy would take my hand and shake it just a little too hard, testing his strength. I had learned not to wince when this occurred, for then Jimmy would say, 'Ah, he has a way to go yet,' and shake his head in mock disappointment. But if my face remained still, and I returned the grip as best I could, Jimmy would smile and slip me a dollar, with the admonition: 'Don't spend it all on booze, now.'

I didn't spend it all on booze. In fact, until I turned fifteen, I didn't spend any of it on booze. I spent it on candy and comic books, or saved it for our summer vacation in Maine, when we would stay with my grandfather in Scarborough and I would be taken to Old Orchard Beach and allowed to run riot on the rides. As I grew older, though, booze became a more attractive option. Carrie Gottlieb's brother, Phil, who worked for the railroad and was believed to be of slightly subnormal intelligence, was known to be willing to buy beer for underage kids in return for one bottle out of every six. One evening, two of my friends and I pooled our cash for a couple of six-packs of PBR that Phil picked up for us, and we drank most of them in the woods one night. I had liked the taste less than the frisson of pleasure I experienced from breaking both the law and a rule of the house, for my father had made it clear to me that there was to be no drinking until he said it was okay. Like young men the world over, I took this and other rules to refer only to things about which my father knew since, if he didn't know about them, then they couldn't possibly be of any consequence to him.

Unfortunately, I had brought home one of the bottles and stashed it in the back of my closet for future use, which was where my mother found it. I'd taken a cuff on the head for that, and was grounded, *and* required to take an involuntary vow of poverty for at least a month. That afternoon, which was a Sunday, Jimmy

Gallagher had come by the house. It was Jimmy's birthday, and he and my father were going to hit the town, as they always did when one of them celebrated another year of not being shot, stabbed, beaten to a pulp, or run over. He had smiled mockingly at me, a dollar bill held between the index and middle fingers of his right hand.

'All those years,' he said, 'and you never listened.'

And I had answered sullenly: 'I did listen. I didn't spend it *all* on booze.'

Even my father had been forced to laugh.

But Jimmy didn't give me the dollar, and after that he never gave me money again. He never got the chance. Six months later, my father was dead, and Jimmy Gallagher stopped coming around with dollar bills in his hand.

They had questioned my father after the killing, for he admitted his involvement as soon as they confronted him. They treated him sympathetically, trying to understand what had taken place so that they could begin to limit the damage. He had ended up at the Orangetown PD, since the local cops were the primaries. IAD had been involved, as had an investigator from the Rockland County DA's office, a retired NYPD cop himself who knew how these things were done, and who would smooth the feathers of the local boys prior to taking over the investigation.

My father had called my mother shortly after they came for him, and told her what he had done. Later, a courtesy call was paid to the house by a pair of local cops, one of them Jimmy Gallagher's nephew, who worked out of Orangetown. Earlier that evening, when he was not yet on duty, he had come to our house in his casual clothes and had sat in our kitchen. He had a gun on his belt. He and my mother had pretended that it was merely a normal visit, but he had stayed too long for that, and I had seen the tension on my mother's face as she served him coffee and cake that he barely touched. Now, as he stood again in our house, this time in uniform, I understood that his earlier presence had been connected to the shootings, but I did not yet know how.

Jimmy's nephew confirmed for her all that had occurred, or appeared to have occurred, on the patch of waste ground just a short distance from the house, without ever referring to the fact that it was his second visit to our home that evening. She had wanted to join her husband, to offer him support, but he told her that there would be no point. The questioning would go on for some time, and then he would probably be suspended on full pay pending an investigation. He would be home soon, he promised her. Sit tight. Keep an eye on the boy. Tell him nothing for now. It's up to you, but, you understand, it might be better to wait until we all know more . . .

I heard her crying after my father's call, and I went down to her. I stood before my mother, dressed in my pajamas, and said: 'What's wrong? Mom, what's the matter?'

She had looked at me, and for a moment I felt sure that she had failed to recognize me. She was upset and in shock. What my father had done had frozen her responses, so that I seemed a stranger. Only that could explain the coldness of her stare, the distance it placed between us, as though the air had frozen solid, cutting us off from each other. I had seen that expression on her face before, but only when I had done something so terrible that she was unable to bring herself to speak: the theft of money from her kitchen fund, or, in an abortive attempt to create a bobsled for my G.I. Joe, the destruction of a plate bequeathed to her by her grandmother.

There was, I thought, blame in her eyes.

'Mom?' I said again, uncertain now, frightened. 'Is it Dad? Is he okay?'

And she found it in herself to nod, her upper teeth clamped down hard on her lower lip, so hard that, when she spoke, I saw blood against the white.

'He's okay. There was a shooting.'

'Was he hurt?'

'No, but some people . . . some people died. They're talking to your father about it.'

'Did Dad shoot them?'

But she would not say anything more.

'Go back to bed,' she said. 'Please.'

I did as I was told, but I could not sleep. My father, the man who could barely bring himself to cuff the back of my head, had drawn his gun and killed someone. I was sure of it.

I wondered if my father would get into trouble.

Eventually, they released him. Two IAD goons escorted him home, then sat outside reading the newspapers.

I watched them all from my window. My father looked old and crumpled as he walked up the path. His face was unshaven. He glanced up at the window and saw me there. He raised his hand in greeting, and tried to smile. I waved back before leaving my room, but I did not smile.

When I padded halfway downstairs, my father was holding my mother tightly as she wept against him, and I heard him say: 'He told us they might come.'

'But how could that be?' my mother asked. 'How could it be the same people?'

'I don't know, but it was. I saw them. I heard what they said.'

My mother began to cry again, but the tone had changed: it was now a high keening, the sound of someone breaking apart. It was as though a dam had burst inside her, and all that she had kept hidden away was pouring through the breach, sweeping away the life she once had in a great torrent of grief and violence. Later, I would wonder if, had she managed to hold herself together, she might have been able to prevent what happened next, but she was so caught up in her own sorrows that she failed to see that, in killing those two young people, her husband had destroyed something crucial to his own existence in the process. He had murdered a pair of unarmed teenagers, and, despite what he had said to her, he was not sure why; that, or he was unable to live with the possibility that what he had told her was true. He was tired, wearier than he had ever been. He wanted to sleep. He wanted to sleep and never wake up.

They became aware of my presence, and my father removed his right arm from around my mother, and he welcomed me into their embrace. We remained that way for a minute until my father patted us both on the back.

'Come on,' he said. 'We can't stay like this all day.'

'Are you hungry?' my mother asked, wiping her eyes on her apron. There was no emotion to her voice now as though, having given vent to her pain, she had nothing else left to give.

'Sure. Eggs would be good. Bacon and eggs. You want some bacon and eggs, Charlie?'

I nodded, although I was not hungry. I wanted to be near my father.

'You should take a shower, change your clothes,' my mother said.

'I'll do that. I just need to do something else first. You worry about those eggs.'

'Toast?'

'Toast would be good. Wheat, if you have it.'

My mother began bustling around the kitchen. When her back was to us, my father held my shoulder tightly and said: 'It'll all be fine, understand? You help your mother, now. Make sure she's okay.'

He left us. The back door opened, then closed again. My mother paused and listened, like a dog sensing some disturbance, then returned to heating the oil in the pan.

She had just broken the first egg when we heard the shot.

3

The movement of the clouds against the sun caused the light to change rapidly, disconcertingly, brightness briefly fading to a wintry dusk in the blink of an eye, a taste of the greater darkness that would soon encroach. The front door opened and the old man appeared on his doorstep. He was wearing a hooded jacket, but he still had his slippers on. He trotted to the end of the path and stopped at the edge of his property, his toes lined up with the lawn, as though the sidewalk were a body of water and he was fearful of falling from the bank.

'Can I help you with something, son?' he called.

Son.

I crossed the street. He tensed slightly, wondering now if it had been such a good idea to confront a stranger after all. He glanced down at his slippers, probably thinking that he should have taken the time to put on his boots. He would have felt less vulnerable in boots.

Up close, I could see that he was seventy or more, a small, fragile-looking man yet with enough inner strength and confidence to face down a stranger who was staking out his home. There were men younger than he was who would simply have called the police. His eyes were brown and rheumy, but the skin on his face was relatively unwrinkled for someone his age. It was especially taut around his eye sockets and cheekbones, giving the impression that his skin had begun to shrink, not loosen, against his skull.

'I once lived here, in this house,' I said.

Some of the wariness left him.

'You one of the Harrington boys?' he asked, squinting as he tried to identify me.

'No, I'm not.'

I didn't even know who the Harringtons were. The people who bought the house after we left were named Bildner. A young couple, with a baby daughter. But then, over a quarter of a century had passed since I had last seen the house. I had no idea how many times it might have changed hands over the years.

'Huh. What's your name, son?'

And each time he said that word, I heard the echo of my father's voice.

'Parker, Charlie Parker.'

'Parker,' he repeated, chewing on the word as though it were a piece of meat. He blinked rapidly three times, and his mouth tightened in a wince. 'Yes, I know who you are now. My name's Asa, Asa Durand.'

He held out his hand, and I shook it.

'How long have you lived here?'

'Twelve years, give or take. The Harringtons were here before us, but they sold it and moved to Dakota. Don't know if it was North or South. Don't suppose it matters much, seeing as how it was Dakota.'

'You been to Dakota?'

'Which one?'

'Either.'

He smiled mischievously, and I saw clearly the young man now trapped in an old man's body. 'Why would I want to go to Dakota?' he asked. 'You care to come inside?'

I heard myself say the words before I even realized I had made the decision.

'Yes,' I said, 'if it's not an imposition.'

'Not at all. My wife will be home soon. She plays bridge on Sunday afternoons, and I cook dinner. You're welcome to stay, if you're hungry. It's pot roast. Always pot roast on Sundays. It's the only thing I can cook.'

'No, thank you. It's good of you to offer, though.'

I walked alongside him up the path. His left leg dragged slightly.

'What do you get in return for cooking dinner, or am I allowed to ask?'

'An easier life,' said Durand. 'To sleep in my bed without fear of suffocation.' The smile came again, soft and warm. 'And she likes my pot roast, and I like it that she does.'

We reached the front door. Durand went ahead and held it open. I paused on the step for a moment then followed him inside, and he closed the door behind me. The hallway was brighter than I remembered. It had been painted yellow with white trim. When I was a boy, the hallway had been red. To the right was a formal dining room, with a mahogany table and chairs not dissimilar to the set we had once owned. To the left was the living room. There was a flat-screen high-definition TV where our old Zenith used to stand, in the days when VCRs were still a novelty and the networks had instituted a family hour to protect the young from sex and violence. When was that, '74, '75? I couldn't recall.

There was no longer a wall between the kitchen and the living room. It had been removed to create a single, open-plan space, so that the little kitchen of my youth, with its four-seat table, was now entirely gone.

I could not picture my mother in the new space.

'Different?' asked Durand.

'Yes. This is all different.'

'The other people did that. Not the Harringtons, the Bildners. They the ones you sold to?'

'That's right.'

'It was vacant for a time too. Couple of years.' He looked away, troubled by the direction the conversation was taking. 'Would you like a drink? There's beer, if you want. I don't drink so much now. Goes through me like water down a pipe. Hardly in one end before it's out the other. Then I have to nap.'

'It's a little early for me. I'll take a cup of coffee, though, if I don't have to drink it alone.'

'Coffee we can do. At least I don't have to nap after it.'

He switched on the coffeemaker, then rounded up some cups and spoons.

'Would you mind if I looked in my old bedroom?' I asked. 'It's the small one to the front, with the broken pane.'

Durand winced again, and looked a little embarrassed. 'Damned pane. Kids broke it playing baseball. I just didn't get around to fixing it. And then, well, we don't use that room for much other than storage. It's full of boxes.'

'It doesn't matter. I'd still like to see it.'

He nodded, and we went upstairs. I stood at the threshold of my old bedroom, but I did not enter. As Durand had said, it was a mass of boxes, files, books, and old electrical equipment that was now gathering dust.

'I'm a packrat,' said Durand apologetically. 'All that stuff still works. I keep hoping someone will come along who might need it and take it off my hands.'

As I stood there, the boxes disappeared, vanishing along with the junk and the books and the files. There was only a room carpeted in gray; white walls covered with pictures and posters; a closet with a mirror on the front in which I could see myself reflected, a man in his forties with graying hair and dark eyes; shelves lined with books, carefully ordered according to author; a nightstand with a digital alarm clock, the height of technology, showing a time of 12:54 p.m.

And the sound of the gunshot carrying from the garage at the back of the house. Through the window, I saw men running—

'Are you okay, Mr. Parker?'

Durand touched my arm gently. I tried to speak, but I could not.

'Why don't we go downstairs? I'll make you that cup of coffee.'

And the figure in the mirror became the ghost of the boy that I once was, and I held his gaze until he slowly faded away and was gone.

We sat in the kitchen, Asa Durand and I. Through the window, I could see a copse of silver birch where the garage used to be. Durand followed my gaze.

'I heard about what happened,' he said. 'A terrible thing.'

The room was filled with the aroma of Durand's pot roast. It smelled good.

'Yes, it was.'

'They knocked it down, the garage.'

'Who did?'

'The Harringtons. The neighbors, Mr. and Mrs. Rosetti – they were probably after your time by a couple of years – told me about it.'

'Why did they knock it down?' But even as I asked the question, I already knew the answer. The only surprise was that it had stayed intact for as long as it had.

'I guess there are those who feel that, when something bad happens in a place, the echo of it remains,' said Durand. 'I don't know if that's true. I'm not sensitive to such things myself. My wife believes in angels—' He pointed at a wispily clothed winged figure hanging from a hook on the kitchen door '—except all her angels look like Tinkerbell to me. I don't think she can tell the difference between angels and fairies.

'Anyway, the Harrington kids didn't like going into

the garage. The youngest one, the little girl, she said it smelled bad. The mother, she told Mrs. Rosetti that sometimes it smelled—'

He paused, and winced for a third time. It seemed to be an involuntary response when anything discomfited him.

'It's okay,' I said. 'Go on, please.'

'She told her that it smelled like a gun had gone off in there.'

We were both silent for a time.

'Why are you here, Mr. Parker?'

'I'm not sure. I think I have some questions I need answered.'

'You know, you get the urge, at a certain point in your life, to go digging around in the past,' said Durand. 'I sat my mother down before she died and made her go through our whole family history, everything that she could remember. I wanted to have that knowledge, I guess, to understand what I was part of before anyone who could clear that stuff up for me was gone forever. And that's a good thing, to know where you came from. You pass it on to your children, and it makes everyone feel less adrift in life, less alone.

'But some things, they're better left in the past. Oh, I know that psychiatrists and therapists and Lord knows who else will tell you different, but they're wrong. Not every wound needs to be poked and opened, and not every wrong needs to be reexamined, or dragged kicking and screaming into the light. Better just to let the wound heal, even if it doesn't heal quite right, or to leave the wrongs in the dark, and remind yourself not to go stepping into the shadows if you can avoid it.'

'Well, that's the thing of it,' I said. 'Sometimes you can't avoid those shadows.'

Durand pulled at his lip. 'No, I guess not. So, is this the beginning, or the end?'

'The beginning.'

'You got a long road ahead of you, then.'

'I think so.'

I heard the front door open. A small, slightly overweight woman with permed silver hair stepped into the hallway.

'It's me,' she said. She didn't look toward the kitchen. Instead, she first removed her coat, gloves, and scarf, and checked her hair and face in the mirror on the coat rack. 'Smells fine,' she said. She turned to the kitchen and saw me.

'Goodness!'

'We got company, Elizabeth,' said Durand, and I stood as his wife entered the room.

'This is Mr. Parker,' said Durand. 'He used to live here, when he was a boy.'

'Pleased to meet you, Mrs. Durand,' I said.

'Well, you're—'

She paused as she made the connection, and I watched the emotions play upon her face. Eventually, her features settled into what I suspected was their default mode: kindness, tinged with just the hint of sadness that comes with a lifetime of experience, and the knowledge that it was all drawing to a close.

'You're welcome,' was what she settled upon. 'Sit, sit. You'll stay for dinner?'

'No, I can't. I have to get going. I've taken up too much of your husband's time as it is.'

Despite her inherent decency and good nature, I could see that she was relieved.

'If you're sure.'

'I am. Thank you.'

I stayed on my feet to put on my coat, and Durand showed me to the door.

'I ought to tell you,' he said, 'that when I first saw you I thought that you were someone else, and I don't mean one of the Harrington boys. Just for a second, mind.'

'Who did you think I was?'

'There was a man came here, couple of months back. It was evening, darker than it is now. He did what you did: stared at the house for a time, even went as far as to come onto the lawn so he could take a look at the back of the house, out where the garage used to be. I didn't like it. I ventured out to ask him what he thought he was doing. Haven't seen him since.'

'You think he was casing the house for a robbery?'

'At first, except that when I challenged him, that's not what he said. Not that a burglar would tell you he was casing a place, not unless he was dumb as dirt.'

'What did he say?'

'"Hunting." That's what he said. Just that one word: "Hunting." Now what do you think that means?'

'I don't know, Mr. Durand,' I said, and his eyes narrowed as he wondered if he was being lied to.

'Then he asked me if I knew what had happened here, and I said I didn't know what he was talking about, and he said that he thought I did. I didn't care for his tone, and told him to be on his way.'

'Do you remember what he looked like?'

'Not so well. He was wearing a wool hat, pulled down over his hair, and he had a scarf around his neck and chin. It was a cold night, but not that cold. Younger than you. Late twenties, maybe older. A little taller, too. I'm nearsighted, and I didn't have my spectacles. Keep leaving them places. I should buy a chain.' He realized that he was drifting from the subject at hand, and returned to it. 'Apart from that, I don't recall much about him, except—'

'What?'

'I was glad to see him leave, that's all. He made me uneasy, and not just because he was on my lawn, snooping around on my property. There was a thing about him.' Durand shook his head. 'I can't explain it right. I could say to you that he wasn't from around here, and that would be as close as I could get. He wasn't from anywhere like here, anywhere at all.'

He looked out over the town, taking in the cars moving on the streets, the lights of the bars and stores near the train station, the dim shapes of people heading home to their families. It was normality, and the man who had stood on his lawn did not belong in it.

Night had now come. The streetlights caught the patches of frozen snow, making them shine in the gloom. Durand shivered.

'You be careful, Mr. Parker,' he said. We shook

hands. He stayed on the step until I reached the sidewalk, then he waved once and closed the door. I looked up at the window with the broken pane, but there was nobody there. That room was empty. Whatever remained there had no form; the ghost of the boy was inside me, where he had always been.

4

I met Angel and Louis for dinner that night at the Wildwood BBQ on Park Avenue, not far from Union Square. It was tough to make the call between Wildwood and Blue Smoke up on 27th, but novelty won out; novelty, and, for Louis, the prospect of beans that had pieces of steak added to them. When it came to rib joints, Louis liked extra meat with everything, probably including the Jell-O. If he was going to die of a coronary, he was going to do it in style.

These two men, both of whom had killed, yet only one of whom, Louis, could truly be called a natural killer, were now my closest friends. I hadn't seen them since late the previous year, when they had managed to get themselves into some trouble in upstate New York and I'd followed their tracks to see if I could help. It hadn't ended well, and we'd kept some distance from one another since then; not due to any ill will, but because Louis was concerned about the possible fallout from what had occurred, and didn't want to see me contaminated by association. Now, though, he appeared content, figuring that the worst was over, or as content as Louis ever seemed to be. In truth, it was hard to tell. After all, it wasn't that when Louis laughed, the world laughed with him. When Louis laughed, the world tended to look around to see who had fallen over and impaled himself on a spike.

It was always an entertaining spectacle, seeing Angel and Louis eat ribs, because some kind of role reversal seemed to occur. Louis – tall, black, and dressed like a showroom dummy that has suddenly decided to take flight and seek better accommodations elsewhere – ate ribs in the manner of a man who fears that his plate could be whisked away at any point, and he should therefore consume as many as possible as quickly as possible. Angel, on the other hand, who was small and white (or, as he liked to put it, 'white-ish'), and who not only looked like he'd slept in his clothes but like other people might have slept in them too, nibbled his food in an almost delicate manner, the way a small bird might if it could hold a short rib in its claws. They were drinking ale. I was sipping a glass of red wine.

'Red wine,' said Angel. 'In a rib joint. You know, we're gay, and even we don't drink wine in a rib joint.'

'Then I guess if I were gay, I'd just be a more sophisticated homosexual than you. In fact, regardless of my sexuality, I'm still more sophisticated than you.'

'You not eating?' asked Louis, pointing with the end of a mostly demolished rib at the small pile of bare bones on my plate.

'I'm not so hungry,' I said. 'Anyway, after watching you two, I'm considering vegetarianism, or just never eating again. At least, not in public, and certainly not with you.'

'What the hell is wrong with us?' Angel sounded spectacularly aggrieved.

'You eat like an old lady. He eats like they just thawed him out next to a mammoth.'

'You want us to use a knife and fork?'

'Do you *know* how to use a knife and fork?'

'Don't tempt me, Miss Manners. The knives are sharp here.'

Louis finished his final rib, wiped his face with his napkin, and sat back with a sigh. If his heart could have sighed with relief, it would have echoed him.

'Glad I wore my buffet pants tonight,' he said.

'Me too,' I said. 'You'd worn your regular pants, one of your buttons would have taken someone's eye out by now.'

He arched an eyebrow.

'Sorry,' I said. 'You continue to be boyishly slim.'

Angel signaled the server for another beer.

'You want to tell us about it?' he said.

They knew most of it already. I had lost my Maine private investigator's license, and my lawyer, Aimee Price, was still fighting to have it restored to me, hampered at every turn by the objections of the state police and, it appeared, a detective named Hansen in particular. From what Aimee could establish, the order to revoke my license had come from high up, and Hansen was just the messenger. A court challenge was still an option, but Aimee wasn't sure that it would be useful. The state police were the final arbiters when it came to licensing, and any court in Maine would probably be guided by their decision.

My firearms permit had also been revoked, although the precise nature of the revocation was still unclear to me and to my lawyer. I had initially been ordered to hand over every gun in my possession pending what was vaguely termed 'an inquiry,' and was told that it would be only a temporary matter.

I had surrendered my licensed firearms (and hidden the unlicensed ones, after an anonymous tip that the cops were coming with a warrant), which had subsequently been returned to me when it became apparent that the surrender notice was of dubious legality, and possibly in breach of the Second Amendment. Less open to argument was the decision to rescind my permit to carry a concealed weapon in the state of Maine, on the grounds that my previous actions had revealed me as an 'unsafe' person. Aimee was working on that one too, but so far a brick wall would have been more yielding than the state police. I was being punished, but just how long that punishment would continue remained to be seen.

Now I was working as bar manager at the Great Lost Bear in Portland, which wasn't bad work and usually only took up four days each week, but it wasn't what I was good at. There wasn't a great deal of sympathy for my plight in the local law enforcement community. I couldn't recall how I'd made so many enemies until Aimee took the trouble to explain, and then it all became a little clearer.

Strangely, I didn't care about what had occurred as much as Hansen and his superiors might have thought. It had dented my pride, and my lawyer was fighting in my name partly on principle and mostly because I didn't want them to think that I would just roll over and die on their say-so, but in a sense I was satisfied that I couldn't practice as a PI. It left me free, relieving me of the obligation to help others. If I were to take on a case, however informally, it would probably land me in jail. The state police's actions had given me permission to be selfish, and to pursue my own aims. It had taken me some months to decide that that was what I was going to do.

Despite what the old man, Durand, might have thought earlier that day, I hadn't chosen lightly to delve into my past and to question the circumstances of my father's death. A man, a foul man who used the name Kushiel but was better known as the Collector, had whispered to me that my family had secrets, that my blood group could not have been the result of my assumed parentage. For a time, I tried to hide from myself what he had said. I did not want to believe it. I think that I took the job in the bar as a form of escape. I replaced my obligations to clients with my obligations to Dave Evans, one of the owners of the Bear and the man who had offered me the job. But as time passed, and winter came again, I made a decision.

Because the Collector had not been lying, not entirely. The blood groups did not match.

When the new year dawned, I started asking questions. I began trying to contact those who had known my father, and especially the cops who had worked alongside him. Some were dead. Others had fallen off the radar after retirement, as sometimes happens with those who have served their time and desire only to collect their pensions and walk away from it all. But I knew the names of the two men to whom my father had been particularly close, beat cops who had graduated from the academy alongside him: Eddie Grace, who was a couple of years older than my father, and Jimmy Gallagher, my father's old partner and closest friend. My mother had sometimes referred semifondly to my father and Jimmy as the 'Birthday Boys,' a reference to their twice yearly nights on the town. Those were the only times when my father would stay out all night, eventually reappearing shortly before noon the following day, when he would return quietly, almost apologetically, slightly the worse for wear but never sick or stumbling, and sleep until the evening. My mother never commented on it. It was an indulgence that she permitted him, and he was a man of few indulgences, or so it seemed to me.

And then there was Jimmy Gallagher himself. I hadn't seen him since shortly after the funeral, when he had come to the house to ask how my mother and I were doing, and she had told him that she intended to leave Pearl River and return to Maine. My mother had sent me to bed, but what teenager would not have listened at the top of the stairs, seeking some of the information that he was certain was being withheld from him? And I heard my mother say: 'How much did you know, Jimmy?'

'About what?'

'About all of it: the girl, the people who came. How much did you know?'

'I knew about the girl. The others . . .'

I could almost see him shrugging.

'Will said they were the same people.'

Jimmy did not answer for a time. Then: 'That's not possible. You know it's not. I killed one of them, and the other died months before. The dead don't return, not like that.'

'He whispered it to me, Jimmy.' The tears were being held back, but only barely. 'It was one of the last things he said to me. He said it was them.'

'He was frightened, Elaine, frightened for you and the boy.'

'But he killed them, Jimmy. He killed them, and they weren't even armed.'

'I don't know why—'

'*I* know why: he wanted to stop them. He knew that they would come back in the end. They wouldn't need guns. They'd use their bare hands if they had to. Maybe—'

'What?'

'Maybe they'd even have preferred it that way,' she concluded.

Now she began to cry. I heard Jimmy stand, and I knew that he was putting his arms around her, consoling her.

'This I do know: he loved you. He loved you both, and he was sorry for all that he did to hurt you. I think he spent sixteen years trying to make it up to you, but he never could. It wasn't your fault. He couldn't forgive himself, that's all. He just couldn't do it . . .'

My mother's sobbing increased in intensity, and I turned away and went as quietly as I could to my room, where I watched the moon from my window and stared out at Franklin Avenue, and the paths that my father would never walk again.

The server came to take away our plates. He seemed impressed with Angel and Louis's demolition of their food, and commensurately disappointed in me. We ordered coffee, and watched the place begin to empty.

'Is there anything we can do?' asked Angel.

'No. I think this one is mine.'

He must have spotted something playing on my mind, its movements replicated on my face.

'What aren't you telling us?' he said.

'Durand said that a young man – late twenties, according to him, maybe a little older – had come to his house a couple of months ago. He was snooping around. Durand called him on it, and the guy said he was "hunting."'

'In Pearl River?' said Angel. 'What was he hunting: leprechauns?'

Louis spoke. 'Might be nothing to do with you.'

'Might not,' I agreed. 'But he asked if Durand knew what had happened there.'

'Thrill seeker. Murder tourist. You've had them before.'

'Durand said that the guy made him uneasy, that's all. He couldn't put his finger on why.'

'Not much you can do, then, unless he shows up again.'

'Yeah, a late twenty-something guy in New York who makes people uneasy. Shouldn't be hard to spot. Hell, that description even covers half of the Mets' starting lineup.'

We paid the tab, and headed out into the night.

'You call us, anytime,' said Angel. 'We're around.'

They hailed a cab, and I watched them head uptown. When they were gone from sight, I went back into the restaurant and sat at the bar, sipping another glass of wine. I thought about the hunter, and wondered if it was me he was hunting.

And part of me willed him to come.

5

The Great Lost Bear was a Portland institution. It occupied a space on Forest Avenue, away from the main tourist drag of the Old Port, that had once housed a bar called Bottom's Up. Semi–big bands used to play there, groups that were either on their way up, or on their way down, or had just reached a plateau where all that mattered was a paying gig in front of a decent-size crowd, preferably one that wasn't about to start hurling bottles when they departed from the hits to play a new song.

The stage lighting was still in place in the restaurant area, which always gave the impression that either the diners were only a prelude to the main act, or they *were* the main act. Half of the building also used to be a bakery, and at 11:30 p.m., as the bar was serving last rounds, the place would fill with the smell of baking bread, driving the customers into paroxysms of the munchies just after the kitchens had closed.

When the bar changed hands in 1979 it became known as the Grizzly Bear, until a pizza chain on the West Coast objected and the name was changed to the Great Lost Bear, which was more evocative anyway. The Bear's main claim to fame, apart from its general conviviality and the fact that it served food until late, was its beer selection: fifty-six draft beers at any one time, sometimes even sixty. Despite its location in a quiet part of the city not far from the University of Southern Maine's campus, it had built up a considerable reputation over the years and now the summer, which used to be slow, was its busiest time.

As well as locals, the Bear attracted the beer aficionados, most of whom were men, and men of a certain age. They didn't cause trouble, they didn't overindulge, and mostly they were content to talk about hops and casks and obscure microbreweries of which even some of the bartenders had never heard. In fact, the more obscure they were, the better, for there was a kind of competitiveness among a certain group of drinkers at the Bear. Occasionally, the sight of a woman might distract them from the task at hand for a time, but there would be other women. There wouldn't always be a guy sitting next to them who had tried every microbrew in Portland, Oregon, but knew squat about Portland, Maine.

I had been working as the bar manager in the Bear for a little over four months. I wasn't hurting for money, not yet, but it made sense to find some kind of work while Aimee Price fought my case. I had a daughter to support, even if her mother wasn't pressing me for payments. I sometimes wondered if Rachel might have preferred it if I wasn't part of Sam's life at all, although she had never said anything that might have led me to that conclusion. I was allowed to visit Sam over in Vermont any time that I chose, as long as I gave Rachel some notice. Even then, I had sometimes felt the urge to see Sam (and, truth be told, Rachel, for there was unfinished business between us) and had traveled to Burlington on a whim. Apart from the occasional disapproving look from Rachel's father, for she and Sam lived in the adjoining cottage on her parents' property, such unscheduled visits had so far caused no friction between us.

Rachel and I had slept together a couple of times since the separation, but neither of us had raised the possibility of a reconciliation. I didn't think that one was possible, not now, but it didn't prevent me from loving her. Still, it was a situation that couldn't last. We were drifting further and further apart. It was over, but neither of us had spoken the words yet.

It was a little after four on Thursday afternoon, and the Bear was quiet for now. Well, relatively quiet. Three men were seated at the bar. Two were regulars, classic Maine winter types in worn boots, Red Sox caps, and enough layers of clothing to ward off the effects of a second Ice Age until someone got around to opening a bar in a cave and began brewing beer again. Their names were Scotty and Phil. Usually, there was a third guy with them called Dan, or variously 'Dan the Man,' 'Danny Boy,' or, when he wasn't within earshot, 'Dan the Dummy,' but on this particular occasion, Dan was absent, and taking his place was a man who was not considered a regular, but looked like he was about to become one now that I was working there.

This was not necessarily a good thing. I liked Jackie

Garner. He was loyal and brave, and he kept his mouth shut about the things that he had done in my name, but something rattled in his head when he walked, and I wasn't certain that he was entirely sane. He was the only person I knew who had volunteered to attend military school instead of a regular high school, since he liked the idea of being taught how to shoot, stab, and blow things up. He was also the only person I knew who had been quietly expelled from military school for his excessively enthusiastic attitude toward shooting, stabbing, and, most particularly, blowing things up, an enthusiasm that made him as potentially lethal to his comrades as to his enemies. Eventually, the army found a place for him in its ranks, but it had never quite managed to control him, and it was hard not to feel that the US military had raised a discreet cheer when Jackie was eventually invalided out.

Worse, where Jackie went, the Fulci brothers, Tony and Paulie, frequently went too, and the Fulcis, blockhouses in human form, made Jackie look like Mother Teresa. So far, they hadn't graced the Bear with their presence, but it was only a matter of time. I still hadn't worked out how to tell Dave that he'd have to get a couple of chairs reinforced for them. I figured that when he heard the Fulcis might be about to become regulars, he'd just fire me; that, or load up with guns and prepare for a siege.

'Dan not around?' I asked Scotty.

'Nah, he's back in the hospital. He thinks he might be schizophrenic.'

It figured. He was certainly something ending in -ic. Schizophrenic would do to be getting along with.

'He still dating that girl?' asked Phil.

'Well, one of him is,' said Scotty, and laughed.

Phil frowned. He wasn't as smart as Scotty. He had never voted because he claimed the machines were too complicated. One of his brothers, who was even less intellectually endowed than Phil, had ended up in jail after writing to *Dateline* NBC's 'To Catch a Predator' asking them to fix him up with a date.

'You know the one: not so smart,' continued Phil, as though Scotty hadn't spoken. He thought for a moment. 'Lia, that's it. Dumb as a box of donuts.'

That old proverb about people in glass houses had clearly never made an impact on Phil. He was the kind of guy who would throw a stone in a glass house, and then be surprised when it didn't bounce.

'Understatement,' said Scotty. 'Girl gave herself a jailhouse tattoo, couldn't even spell her own name right. Three fucking letters. How hard could it be? Now she has "Lai" tattooed on her arm, goes around telling people she's half Hawaiian.'

'Wasn't she in a cult?'

'Yeah. Couldn't spell that right either, or else her hand slipped. Now she has to keep her left arm covered up, especially in church.'

'Yeah, well, it's not like Dan the Man is anybody's idea of a catch,' said Jackie. 'He lives with his mother and sleeps in a NASCAR bed.'

'Jackie,' I pointed out, 'you live with your mother.'

'Yeah, but I don't sleep in no NASCAR bed.'

I left them to it, wondering if those three should be the first guys I banned from the bar, and went to help Gary Maser stock the domestic bottles. I'd hired Gary shortly after I became bar manager, and he was working out well. When we'd finished, and I'd poured us both a cup of coffee, Jackie, Phil, and Scotty were still around, unfortunately. Jackie was reading aloud from the newspaper.

'It's that guy again, the one from Ogunquit who got abducted by aliens,' he explained. 'Says he can't turn on his TV no more. Says the channels keep changing without him touching the clicker, and it makes his head buzz.' Jackie considered this for a time. 'How come it's always guys from Ogunquit that these things happen to?'

'Or Fort Kent,' said Scotty.

'Ayuh, Fort Kent,' said Phil. All three nodded in solemn understanding. It was a widely held belief down east that once you got a certain distance north in Maine, people became very strange indeed. Given that Fort Kent was about as far north as a person could go without taking out Canadian citizenship, it followed that its denizens had strangeness all wrapped up.

'I mean,' Jackie continued, 'what do the aliens think they're going to learn from sticking a probe up the ass of some fella from Ogunquit?'

'Apart from the obvious,' said Phil.

'Like not to do it again,' said Scotty.

'You'd think they'd abduct nuclear scientists, or generals,' said Jackie. 'Instead, all they seem to do is take crackers and rubes.'

'Foot soldiers,' said Phil.

'First wave,' said Scotty. 'They're the ones the aliens will have to, y'know, subdue.'

'But why the probing?' asked Jackie. 'What's with that?'

'Could be someone was yanking their chain,' said Phil. 'Some Venusian: "Yah, you stick a probe up their asses, and they light up."'

'"They play a tune,"' said Scotty.

'I just don't understand it,' Jackie concluded.

At the end of the bar, there was a man scribbling in a notebook. His face looked familiar, and I thought he might have been in the previous week, although he wasn't a regular. He was in his early fifties and wore a brown tweed jacket and an open-collared white shirt. His hair was short, and either he was aging well or he was spending a lot on Grecian. When I'd served him earlier, I'd caught a hint of expensive aftershave. Now he had a finger width of beer at the bottom of his glass. I wandered over to him.

'Get you another?'

As he saw me approach, he closed the notebook and glanced at his watch.

'Just the check, thanks.'

I nodded and slipped him the tab.

'Nice place,' he said.

'Yeah, it is.'

'You been working here long?'

'Nope. Wouldn't even be working today if one of the regular bartenders wasn't sick.'

'So, what? You the manager?'

'The bar manager.'

'Huh.' He chewed his bottom lip, and seemed to consider me for a moment or two. 'Well, I'll be on my way. Next time.'

'Sure,' I said. I watched him leave. Jackie caught the look on my face.

'Something?' he asked.

'Probably nothing.'

I didn't have time to think about the stranger for the rest of the evening. Thursday was always microbrew night at the Bear, with beer specials, and that night we were hosting a small brewery named Andrew's Brewing Company, a father-and-son operation out of Lincolnville. Minutes later we were swamped, and it was all that I could do to keep us out of the weeds for the evening. Two large birthday groups, one almost entirely male, the other exclusively female, hit the restaurant simultaneously and over the course of the night began to meld into one indistinguishable whole of booze-fueled carnality. Meanwhile, there was rarely more than one seat free at the bar, and everyone seemed to want to eat as well as drink. Shorthanded as we were, it meant that Gary and I were working flat out for six hours solid. I didn't even remember seeing Jackie leave; I must have been changing a keg when he wandered into the night.

'This is still February, right?' asked Gary as he made a batch of margaritas for Sarah, one of the regular waitresses who always kept her head covered with a scarf, which made her easy to spot on nights like this one.

'I think so.'

'Then where the hell did all these people come from? It's *February*.'

At about ten-thirty, things quieted down some, and there was time to restock and deal with our casualties. One of the line chefs had sliced himself badly across the palm of the hand with a paring knife, and the wound needed stitches. Now that the Bear was a little calmer, he was free to drive himself to the emergency room. Apart from that, there were the usual minor burns and heated tempers in the kitchen. I'd give the line chefs this much: they were always entertaining. The ones who worked at the Bear were better than most. I knew people in the business who spent a significant portion of their time bailing their chefs out of jail, finding places for them to sleep when their old ladies threw their asses out on the street, and, occasionally, beating them into submission just to keep them under control.

A group of Portland cops had taken up position near the door. Gary had been looking after them for most of the evening. The Bear was a popular hangout for local law enforcement: there was parking, the beer was good, it served food until closing, and it was far enough away from the Old Port and Portland PD headquarters to make them feel that they were off the radar. Perhaps its bunkerlike aspect appealed to them as well. The Bear didn't have many windows, and if all of the lights were switched off, it was pitch black inside.

Now, as I watched, the crowd of cops parted slightly,

and a familiar figure made his way to the bar. I had assumed that they were all Portland cops, but I was wrong. One of them, at least, was a statie: Hansen, the detective out of the barracks in Gray who, more than anyone else, was relishing my current situation. He was fit looking, his eyes more green than blue, with very black hair and a permanent dark shadow on his face from years of shaving with an electric razor. As usual, he was better dressed than the average cop. He wore a well-cut dark blue suit and a blue paisley tie. A gold tie pin twinkled as it caught the lights above the bar.

He took a seat away from the main group and placed his near-empty glass on the bar, then put his hands together and waited for me to come over. I let a couple of seconds go by, then resigned myself to having to deal with him.

'What can I get you, Detective?'

He didn't reply. His jaw moved as his bottom teeth worried against his incisors. I wondered how much he'd had to drink, and decided that it probably wasn't much. He didn't seem like a man who liked to cut loose.

'I heard you were working here,' he said.

'Took you a while to drop by.'

'This isn't a social call.'

'I guessed that. I don't think sociability is in your makeup.'

He looked away, shaking his head slightly, a reasonable man faced with an unreasonable one.

'What are you doing here?' he asked, gesturing with

disdain at the bar, the clientele, maybe even the world itself.

'Making a living. You and your buddies dug up my chosen career path. I picked another temporarily.'

'"Temporarily"? You think so? I hear your lawyer is making a lot of calls on your behalf. Good luck to her. Better rack up the tips. She doesn't work cheap.'

'Well, here's your chance to contribute to the cause. You want a refill on that, or should I just leave you to fill it yourself with piss and vinegar?'

Hansen leaned forward. His eyes, I now saw, were slightly glazed. Either he'd had more than I thought, or he just couldn't hold his booze.

'This is a cop place. Don't you have any dignity? You let good police see you like this, working behind a bar. What are you trying to do, rub it in their faces?'

It was a question that I'd asked myself. Even Dave had said, when he offered me the job, that he would understand if I didn't want to take it because of the cops who drank there. I told him I didn't much care what anyone thought, but maybe Hansen was hitting closer to the mark than I wanted to give him credit for. There was an element of cussedness about my decision to work at the Bear. I wasn't going to slink away after what had happened. True, some of the cops who came to the bar seemed embarrassed by my presence there, and a couple were openly contemptuous of me, but they were guys who'd never much cared for me anyway. Most of the rest were just fine, and some had let me know how sorry they were for what had been done. It didn't matter much either way. I was content to let things rest, for now. It gave me time to do what I wanted to do.

'You know, Detective, if I didn't know better, I'd think that you had a hard-on for me. Maybe I could introduce you to some people? Might help relieve some of that tension. Or you could take out an ad in the *Phoenix*. Lot of guys out there aching for a man with a uniform in his closet.'

Hansen expelled a single humorless laugh, like a poison dart being blown from a pipe.

'You'd better hold on to that dry wit,' he said. 'A man who goes home smelling of stale beer to an empty house needs something to laugh about.'

'It's not empty,' I said. 'I have a dog.'

I picked up his glass. I figured he was drinking Andrew's Brown, so I poured him a refill and placed it before him.

'On the house,' I said. 'We like to keep good customers happy.'

'You drink it,' he replied. 'We're done here.'

He took his wallet from his pocket and put down a twenty.

'Keep the change. Won't buy you much, but it'll buy you even less in New York. You want to tell me what you were doing down there?'

I shouldn't have been shocked. I'd been stopped five times by state troopers on the highway in recent months. It was someone's way of letting me know that I hadn't been forgotten. Now a cop at the Portland Jetport had probably recognized me when I was traveling either to or from New York, and had made a call. I'd need to be more careful in the future.

'I was visiting friends.'

'That's good. A man needs friends. But I find that you're working a case, and I'll break you.'

He turned away, said his good-byes to his buddies, and left the bar. Gary sidled over to me as the door closed behind Hansen.

'Everything okay?'

'Everything's fine.' I handed him the twenty. 'I think he was one of yours.'

Gary looked at the untouched beer.

'He didn't finish his beer.'

'He didn't come here to drink.'

'Then why did he come here?'

It was a good question.

'For the company, I guess.'

6

I took Walter, my Labrador retriever, for a walk when I got home shortly after eleven. The novelty of snow had eventually worn off for him, as it did for most creatures, man or beast, who spent longer than a week in Maine in winter, so that now he contented himself with a few desultory sniffs before doing what he had to do and indicating his preference for returning to his warm basket by turning around and heading straight back to the house. He had matured a lot in the last year. Perhaps it was because the house was quieter than it was before, and he had accommodated himself somewhat to the fact that Rachel and Sam were no longer part of its, and his, routines. I liked having him in the house for a whole lot of reasons: security, company, and maybe because he was a link to the family life that was no longer mine. Two families lost now: Rachel and Sam to Vermont, and Susan and Jennifer to a man who had torn them apart, and who had died in turn by my hand. But I also felt guilty about the amount of time I was leaving Walter alone, or with my neighbors, the Johnsons. They were happy to look after him when I wasn't around, but Bob Johnson wasn't so good on his feet anymore, and it was asking a lot of him to exercise a frisky dog regularly.

I locked the doors, patted Walter, then went to bed and tried to sleep, but when it came it brought with it strange dreams, dreams of Susan and Jennifer so vivid that I woke in the darkness, convinced that I had heard someone speak. It had been many months since I had dreamed of them in such a way.

What do I call them? Even now, after all these years, how do I say it? My murdered wife? My late daughter? They died, but I held something of them inside me for too long, and that in turn manifested itself as phantasms, echoes of the next life in this one, and I could not bring myself to call these remnants by the names of those whom I had loved. We haunt ourselves, I sometimes think; or, rather, we choose to be haunted. If there is a hole in our lives, then something will fill it. We invite it inside, and it accepts willingly.

But I had made my peace with them, I thought. Susan, my wife. Jennifer, my daughter. Beloved of me, and I, beloved of them.

Susan once said to me that, if anything happened to Jennifer, if she were to die before her time, before her mother, then I should not tell Susan what had occurred. I should not try to explain to her that her child was gone. I must not do that to her. If Jennifer were to die, I was to kill Susan. There should be no words, no warning. She should not have time to look at me and understand why. I was to take her life, for she did not believe that she could live with the loss of her child. It would be too much to bear; she would not be able to withstand such pain. It would not kill her, not at first, but it would draw the life from her just the same, and all that would be left would be a hollow shell, a woman resonant with grief.

And she would hate me. She would hate me for putting her through such sorrow, for not loving her enough to spare her. I would be a coward in her eyes.

'Promise me,' she said, as I held her in my arms. 'Promise me that you won't let that happen. I don't ever want to hear those words. I don't want to have to hurt that much. I couldn't bear it. Do you hear me? This isn't a joke, a "what-if?" I want you to promise me that I will never have to endure that pain.'

And I promised. I knew that I could not have done what she asked, and perhaps she knew that too, but I made the promise just the same. That is what we do for the ones we love: we lie to protect them. Not all truths are welcome.

But what she did not explain, what she did not consider, was what would happen if they were both wrenched from me. Should I take my own life? Should I follow them into that dark place, tracing their steps through the underworld until I found them at last, a sacrifice to no purpose other than the denial of loss? Or should I continue, and if I should, then how? What form should my life take? Should I die alone, worshipping at the shrine of their memory, waiting for time to do what I could not do for myself; or would I try to find a way to live with their loss, to survive without betraying their memory? What acts do those who are left behind have to perform to honor the memory of the departed, and how far can they go before they betray that memory?

I lived. That is what I did. They were taken, but I stayed. I found the one who had killed them, and I killed him in turn, but it gave me no satisfaction. It did not assuage the burning grief. It did not make their loss any easier to endure, and it almost cost me my soul, if, indeed, I have a soul. The Collector, that repository of old secrets, once told me that I did not, and sometimes I am inclined to believe him.

I still feel their loss every day. It defines me.

I am the shadow cast by all that once was.

7

Daniel Faraday sat in the basement room and felt his grief slowly give way to anger. His son had been dead for four days, and his body still lay in the morgue. They had been assured that he would be released for burial the next day. The chief had promised them as much during his visit earlier that afternoon.

In the days since the discovery of Bobby's remains, Daniel and his wife had become ghosts in their own home, creatures defined only by loss, and absence, and grief. Their only son was gone, and Daniel knew that his passing signaled also the death of their marriage in all but name. Bobby had kept his parents together, but his father had not realized the extent of their debt to him until he had left for college, and then returned. So much of their conversation had revolved around the activities of their beloved son: their hopes for him, their fears, their occasional disappointments, although the latter now seemed so trivial that Daniel silently berated himself for ever having raised them with the boy. He regretted every harsh word, every argument, every hour of sullen silence that had passed in the aftermath of conflict. Even as he did so, he recalled the circumstances of each disagreement, and knew that every word spoken in anger had also been spoken out of love.

This had been his son's space. There was a TV, and a stereo, and a dock for his iPod, although Bobby was one of the only kids in town who still preferred to listen to music on vinyl when he was at home. He had inherited his father's old record collection, most of it classic stuff from the sixties and seventies, adding to it from the racks of used record stores and the occasional yard sale. There was still an LP sitting on the turntable, an original copy of *After the Gold Rush* by Neil Young, its surface a network of tiny scratches yet clearly, as far as Bobby had been concerned, still listenable, the pops and hisses a part of the record's history, its warmth and humanity enhanced by the flaws it had accumulated over the years.

Most of the basement floor was covered by a huge rug that always smelled faintly of spilled beer and old potato chips. There were bookshelves, and a gunmetal gray filing cabinet whose drawers had been used mainly for storing old photographs, college notes, textbooks, and, unbeknownst to the boy's mother, some mild pornography. There was a battered red couch with a stained blue pillow at one end facing the TV. The pillow still bore the imprint of his son's head and the couch had retained the shape of his body so that, in the dim light cast by the basement's sole lamp, it seemed that the ghost of his son had somehow returned to this place, occupying his old familiar position, a thing invisible yet with weight and substance. Daniel wanted to curl up there, to mold his body into the ridges and hollows of the couch, to become one with his lost son, yet he did not. To do so would be to disturb the impression that remained, and with it to banish something of the boy's essence. He would not lie there. Nobody would lie there. It would remain as a memorial to all that had been taken from him, from them.

At first, there had been only shock. Bobby could not be gone. He could not be dead. Death was for the old and the sick. Death was for the children of other men. His son was mortal, but not yet shadowed by mortality. His passing should have been a distant thing, and his father and mother should have predeceased him. He should have mourned them. It was not right, not natural, that they should now be forced to cry over his remains, to watch as his coffin was lowered into the ground. He remembered again the sight of his son's body on the gurney in the morgue, draped with a sheet, swollen with the gases of decay, a deep red line circling his throat where the rope had cut into him.

Suicide. That had been the initial verdict. Bobby had asphyxiated himself by tying a rope to a tree, dropping the noose at the other end around his neck, and leaning forward with the full weight of his body. At some point, he had realized the awfulness of what was about to happen and had struggled to release himself, scratching and tearing at his flesh, even ripping loose one of his fingernails, but by then the rope had cinched itself tight, the knot designed so that, if his courage failed him, the instrument of his self-destruction would not.

The chief had asked them, in those first hours, if they knew why Bobby might have wanted to kill himself. Was he unhappy? Were there unusual stresses and tensions in his life? Did he owe money to anyone? The autopsy showed that he had been drinking heavily before he died, and his motorcycle was found in a ditch at the edge of the field. It was a wonder, the coroner said, that the boy had managed to ride the bike so far considering the amount of alcohol he had consumed.

And all Daniel Faraday could think of was the girl, Emily, the one for whom his son had not been good enough.

But then the chief had returned that afternoon, and everything had changed. It was a question of angles and force, he had told them, although he, and the state police detectives, had already voiced their suspicions among themselves, given the nature of the wounds that the rope had left on his skin. There had been two injuries to his son's neck, but the first had been obscured by the second, and it had taken the state's chief medical examiner to confirm the suspicions of her deputy. Two injuries: the first inflicted by asphyxiation from behind, possibly while the boy was lying flat on the ground, judging by some bruises to his back where his attacker had perhaps knelt upon him. The initial injury was not fatal, but had resulted in a loss of consciousness. Death had occurred from the second injury. The noose had been kept around the boy's neck as he was lifted to his knees, the other end of the rope secured around the trunk of the tree.

His killer, or killers, had then put further pressure on his back, forcing him forward so that he slowly strangled.

The chief had said that it must have taken considerable strength and effort to kill big, strong Bobby Faraday in that way. The rope was being tested for traces of DNA, as was the lower part of the tree, but—

They had waited for him to continue.

The person or persons responsible for Bobby's death had been careful, he told them. Bobby's hair and clothing had been soaked with pond water and mud, along with his fingernails and the skin of his hands. The intention had clearly been to corrupt any trace evidence, and it had been successful. The authorities weren't going to give up on finding Bobby's killer, he reassured them, but their task had been made a great deal more difficult. He had asked them to keep this information to themselves for the time being, and they had agreed to do so.

After the chief left, Daniel held his wife as she wept in his arms. He was not sure why she was crying, only surprised that she had any tears left to shed. Perhaps she was weeping at the horror of it, or because this was a new grief that her son had not taken his own life, but had his life taken from him by others. She did not say, and he did not ask her. But when he felt the first of his own tears slide down his cheek, he understood that his were not tears of loss, or of horror, or even of anger. He was relieved. He realized that he had felt a kind of hatred for his son for killing himself. He had been raging at the selfishness of the act, the stupidity of it, that Bobby had not turned to those who loved him in his moment of direst need. He had hated his son for rendering his father powerless, and for leaving his parents to bear the weight of his grief in his stead. For the time that he had believed his son had died at his own hand, Daniel had contemplated the horror of the act during the long, still days and nights, the hours creeping by with relentless sloth. Grief, it seemed, was a kind of matter: it could not be created or destroyed, but merely altered its form. In dying, the sadness that might have driven Bobby to such an act had not dissipated, but had merely transferred itself to those left behind. There had been no note, no explanation, as though any explanation could have sufficed. There had only been unanswered questions, and the gnawing sense that they had failed their son.

Daniel's first instinct had been to blame the girl. Bobby had not been the same since she had broken off their relationship. Despite his size, and his apparent ease with the world, there was a sensitivity to him, a softness. He had dated before, and there had been break-ups and teenage traumas, but he had fallen heavily for the slim young woman with the dark hair and pale green eyes. She was a few years older than Bobby, and she had something special; that was undeniable. There had been rivals for her affections, but she had chosen him. His son knew that. The power had been hers, and he had always struggled slightly with the imbalance that it created in the relationship.

Daniel believed, as most fathers did, that his son

was the finest young man in town, maybe even the finest young man he had ever known. He deserved the very best in life: the most rewarding of jobs, the most beautiful of women, the most loving of children. That Bobby did not share this view was both one of his best and worst qualities: admirable in its natural humility, yet frustrating in the way in which it stifled his ambition and caused him to doubt himself. Daniel believed that the girl was clever enough to play on that disparity, but then that was true of all her sex. Daniel Faraday had always been suspicious of women. He admired them, and was attracted to them (in truth, more than his wife knew, or pretended to know, for he had acted on that attraction with others more than once during their marriage), but he had never come close to understanding them, and by engaging in casual conquests and then casting them aside he was able to balance this lack of comprehension with a degree of contempt. He had watched as the girl manipulated his son, twisting and turning him as though he were caught on a silken thread that could draw him closer or keep him dangling at a distance, as she chose. Bobby knew what was being done, and yet he was so smitten that he could not bring himself to break the bond. His father and mother had discussed it more than once over a bottle of wine, but had differed in their interpretations of the relationship. While Daniel's wife had acknowledged that the girl was clever, still she felt that there was nothing unusual in her behavior. She was merely doing what all young girls did, or what those who understood the nature of the balance of power between the sexes generally did. The boy wanted her, but as soon as she gave herself to him unconditionally she would cede control of the relationship. Better to force him to prove his loyalty before she surrendered herself fully.

Daniel had to concede that his wife had a point, but he disliked seeing his son being played for a fool. Bobby was comparatively naive and inexperienced, even though he was almost twenty-two. He had not yet had his heart truly broken. Then the girl had ended the relationship after Bobby came back from college for the holidays, and that experience had been forced upon him. There had been no warning, and no explanation was given beyond the fact that she believed Bobby was not the man for her. His son had taken it badly, to the extent that it had caused him actual, physical pain, he said: an ache deep in his belly that would not subside.

The break-up had also plunged him into depression, a depression exacerbated by the fact that this was a small town: there were only so many places one could go to drink, to eat, to see a movie, to pass the time. The girl worked behind the bar at Dean's Place, and Dean's was where the young people of the town – and many of the older ones too – had for generations gone to congregate. If Bobby wanted to socialize, then Dean's could be avoided for only so long. Daniel knew that following the break-up there had been encounters at Dean's between the two young people. Even then, the girl had enjoyed the upper hand. His son had been drinking, while she had not. After one particularly loud exchange, old Dean himself, who ruled his bar like a benevolent dictator, had been forced to warn Bobby against bothering the staff. As a result, Bobby had stayed away from Dean's for a week, returning home from work each evening and heading straight for his basement hideaway, barely pausing to greet his parents and emerging only to raid the refrigerator or to share an awkward meal at the kitchen table. Sometimes he slept on the couch instead of in the adjoining bedroom, not even bothering to undress. Only after some of his friends came by and cajoled him out did the clouds above his head seem to break for a time, and then only for as long as he avoided seeing the girl.

When his body was discovered, Daniel's first thought was that he had killed himself out of some misplaced devotion to Emily. After all, there seemed to be nothing else troubling him. He was saving for college, and seemed to have every intention of returning to further study, hinting that perhaps Emily might come with him and get a job in the city; he was popular with his friends both there and at home; and his natural disposition had always tended toward the optimistic, or had until the dissolution of his relationship.

Emily should have stayed with his son, thought Daniel. He was a fine boy. She should not have broken his heart. When she had arrived at the death site, just as the body was being carried across the fields to the waiting ambulance, Daniel had been unable to speak to her. She had approached him, her eyes glistening, her arms raised to hold him and to be held in turn, but he had turned away from her, one hand outstretched behind him, the palm raised in a gesture that was plain to all who had witnessed it, and in that way he had made it clear where he felt the blame for his son's death lay.

And so Bobby's mother had wept tears of grief and pain at the news that her son's life had been taken from him by others, of incomprehension at the manner of her son's death, while his father had felt some of the weight lifted from his shoulders, and he marveled at his own selfishness. Now, in the basement, the anger came back, and his hands formed themselves into fists as he raged at the faceless thing that had killed his son. Somewhere above him the doorbell rang, but he barely heard it over the roaring in his head. Then his name was called, and he allowed the tension to ease from his body. He released a ragged breath.

'My boy,' he said softly. 'My poor boy.'

Emily Kindler was sitting at the kitchen table. Behind her, his wife was making tea.

'Mr. Faraday,' said Emily.

He found that he was able to smile at her. It was a small thing, but there was genuine warmth in it. There was no longer any hint of blame attaching to her for what had occurred, and she seemed more like a link to his son, fuel for the fire of his memory.

'Emily,' he said. 'How are you doing?'

'Okay, I guess.' She could not look at his face. He knew that his rejection had wounded her deeply, and if he had absolved her of all blame, she had yet to do the same for him. They had never discussed what had happened that day, so it was true to say that he had not made any recompense for it.

His wife came over and touched the girl's hair gently with the palm of her hand, smoothing down some loose strands. Daniel thought that they looked a little alike: both were pale and without makeup, and there were dark circles of grief beneath their eyes.

'I've come to tell you that I'm leaving after the funeral.'

He struggled to find something to say.

'Listen, honey,' he said, 'I owe you an apology.' He reached for her hand, and she allowed him to take it. 'That day, the day they found Bobby, I wasn't myself. I was just so hurt, so shocked, that I couldn't . . . I couldn't . . .'

Words failed him. He did not want to lie to her, and he did not want to tell her the truth.

'I know why you couldn't look at me,' she said. 'You thought it was my fault. Maybe you still do.'

He felt his chin begin to tremble, and his eyes grew hot. He did not want to cry in front of her. He shook his head.

'I'm sorry,' he said. 'I apologize for ever thinking that of you.'

Now she gripped his hand tentatively as his wife placed three cups on the table and poured tea from an old china pot. 'Thank you.'

'Chief Dashut came by earlier,' he continued. 'He said that Bobby didn't take his own life. He was murdered. He asked us to keep it quiet for now. We've told nobody else, but you, you should know.'

The girl made a small mewling sound. The little blood she had left seemed to drain from her face.

'What?'

'The injuries, they're not consistent with suicide.' He was crying now. 'Bobby was killed. Someone choked him until he was unconscious, then tightened the rope around him until he died. Who would do that? Who would do such a thing to my boy?'

He tried to hold on to her, but her hand slipped from his. She stood up, teetering on her low heels.

'No,' she said. She turned suddenly, her right hand trailing. It caught the nearest cup and sent it falling to the floor, where it shattered on the tiles. 'I have to go,' she said. 'I can't stay here.'

And there was something in her voice that caused Daniel's tears to cease.

'What do you mean?'

'I just can't stay. I have to leave.'

There was knowledge in her eyes. Daniel saw it.

'What do you know?' he said. 'What do you know about my boy's death?'

He heard his wife speak, but it meant nothing to him. All of his attention was focused on the girl. Her eyes were huge. They were staring at the window behind him, where her face was reflected in the glass. She looked confused, as though the image there was not the one that she had expected to see.

'Tell me,' he said. 'Please.'

She did not speak for a time. Then, softly: 'I caused this.'

'What? How?'

'I'm bad luck. I bring it with me. It *follows* me.'

She looked at him for the first time, and he shivered. He had never seen such desolation in the eyes of another human being, not even in his wife's eyes when he'd told her that their son was gone, not even in his own as he looked in the mirror and saw the father of a dead child.

'What follows you?'

The first of her tears began to fall. She continued speaking, but he felt as though their presence in the room was immaterial to her. She was talking to another, or perhaps to herself.

'There's something haunting me,' she said, '*someone* haunting me, following in my footsteps. It won't give me peace. It won't leave me alone. It hurts the people I care about. I bring it down on them. I don't want to, but I do.'

Slowly, he approached her. 'Emmy,' using his son's pet name for her, 'you're not making any sense. Who is this person?'

'I don't know,' she said, her head low. 'I don't know.'

He wanted to shake her, to pummel the information from her. He did not know if she was talking about a real person or some imagined shadow, a ghost conjured up to explain her own torment. An unknown entity had killed his son. Now here was his ex-girlfriend talking about someone following her. It needed to be explained.

She seemed to sense what he was thinking, for as he moved to take hold of her, she slipped away.

'Don't touch me!' The ferocity with which she spoke the words caused him to yield to her.

'Emily, you need to explain yourself. You have to tell the police what you've told us.'

She almost laughed. 'Tell them what? That I'm haunted?' She was in the hallway now, backing toward the door. 'I'm sorry for what happened to Bobby, but I won't stay here. It's found me. It's time to move on.'

Her hand found the door handle and twisted it. Outside, Daniel felt snow coming. This strange spell of warmth was coming to an end. Soon, they would be lost in drifts, and his son's grave would gape darkly like a wound amid the whiteness as they lowered him into the ground.

He began running as Emily turned to leave, but she was too fast for him. His fingers touched the material of her shirt, and then he stumbled on the porch step and dropped heavily to his knees. By the time he got to his feet, she was already running down the street. He tried to follow, but his legs hurt and he had been shocked by the fall. He leaned against the gate, his face contorted in pain and frustration, as his wife held his shoulders and asked him questions that he could not answer.

Daniel called the police as soon as he was inside the house. The dispatcher took his name and number and promised to pass his message on to the chief. He told her that it was urgent, and demanded that she give him Dashut's cell phone number, but she informed him that the chief was out of town and had given orders that, for this night at least, he was not to be disturbed. Eventually, she promised to call the chief as soon as Daniel was off the line. With no other option, Daniel thanked her and hung up.

The chief did not call back that night, even though the dispatcher had informed him of Daniel Faraday's call. He was having a good time with his family at his brother's fortieth birthday party, and he believed that he had earned it. He had not told Daniel Faraday and his wife all that he had learned. That morning, one of his men had called Dashut's attention to the base of the tree to which Bobby Faraday had been tied. Initials had been carved into its bark by the kids who had gone there to make out over the years, transforming it into a monument to love and lust, both passing and undying.

But something else had been hacked into the bark, and recently too, judging by the color of the exposed flesh beneath: a symbol of some kind, but unlike anything that Dashut had seen before.

He made sure that a photograph was taken of it, and he intended to seek advice about it the next day.

The symbol might mean nothing, of course, or be entirely unconnected to the Faraday killing, but its presence at the murder scene troubled him. Even at the party, as he tried to put it from his mind, it came back to him, and, with a damp finger, he found himself tracing it upon a table, as if by doing so it might reveal its meaning.

By the time the party was over, it was after 2 a.m. Daniel Faraday, the chief decided, would have to wait until the morning.

Daniel Faraday and his wife died that night. The rings on their gas stove had been turned to full. The windows, and the front and back doors, all fitted perfectly in their frames, for Daniel worked as a supervisor for one of the local utility companies and knew the cost of heat leakage in winter, so no gas escaped from the house. It seemed that his wife must have had second thoughts at some point (that, or there was the dreadful possibility that it was not a pact, but a murder-suicide on the part of her husband), for her body was found lying on the bedroom floor. On the kitchen table was a photograph of the Faradays with their son, along with a bunch of winter flowers. It was assumed that they had killed themselves out of grief, and the chief was overwhelmed by guilt for failing to return their call. It made him more determined than ever to find whomever was responsible for Bobby Faraday's death, even as he slowly began to wonder about three apparent suicides, all involving a single family, one of which had already proven to be something other than what it first appeared.

Emily finished packing her bags after leaving the Faradays. She had been preparing to leave town ever since Bobby had gone missing, sensing somehow (although she did not speak the words aloud) that Bobby would not be returning, that something terrible had befallen him. The discovery of his body, and the nature of his death, only confirmed what she already knew. She had been discovered. It was time to move on again.

Emily had been running for years from the thing that was pursuing her. She was getting better and better at concealing herself from it, but not good enough to hide from it forever. Eventually, she feared, it would trap her.

It would trap her, and it would consume her.

8

I had the next day off, and it was the first opportunity I had been given in some time to see how unsettled Walter had become. He would paw at the door to be let out, then minutes later would beg to be let in again. He seemed not to want to leave my side for too long, but struggled to sleep. When Bob Johnson came over to say hi while out for his morning constitutional, Walter would not go to him, not even when Bob offered him half a cookie from his pocket.

'You know,' said Bob, 'he was like that while you were away in New York. I thought he might just be ailing that weekend, but it doesn't seem to have gotten any better.'

I took Walter to the vet that afternoon, but the vet could find nothing wrong with him.

'Is he alone for long periods?' she asked me.

'Well, I work, and sometimes I have to stay away from home for a night or two. The neighbors look after him when I'm gone.'

She patted Walter. 'My guess is he doesn't like that very much. He's still a young dog. He needs company and stimulation. He needs a routine.'

Two days later, I made the decision.

It was Sunday, and I was on the road early, Walter on the front seat beside me, alternately dozing and watching the world go by. I reached Burlington before noon, and stopped at a little toy store I knew to buy a rag doll for Sam, and at a bakery to pick up some muffins. While I was there, I bought a coffee at a place on Church Street and tried to read *The New York Times*, Walter at my feet. Rachel and Sam lived only ten minutes outside town, but still I lingered. I couldn't concentrate on the newspaper. Instead, I stroked Walter, and his eyelids drooped with pleasure.

A woman emerged from the gallery across the street, her red hair loose upon her shoulders. Rachel was smiling, but not at me. A man was behind her, saying something that was making her laugh. He looked older than she did, comfortable and paunchy. He placed the palm of his hand lightly against the small of her back as they walked together. Walter spotted Rachel and tried to rise, his tail wagging, but I held him back with his collar. I folded the newspaper and tossed it aside.

Today was going to be a bad day.

When I reached Rachel's parents' property, her mother, Joan, was outside the main house, playing ball with Sam. Sam was two now, and was already at that point where she knew the names of her favorite foods, and understood the concept of 'mine,' which pretty much covered everything she had developed a liking for, from other people's cookies to the occasional tree. I envied Rachel the opportunity she had to watch Sam develop. I seemed to see it only in fits and starts, like a jerky film from which crucial frames had been excised.

Sam recognized me as I stepped from the car. Actually, I think she recognized Walter before me, because she called out a mangled version of his name that sounded like 'Walnut' and spread her arms in welcome. She had never been afraid of Walter. Walter fell into the category of 'mine' where Sam was concerned, and Walter, I suspected, regarded Sam in much the same way. He bounded up to her, but slowed down when he was a couple of feet away, so that he wouldn't knock her over. She threw her arms around him. After licking her some, he lay down and let her fall upon him, his tail wagging happily.

If Joan had been gifted with a tail, I don't think it would have been wagging. She struggled to put a smile on her face as I approached, and kissed me lightly on the cheek.

'We weren't expecting you,' she said. 'Rachel went into town. I'm not sure when she'll be back.'

'I can wait,' I said. 'Anyway, I came to see Sam, and to ask a favor.'

'A favor?' The smile wavered again.

'It'll hold until Rachel returns.'

Sam relinquished her grip on Walter for long enough to toddle up to me and put her arms around my legs. I lifted her up and stared into her eyes as I gave her the doll.

'Hey, beautiful,' I said. She laughed and touched my face.

'Daddy,' she said, and my eyes grew warm.

Joan invited me inside and offered coffee. I'd had my fill of coffee for the day, but it gave her something to do. Otherwise, we'd simply have ended up staring at each other, or using Sam and Walter as a distraction. Joan excused herself, and I heard a door close and then her voice speaking in a low tone. I guessed that she was calling Rachel. While she was gone, Sam and I played with Walter, and I listened to her speaking a mixture of recognizable words and her own private language.

Joan returned and poured the coffee, then put some milk in a plastic cup for Sam, and we picked at the muffins while talking about nothing at all. After about fifteen minutes, I heard a car pull up outside, then Rachel entered the kitchen, looking flustered and angry. Sam immediately went to her, then pointed at the dog and said 'Walnut' again.

'This is a surprise,' said Rachel, making it clear that, as surprises went, it was right up there with finding a corpse in one's bed.

'A spur of the moment decision,' I said. 'Sorry if I disrupted your plans.'

Despite my best efforts, or maybe they just weren't very good to begin with, there was an edge to my voice. Rachel picked up on it, and frowned. Joan, ever the diplomat, took Sam and Walter outside to play as Rachel removed her coat and tossed it on a chair.

'You should have called,' she said. 'We might have been out, or away somewhere.'

She made an attempt to clear some plates from the draining board, then gave up.

'So,' she said. 'How have you been?'

'I've been okay.'

'You still working at the Bear?'

'Yeah. It's not so bad.'

She did a good imitation of her mother's pained smile. 'I'm glad to hear that.'

There was silence for a time, then: 'We need to formalize these visits, that's all. It's a long way to come on a whim.'

'I try to come as often as I can, Rach, and I do my best to call. Besides, this isn't quite a whim.'

'You know what I mean.'

More silence.

'Mom said you had a favor to ask.'

'I want you to keep Walter.'

For the first time she showed some emotion other than frustration and barely restrained anger.

'What? You love that dog.'

'Yes, but I'm not around enough for him, and he loves you and Sam at least as much as he loves me. He's cooped up in the house when I'm working, and I keep having to ask Bob and Shirley to look after him when I leave town. It's not fair to him, and I know your mom and dad like dogs.'

Rachel's parents had kept dogs until very recently, when their two old collies had both died within months of each other. Since then, they'd talked about getting another dog, but hadn't quite been able to bring themselves to do it.

Rachel's face softened. 'I'll have to ask mom,' she said, 'but I think it'll be fine. Are you sure, though?'

'No,' I said, 'but it's the right thing to do.'

She walked over and, after a moment's hesitation, hugged me.

'Thank you,' she said.

I'd put Walter's basket and toys in the trunk, and I handed them over to Joan once it was clear that she was content to take him. Her husband Frank was away on business, but she knew that he wouldn't object, especially if it made Sam and Rachel happy. Walter seemed to know what was happening. He went where his basket went, and when he saw it being placed in the kitchen he understood that he was staying. He licked my hand as I was leaving, then sat himself down beside Sam in recognition of the fact that his role as her guardian had been restored to him.

Rachel walked me to the car.

'I'm just curious,' she said. 'How come you're away so much if your job is at the Bear?'

'I'm looking into something,' I replied.

'Where?'

'New York.'

'You're not supposed to be working. It could prevent you from getting your license back.'

'It's not business,' I said. 'It's personal.'

'It's always personal with you.'

'Hardly worth doing if it isn't.'

'Well, just be careful, that's all.'

'I will.' I opened the car door. 'I have to tell you something. I was in town earlier. I saw you.'

Her face froze.

'Who is he?'

'His name is Martin,' she said, after a moment.

'How long have you been seeing him?'

'Not long. A month, maybe.' She paused. 'I don't know how serious it is yet. I was going to tell you. I just hadn't figured out how.'

I nodded. 'I'll call next time,' I said, then got into the car and drove away.

I learned something that day: there may be worse things than arriving somewhere with your dog and leaving without him, but there aren't many.

It was a long, quiet ride home.

II

A false friend is more dangerous than an open enemy.

Francis Bacon (1561–1626),
'A Letter of Advice . . . to the Duke of Buckingham'

9

Nearly a week went by before I could make another trip to New York. Not that it mattered so much: the Bear was short-staffed again, and I ended up working extra days to take some of the load, so there was no way that I could have gone down there even if I had wanted to.

I had been trying to contact Jimmy Gallagher for almost a month, leaving messages on the machine at his home, but there had been no reply until that week. I received a letter, not a phone call, informing me that he'd taken a long vacation to free himself from the New York winter, but now he was back in town and would be happy to meet with me. The letter was handwritten. That was very much Jimmy's style: he wrote letters in perfect copperplate, shunned computers, and thought that telephones were for his convenience, not for other people's. It was a miracle that he even had an answering machine, but Jimmy still liked to socialize, and the machine made sure that he didn't miss anything important while enabling him to ignore anything that didn't appeal. As for cell phones, I was pretty sure that he regarded them as the devil's work, on a par with poisoned arrowheads and people who used salt on their food without tasting it first. His letter said that he would be free to meet me on Sunday at midday. Again, that precision was typical of Jimmy Gallagher. My father used to say that Jimmy's police reports were works of art. They would show them to classes at the academy as perfect examples of paperwork, which was like showing the ceiling of the Sistine Chapel to a bunch of trainee painters and explaining that this was what they should be aiming for when they were working on the walls of apartment blocks.

I booked the cheapest flight that I could find, and got into JFK shortly before 9 a.m., then took a cab to Bensonhurst. Ever since I was a boy, I had struggled to associate Jimmy Gallagher with Bensonhurst. Of all the places that an Irish cop, and a closeted homosexual to boot, might have called home, Bensonhurst seemed about as likely a choice as Salt Lake City, or Kingston, Jamaica. True, there were now Koreans, and Poles, and Arabs, and Russians in the neighborhood, and even African Americans, but it was the Italians who had always owned Bensonhurst, figuratively if not literally. When Jimmy was growing up, each nationality had its own section, and if you wandered into the wrong ones you were likely to get a beating, but the Italians gave out more beatings than most. Now, even their age was passing. Bay Ridge Parkway was still pretty solidly Italian, and there was one mass said each day in Italian at St. Domenic's at 20th Street, but the Russians, Chinese, and Arabs were slowly encroaching, taking over the side streets like ants advancing on a millipede. The Jews and Irish, meanwhile, had been decimated, and the blacks, whose roots in the area dated back to the Underground Railroad, had been reduced to a four-block enclave off Bath Avenue.

I was still two hours early for my meeting with Jimmy. I knew that he went to church every Sunday, but even if he were home he would resent it if I arrived early. That was another thing about Jimmy. He believed in punctuality, and he didn't care for people who erred on the side of early or late, so while I waited I took a walk along 18th Avenue to get breakfast at Stella's Diner on 63rd, where my father and I had eaten with Jimmy on a couple of occasions because, even though it was nearly twenty blocks from where he lived, Jimmy was close to the owners, and they always made sure that he was taken care of.

While 18th still bore the title of Cristoforo Colombo Boulevard, the Chinese had made their mark, and their restaurants, hair salons, lighting stores, and even aquarium suppliers now stood alongside Italian law firms, Gino's Foccaceria, Queen Ann's Gourmet Pasta, and the Arcobaleno Italiano music and DVD store, where old men sat on benches with their backs to the avenue, as though signaling their dissatisfaction with the changes that had occurred there. The old Cotillion Terrace was boarded up, twin pink cocktails on either side of the main marquee still bubbling sadly.

When I got to Stella's, it too was no more. The name remained, and I could see some of the stools were still in place in front of the counter, but otherwise the diner had been stripped bare. We had always sat at Stella's counter when we ate there, Jimmy to the left, my father in the middle, and I at the end. For me, it was as close as I could get to sitting at a bar, and I would watch as the waitresses poured coffee and the plates moved back and forth between the kitchen and the diners, listening to snatches of conversation from all around while my father and Jimmy talked quietly of adult things. I tapped once upon the glass in farewell, then took my *New York Times* down to the corner of 64th and ate a slice at J & V's pizzeria, which had been in existence for longer than I had. When my watch showed 11:45 a.m., I made my way to Jimmy's house.

Jimmy lived on 71st, between 16th and 17th, a block that consisted mostly of narrow row homes, in a small, one-family semi-detached stucco house with a wrought-iron fence surrounding the yard and a fig tree in the backyard, not far from the area still known as New Utrecht. This had been one of the six original towns of Brooklyn, but then it was annexed to the city in the 1890s and lost its identity. It had been mostly farmland until 1885, when the coming of the Brooklyn, Bath and West End Railroad opened it up to developers, one of whom, James Lynch, built a suburb, Bensonhurst-by-the-Sea, for a thousand families. With the railroad arrived Jimmy Gallagher's grandfather, who had been a supervising engineer on the project, and his family. Eventually, after some shuffling around, the Gallaghers returned to Bensonhurst and settled in the house that Jimmy still occupied, not too far from the landmark New Utrecht Reformed Church at 18th and 83rd.

In time, the subway came, and with it the middle classes, including Jews and Italians who were abandoning the Lower East Side for the comparatively wide open spaces of Brooklyn. Fred Trump, the Donald's father, made his name by building the Shore Haven Apartments near the Belt Parkway, at five thousand units the largest private housing development in Brooklyn. Finally, the Southern Italian immigrants arrived in force in the 1950s, and Bensonhurst became eighty percent Italian by blood, and one hundred percent Italian by reputation.

I had visited Jimmy's house on only a couple occasions with my father, one of which was to pay our respects after Jimmy's father died. All I could recall of that occasion was a wall of cops, some in uniform, some not, with red-eyed women passing around drinks and whispering memories of the departed. Shortly after, his mother had moved out to a place on Gerritsen Beach to be closer to her sister. Since then, Jimmy had always lived alone in Bensonhurst.

The exterior of the house was much as I remembered it, the yard tidy, the paintwork recently refreshed. I was reaching for the bell when the door opened, saving me the trouble of ringing, and there was Jimmy Gallagher, older and grayer but still recognizably the same big man who had crushed my hand in his grip so that I might earn the dollar that was on offer. His face was more florid now and, although he had clearly had some sun while he was away, a roseate tinge to his nose suggested that he was hitting the booze more often than was wise.

Otherwise, he was in good shape. He wore a freshly pressed white shirt, open at the collar, and gray trousers with a razor pleat. His black shoes were buffed and polished. He looked like a chauffeur who was enjoying his final moments of leisure before adding the finishing touches to his uniform.

'Charlie,' he said. 'It's been a long time.' We shook hands and he grinned warmly, patting me on the shoulder with a meaty left paw. He was still four or five inches taller than I, and I instantly felt as if I was twelve years old again.

'Do I get a dollar now?' I asked as he released his grip.

'You'd only spend it on booze,' he said, inviting me inside. The hallway boasted a huge coat rack, and a grandmother clock that still appeared to be keeping perfect time. Its loud ticking probably echoed through the house. I wondered how Jimmy could sleep with the sound of it in his head, but I supposed that he had been listening to it for so long he hardly noticed it anymore. A flight of carved mahogany stairs led up to the second floor, and to the right was the living room, furnished entirely with antiques. There were photographs on the mantel and on the walls, some of them featuring men in uniform. Among them I saw my father, but I did not ask Jimmy if I might look more closely at them. The wallpaper in the hallway was a red and white print that seemed new, but had a turn-of-the-century look that fit in with the rest of the decor.

There were two cups on the kitchen table, along

with a plate of pastries, and a coffeepot was brewing on the stove. Jimmy poured the coffee, and we took seats at opposite ends of the small kitchen table.

'Have a pastry,' said Jimmy. 'They're from Villabate. Best in town.'

I broke one apart and tasted it. It was good.

'You know, your old man and I used to laugh about that booze you bought with the money I gave you. He'd never have told you, because your mother thought it was the end of the world when she found that bottle, but he saw that you were growing up, and he got a kick out of it. Mind you, he used to say that I'd put the idea in your head to begin with, but he could never be angry at anyone for long, and especially not you. You were his golden boy. He was a good man, God rest him. God rest them both.'

He nibbled thoughtfully at his pastry, and we were quiet for a time. Then Jimmy glanced at his watch. It wasn't a casual gesture. He wanted me to see him do it, and a warning noise went off in my brain. Jimmy was uneasy. It wasn't simply that the son of his old friend, a man who had killed two others and then himself, was here in his kitchen clearly seeking to rake over the ashes of long-dead fires. There was more to it than that. Jimmy didn't want me here at all. He wanted me gone, and the sooner the better.

'I got a thing,' he said, as he saw me take in the movement. 'Some old friends getting together. You know how it is.'

'Any names I might recognize?'

'No, none. They're all after your father's time.' He

leaned back in his seat. 'So, this isn't a casual call, is it, Charlie?'

'I have some questions,' I said. 'About my father, and about what happened on the night those kids died.'

'Well, I can't help you much with the killings. I wasn't there. I didn't even see your father that day.'

'No?'

'No, it was my birthday. I wasn't working. I made a good collar for some grass and got my reward. Your old man was supposed to join me after his tour finished, the way he always did, but he never made it.' He twisted his cup in his hands, watching the patterns that resulted on the surface of the liquid. 'I never celebrated my birthday the same way after that. Too many associations, all of them bad.'

I wasn't letting him off the hook that easily. 'But your nephew was the one who came to the house that night.'

'Yeah, Francis. Your father called me at Cal's, told me that he was worried. He thought somebody might be trying to hurt you and your mother. He didn't say why he believed that.'

Cal's was the bar that used to stand next door to the Ninth's precinct house. It was gone now, like so much else from my father's time.

'And you didn't ask?'

Jimmy puffed out his cheeks. 'I might have asked. Yeah, I'm sure I did. It was out of character for Will. He didn't go jumping at shadows, and he didn't have any enemies. I mean, there were guys he might have crossed, and he put some bad ones away, but we all did. That was business, not personal. They knew the difference back then. Most of them, anyway.'

'Do you remember what he said?'

'I think he told me just to trust him. He knew that Francis lived in Orangetown. He asked if maybe I could get him to look out for you and your mother, just until he had a chance to get back to the house. Everything happened pretty fast after that.'

'Where did my father call you from?'

'Jeez.' He appeared to be trying to remember. 'I don't know. Not the precinct, that's for sure. There was noise in the background, so I guess he was using the phone at a bar. It was a long time ago. I don't recall everything about it.'

I drank some coffee, and spoke carefully. 'But it wasn't a typical night, Jimmy. People got killed, and then my father took his own life. Things like that, they're hard to forget.'

I saw Jimmy tense, and I felt his hostility rise to the surface. He had been good with his fists, I knew; good, and quick to use them. He and my father balanced each other well. My father kept Jimmy in check, and he in turn honed an edge in my father that might otherwise have remained blunted.

'What is this, Charlie? You calling me a liar?'

What is it, Jimmy? What are you hiding?

'No,' I said. 'I just don't want you to keep anything from me because, say, you're trying to spare my feelings.'

He relaxed a little. 'Well, it was hard. I don't like

thinking about that time. He was my friend, the best of them.'

'I know that, Jimmy.'

He nodded. 'Your father asked for help, and I made a call in return. Francis stayed with you and your mother. I was in the city, but I thought, you know, I can't stay here when something bad might be happening. By the time I got to Pearl River, those two kids were dead and your father was already being questioned. They wouldn't let me talk to him. I tried, but Internal Affairs, they were tight around him. I went to the house and talked to your mother. You were asleep, I think. After that, I only saw him alive one other time. I picked him up after they'd finished the interview. We went for breakfast, but he didn't talk much. He just wanted to collect himself before he went home.'

'And he didn't tell you why he'd just killed two people? Come on, Jimmy. You were close. If he was going to talk to anyone, it would have been you.'

'He told me what he told IAD, and whoever else was in that room with him. The kid kept pretending to reach inside his jacket, taunting Will, as if he had a gun there. He'd go so far, then pull back. Will said that, the final time, he went for it. His hand disappeared, and Will fired. The girl screamed and started pulling at the body. Will warned her before he shot her too. He said something snapped inside him when that kid started yanking his chain. Maybe it did. Those were different times, violent times. It never paid to take chances. We'd all known guys who'd taken one on the streets.

'The next time I saw Will, he was under a sheet, and there was a hole in the back of his head that they were going to have to pack before the funeral. Is that what you wanted to know, Charlie? Do you want to hear how I cried over him, about how I felt because I wasn't there for him, about how I've felt all these years? Is that what you're looking for: someone to blame for what happened that night?'

His voice was raised. I could see the anger in him, but I couldn't understand its source. It seemed manufactured. No, that wasn't true. His sadness and rage were genuine, but they were being used as a smokescreen, a means of hiding something from both me, and himself.

'No, that's not what I'm looking for, Jimmy.'

There was a weariness, and a kind of desperation, to what he said next.

'Then what *do* you want?'

'I want to know why.'

'There is no "why." Can't you get that into your head? People have been asking "why?" for twenty-five years. I've been asking why, and there's no answer. Whatever the reason was, it died when your father died.'

'I don't believe that.'

'You've got to let it go, Charlie. No good can come of this. Let them rest in peace, both of them, your father and your mother. This is all over.'

'You see, that's the problem. I can't let them rest.'

'Why not?'

'Because one, or both, of them was not related by blood to me.'

It was as if someone had taken a pin and punctured Jimmy Gallagher from behind. His back arched, and some of his bulk seemed to dissipate. He slumped back in the chair.

'What?' he whispered. 'What kind of talk is that?'

'It's the blood types: they don't match. I'm type B. My father was type A, my mother type O. There's no way that parents with those two blood types could produce a child with type B blood.'

'But who told you this?'

'I spoke to our family doctor. He's retired now, but he'd kept his records. He had them checked, and sent me copies of two blood tests from my father and my mother. That confirmed it for me. It's possible that I'm my father's son, but not my mother's.'

'This is madness,' said Jimmy.

'You were closer to my father than any of his other friends. If he had told anyone about it, he would have told you.'

'Told me what? That there was a cuckoo in the nest?' He stood up. 'I can't listen to this. I won't listen to it. You're mistaken. You must be.'

He picked up the coffee cups and emptied their contents into the sink, then left them there. His back was to me, but I could see that his hands were shaking.

'I'm not,' I said. 'It's the truth.'

Jimmy spun around and moved toward me. I felt sure that he was going to take a swing at me. I stood and kicked the chair away, tensing for the blow, waiting to block it if I had time to see it, but it did not come. Instead, Jimmy spoke calmly and deliberately.

'Then it's a truth that they didn't want you to know, and one that can't help you. They loved you, both of them. Whatever this is, whatever you think you've discovered, leave it alone. It's only going to hurt you if you keep searching.'

'You seem very sure of that, Jimmy.'

He swallowed hard.

'Fuck you, Charlie. You need to go now. I have things to do.'

He waved a hand in dismissal and turned his back on me once more.

'I'll be seeing you, Jimmy,' I said, and I knew that he heard the warning in my voice, but he said nothing. I let myself out and walked back to the subway.

Later I would learn that Jimmy Gallagher waited only until he was certain that I would not return before making the call. It was a number that he had not dialed in many years, not since the day after my father's death. He was surprised when the man answered the phone himself, almost as surprised as he was to discover that he was still alive.

'It's Jimmy Gallagher.'

'I remember,' said the voice. 'It's been a long time.'

'Don't take this the wrong way, but not long enough.'

He thought he heard something that might have been a laugh. 'Well, what can I do for you, Mr. Gallagher?'

'Charlie Parker was just here. He's asking questions about his parents. He said something about blood types. He knows about his mother.'

There was silence on the other end of the line, then: 'It was always going to happen. Eventually he had to find out.'

'I didn't tell him anything.'

'I'm sure that you didn't, but he'll come back. He's too good at what he does not to discover that you've lied to him.'

'And then?'

The answer, when it came, gave Jimmy his final surprise on a day already filled with unwanted surprises.

'Then you might want to tell him the truth.'

10

I spent that night at the home of Walter Cole, the man after whom I'd named my dog and my former partner and mentor in the NYPD, and his wife, Lee. We ate dinner together, and talked of mutual friends, of books and movies and how Walter was spending his retirement, which seemed to consist of little more than napping a lot and getting under his wife's feet. At 10 p.m. Lee, who was nobody's idea of a night owl, kissed me on the cheek and went to bed, leaving Walter and me alone. He threw another log on the fire and filled his glass with the last of the wine, then asked me what I was doing in the city.

I told him of the Collector, a raggedy man who believed himself to be an instrument of justice, a foul individual who killed those whom he considered to have forfeited their souls due to their actions. I recalled the nicotine stink of his breath as he spoke of my parents, the satisfaction in his eyes as he spoke of blood types, of things that he could not have known but did, and of how all that I had believed about myself began to fall away at that moment. I told him of the medical records, my meeting earlier that day with Jimmy Gallagher, and of how I was convinced that he had knowledge he was not sharing with me. I also told him one thing that I had not discussed with Jimmy. When my mother died of cancer, the hospital had retained samples of her organs. Through my lawyer, I'd had a DNA test conducted, comparing a swab taken from my cheek with my mother's tissue. There was no match. I had not been able to carry out a similar test on my father's DNA. There were no samples available. It would require an exhumation order on his remains for such a test, and I was not yet willing to go that far. Perhaps I was frightened of what I might find. After discovering the truth about my mother, I had wept. I was not sure that I was ready to sacrifice my father on the same altar as the woman I had called my mother.

Walter sipped his wine and stared into the fire, not speaking until I was done.

'Why did this man, this "Collector," tell you all of this, all these truths and half-truths, to begin with?' he asked. It was a typical cop move: don't go straight to the main issue, but skirt it. Probe. Buy time in which to start connecting small details to larger ones.

'Because it amused him,' I replied. 'Because he's cruel in ways that we can't even begin to imagine.'

'He doesn't sound like the kind of guy who drops hints lightly.'

'No.'

'Which means he was goading you into acting. He knew you couldn't let this slide.'

'What are you saying?'

'I'm saying that, from what you've told me, he's

used people before to achieve his own ends. Hell, he's even used you. Just be careful that he's not using you again to flush someone out.'

Walter was right. The Collector had used me to establish the identities of the depraved men he was seeking so that he could punish them for their failings. He was cunning, and absolutely without mercy. Now he had hidden himself away again, and I had no desire to find him.

'But if that's true, then who is he looking for?'

Walter shrugged. 'From what you've told me, he's always looking for somebody.'

Then we came to it.

'As for this blood thing, well, I don't know what to say. What are the options? Either you were adopted by Will and Elaine Parker, and they kept that from you for reasons of their own, or Will Parker fathered you by another woman, and he and Elaine raised you as their own child. That's it. Those are the choices.'

I couldn't disagree. The Collector had told me that I was not my father's son, but the Collector, from my past experience of him, never told the truth, not entirely. It was all a game to him, a means of furthering his own ends, whatever they might be, but always leavened with a little cruelty. But it might also have been the case that he simply did not know the entire truth, only that something in my parentage did not add up. I still did not believe that I had no blood ties to my father. Everything in me rebelled against it. I had seen myself in him. I recalled how he had spoken to me, how he had looked at me. It was different from the woman I had known as my mother. Perhaps I simply did not want to admit the possibility that it was all a lie, but I would not accept such a thing until I had irrefutable proof.

Walter walked to the fire, then squatted to stab at it with the poker.

'I've been married to Lee for thirty-nine years now. If I'd cheated on her, and the other woman became pregnant, I don't think Lee would have taken kindly to a suggestion that we raise the child alongside our own daughters.'

'Even if something had happened to the mother?'

Walter thought about it. 'Again, I can only speak from my own experience, but the strain that would put on a marriage would be almost unendurable. You know, to be faced every day with the fruit of your husband's infidelity, to have to pretend that this child was loved as much as the others, to treat it the same way as one's own children.' He shook his head. 'No, it's too difficult. I'm still inclined toward the first option: adoption.'

But they had no other children, I thought. Would that have changed things?

'But why keep it from me?' I asked, putting that thought aside. 'There's no shame to it.'

'I don't know. Maybe it wasn't an official adoption, and they were frightened that you might be taken from them. In that case, it would have been better to keep it quiet until you were an adult.'

'I was a student when my mother died. Enough time had passed by then for her to have told me.'

'Yeah, but look at what she'd gone through. Her husband takes his own life, branded a killer. She leaves the state, takes her son back to Maine with her, then she contracts cancer. It could be that you were all she had left, and she didn't want to lose you as her son, whatever the truth might have been.'

He rose from the fire and resumed his seat. Walter was older than me by almost twenty years and, in that moment, the relationship between us seemed more like that of a father and a son than two men who had served together.

'Because here's the thing of it, Charlie: no matter what you discover, they were your mother and your father. They were the ones who raised you, who sheltered you, who loved you. What you're chasing is some kind of medical definition of a parent, and I understand that. It has meaning for you. In your shoes, I'd probably do the same. But don't mistake this for the real thing: Will and Elaine Parker were your father and your mother, and don't let anything that you discover obscure that fact.'

He gripped my arm once, tightly, before releasing me.

'So what now?'

'My lawyer has the papers prepared for an exhumation order,' I said. 'I could have my DNA checked against my father's.'

'You could, but you haven't. Not ready for that yet, right?'

I nodded.

'When do you go back to Maine?'

'Tomorrow afternoon, after I speak to Eddie Grace.'

'Who?'

'Another of my father's cop friends. He's been ill, but his daughter says that he might be up to a few minutes with me now, if I don't tax him.'

'And if you don't get anything from him?'

'I put the squeeze on Jimmy.'

'If Jimmy's hidden something, then he's hidden it well. Cops gossip. You know that. They're like fishwives: hard to keep anything quiet once it gets out. Even now, I know who's screwing around behind his wife's back, who's fallen off the wagon, who's using blow or taking kickbacks from hookers and dealers. It's the way of things. And after those two kids died, IAD went over your father's life and career with a magnifying glass and tweezers in an effort to find out why it happened.'

'The official investigation uncovered nothing.'

'Screw the official investigation. You, more than anyone, should know how these things work. There would have been the official inquiry, and the shadow one: one that was recorded and open to examination, and one that was conducted quietly and then buried in a pit.'

'What are you saying?'

'I'm saying I'll ask around. I still have favors owed. Let's see if there was a loose thread anywhere that somebody pulled. In the meantime, you do what you have to do.'

He finished his wine.

'Now, we'll call it a night. In the morning, I'll give you a ride out to Pearl River. I always did like to see how the Micks live. Made me feel better about not being one.'

11

Eddie Grace had recently been released from the hospital into the care of his daughter, Amanda. Eddie had been ailing for a long time, and I'd been told he spent most of his time sleeping, but it seemed that he had rallied in recent weeks. He wanted to return home, and the hospital was content to let him leave, as there was nothing more that its staff could do for him. The medication to control his pain could just as easily be given to him in his own bed as in a hospital room, and he would be less anxious and troubled if surrounded by his family. Amanda had left a message on my phone in response to my earlier inquiries, informing me that Eddie was willing and, it appeared, able to meet with me at her home.

Amanda lived up on Summit Street, within praying distance of St. Margaret of Antioch Church and on the other side of the tracks from our old house on Franklin Street. Walter dropped me off at the church and went for a coffee. Amanda answered the door seconds after I rang the bell, as though she had been waiting in the hallway for me to arrive. Her hair was long and brown, with a hint of some tone from a bottle that was not so far from her natural color as to be jarring. She was small, a little over five-two, with freckled skin and very light brown eyes. Her lipstick looked freshly applied, and she smelled of some citrus fragrance that, like her, managed the trick of being both unassuming yet striking.

I'd had a crush on Amanda Grace while we were at Pearl River High School together. She was a year older than I was, and hung with a crowd that favored black nail polish and obscure English groups. She was the kind of girl jocks pretended to abhor but about whom they secretly fantasized when their perky blond girlfriends were performing acts that didn't require their boyfriends to look them in the eyes. About a year before my father died, she began dating Michael Ryan, whose main aims in life were to fix cars and open a bowling alley, not worthless ends in themselves but not the level of ambition that was going to satisfy a girl like Amanda Grace. Mike Ryan wasn't a bad guy, but his conversational skills were limited, and he wanted to live and die in Pearl River. Amanda used to talk about visiting Europe, and studying at the Sorbonne. It was hard to see where common ground could lie between her and Mike, unless it was somewhere on a rock in the mid-Atlantic.

Now here she was, and although there were lines where there had not been lines before, she was, like the town itself, largely unaltered. She smiled.

'Charlie Parker,' she said. 'It's good to see you.'

I wasn't sure how to greet her. I reached out a hand, but she slipped by it and hugged me, shaking her head against me as she did so.

'Still the same awkward boy,' she said, not, I thought, without a hint of fondness. She released her hold, and looked at me with amusement.

'What's that supposed to mean?'

'You visit a good-looking woman, and you offer to shake her hand.'

'Well, it's been a long time. I don't like to make assumptions. How's your husband? Still playing with bowling pins?'

She giggled. 'You make it sound kind of gay.'

'Big man, stroking hard phallic objects. Difficult not to draw those conclusions.'

'You can tell him that when you see him. I'm sure he'll take it under advisement.'

'I'm sure; that, or try to kick my ass from here to Jersey.'

The look on her face changed. Something of the good humor vanished, and what replaced it was speculative.

'No,' she said, 'I don't think he'd try that with you.'

She stepped back into the house and held the door open for me.

'Come in. I've made lunch. Well, I bought some cold cuts and salads, and there's fresh bread. That'll have to do.'

'It's more than enough.' I moved into the house, and she closed the door behind me, squeezing past me to lead me to the kitchen, her hands resting for a moment at my waist, her stomach brushing my groin. I let out a deep sigh.

'What?' she said, wide-eyed and radiating innocence.

'Nothing.'

'Go on, say it.'

'I think you could still flirt for your country.'

'As long as it's in a good cause. Anyway, I'm not flirting with you, not much. You had your chance a long time ago.'

'Really?' I tried to remember any chance I'd had with Amanda Grace, but nothing came to me. I followed her into the kitchen and watched her fill a jug from a purified water faucet.

'Yeah, really,' she said, not turning. 'You only had to ask me out. It wasn't complicated.'

I sat down. 'Everything seemed complicated back then.'

'Not to Mike.'

'Well, he wasn't a complicated guy.'

'No, he wasn't.' She turned off the faucet and placed the jug on the table. 'He still isn't. As time goes on, I've come to realize that's no bad thing.'

'What does he do?'

'He runs an auto shop in Orangetown. Still bowls, but he'll die before he ever owns an alley of his own.'

'And you?'

'I used to teach elementary school, but I gave it up when my second daughter was born. Now I do some part-time work for a company that publishes school-books. I guess I'm a saleswoman, but I like it.'

'You have kids?' I hadn't known.

'Two girls. Kate and Annie. They're at school today. They're still adjusting to having my dad here, though.'

'How is he?'

She grimaced. 'Not good. It's just a matter of time.

The drugs make him sleepy, but he's usually good for an hour or two in the afternoon. Soon, he'll have to go to a hospice, but he's not ready for that, not yet. For now, he'll stay here with us.'

'I'm sorry.'

'Don't be. He's not. He had a great life, and he's ending it with his family. He's looking forward to seeing you, though. He liked your father a lot. Liked you too. I think he'd have been happy if we'd ended up together, once.'

Her face clouded. I think she had made a series of unspoken connections, creating an alternative existence in which she might have been my wife.

But my wife was dead.

'We read about all that happened,' she said. 'It was awful, all of it.'

She was silent for a time. She had felt obliged to raise the subject, and now she did not know what to do to dispel the effect it had had.

'I have a daughter too,' I told her.

'Really? That's great,' she said, with a little too much enthusiasm. 'How old is she?'

'Two. Her mother and I, we're not together anymore.' I paused. 'I still see my daughter, though.'

'What's her name?'

'Samantha. Sam.'

'She's in Maine?'

'No, Vermont. When she's old enough, she can vote socialist and start signing petitions to secede from the union.'

She raised a glass of water. 'Well, to Sam, then.'

'To Sam.'

We ate and talked about old school friends, and her life in Pearl River. It turned out that she had made it to Europe after all, with Mike. The trip had been a gift for their tenth wedding anniversary. They went to France and Italy and England.

'And was it what you'd expected?' I asked.

'Some of it. I'd like to go back and see more but it was enough, for now.'

I heard movement above us.

'Dad's awake,' she said. 'I just need to go help him get organized.'

She left the kitchen and went upstairs. After a moment or two, I could hear voices, and a man coughing. The coughs sounded harsh and dry and painful.

Ten minutes later, Amanda led an old, stooped man into the room, keeping a reassuring arm around his waist. He was so thin that her arm circled him, but even bent over he was nearly as tall as I was.

Eddie Grace's hair was gone. Even his facial hair had disappeared. His skin looked clammy and transparent, tinged with yellow at the cheeks and a reddish-purple below the eyes. There was very little blood in his lips, and when he smiled, I could see that he had lost many of his teeth.

'Mr Grace,' I said. 'It's good to see you.'

'Eddie,' he said. 'Call me Eddie.' His voice was a rasp, like a plane moving over rough metal.

He shook my hand. His grip was still strong.

His daughter stayed with him until he had seated himself.

'You want some coffee, Dad?'

'Nah, I'm good, thank you.'

'There's water in the jug. You want me to pour some for you?'

He raised his eyes to heaven.

'She thinks that, because I walk slow and sleep a lot, I can't pour my own water,' he said.

'I know you can pour your own water. I was just trying to be nice. Jeez, but you're an ungrateful old man.' She said it with affection, and when she hugged him he patted her hand and grinned.

'And you're a good girl,' he said. 'Better than I deserve.'

'Well, as long as you understand that.' She kissed his bald pate. 'I'll leave you two alone to talk. I'll be upstairs if you need me.'

She looked at me from behind him, and asked me silently not to tire him out. I nodded slightly, and she left us once he was comfortably seated, but not before touching him gently on the shoulder as she pulled the door half closed behind her.

'How are you doing, Eddie?' I asked.

'So-so,' he said. 'Still here, though. I feel the cold. I miss Florida. Stayed as long as I could, but I wasn't able to look after myself, once I started getting sick. Andrea, my wife, she died a few years back. I couldn't afford a private nurse. 'Manda brought me up here, said she'd look after me if the hospital agreed. And I still got friends, you know, from the old days. It's not so bad. It's just the damn cold that gets me.'

He poured himself some water, the jug shaking only slightly in his hand, then took a sip.

'Why'd you come back here, Charlie? What are you doing, talking to a dying man?'

'It's about my father.'

'Huh,' he said. Some of the water dribbled from his mouth and ran down his chin. He wiped at it with the sleeve of his gown.

'I'm sorry,' he said, clearly embarrassed. 'It's only when someone new comes along that I forget how little dignity I have left. You know what I've learned from life? Don't get old. Avoid it for as long as you can. Getting sick don't help none either.'

He seemed to drift and his eyes grew heavy momentarily.

'Eddie,' I said gently. 'I wanted to talk to you about Will.'

He grunted and turned his attention back to me. 'Yeah, Will. One of the good ones.'

'You were his friend. I hoped that you might be able to tell me something about what happened, about why it happened.'

'After all this time?'

'After all this time.'

He tapped his fingers on the table.

'He did things the quiet way, your old man. He could talk people down, you know? That was his thing. Never got real angry. Never had a temper. Even the move for a time from the Ninth to Uptown, that was his decision. Probably didn't do much for his record, requesting a transfer that early in his career, but he did it for a quiet life. Of all the men who might have done what he did, he wasn't the one I'd have picked, not in a million years.'

'Do you remember why he requested the transfer?'

'Ah, he wasn't getting on with some of the brass in the Ninth, he and Jimmy both. They were some team, those two. Where one led, the other followed. Between them, I think they managed to spit in the eye of everyone who mattered. That was the flipside of your father. He had a devil in him, but he kept it chained up most of the time. Anyway, there was a sergeant in the Ninth name of Bennett. You ever hear of him?'

'No, never.'

'Didn't last long. He and your father, they locked horns, and Jimmy backed Will, same as always.'

'You remember why they didn't get on?'

'Nah. Clash of personalities, I think. Happens. And Bennett was dirty, and your father didn't care much for dirty cops, didn't matter how many stripes they carried. Anyway, Bennett found a way to unlock the devil in your father. Punches were thrown one night, and you didn't do that while in uniform. It looked bad for Will, but they couldn't afford to lose a good cop. I guess some calls were made on his behalf.'

'By whom?'

Eddie shrugged. 'If you do right by others, you build up favors you can call in. Your old man had friends. A deal was cut.'

'And the deal was that my father would request a transfer.'

'That was it. He spent a year in the wilderness, until Bennett took a beating from the Knapp Commission for being a meat eater.'

The Knapp Commission, which investigated police corruption in the early seventies, came up with two definitions of corrupt cops: the 'grass eaters,' who were guilty of petty corruption for tens and twenties, and the 'meat eaters,' who shook down dealers and pimps for larger amounts.

'And when Bennett was gone, my father returned?'

'Something like that.' Eddie made a movement with his fingers, as of someone dialing a rotary phone.

'I didn't know my father had those kinds of friends.'

'Maybe he didn't either, until he needed them.'

I let it go.

'Do you remember the shooting?' I asked.

'I remember hearing about it. I was four-twelve that week. Me and my partner, we met up with two other guys, Kloske and Burke, for coffee. They'd been over at the precinct house when the call came in. Next time I saw your father, he was lying in a box. They did a good job on him. He looked like he'd always done, I suppose, like himself. Sometimes, these embalmers, they make you look like a wax dummy.' He tried to smile. 'I got these things on my mind, as you can imagine.'

'They'll see you right,' I said. 'Amanda wouldn't have it any other way.'

'I'll look better dead than I ever did alive, she has her way. Better dressed too.'

I brought us back to my father. 'You have no idea why my father might have killed those kids?'

'None, but like I said, it took a lot to make Will see red. They must have turned it on real bad.'

He sipped some more water, keeping his left hand beneath his chin to stop it from spilling. When he lowered the glass he was breathing heavily, and I knew that my time with him was growing short.

'What was he like, in the days before it happened? I mean, did he seem unhappy, distracted?'

'No, he was the way he always was. There was nothing. But then, I didn't see him much that week. He was eight-four, I was four-twelve. We said hello when we passed each other, but that was about it. No, he was with Jimmy Gallagher that week. You should talk to him. He was with your old man on the day of the shooting.'

'What?'

'Jimmy and your old man, they always hooked up for Jimmy's birthday. Never missed it.'

'He told me that they didn't see each other that day. Jimmy was off. He'd made a good collar, he said, some drug thing.'

A day off was a reward for a solid arrest. You filled out a '28', then submitted it to the precinct's clerical guy, the captain's man. Most cops would slip him a couple of dollars, or maybe a bottle of Chivas earned from escorting a liquor store owner to the bank, in order to ensure a prime day. It was one of the benefits of handling paperwork for the precinct.

'Maybe,' said Eddie, 'but they were together on the

day that your father shot those two kids. I remember. Jimmy came in to meet your old man when he came off duty.'

'You're sure?'

'Sure I'm sure. He came down to the precinct. I even covered for Will so that he could leave early. They were going to start drinking in Cal's then finish up at the Anglers' Club.'

'The what?'

'The Greenwich Village Anglers' Club. It was kind of a private members' place on Horatio Street. A quarter for a can.'

I sat back. Jimmy had assured me that he wasn't with my father on the day of the shooting. Now Eddie Grace was directly contradicting him.

'You saw Jimmy at the precinct house?'

'You deaf? That's what I said. I saw him meet your old man, saw the two of them leave together. He tell you something different?'

'Yes.'

'Huh,' said Grace again. 'Maybe he's misremembering.'

A thought struck me. 'Eddie, do you and Jimmy stay in touch?'

'No, not so much.' His mouth twitched, an expression of distaste. It gave me pause. There was something here, something between Jimmy and Eddie.

'So does he know that you're back in Pearl River?'

'If someone told him, maybe. He hasn't been to visit, if that's what you mean.'

I realized that I was tensed, sitting forward in my chair. Eddie saw it too.

'I'm old and I'm dying,' he said. 'I got nothing to hide. I loved your father. He was a good cop. Jimmy was a good cop too. I don't know what reason he'd have to lie to you about your old man, but you can tell him that you talked to me. Tell him that I said he should tell the truth, if that's what you want.'

I waited. There was more coming.

'I don't know what you expect to get out of this,' said Eddie. 'Your father did what they accused him of doing. He shot those two young people, and then he shot himself.'

'I want to know why.'

'Maybe there isn't a why. Can you deal with that?'

'As long as I tried.'

I debated telling him more, but instead asked: 'You'd have known if my father was . . . screwing around, right?'

Eddie reeled slightly, then laughed. It brought on another fit of coughing, and I had to get him some more water.

'Your old man didn't "screw around,"' he said, when he'd recovered. 'That wasn't his style.'

He took some deep breaths, and I caught a gleam in his eye. It wasn't pleasant, as though I'd seen him eyeing a young girl up and down on the street and had watched as the sexual fantasy played out in his mind.

'But he was human,' he continued. 'We all make mistakes. Who knows? Someone say something to you?'

He looked at me closely, and that gleam remained.

'No,' I replied. 'Nobody said anything.'

He held my gaze for a while longer, then nodded. 'You're a good son. Help me up, will you? I think I'll watch some TV. I've got an hour in me yet before those damn drugs send me to sleep again.'

I assisted him in getting out of the chair, and helped him into the living room where he settled himself on the sofa with the remotes, and turned on a game show. The sound drew Amanda from upstairs.

'You two all done?' she asked.

'I believe so,' I said. 'I'll be going now. Thanks for your time, Eddie.'

The old man raised the remote control in farewell, but he didn't look away from the TV. Amanda was escorting me to the door when Eddie spoke again.

'Charlie!'

I went back to him. His eyes were fixed on the television.

'About Jimmy.'

I waited.

'We were friendly but, you know, we were never really close.' He tapped the remote on the armrest of his chair. 'You can't trust a man who spends his whole life living a lie. That's all I wanted to say to you.'

He hit a button, changing the channel to an afternoon soap. I returned to where Amanda was waiting.

'Well, was he helpful?'

'Yes,' I said. 'You both were.'

She smiled, and kissed me on the cheek. 'I hope you find what you're looking for, Charlie.'

'You have my number,' I said. 'Let me know how things go with your father.'

'I will,' she said. Then she took a piece of paper from the telephone table and scribbled a number on it. 'My cell phone,' she said. 'Just in case.'

'If I'd known it was that easy to get your number, I'd have asked a long time ago.'

'You had my number,' she said. 'You just never used it.'

With that, she closed the door, and I walked back down the hill to the Muddy Brook Café, where Walter was waiting to take me to the airport.

12

I was frustrated to be forced to leave New York with questions unanswered about Jimmy Gallagher's whereabouts on the day my father became a killer, but I had no choice: I owed Dave Evans, and he had made it clear that he needed me at the Bear for most of the coming week. I also had only Eddie's word that Jimmy and my father had met that day. It was possible that he could have been mistaken, and I wanted to be sure of the facts before I called Jimmy Gallagher a liar to his face.

I picked up my car at the Portland Jetport, and got back to my house in time to shower and change my clothes. For a moment, I found myself walking in the direction of the Johnson place to pick up Walter, but then I remembered where Walter was and it put me in a black mood that I knew wouldn't lift for the rest of the night.

I spent most of the evening behind the bar with Gary. Business was steady, but there was still time for me to talk with customers and even get a little paper-work done in the back office. The only moment of excitement came when a steroid jockey, who had stripped down his winter layers to only a wife-beater and a pair of stained gym pants, came on to a woman named Hillary Herman who was five-two, blond, and looked as if a soft breeze would carry her away like a leaf. When Hillary turned her back on him and his advances, he was dumb enough to lay a hand on her shoulder in an effort to regain her attention, at which point Hillary, who was the Portland PD's resident judo expert, spun and twisted her would-be suitor's arm so far behind his back that his forehead and his knees hit the ground simultaneously. She then escorted him to the door, dumped him in the snow, and threw his clothes out after him. His buddies seemed tempted to make their displeasure known, but the intervention of the other Portland cops with whom Hillary was drinking saved her from having to kick their asses as well.

When it was clear that everything had calmed down, and nobody was hurt who didn't deserve to be, I started bringing cases to the bottle coolers from the walk-in. It was still an hour before closing, but it didn't look as if we were about to be hit by an unanticipated rush, and it would save me time later. As I was bringing out the third case I saw the man who had taken a seat at the far end of the bar. He was wearing the same tweed jacket, and he had a notebook open beside his right hand. It was Gary's end of the bar, but as he moved to serve the new arrival I indicated to him that I wanted to take care of it, and he went back to talking to Jackie Garner, for whom he seemed to have developed a worrying fondness. Even though Jackie was trying to talk to a pretty but shy redhead in her forties, he seemed grateful for Gary's company. Jackie didn't do well with women. In fact, I couldn't recall Jackie even dating a woman. Usually when a member of the opposite sex talked to him, he developed a confused expression, like an infant being spoken to in a foreign language. Now he was blushing, and so was the redhead. It looked as if Gary was acting as a go-between in order to keep the conversation flowing. If he hadn't been helping them along, they might have lapsed into total silence or, if they blushed any more, simply exploded.

'How you doin'?' I said to Notebook Man. 'Back for more?'

'Guess so,' he replied. He was shrugging off his jacket. His shirtsleeves were rolled up to his elbows, his tie was loose, and the top button of his white shirt was undone. Despite the casualness of his attire, he gave the impression that he was about to get down to some serious work.

'What can I get you?'

'Just coffee, please.' When I came back with a cup of fresh brew, and some creamer and sweeteners, there was a card beside the notebook, facing me. I placed everything on top of the card without looking at what was written on it.

'Beg your pardon,' said the man. He lifted his cup, then picked up the card and handed it to me. I took it, read it, then put it back on the bar.

'Nice card,' I said, and it was. His name, Michael Wallace, was embossed on it in gold, along with a box number in Boston, two telephone numbers, an e-mail address, and a website. The card named his profession as 'Writer and Reporter.'

'Hold on to it,' he said.

'No thanks.'

'Seriously.'

There was a set look on his face that I didn't much like, the kind that cops wore when they were door-stepping a suspect who wasn't getting the message.

'"Seriously"?' I didn't care for his tone.

He reached into his satchel and removed a pair of nonfiction paperback books. I thought that I recognized the first from bookstores: it detailed the case of a man in northern California who had almost managed to get away with killing his wife and two children by claiming that they had drowned when their boat got caught up in a storm. He might have succeeded had a lab technician not spotted tiny chemical traces in the saltwater found in the lungs of the recovered bodies, and matched it to solvent stains found in the sink of the boat's galley, indicating that the husband had drowned all three victims in the sink before tossing their bodies overboard. His reason for the killings, when he eventually confessed, was that 'they were never on time for anything.' The second book seemed to be an older work, a standard serial-killer volume concentrating on sex murderers. Its title was almost as lurid as its subject matter. It was called *Blood on the Sheets*.

'That's me,' he said, somewhat unnecessarily. 'Michael Wallace. This is what I do. I write true crime books.' He reached out a hand. 'My friends call me Mickey.'

'We're not about to become friends, Mr. Wallace.'

He shrugged, as if he had expected as much.

'Here's the thing of it, Mr. Parker. I've read a lot about you. You're a hero. You've brought down some real bad people, but until now nobody has written the full history of what you've done. I want to write a book about you. I want to tell your story: the deaths of your wife and child, the way you hunted down the man responsible, and the way you've hunted down others like him since then. I already have a publisher for it, and a title. It's going to be called *The Avenging Angel*. Good, don't you think?'

I didn't reply.

'Anyway, the advance isn't huge – mid five-figure sum, which still isn't too shabby for this kind of work – but I'll split it with you fifty-fifty in return for your cooperation. We can negotiate on the royalties. My name will be on the cover, but it will be your story, as you want to tell it.'

'I don't want to tell my story, sir. This conversation is over. The coffee is on me, but I wouldn't advise you to linger over it.'

I turned away, but he kept talking.

'I don't think you understand, Mr. Parker. I don't mean to be confrontational, but I'm writing this book whether you choose to help me or not. There's a lot that's already public record, and I'll find out more as the interview process goes on. I've already done a degree of background work, and I've lined up a couple of people in New York who are willing to talk. Then there'll be folks from your old neighborhood, and from around here, who can provide insights into your life. I'm giving you the chance to shape the material, to respond to it. All I want is a few hours of your time over the next week or two. I work quickly, and I won't intrude any more than is absolutely necessary.'

I think he was surprised by how fast I moved, but to his credit he didn't flinch, even when I was in his face.

'You listen to me,' I said softly. 'This isn't about to happen. You're going to get up, and you're going to walk away, and I'm never going to hear from you again. Your book dies here. Am I clear?'

Wallace picked up his notebook and tapped it once on the bar, then slipped it back into his pocket. He put his jacket on, wrapped his scarf around his neck, then put three dollars on the bar.

'For the coffee, and the tip,' he said. 'I'll leave the books with you. Take a look at them. They're better than you think they are. I'll call again in a day or two, see if you've reconsidered.'

He nodded in farewell, then left. I swept his books into the trash can under the bar. Jackie Garner, who had been listening to the whole exchange, climbed from his stool and walked around to face me.

'You want me to, I can take care of this,' he said. 'That asshole's probably still in the parking lot.'

I shook my head. 'Let him go.'

'I ain't going to talk to him,' said Jackie. 'And if he tries to talk to Paulie and Tony, they'll drop his body in Casco Bay.'

'Thanks, Jackie.'

'Yeah, well . . .'

A car engine started up in the Bear's lot. Jackie walked to the door and watched as Wallace departed.

'Blue Taurus,' he said. 'Mass plates. Old, though. Not a rental. Not the kind of car a big-shot writer would drive.' He returned to the bar. 'You think you can make him stop?'

'I don't know. I can try.'

'He looks like the persistent type.'

'Yeah, he does.'

'Well, you remember: that offer still stands. Tony and Paulie and me, we're good with persistence. We see it as a challenge.'

Jackie hung around after the bar had closed, but it was clear that it wasn't out of any concern for me. He only had eyes for the woman, whose name, he whispered to me, was Lisa Goodwin. I was tempted to tell her if she was seriously considering dating Jackie to run and never look back, but that didn't seem fair to either of them. According to Dave, who knew a little about her from previous visits she'd paid to the Bear, she was a nice woman who had made some bad choices in the past when it came to men. By comparison with most of her former lovers, Jackie was practically Cary Grant. He was loyal, and good-hearted, and, unlike some of this woman's exes, he would never resort to violence against her. True, he lived with his mother and had a fondness for home-made munitions, and the munitions were less volatile than his mother, but Lisa could deal with those issues if and when they arose.

I filled a mug with the last of the coffee from the pot and went out to the back office. There I turned on the computer and found out all that I could about Michael Wallace. I visited his website, then read some of his newspaper stories, which came to an end after 2005, and reviews of his first two books. After an hour, I had his home address, his employment history, and details of his divorce in 2002 and a DUI that he'd incurred in 2006. I'd have to talk to Aimee Price about Wallace. I wasn't sure what action, if any, I could legally take to prevent Wallace from writing about me, but I just knew that I didn't want my name on the cover of a book. If Aimee couldn't help, I'd be forced to lean on Wallace, and something told me that he wouldn't respond well to that kind of pressure. Reporters rarely did.

Gary entered as I was finishing up.

'You okay?' he asked.

'Yeah, I'm fine.'

'Well, we're all done out here.'

'Thanks. Go home, get some sleep. I'll lock up.'

'Good night, then.' He lingered at the door.

'What is it?'

'If that guy comes back, the writer, what should I do?'

'Poison his drink. Be careful where you dump the body, though.'

Gary looked confused, as if uncertain whether or not I was being serious. I recognized the look. Most of the people who worked at the Bear knew something about my past, especially the locals who'd been there for a few years. Who could guess what kind of stories they'd been telling Gary when I wasn't around?

'Just let me know if you see him,' I said. 'Maybe you could spread the word that I'd appreciate it if nobody spoke to him about me.'

'Sure thing,' said Gary, brightening noticeably, then left. I heard him talking to Sergei, one of the line chefs, and then a door closed behind them and all was quiet.

The coffee had gone cold. I poured it down a sink, printed out all that I had learned about Wallace, and went home.

Mickey Wallace sat in his motel room out by the Maine Mall and wrote up the notes on his encounter with Parker. It was a trick he'd learned as a reporter: write everything down while it was still fresh, because even after a couple of hours the memory began to play tricks. You could fool yourself into thinking that you were remembering only the important stuff, but that wasn't the case. You were just remembering what you hadn't forgotten, important or not. Mickey was in the habit of recording his material in longhand in a series of notebooks, and then transferring it to his computer, but the notebooks remained the primary record, and it was to them that he always returned during the process of writing a book.

He hadn't been disappointed or surprised by Parker's response to his initial overture. In fact, he regarded the man's possible participation in the venture as something of a long shot to begin with, but it never hurt to ask. What was more surprising to him was that someone hadn't written a book about Parker already, given all that he'd done, and the cases with which he'd been involved, but that was just one of the many strange things about Charlie Parker. Somehow, despite his history and his actions, he had managed to remain just slightly off the radar. Even in the coverage of the most high profile cases, his name usually appeared buried in the fine print somewhere. It was almost as if there was an element of collusion when it came to him, an unspoken understanding that his part should be played down.

And those were just the ones that had made it into the public arena. Wallace had already done more than a little snooping, and Parker's name had been mentioned in connection with some business in upstate New York involving Russian mobsters, or so the story went. Mickey had managed to get a local cop in Massena to talk to him over some beers and quickly came to realize that something was being covered up in a big way, but when he tried to talk to the cop again the next day, Mickey was run out of town and warned, in no uncertain terms, never to come back. The trail had died after that, but Mickey's curiosity had been piqued.

He could smell blood, and blood sold books.

13

Emily Kindler left the little town in which she had been living for the past year shortly after the funeral for her deceased boyfriend's parents. An open verdict was delivered as to the cause of their deaths, but it was understood in the town that they had taken their own lives, although Chief Dashut increasingly wondered why they had done so before they'd had a chance to bury their son properly. He couldn't think of any parents who would not want to do right by their deceased child, no matter how traumatized they were by what had occurred. He questioned the verdict, both publicly and privately, and yoked the deaths of the parents to the murder of their son in both his mind and his own investigation.

There had been no denying that Emily Kindler's shock at their deaths was genuine. One of the local doctors had been forced to give her a sedative to calm her down, and there were concerns that she might have to be admitted to a psychiatric facility. She told the chief that she had visited the Faradays on the evening before they died, and Daniel Faraday in particular had appeared distressed, but there had been no indication that one or both of the Faradays might have been planning suicide.

The only lead so far in the killing of Bobby Faraday had come from the state police, who had discovered that Bobby had been involved in an altercation in a bar in Mackenzie, some eight miles from town, two weeks before his death. The bar in question was a roadside gin mill popular with bikers, and it seemed that Bobby, while intoxicated, had put the moves on a girl who was peripherally involved with the Crusaders biker gang. The Crusaders' base was in Southern California, but their reach extended as far as Oklahoma and Georgia. Words had been exchanged, and a couple of punches thrown, before Bobby was dumped in the parking lot and given a kick in the ass to send him home. He was lucky not to have been stomped, but someone at the bar who knew Bobby had intervened on his behalf, arguing that he was just a kid who didn't know any better, a kid, what's more, who was hurting over the end of a relationship. Common sense had prevailed; well, common sense and the fortuitous arrival of a state police cruiser just as the Crusaders were debating the wisdom of giving Bobby some serious physical pain to distract him from his emotional distress. The Crusaders were bad, but the chief didn't see them strangling a boy just because he'd crossed them. Still, the state police detectives seemed to feel that it was worth pursuing, and were now engaged in a game of catch-up with the Crusaders, assisted by the FBI. In the meantime, Dashut had pointed out to the state police the symbol carved into the beech tree, and additional photographs had been taken, but he had heard nothing more about it.

Emily Kindler had been home alone at the time her boyfriend was believed to have been killed, which meant that she didn't have an alibi, but that counted for half of the town too. The gas in the Faraday house had been turned on sometime after midnight and before 2 a.m., at best reckoning. Again, most of the people in town were home in bed at that time.

But the chief didn't really suspect the Kindler girl of any involvement in Bobby Faraday's death and, by extension, any suspicions that he had about how Bobby's parents had met their end did not center on her, even though he considered the possibility of her involvement out of due diligence. When the chief had quietly mentioned Emily as a suspect to Homer Lockwood, the assistant ME, who was a resident in the town and knew both Emily and the Faradays by sight, the old man had just laughed.

'She doesn't have the strength, not to do what was done to Bobby Faraday,' he told the chief. 'Those aren't arms of steel.'

So when Emily told the chief that she planned to leave town, he could hardly blame her. He did request that she notify him when she settled down somewhere, and keep him apprised of her movements for a time, and she agreed, but he had no reason to prevent her from going. She gave the chief a cell phone number at which she could be contacted, and the address of a resort hotel in Miami where she intended to seek work as a waitress, and told him that she would be willing to return at any time if she could be of help in the investigation, but when Dashut eventually tried to contact her, the cell phone number was no longer in use, and the manager of the Miami resort told him that she had never taken up his offer of a job.

Emily Kindler, it seemed, had vanished.

Emily headed northeast. She wanted to smell the sea, to clear her senses. She wanted to try to shake whatever was shadowing her. It had found her in that small midwestern town, though, and it had taken the Faradays. It would find her again, she knew, but she wasn't prepared simply to lie down in a dark corner and wait for it to happen. She set her eyes on distant places, maybe even Canada.

Men looked at her as she sat on the Greyhound bus, watching the monotonous flat landscape gradually transform into gentle hills, snow still thick upon them. A guy in a worn leather jacket who smelled of sweat and pheromones tried to talk to her at one of the rest stops, but she turned away from him and resumed her seat behind the driver, a man in his late fifties who sensed her vulnerability but, unlike others, had no intention of exploiting it. Instead, he had taken her under his wing, and glared balefully at any male below the age of seventy who threatened to take the empty seat beside the girl. When the man in the leather jacket got back on the bus and seemed intent upon changing seats to be closer to the object of his interest, the driver told him to sit his ass back down and not to move again until they hit Boston.

Still, the man's attentions made Emily think of Bobby, and she felt tears well. She had not loved him, but she had liked him. He was funny and sweet and awkward, at least until he started drinking, when some of his anger and frustration at his father, the small town, even her, would bubble to the surface.

She had never been entirely sure what she wanted in a man. Sometimes, she thought that she caught some inkling of it, a brief flash of what she sought, like a light glimpsed in the darkness. She would respond to it, and then the man would respond in turn. Sometimes, it had been too late for her to retreat, and she had suffered the consequences: verbal abuse, sometimes even physical violence, and once very nearly worse than that.

Like some young men and women her age, she had struggled to find a sense of purpose. The path that she wanted her life to take had not yet become clear to her. She thought that she might become an artist, or a writer, for she loved books and paintings and music. In big cities, she would while away hours in museums and galleries, standing before the great canvases as though she hoped that by doing so she might be absorbed into them, becoming one with their world. When she could afford it, she would buy books. When money was not so freely available, she would go to a library, although the experience of reading a book that she could not call her own was not the same. Still, they gave her a sense of possibility so that she did not feel so adrift in the world. Others had struggled with some of the same problems and they had triumphed over them.

She did not make it as far as the Canadian border, but stopped off at a town in New Hampshire. She could not have said why, but she had learned to trust her instincts. After a week there, she still had developed no fondness for it, but she stayed despite herself. This was not a community of art or culture. It had one tiny museum, a mishmash of history, most of it local, and art, most of that local too. Any other acquisitions felt like an afterthought, the impulse of those who did not have the funds to match their taste, or, perhaps, the taste to match their funds, in a town that felt a museum was appropriate, even necessary, without fully understanding why. This attitude seemed to have permeated all of its strata, and she could not recall another environment in which creativity was so stifled; or, at least, she could not until she remembered the small town that she had once called home. Art and beauty had no place there either, and the house in which she had grown up was barren of all such fripperies. Even magazines had no place in it, unless one counted her father's stash of porn.

She had not thought of him in so long. Her mother had left when she was still a child, promising to return for her, but she never came back, and in time word came that she had died somewhere in Canada, and had been buried by her new boyfriend's family. Emily's father did what was necessary for her education and survival, but little more. She went to school, and always had money for books. They ate adequately, but only at home and never in restaurants. Some money was put aside in a jar for household expenses, and he gave her a little for herself, but she did not know where the rest of his money went. He did not drink to excess, and he did not take drugs. Neither did he ever lay a hand upon her in affection or anger and, as she grew older and her body matured, he was careful never to do or say anything that might be deemed inappropriate. For this she was more grateful than he would ever know. She had heard the tales told by some of the other girls in her school, stories of fathers and stepfathers, of brothers and uncles, of the new boyfriends of tired, lonely mothers. Her father was not such a man. Instead, he maintained his distance and kept his conversations with her to a minimum.

Yet she had never regarded herself as neglected. When she began having trouble at school – acting up in class, crying in the restrooms – as she entered adolescence, he spoke to the principal and arranged for Emily to see a psychologist, although she chose to share as little with the kindly, soft-spoken man in the rimless glasses as she did with her father. She did not want to speak with a psychologist. She did not want to be perceived as different in any way, and so she did not tell him of the headaches, or the blackouts, or the dreams that she had in which something was emerging from a dark pit in the ground, a thing with teeth that gnawed at her soul. She did not speak of her paranoia, or the sense that her identity was a fragile thing that could be lost and broken at any time. After ten sessions, the psychologist concluded that she was a normal, if sensitive, girl who would, in time, find her place in the world. There was the possibility that her difficulties presaged something more serious, a form of schizophrenia, perhaps, and he advised both her and, particularly, her father to be aware of any significant changes in her behavior. Her father had looked at her differently after that, and twice in the months that followed she had woken to find him standing at the door to her room. When she'd asked what was wrong, he told her that she had been shouting in her sleep, and she wondered if he had heard what she might have said.

Her father worked as a driver for a furniture warehouse: Trejo & Sons, Inc., Mexicans who had made good. Her father was the only non-Mexican who worked for the Trejos. She did not know why this was. When she asked her father he admitted that he did not know either. Maybe it was because he drove his truck well, but she thought it might have been the fact that the Trejos sold many types of furniture, some of it expensive and some of it not, to many different types of people, some of them Mexicans and some of them not. Her father had a sense of authority about him, and he spoke well. For their wealthier customers, he was the acceptable face of the Trejos.

Every piece of furniture in their home had been bought at a discount from his employers, usually because it was damaged, or torn, or so ugly that all hope of ever selling it had been abandoned. Her father had cut and sanded the legs on the kitchen table in an effort to make them even, but the result was that the table seemed too low, and the chairs could not be pushed under it when they had finished eating.

The couches in the living room were comfortable but mismatched, and the rugs and carpets were cheap but hard-wearing. Only the succession of TVs that graced one corner of the room were of any quality, and her father regularly upgraded the sets when a better model came on the market. He watched history documentaries and game shows. He rarely watched sports. He wanted to know things, to learn and, in silence, his daughter learned alongside him.

When she finally left, she wondered if he would even notice. She suspected that he might be grateful for her absence. Only later did it strike her that he had appeared almost frightened of her.

She found another waitressing job, this one in the closest thing to a boho coffeehouse the town could boast. It didn't pay much, but then her rent wasn't very much either, and at least they played good music and the rest of the staff weren't total assholes. She was supplementing her income with weekend bar work, which wasn't so pleasant, but she had already met a guy who seemed to like her. He had come in with some of his buddies to watch a hockey game, but he was different from them, and he had flirted with her some. He had a nice smile, and he didn't swear like his buddies, which she admired in a man. He'd returned a couple of times since then, and she could feel him working up the courage to ask her out. She wasn't sure that she was ready yet, though, not after what had happened before, and she still wasn't certain about him. There was something there, though, something that interested her. If he asked, she would say yes, but she would keep some space between them as she tried to find out more about him. She did not want things to turn out the way they had with Bobby, at the end.

On her fourth night in the new town, she woke to a vision of a man and a woman walking up the street toward her rented apartment. It was so vivid that she went to the window and looked out at the world beyond, expecting to see two figures standing beneath the nearest streetlight, but the town was quiet, and the street was empty. In her dream, she had almost been able to see their faces. The dream had been coming to her for many years now, but it was only recently that the features of the man and woman had begun to seem clearer to her, growing sharper with each visitation. She could not yet recognize them, but she knew that the time was coming when she would be able to do so.

There would be a reckoning then. Of that, at least, she was certain.

III

So, so, break off this last lamenting kiss,
Which sucks two souls, and vapours both
away,
Turn thou ghost that way, and let me turn
this . . .

John Donne (1572–1631), 'The Expiration'

14

I spent each Friday at the Bear dealing with our biggest distributor, Nappi. The Bear took delivery of beer three times a week, but Nappi accounted for eighty percent of all our taps, so its consignment was a big deal. The Nappi truck always arrived on Fridays, and once the thirty kegs had been checked and stored, and I had paid for the delivery according to the Bear's COD policy, I would buy the driver lunch on my tab, and we would talk about beer, and his family, and the downturn in the economy.

The Bear had a slightly different yardstick from most bars by which to judge how things were going for its customers. The bar had always been popular with repo men, and we had seen increasing numbers of them parking their trucks in the lot. It wasn't a job I would have cared to do, but the majority of them were pretty philosophical about it. They could afford to be. They were, with only a couple of exceptions, big, hard men, although the toughest of them, Jake Elms, who was eating a burger and checking his phone at the bar, was only five-five and tipped the scales at barely 120 pounds. He was soft-spoken, and I had never heard him shout, but the stories that circulated about him were legendary. He traveled with a mangy terrier in the front of his truck, and kept an aluminum baseball bat in a rack beneath the dashboard. As far as I was aware, he did not own a gun, but that bat had broken some heads in its time, and Jake's dog was reputed to have the singular talent of being able to grip a man's testicles in its jaws and then dangle from them, growling, if anyone had the temerity to threaten its beloved owner.

The dog, needless to say, wasn't allowed in the bar.

'I hate this time of year,' said Nathan, the Nappi driver, as he finished off his wrap and prepared to head out into the cold. 'I ought to find me a job down in Florida.'

'You like the heat?'

'No, I don't much care for it. But this—' He gestured at the world beyond the dark cocoon of the Bear as he shrugged on his coat. 'They can call it spring, but it's not. This is still the dead of winter.'

He was right. There were only three seasons in this place, or so it seemed: winter, summer, and fall. There was no spring. Already, it was the middle of February, yet there were no real signs of returning life, no hints of renewal. The streets of the city were fortified with ramparts of snow and ice, the wider sidewalks etched with the treads of the machines that had cleared them over and over. True, the worst of the snow had departed, but in its place had come freezing rain and the dread siege of lingering cold, augmented at times by high winds, but, even in its stillest form, capable of turning ears and noses and fingertips raw. Sheltered streets were caked with patches of ice, some visible and some not. Those that sloped upward from Commercial into the Old Port were treacherous to tackle without grips on one's soles, and the cobblestone paving, so beloved of the tourists, did nothing to make the ascent any less hazardous. The task of sweeping the floors of bars and restaurants was rendered more tedious by the accumulation of slush and ice, of grit and rock salt. In places – by the parking lots on Middle Street, or down by the wharfs – the accumulated piles of snow and ice were so high as to give the impression that pedestrians were engaged in a form of trench warfare. Some of the ice chunks were as big as boulders, as though expelled from the depths of some strange, near-frozen volcano.

On the wharfs, the lobster boats were shrouded in snow. Occasionally, a brave soul would make a foray out onto the bay and, when he returned, the blood of the fish would stain the ice pink and red, but mostly the seagulls fluttered disconsolately, waiting for summer and the return of easy pickings. At night, there was the sound of tires seeking purchase on treacherous ice, of feet stamping impatiently as keys were sought, and of laughter that teetered on the brink of tears at the pain that the cold brought.

And March still waited in the wings, a miserable month of dripping ice and melting snow and the last vestiges of winter lurking filthily in shadowy places. Then April, and May. Summer, and warmth, and tourists.

But, for now, there was only winter without the promise of spring. Here there were only ice and snow, and the traces of old footprints retained amid the crystals like unwanted memories that refused to die. The people huddled together, and waited for the siege to break. But that day, the day that Nathan spoke of the dead of winter, brought something strange and different to this part of the world.

It brought the mist.

It brought *them*.

It had been bitterly cold for days, weeks, unusually so even for the time of year. Snow had fallen day after day, and then, just before Valentine's Day, it turned to freezing rain that flooded streets and turned the drifts of accumulated snow to rugged slabs of ice. Then the rain stopped, but the cold stayed, until at last the weather broke, and temperatures climbed.

And the mist rose off the white fields like smoke from a cold burning, carried by air currents unfelt by man so that it seemed almost a living thing, a pale manifestation with a purpose untold and unknown. The shapes of the trees became indistinguishable, the forests lost to the enveloping fog. It did not diminish or falter, but appeared to grow denser and deeper as the day drew on, dampening the towns and cities and falling like soft rain on windows and cars and people. By nightfall visibility was down to a matter of feet, and the highway signs flashed warnings about speed and distance.

And still the mist came. It took over the city, turning the brightest lights to ghosts of themselves, cutting off those who walked the streets from others like them, so that all felt alone in the world. In its way, it brought closer together those with families and other loved ones for they sought solace with one another, a point of contact in a world that had grown suddenly unfamiliar.

Perhaps that was why they came back, or did I still believe that they had never quite departed to begin with? I had set them free, these ghosts of my wife and child. I had asked their forgiveness for my failings, and I had taken all that I had retained of their lives – clothes and toys, dresses and shoes – and burned them in my yard. I had felt them leave, following the marsh streams into the waiting sea beyond, and when I set foot in the house again, the smell of smoke and lost things thick upon me, it seemed different to me: lighter, somehow, as though a little of the clutter had been cleared from it, or an old, stale odor banished by the breezes through open windows.

They were my ghosts, of course. I had created them, in my way. I had given form to them, making my anger and grief and loss their own, so that they became to me hostile things, with all that I had once loved about them gone, and all that I hated about myself filling the void. And they took that shape and accepted it, because it was their way to return to this world, my world. They were not ready to slip into the shadows of memory, to relinquish their place in this life.

And I did not understand why.

But that was not them. That was not the wife I had loved, however poorly, and the daughter I had once cherished. I had caught glimpses of them as they truly were, before I allowed them to be transformed. I saw my dead wife leading the ghost of a boy into a deep forest, his small hand in hers, and I knew that he felt no fear of her. She was the Summer Lady, taking him to those whom he had lost, accompanying him on his last journey through the thickets and trees. And so that he would not be frightened, so that he would not be alone, there was another with him, a girl close to his own age who skipped in winter sunlight as she waited for her playmate to arrive.

This was my wife and child. This was their true form. What I released in smoke and flames were my ghosts. What returned with the mist were their own.

I worked that night. I was not scheduled to do so, but Al and Lorraine, two of the regular bartenders who had been living together for almost as long as they had been working at the Bear, were involved in a collision on Route 1 not far from Scarborough Downs, and both were taken to the hospital as a precaution. With nobody to cover for them, I had to spend another night behind the bar. I was still tired from the night before, but there was nothing to be done except to keep going. I figured that I could probably get an extra day in comp time from Dave, which would give me a few more hours to spend in New York the following week, but for now it was just me and Gary and Dave, serving up beers and burgers and trying to keep our heads above water.

Mickey Wallace had planned to talk to Parker again at the Bear that day, but an incident in the motel parking lot had caused him to reconsider. A man who had been sitting at the bar earlier in the week, the one who had been flirting with the little redhead, was waiting beside Mickey's car when he went outside shortly after 3 p.m., both car and man barely visible in the thickening fog. The man, who didn't introduce himself but who Mickey remembered was called Jackie, had made it clear to Mickey that he didn't approve of him bothering Parker, and if Mickey continued to do so he threatened to acquaint him with two gentlemen who were both bigger and less reasonable than he, Jackie, was, and who would fold Mickey into a packing crate, breaking limbs if they had to in order to make him fit, and then mail him to the darkest hole in Africa by the slowest and most circuitous route possible. When Mickey asked Jackie if Parker had put him up to this, Jackie had replied in the negative, but Mickey wasn't sure whether to believe him. It didn't matter, in the end. Mickey wasn't above playing dirty himself. He called the Bear to make sure that Parker was still working, and when he was asked if he wanted to talk to him, Mickey said that it was okay, he'd drop by and see him in person.

As darkness settled on the city, and while the mist was still heavy on the land, Mickey drove out to Scarborough.

It was past 8 p.m. as Mickey moved through the fog toward the house on the hill. He knew that Parker would not return until one or two in the morning, and the house next door was dark. An old couple, the Johnsons, lived there, but they seemed to be out, or away. What was it that they called people who left for Florida when the cold began to bite? Birds? No, 'snowbirds,' that was it.

Even if they were home, it wouldn't have deterred him from what he was planning to do. It would just have meant a longer walk. With them gone, he could park his car close to the house and not have to get his feet cold and wet, or risk being asked by a curious cop what he happened to be doing walking down a marsh road in the winter darkness.

He had already driven by the subject's house a couple of times in daylight, but he couldn't take the chance of looking at it up close without the risk of being seen. Now that he wasn't working as a PI any longer, Parker spent more of his time at home, but Mickey hadn't been allowed the luxury of watching the house for long enough to establish his routines. That would come in time.

Mickey still entertained the possibility that he could wear down Parker's defenses and receive at least a modicum of cooperation from him. Mickey was tenacious, in a quiet way. He knew that most people wanted to talk about their lives, even if they didn't always realize it. They wanted a sympathetic ear, someone who would understand. Sometimes all it took was a cup of coffee, but he'd seen it take a bottle of bourbon too. They were the two extremes, and the rest of humanity, in Mickey's experience, slotted into various points between.

Mickey Wallace had been a good reporter. He was genuinely interested in those whose stories he wrote.

He didn't have to fake it. Human beings were just endlessly fascinating to him, and even the dullest had a story worth telling, however short, buried somewhere deep inside. But, in time, journalism began to weary him. He didn't have the energy for it that he had once enjoyed, or the hunger to go chasing people day after day just for the stories that he uncovered to be forgotten before the weekend. He wanted to write something that would last. He thought about writing novels, but it wasn't for him. He didn't read them, so why would he want to write them? Real life was curious enough without the embellishments of fiction.

No, what interested Mickey was good and evil. It always had, ever since he was a kid watching *The Lone Ranger* and *The Virginian* on TV. Even as a reporter, it was the crime stories to which he was most drawn. True, they were more likely to appear above the fold, and Mickey liked seeing his name as close to the masthead as possible, but he was also fascinated by the relationship between killers and their victims. There was an intimacy, a bond between a murderer and a victim. It seemed to Mickey that a little of the victim's identity was transferred to the killer, passed on at the moment of death, retained deep within his soul. He also believed, somewhat more controversially, that the victims' deaths were what gave meaning to their lives, what raised them from the anonymity of day-to-day ordinariness and bequeathed a kind of immortality on them, or as close to immortality as the temporary nature of public attention could allow. Mickey supposed that it wasn't quite immortality, especially since the victims in question were dead, but it would do until he could think of a better word.

It was as a reporter that he had first come into indirect contact with Parker. He had been among the throng outside the little house in Brooklyn on the night that Parker's wife and child were killed. He had reported on the case, the stories getting smaller and smaller, and falling deeper and deeper into the main body of the paper, as lead after lead dried up. Eventually, even Mickey gave up on the Parker killings, and put them on the back burner. He had heard rumors that the feds were looking at a possible serial-killer connection, but the price of that information was a promise that he would sit on it until the time was right.

While Mickey was genuinely interested in human beings and their stories, he also acknowledged to himself a kind of numbness of the heart that afflicted many in his trade. He was curious about people, but he did not care about them, or not enough to feel their pain as his own. He sympathized with them, a temporary, shallow emotion, but he did not empathize. Perhaps it was a consequence of his work, of being forced to deal with story after story in close succession, the depth and duration of his involvement dependent entirely on the public's appetite and, by extension, his newspaper's. That was, in part, why he had decided to leave the world of journalism behind, and devote himself to books. By immersing himself in only a handful of cases, he hoped to sensitize himself anew. That, and make a little money along the way. He just needed to find the right story to tell, and he was convinced that, in Charlie Parker, he had found that story.

Mickey could recall the moment he had become convinced that there was something different about the man. He hadn't faded away after the deaths of his family. Neither had he gone on daytime shows to talk about his pain, in an effort to keep the killings in the public eye and ensure that the pressure on the law enforcement community to track down their killer remained constant. No, he had picked up a PI's license, and then he had gone hunting, both for the killer, the one who would come to be called the Traveling Man, and for others. The first one he found was the Modine woman, and that was when the bells starting ringing for Mickey. That was a story in itself right there, worthy of a Sunday supplement: father loses his wife and child to a killer, then hunts down a pair of child killers in turn. It had everything that a jaded public could desire.

Except Parker wouldn't tell it. Requests for interviews were politely, and sometimes impolitely, declined. Then – bang! – there he was again, and this time it was the big one he was trying to hook, the Traveling Man. Over the years that followed, it became clear to Mickey, and to others like him, that there was something quite exceptional going on here. This man had a gift of sorts, although it wasn't a gift that anybody in his right mind would wish to have: it seemed that he was drawn to evil, and evil, in turn, was drawn to him. And when he found it, he destroyed it. It was as simple, or as complex, as that, depending upon how you chose to view it, because Mickey Wallace was not dumb, and he knew that a man couldn't do what Parker had done and not suffer serious damage along the way. Now here he was, working in a bar in a northeastern city, separated from his girlfriend, seeing the child he'd had with her maybe once or twice each month, and living alone in the big house upon which Mickey was now carefully shining his flashlight.

Mickey wanted to go inside. He wanted to poke around in desk drawers, to open files in cabinets and on computers, to see where the subject ate, sat, slept. He wanted to walk in his footsteps, because what Mickey proposed to do was to give Parker a voice, to take his words, his experiences, and improve upon them, creating a new version of him that was somehow greater than the sum of his parts. To do that, Mickey needed to *become* him for a time, to understand the reality of his existence.

And if Parker ultimately decided not to cooperate? Mickey was trying not to think about that. He had spoken to his publisher that morning, and the publisher had made clear his preference for Parker being involved with the project. It wasn't a deal breaker, but it would affect the number of copies that would be printed, and the nature of the publicity for the book. His view was understandable, but it would make Mickey's task more difficult. Anyone could put together a cut-and-paste job, although not as good a cut-and-paste job as Mickey could, but that wasn't what the big bucks would be paid for. It wasn't just about the money, either: there was a real story here, something deep and peculiar and unsettling, and the words had to come from the subject's own mouth. Mickey would wear him down, of that he was certain, or reasonably certain. In the meantime, he had begun making contact with other prospective interviewees in the hope of establishing a more detailed background dossier about the subject, because Mickey wanted to know more about Parker than Parker did about himself.

Except, the people who were close to him were also loyal, and so far all that Mickey had to show for his efforts was a series of rebuffs. True, he had sessions lined up, both on and off the record, with a couple of ex-cops who remembered Parker from New York, and a former captain from Internal Affairs who, Mickey was reliably informed, believed that the subject should be behind bars; the subject, and his buddies. They interested Mickey too. All he knew were their names: Angel and Louis. The captain said that he could help with them too, just not as much. He was only willing to talk off the record, but he had promised Mickey copies of investigation reports, and some juice that a good reporter like he was would easily be able to corroborate. It was a start, but Mickey wanted more.

His clothes felt damp. The mist was a blessing in that it concealed him from any casual observer passing on the road below, and even someone coming up the drive would struggle to see his car, or him, until they reached the house itself. In fact, Mickey had parked the car beneath a copse of trees, and unless somebody was actively looking for it, he was pretty certain that it would pass unnoticed. Even if Parker returned unexpectedly, Mickey was convinced that he would drive right by it. But the mist was also cold and wet, and so thick that Mickey felt he might almost clasp a clump of it in his hand if he tried, like cotton candy.

In the pocket of his coat he had a set of lock picks. He climbed up to the porch of the house and, more out of hope than expectation, tried the door. It was locked. He thought for a moment, then gave the door a hard push with his shoulder, rattling it in its frame. No alarm went off. Good, thought Mickey. Another lucky break, to add to the absent neighbors and the fact that Parker no longer seemed to have a dog. He'd heard him talking about it with one of the bartenders shortly before Parker gave Mickey the bum's rush.

He moved to the left and peered in the window. There was a night-light burning in the kitchen at the back of the house that shed a little illumination into the living room. It looked like it was comfortably furnished, with a lot of books. To the right of the front door was a small office, with a computer on a desk, papers piled neatly around it, and on the floor. Mickey knew that Parker had been down in New York recently. He wondered why. He desperately wanted to look through those papers.

He walked to the back of the house, and stood in the segmented square of illumination cast by the night-light. The mist seemed thicker here, and when he looked behind him it formed a near-impenetrable wall of white, obscuring the trees and the marshes beyond. Mickey shivered. He tried the back door, with no result. Once again, he pressed his face to the glass.

And something moved inside the house.

For a moment, he thought that it was reflected light, or a car on the road creating shadows in the room beyond the kitchen, but he had heard no car. He blinked, and tried to recall what he had seen. He couldn't be sure, but he thought it might have been a woman, a woman in a dress that hung just below her knees. It wasn't the kind of dress anyone would usually wear at this time of year. It was a summer dress.

He considered leaving, but then he realized that an opportunity to enter the house might just have presented itself without necessitating a breach of the law. If there was someone inside, maybe he could introduce himself as a friend of the detective. There might be a cup of coffee in it for him, or a drink, and once Mickey got himself seated he would be difficult to roust. Cockroaches were harder to get rid of than Mickey Wallace in interrogation mode.

'Hello?' he called. 'Anybody home?' He knocked on the door. 'Hello? I'm a friend of Mr. Parker's. Can you—'

The light went out in the kitchen. The shock was so sudden that Mickey stumbled backward in fright, spots before his eyes as they adjusted to the darkness. He recovered himself, and took a breath. Maybe it was time to leave. He didn't want the woman inside to be frightened and call the cops. Still, he carefully approached the door one more time. His flashlight was in his right hand, and he used it to rap on the door as he leaned against the glass, shielding his eyes with his left hand.

The woman was standing in the doorway between the kitchen and the living room. She was looking right at him, her hands by her sides. He could see the shape of her legs through the thin material, but her face was cast in shadow.

'I'm sorry,' he called. 'I didn't mean to frighten you. My name is Michael Wallace. I'm a writer. Here's my card. I'm going to slide it under the door, so you'll know I'm legit.'

He knelt down and slipped the card through. When he stood up, the woman was gone.

'Ma'am?'

Something white appeared at his feet. His card had been pushed back at him.

Jesus, thought Mickey. She's at the door. She's hiding at the door.

'I just want to talk to you,' he said.

go away

For a moment, Mickey wasn't sure that he'd heard right. The words had been clear enough, but they seemed to come from behind him. He turned around, but there was nothing there, only mist. He put his face to the glass again, trying to catch a glimpse of the woman hiding inside. He could almost see her: a patch of darkness on the floor, a palpable presence. Who is she? he wondered. Parker's girlfriend was supposed to be in Vermont, not here. Mickey planned to try to talk to her sometime over the next couple of weeks. Anyway, they were estranged. There was no reason she should be here, and even less reason for her to try to hide herself if she was.

Something began nagging at Mickey, something that made him uneasy, but he tried to force it from his mind. He only partially succeeded. He felt it lurking at the edge of his consciousness, just like the woman who was squatting in the shadows by the door, an unwelcome presence to which he was frightened of giving his complete attention.

'Please. I just wanted to speak to you for a moment about Mr. Parker.'

Michael

The voice came again, only this time it was closer. He thought that he could feel breath on his neck, or maybe it was just the wind coming in from the sea, except there was no wind. He spun around, breathing heavily. He felt the mist enter his lungs. It made him cough, and he tasted snow and saltwater. He hadn't liked the way the voice had spoken his name. He hadn't liked it one little bit. There was a hint of mockery to it, and an implicit threat. He felt like a recalcitrant child being spoken to by a nanny, except—

Except it was a child's voice that had spoken.

'Who's out there?' he said. 'Show yourself.'

But there was no movement, and no response, not from before him. Instead, he became aware of movement at his back. Slowly, he craned his neck, not wishing to turn away from whatever had spoken to him from the mist, yet anxious to see what was happening behind him.

The woman was standing in the kitchen once again, midway between the back door and the entrance to the living room, but there was a lack of substance to her. She cast no shadow, distorting instead of blocking what little light was filtering through the glass, like a piece of gauze in the shape of a human being.

go away

please

It was the use of the word 'please' that finally got to him. He had heard the word used in that way before, usually before a cop wrestled someone to the ground, or a doorman at a nightclub applied brute force to a drunk. It was a final warning, couched in a version of politeness. He shifted position so that he could see both the door and the mist, then began to retreat, moving toward the corner of the house.

Because the shadow that was troubling him had just assumed a recognizable form, even as he tried to deny the reality of it.

A woman and a child. A little girl's voice. A woman in a summer dress. Mickey had seen that dress before, or one very like it. It was the dress that Parker's wife had been wearing in the pictures that were circulated to the press after her death.

As soon as he was out of sight of the door, Mickey began to run. He slipped once and landed heavily, soaking his trousers and plunging his arms into the icy snow up to his elbows. He whimpered as he got to his feet and brushed himself off. As he did so, he heard a noise from behind him. It was muffled slightly by the mist, but it was still clearly identifiable.

It was the sound of the back door opening.

He ran again. His car came in sight. He found the keys in his pocket and pushed the Unlock button once to turn on the lights. As he did so, he stopped short and felt his stomach lurch.

There was a child, a little girl, on the far side of the car, staring at him through the passenger window. Her left hand was splayed against the glass, while the index finger of her right traced patterns in the moisture. He couldn't see her face clearly, but he knew instinctively that it wouldn't have made any difference if he had been inches away from her instead of feet. She was as insubstantial as the mist that surrounded her.

'No,' said Mickey. 'No, no.' He shook his head. From behind him came the sound of hard snow crunching underfoot, of an unseen figure drawing nearer. Even as he heard it, he sensed that if he were to retrace his steps to the back door he would find only the imprint of his own footsteps. 'Oh Jesus,' whispered Mickey. 'Jesus, Jesus . . .'

But already the little girl was receding into the mist and the trees, her right hand raised in a mocking gesture of farewell. Mickey took his chance and made a final dash for the car. He wrenched the door open, slammed it behind him, and hit the internal locking button. His fingers didn't fumble, despite his fear, as he started the car and pulled onto the driveway, looking neither right nor left but staring only ahead. He hit the road at speed and hung a sharp right, back over the bridge toward Scarborough, the headlight beams assuming a definition of their own as they tried to slice through the mist. Houses appeared, and then, in time, the reassuring lights of the businesses on Route 1. Only when he reached the gas station on his right did he slow down. He pulled into the lot, then leaned back against his seat and tried to get his breathing under control.

The traffic signal at the intersection began to change color. The action drew his attention to the passenger window, and what had seemed at first to be random patterns in the moisture now assumed a definite shape.

On his window, someone had written:

STAY AWAY FROM MY DADDY

Mickey stared at the words for a few moments longer, then hit the button to wind down the window, destroying the message. When he was sure that it was gone, he drove back to his motel and went straight to the bar. It was only after a double vodka that he found it within himself to begin updating his notes, and it took another double to stop his hand from shaking.

That night, Mickey Wallace did not sleep well.

15

I didn't find Wallace's card until I opened the back door on the afternoon of the next day to put out the trash. It lay on the step, frozen to the cement. I looked at it, then went back inside and dialed his cell phone number from my office.

He answered on the second ring. 'Mickey Wallace.'

'This is Charlie Parker.'

He didn't reply for a moment or two, and when he did he sounded uneasy, although, like a true professional, he quickly rallied. 'Mr. Parker, I was just about to call you. I was wondering if you'd considered my offer.'

'I've given it some thought,' I said. 'I'd like to meet.'

'Great.' His voice rose an octave in surprise, then resumed its usual timbre. 'Where and when?'

'Why don't you come out to my place in, say, an hour? Do you know where it is?'

There was a pause. 'No, I don't. Can you give me directions?'

My directions were intricate and detailed. I wondered if he was even bothering to take them down.

'Got that?' I said, when I was done.

'Yeah, I think so.' I heard him take a sip of liquid.

'You want to read them back to me?'

Wallace almost choked. When he had finished coughing, he said: 'That won't be necessary.'

'Well, if you're sure.'

'Thank you, Mr. Parker. I'll be with you shortly.'

I hung up, then went down the drive and found the tire tracks beneath the trees. If it was Wallace who had parked there, he'd left in a hurry. He'd managed to churn up ice and snow to reveal the dirt beneath. I walked back to the house and sat reading the *Press-Herald* and *The New York Times* until I heard a car pulling into the drive, and Wallace's blue Taurus came into view. He didn't park in the same spot as the night before, but drove right up to the house. I watched him get out, take his satchel from the passenger seat, and check his pockets for a spare pen. When he was satisfied that all was in order, he locked the car.

In my drive. In Maine. In winter.

I didn't wait for him to knock. Instead, I opened the door, and hit him once in the stomach. He buckled and dropped to his knees, then doubled over and retched.

'Get up.'

He stayed down. He was struggling for breath, and I thought that he might vomit on my porch.

'Don't hit me again,' he said. It was a plea, not a warning, and I felt like a piece of grit in a dog's eye.

'I won't.'

I helped him to his feet. He sat against the porch rail, his hands on his knees, and recovered himself. I stood opposite him, regretting what I had done. I had allowed my anger to simmer, and then I had taken it out on a man who was no match for me.

'You okay?'

He nodded, but he looked gray. 'What was that for?'

'I think you know. For sneaking around my property. For being dumb enough to drop your card while you were here.'

He leaned against the rail to support himself. 'I didn't drop it.'

'You're telling me you left it for me in the dirt on my back porch? That doesn't sound likely.'

'I'm telling you that I didn't drop it. I slipped it under the door for the woman who was in your house last night, but she just pushed it back.'

I looked away. I saw skeletal trees amid the evergreens, and the channels in the salt marshes shining coldly amid the frozen snow. I saw a single black crow lost against the gray sky.

'What woman?'

'A woman in a summer dress. I tried to speak to her, but she wouldn't say anything.'

I glanced at him. His eyes couldn't meet mine. He was telling a version of the truth, but he had hidden away some crucial element. He was trying to protect himself, but not from me. Mickey Wallace was scared to death. I could see it in the way his eyes kept returning to something behind the window of my living room. I don't know what he expected to see but, whatever it was, he was glad that it hadn't appeared.

'Tell me what happened.'

'I came out to the house. I thought you might be more amenable to a discussion away from the bar.'

I knew that he was lying, but I wasn't about to call him on it. I wanted to hear what he had to say about the events of the previous night.

'I saw a light, and I went around to the back door. There was a woman inside. I slipped my card under the door, and she slid it back. Then—'

He stopped.

'Go on,' I said.

'I heard a girl's voice,' he continued, 'but she was outside. I think the woman joined her at some point, but I didn't look so I can't be sure.'

'Why didn't you look?'

'I decided to leave.' His face, and those four words, spoke volumes.

'A wise choice. It's a shame that you were here in the first place.'

'I just wanted to see where you lived. I didn't mean any harm by it.'

'No.'

He breathed in deeply, and once he was certain that he wasn't going to throw up, he rallied and pulled himself up to his full height.

'Who were they?' he asked, and now it was my turn to lie.

'A friend. A friend and her daughter.'

'Your friend's daughter always go walking in the snow in dense fog, writing things on other people's windows?'

'Writing? What are you talking about?'

Mickey swallowed hard. His right hand was trembling. His left was jammed in his coat pocket.

'There was something written on the window of my car when I got back to it,' he said. 'It said, "Stay away from my daddy."'

It took all of my self-control not to reveal myself to him. I wanted so badly to look up at the attic window, for I remembered a message written on the glass there, a warning left by an entity that was not quite my daughter. Yet the house did not feel the same way that it had felt then. It was no longer haunted by rage and grief and pain. Before, I had sensed their presence in the shifting of shadows and the creaking of boards, in the slow closing of doors where there was no breeze, and in the tapping on windows where there were no branches to touch them. Now the house was at peace, but if Wallace was speaking the truth, then something had returned.

I recalled my mother once telling me, some years after my father died, that on the night his body was brought to the church, she dreamed that she woke to a presence in the bedroom, and thought she could feel her husband close to her. In the far corner of the room there was a chair where he used to sit every night to finish undressing. He would ease himself into it to take off his shoes and socks, and sometimes he would remain there quietly for a while, his bare feet planted firmly on the carpet, his chin resting on the palms of his hands, and reflect upon the day that was coming to a close. My mother said that, in her dream, my father was back in his chair, except she couldn't quite see him. When she tried to focus on the shape in the corner of the room, there was only a chair, but when she looked away a figure shifted position in the corner of her eye. She should have been frightened, but she was not. In her dream, her eyes became heavy. But how can my eyes be heavy, she thought, when I am still asleep? She fought against it, but the urge to sleep was too strong.

And just as she lost consciousness, she felt a hand on her brow, and lips softly brushed her cheek, and she sensed his sorrow and his guilt, and in that moment I think that perhaps she started to forgive him at last for what he had done. For the rest of the night, she slept soundly and deeply, and despite all that had occurred, she did not weep as the final prayers were said for him in the church, and when his body was lowered into the ground, and the flag was folded and laid in her hands, she smiled sadly for her lost man and a single tear exploded in the dirt like a fallen star.

'My friend's daughter,' I said, 'playing tricks on you.'

'Really?' said Wallace, and he did not even try to keep the skepticism from his voice. 'They still here?'

'No. They're gone.'

He let it go. 'That was a low thing you did. You always hit people without warning?'

'It comes from the line of work. If I had told some of them that I was going to hit them, they would have shot me first. A warning tends to dull the impact.'

'You know, right now, I kind of wish someone had shot you.'

'At least you're honest.'

'Is that why you called me out here, to warn me off again?'

'I'm sorry that I hit you, but you need to hear this face to face, and not in a bar either. I'm not going to help you with your book. In fact, I'll do everything in my power to make sure that it never gets beyond some scratches in one of your notebooks.'

'You're threatening me?'

'Mr. Wallace, do you recall the gentleman at the Bear who was discussing the possible motives of alien abductors?'

'I do. In fact, I met him again yesterday. He was waiting for me in the parking lot of my motel. I assumed that you'd sent him.'

Jackie. I should have known that he'd take matters into his own hands in some misguided effort to help me. I wondered how long he'd spent trawling the parking lots of the city's motels, looking for Wallace's car.

'I didn't, but he's the kind of man who can't easily be controlled, and he has two buddies who make him look like a gentle soul. They're brothers, and there are prisons that don't want them back because they frighten the other inmates.'

'So? You're going to set your buddies on me. Tough guy.'

'If I wanted to hurt you that badly, I'd do it myself. There are other ways to deal with the kind of problem that you represent.'

'I'm not a problem. I just want to tell your story. I'm interested in the truth.'

'I don't know what the truth is. If I don't know after all this time, then you're not going to have any more success than I've had.'

His eyes narrowed shrewdly, and some of the color returned to his face. I had made a mistake even discussing the matter with him. He was like an evangelical Christian who finds someone on a doorstep willing to debate theology with him.

'But I can help you,' he said. 'I'm a neutral party. I can find out things. It doesn't all have to go in the book. You'll have control over how your image is presented.'

'My image?'

He realized that he had taken a wrong turn, and backpedaled furiously.

'It's just a phrase. What I meant to say was, this is your story. If it's to be told properly, it has to be told in your voice.'

'No,' I said. 'That's where you're wrong. It doesn't have to be told at all. Don't come to my home, or to my place of work, again. I'm sure you know that I have a child. Her mother won't talk to you. That I can tell you for sure. If you approach them, if you even pass them on the street and catch their eye, I'll kill you and bury you in a shallow hole. You need to let this slide.'

Wallace's face hardened, and I saw the man's own inner strength reveal itself. Instantly, I felt tired. Wallace wasn't going to fade into the night.

'Well, let me tell you something, Mr. Parker.' He mentioned the name of a famous actor, a man around whom rumors of a sexual nature had long circled without finding purchase. 'Two years ago, I agreed to write an unauthorized biography of him. It's not my area, all that Hollywood bullshit, but the publisher had heard of my talents, and the money was good, given the subject. He's one of the most powerful men in Hollywood. His people threatened me with financial ruin, the loss of my reputation, even the loss of limbs, but that book is due to be published in six months' time, and I can stand by every word of it. He wouldn't cooperate, but it didn't matter. The book is still going to appear, and I've found people who've sworn that his whole life is a lie. You made a mistake punching me in the gut. It was the action of a frightened man. For that alone, I'm going to claw and dig in every dirty corner of your life. I'm going to find out things about you that you didn't even know existed. And then I'm going to put them in my book, and you can buy a copy and read about them, and maybe then you'll learn something about yourself, but I can tell you for sure that you'll learn something about Mickey Wallace.

'And if you ever lay a hand on me again, I'll see you in court, you fuck.'

With that, Wallace turned around and trudged back to his car.

And I thought: Aw, hell.

Aimee Price dropped by later that evening, after I had left another message for her at her office detailing most of what had happened since Wallace had appeared at the Bear. She declined coffee and asked if I had any wine uncorked. I didn't, but I was happy to open a bottle for her. It was the least that I could do.

'Okay,' she said, once she had sipped the wine carefully and decided that it wasn't about to send her into convulsions, 'this isn't my area, so I've had to ask around, but here is where we stand, in legal terms, on the book. Potentially, as the subject of an unauthorized biography of your life, you could bring a lawsuit for a number of legal reasons – libel, misappropriation of the right of publicity, breach of confidence – but the most likely avenue in your case would be invasion of privacy. You're not a public figure in the way an actor or a politician might be, so you have a certain right to privacy. We're talking about the right not to have private facts publicized that might prove embarrassing if they're not related to matters of public concern; the right not to have false or misleading statements or suggestions made about you; and protection against intrusion, which means literal physical intrusion on your privacy by entering onto your property.'

'Which Wallace did,' I said.

'Yes, but he could argue that the first time he came by was to remonstrate with you, and to leave his card, and the second time, according to what you've told me, was at your invitation.'

I shrugged. She was right.

'So how did that second visit go?' she asked.

'Could have gone better,' I said.

'In what way?'

'Not punching him in the stomach would have been a start.'

'Oh, Charlie.' She seemed genuinely disappointed, and I felt even more ashamed of my actions. In an effort to make up for my failings, I recounted my conversation with Wallace in as much detail as I could remember, leaving out any mention of the woman and child that he claimed to have glimpsed.

'You're telling me that your friend Jackie threatened Wallace too?' she said.

'I didn't ask him to. He probably thought that he was doing me a favor.'

'At least he exhibited more restraint than you did. Wallace could have you charged with assault, but my guess is that he won't. Clearly he wants to write this book, and that may override any other concerns as long as you didn't do him any lasting damage.'

'He walked away under his own steam,' I said.

'Well, if he knows anything about you at all, he can probably consider himself lucky.'

I took the hit. I wasn't in any position to argue.

'So where does that leave us?'

'You can't stop him writing the book. As he said himself, a lot of the relevant material is a matter of public record. What we can do is request, or otherwise obtain, a copy of the manuscript, and go through it with a fine-tooth comb looking for instances of libel, or egregious invasion of privacy. We could then apply to the courts for an injunction preventing publication, but I have to warn you that the courts are generally reluctant to permit injunctions of this kind in deference to the First Amendment. The best we could hope for would be monetary damages. The publisher has probably had a warranty and indemnity clause inserted into Wallace's contract, assuming the contract has been formally agreed upon. Also, if the whole thing has been handled right, there will be a media-perils insurance policy in place to cover the work. In other words, not only will we not be able to stop this horse from bolting, but we probably won't even be able to do more than close the door halfway once it's gone.'

I sat back in my chair and closed my eyes.

'You sure you don't want some of this wine?' said Aimee.

'I'm sure. If I start, I may not stop.'

'I'm sorry,' she said. 'I'll talk to some more people and see if there are any other avenues open to us, but I don't hold out much hope. And, Charlie?'

I opened my eyes.

'Don't threaten him again. Just keep your distance. If he approaches you, walk away. Don't get drawn into confrontations. That goes for your friends too, regardless of their good intentions.'

Which brought us to another problem.

'Yeah, well, that could be an issue,' I said.

'How?'

'Angel and Louis.'

I had told Aimee enough about them for her to be under no illusions.

'If Wallace starts digging, then their names may come up,' I said. 'I don't think they have any good intentions.'

'They don't sound like the kind of men who leave too many traces.'

'It doesn't matter. They won't like it, Louis especially.'

'Then warn them.'

I thought about it. 'No,' I said. 'Let's see what happens.'

'Are you sure that's a good idea?'

'Not really, but Louis believes in preventive measures. If I tell him that Wallace may start asking questions about him, he could decide that it might be better if Wallace didn't ask any questions at all.'

'I'll pretend I didn't hear that,' said Aimee. She finished her wine in a single gulp, and appeared to be debating whether or not to have more in the hope that it might destroy any memory of what I'd just said. 'Jesus, how did you end up with friends like that?'

'I'm not sure,' I replied, 'but I don't think that Jesus had anything to do with it.'

16

Mickey Wallace left Portland early the next day. He was simmering with resentment and a barely containable anger that was unfamiliar to him, for Mickey rarely got truly angry, but his encounter with Parker, combined with the efforts of Parker's Neanderthal friend to scare him off, had transformed him utterly. He was used to lawyers trying to intimidate him, and had been pushed up against walls and threatened with more serious damage at least twice, but nobody had punched him the way Parker had in many years. In fact, the last time Mickey had been in anything approaching a serious fight was when he was still in high school, and on that occasion he had landed a lucky punch that had knocked one of his opponent's teeth out. He wished he had managed to strike a similar blow at Parker, and as he boarded the shuttle at Logan he played out alternative scenarios in his mind, ones in which he had brought Parker to his knees and had humiliated the detective, not vice versa. He entertained them for a couple of minutes, and then dispensed with them. There would be other ways to make Parker regret what he had done, principal among them the completion of the book on which Mickey had set his heart and, he felt, his reputation.

He was still troubled by his experience at the Parker house on that mist-shrouded night. He had expected the intensity of his responses to it, his fear and confusion, to diminish, but they had not. Instead, he continued to sleep uneasily, and had woken on the first night after the encounter at precisely 4:03 a.m., convinced that he was not alone in his motel room. He had turned on the lamp by his bed, and the eco-friendly bulb had glowed slowly into life, spreading illumination through most of the room but leaving the corners in shadow, which gave Mickey the uncomfortable sensation that the darkness around him had receded reluctantly from the light, hiding whatever presence he had sensed in the places where the lamp could not reach. He remembered the woman crouched behind the kitchen door, and the child moving her finger across the window of his car. He should have been able to glimpse their faces, but he had not, and something told him that he should be grateful for that small mercy at least. Their faces had been concealed from him for a reason.

Because the Traveling Man had torn them apart, that's why, because he left nothing there but blood and bone and empty sockets. And you didn't want to see that, no sir, because that sight would stay with you until your eyes closed for the last time and they pulled the sheet over your own face. Nobody could look upon that degree of savagery and not be damaged by it forever.

And if those were people whom you loved, your wife and your child, well . . .

A friend and her daughter; two visitors: that was how Parker had described them to Mickey, but Mickey didn't accept that explanation for one moment. Oh, they were visitors all right, but not the kind who slept in the spare room and played board games on winter evenings. Mickey didn't understand their nature, not yet, and he hadn't decided whether or not to include his encounter in the book that he would present to his publishers. He suspected that he would not. By including a ghost story in his narrative, he risked undermining the factual basis of his work. And yet this woman and child, and what they had endured, represented the heart of the book. Mickey had always thought of Parker as a man haunted by what had happened to his wife and child, but not literally so. Was that the answer? Was what Mickey had witnessed evidence of an actual haunting?

And all of these thoughts and reflections he added to his notes.

Mickey checked into a hotel over by Penn Station, a typical tourist trap with a warren of tiny rooms occupied by noisy but polite Asians, and families of rubes trying to see New York on the cheap. By late that afternoon he was sitting in what was, by his standards, and the standards of most other people who weren't bums, a dive bar, and considering what he could order without endangering his health. He wanted coffee, but this looked like the kind of place where ordering coffee for any reason unconnected with a hangover would be frowned upon, if not considered actual evidence of homosexual leanings. In fact, thought Mickey, even washing one's hands after visiting the restroom might be viewed as suspect in a hole like this.

There was a bar menu beside him, and a list of specials chalked on a board that might as well have been written in Sanskrit, they'd been there so long and unchanged, but nobody was eating. Nobody was doing much of anything, because Mickey was the only person in the place, the bartender excepted, and he looked like he'd consumed nothing but human growth hormone for the past decade or so. He bulged in places where no normal person should have bulged. There were even bulges on his bald head, as though the top of his skull had developed muscles so as not to feel excluded from the rest of his body.

'Get you something?' His voice was pitched higher than Mickey had anticipated. He wondered if it was something to do with the steroids. There were peculiar swellings on the bartender's chest, where his breasts had grown secondary breasts of their own. He was so tan that he seemed to fade into the wood and grime of the bar. To Mickey, he looked like a pair of women's stockings that had been stuffed with footballs.

'I'm waiting for someone.'

'Well, order something while you're waiting. Look on it as rent for the stool.'

'Friendly place,' said Mickey.

'You want friends, call the Samaritans. This is a business.'

Mickey ordered a light beer. He rarely drank before nightfall, and even then he tended to limit his intake to a beer or two, the night of the visit to Parker's house excepted, and that night had been exceptional in so many ways. He wasn't thirsting for a beer now, and even the thought of sipping it made him feel queasy, but he wasn't about to offend someone who looked like he could turn Mickey inside out and back again before he'd even realized what was happening. The beer arrived. Mickey stared at it, and the beer stared back. Its head began to disappear, as though responding in kind to Mickey's lack of enthusiasm for it.

The door opened, and a man stepped inside. He was tall, with the natural bulk of someone who had never felt the need to use any form of artificial growth enhancers stronger than meat and milk. He wore a long blue overcoat that hung open, revealing a substantial gut. His hair was short and very white. His nose was red, and not just from the cold wind outside. Mickey realized that he'd made the right choice in ordering a beer.

'Hey,' said the bartender. 'It's the Captain. Long time, no see.'

He reached out a hand, and the newcomer took it and shook it warmly, using his free hand to slap the man's substantial upper arm.

'How you doin', Hector? See you're still using that shit.'

'Keeps me big and lean, Captain.'

'You've grown tits, and you must be shaving your back twice a day.'

'Maybe I'll keep it long, give the boys something to hold on to.'

'You're a deviant, Hector.'

'And proud of it. What can I get you? First one is on the house.'

'That's decent of you, Hector. A Redbreast, if you don't mind, to get the cold out of my bones.'

He walked down to the end of the bar where Mickey was sitting.

'You Wallace?' he asked.

Mickey stood up. He was about five-ten, and the newcomer towered over him by seven or eight inches.

'Captain Tyrrell.' They shook hands. 'I appreciate you taking the time to talk to me.'

'Well, after Hector has obliged me, the drinks are on you.'

'It'll be my pleasure.'

Hector placed a substantial glass of whiskey, untroubled by ice or water, beside Tyrrell's right hand. Tyrrell gestured to a booth against the back wall. 'Let's take our drinks down there. You eaten yet?'

'No.'

'They do a good hamburger here. You eat hamburger?'

Mickey doubted that this place did a good anything, but he knew better than to refuse.

'Yes. A hamburger sounds fine.'

Tyrrell raised a hand and shouted the order to Hector: two hamburgers, medium, with all the trimmings. Medium, thought Mickey. Jesus. He'd prefer it charred to within an inch of its life in the hope of killing whatever bacteria might have taken up residence in the meat. Hell, this might be the last burger he ever ate.

Hector duly entered the order on a surprisingly modern-looking register, even if he operated it like a monkey.

'Wallace: that's a good Irish name,' said Tyrrell.

'Irish-Belgian.'

'That's some mix.'

'Europe. The war.'

Tyrrell's face softened unpleasantly with sentimentality, like a marshmallow melting. 'My grandfather served in Europe. Royal Irish Fusiliers. Got shot for his troubles.'

'I'm sorry to hear it.'

'Ah, he didn't die. Lost his left leg below the knee, though. They didn't have prosthetics then, or not like they do now. He used to pin up his trouser leg every morning. Think he was kind of proud of it.'

He raised his glass to Mickey.

'Sláinte,' he said.

'Cheers,' said Mickey. He took a mouthful of beer. Mercifully, it was so cold that he could barely taste it. He reached into his satchel and produced a notebook and pen.

'Straight down to business,' said Tyrrell.

'If you'd prefer to wait . . .'

'Nah, it's good.'

Mickey took a little Olympus digital voice recorder from his jacket pocket, and showed it to Tyrrell.

'Would you object if—?'

'Yes, I would. Put it away. Better still, take the batteries out and leave that thing where I can see it.'

Mickey did as he was told. It would make things more difficult, but Mickey had reasonable shorthand and a good memory. In any case, he wouldn't be quoting Tyrrell directly. This was background, and deep background. Tyrrell had been quite clear about that when he had agreed to meet with Mickey. If his name appeared anywhere near the book, he'd stomp Mickey's fingers until they looked like corkscrews.

'Tell me some more about this book you're writing.'

So Mickey did. He left out the more artistic and philosophical elements of his proposal, and tried to tread as neutral a path as possible as he described his interest in Parker. Although he hadn't yet ascertained Tyrrell's views on the subject, he suspected that they were largely negative, if only because, so far, anyone who liked or respected Parker had refused point-blank to talk to him.

'And have you met Parker?' asked Tyrrell.

'I have. I approached him about an interview.'

'What happened?'

'He sucker-punched me in the gut.'

'That's him all right. He's a sonofabitch, a thug. And that's not the worst of it.'

He took a sip of his whiskey. It was already half gone.

'You want another one?' asked Mickey.

'Sure.'

Mickey turned to the bar. He didn't even have to order. Hector just nodded and went for the bottle.

'So, what do you want to know about him?' said Tyrrell.

'I want to know what you know.'

And Tyrrell began to talk. He spoke first of Parker's father, who had killed two young people in a car and then taken his own life. He could offer no insights into the killings, beyond suggesting there was something wrong with the father that had passed itself on to the son: a faulty gene, perhaps; a predilection toward violence.

The hamburgers arrived, along with Tyrrell's second drink. Tyrrell ate, but Mickey did not. He was too busy taking notes, or that would be his excuse if he were asked.

'We think the first man he killed was named Johnny Friday,' said Tyrrell. 'He was a pimp, beaten to death in the washroom of a bus station. He was no loss to the world, but that's not the point.'

'Why do you suspect Parker?'

'Because he was there. Cameras picked him up entering and leaving the station during the killing window.'

'Were there cameras on the bathroom door?'

'There were cameras everywhere, but he didn't appear on them. We just got him entering and leaving the station.'

Mickey was puzzled. 'How could that be?'

For the first time, Tyrrell looked uncertain. 'I don't know. The cameras weren't fixed then, except for the ones on the doors. It was a cost-cutting measure. They moved from side to side. I guess he timed them, then moved in conjunction with them.'

'Difficult to do, though.'

'Difficult. Not impossible. Still, it was strange.'

'Was he interviewed?'

'We had a witness who placed him at the scene: washroom attendant. Guy was Korean. Couldn't speak more than about three words of English, but he picked out Parker's image from the door cameras. Well, he picked out Parker's image as one of five possibles from a series of images. Trouble was, we all looked alike to him. Of those five people, four were as different from one another as I am from you. Anyway, Parker was hauled in, and agreed to be questioned. He didn't even lawyer up. He admitted to being at the bus station, but nothing more than that. Said it was in connection with some runaway he'd been asked to find. It checked out. He was working a teen case at the time.'

'And that's as far as it went?'

'There wasn't enough to charge him on, and no appetite for it anyway. Here was an ex-cop who had lost his wife and child only months before. He may not have been loved by his fellow officers, but cops support their own in times of trouble. It would have been a more unpopular case to prosecute than charging Goldilocks with burglary. And like I said, Johnny Friday was no Eagle Scout. A lot of people out there felt that someone had done humanity a service by taking him off the team permanently.'

'Why wasn't Parker popular?'

'Dunno. He wasn't meant to be a cop. He never fit in. There was always something odd about him.'

'So why did he join?'

'Some misplaced loyalty to his old man's memory, I suppose. Maybe he thought he could make up for those kids' deaths by being a better cop than his father was. You ask me, it's about the only admirable thing he ever did.'

Mickey let that slide. He was startled by the depths of Tyrrell's bitterness toward Parker. He couldn't figure out what Parker might have done to deserve it, short of burning Tyrrell's house down and then screwing his wife in the ashes.

'You said that Johnny Friday was the first killing. There were others?'

'I'd guess so.'

'You'd guess?'

Tyrrell signaled for a third whiskey. He was slowing down some, but he was also getting tetchy.

'Look, most are a matter of record: here, in Louisiana, in Maine, in Virginia, in South Carolina. He's like the Grim Reaper, or cancer. If those are the ones that we know about, don't you think there are others that we don't know about? You think he called the cops every time he or one of his buddies punched someone's clock?'

'His buddies? You mean the men known as Angel and Louis?'

'Shadows,' said Tyrrell softly. 'Shadows with teeth.'

'What can you tell me about them?'

'Rumors, mostly. Angel, he did time for theft. From what I can tell, Parker might have used him as a source, and in return he offered him protection.'

'So it started out as a professional relationship?'

'You could say that. The other one, Louis, he's harder to pin down. No arrests, no history: he's a wraith. There was some stuff last year. An auto shop he was reputed to have a silent interest in got targeted. A guy, one of the shooters, ended up in the hospital, then died a week later of his injuries. After that—'

Hector appeared at his elbow and replaced an empty glass with a full one. Tyrrell paused to take a mouthful.

'Well, this is where it gets weird. One of Louis's friends, business partners, whatever, he died too. They said that he had a heart attack, but I heard different. One of the mortuary attendants said that they had to fill in a bullet hole in his throat.'

'Who did it? Louis?'

'Nah, he doesn't hurt those close to him. He's not that kind of killer. The whispers were that this was a revenge raid gone wrong.'

'That's what he was doing up in Massena,' said Mickey, more to himself than to Tyrrell, who didn't seem to notice anyway.

'They're like him: they're being looked after,' said Tyrrell.

'Looked after?'

'A man doesn't get to do what Parker has done, to kill with impunity, unless someone is watching his back.'

'The ones on record were justifiable homicides, I heard.'

'Justifiable! You don't find it strange that none of them ever even made it to the steps of a court, that every investigation into his actions exonerated him or just petered out?'

'You're talking about a conspiracy.'

'I'm talking about *protection*. I'm talking about people with a vested interest in keeping Parker on the streets.'

'Why?'

'I don't know. Could be because they approve of what he's done.'

'But he's lost his PI's license. He can't own a firearm.'

'He can't *legally* carry a firearm in the state of Maine. You can be damned sure he has guns squirreled away somewhere.'

'What I'm saying is, if there was a conspiracy to protect him, then something has changed.'

'Not enough to land him behind bars, where he belongs.' Tyrrell rapped an index finger on the table to emphasize his point.

Mickey leaned back. He had filled pages and pages of notes. His hand ached. He watched Tyrrell. The older man was staring into his third glass. They'd been huge measures, as big as any Mickey had ever seen poured in a bar. Had he himself drunk that much alcohol he would be asleep by now. Tyrrell was still upright, but he was on the ropes. Mickey wasn't going to get anything more of use from him.

'Why do you hate him so much?'

'Huh?' Tyrrell looked up. Even through a fug of progressive intoxication, he was still surprised by the directness of the question.

'Parker. Why do you hate him?'

'Because he's a killer.'

'Just that?'

Tyrrell blinked slowly. 'No. Because he's wrong.

He's all wrong. It's like – It's like he doesn't cast a shadow, or there's no reflection when he looks in a mirror. He seems normal, but then you look closer and he isn't. He's an aberration, an abomination.'

Christ, thought Mickey.

'You go to church?' asked Tyrrell.

'No.'

'You should. A man ought to go to church. Helps him to keep himself in perspective.'

'I'll remember that.'

Tyrrell looked up, his face transformed. Mickey had overstepped the mark.

'Don't get smart with me, *boy*. Look at you, scrabbling in the dirt, hoping to make a few bucks off another man's life. You're a parasite. You don't believe in anything. *I* believe. I believe in God, and I believe in the law. I know right from wrong, good from evil. I've spent my life living by those beliefs. I cleaned out precinct after precinct in this city, rooting out the ones who thought that being lawmen made them above the law. Well, I showed them the error of their ways. Nobody should be above the law, especially not cops, doesn't matter if they wear a badge now or wore one ten years ago, twenty years ago. I found the ones who stole, who ripped off dealers and whores, who dispensed their version of street justice in alleyways and empty apartments, and I brought them to book. I called them on it, and I found them wanting.

'Because there is a *process* in place. There is a system of justice. It's imperfect, and it doesn't always work the way it should, but it's the best we have. And anyone – *anyone* – who steps outside that system to act as judge, jury, and executioner on others is an enemy of that system. Parker is an enemy of that system. His friends are enemies of that system. By their actions, they render it acceptable for others to act the same way. Their violence begets more violence. You cannot perform acts of evil in the name of a greater good, because the good suffers. It is corrupted and polluted by what has been done in its name. Do you understand, Mr. Wallace? These are *gray men*. They shift the boundaries of morality to suit themselves, and they use the ends to justify the means. That is unacceptable to me, and if you have a shred of decency, it should be unacceptable to you too.' He pushed the glass away. 'We're finished here.'

'But what if others won't act, can't act?' asked Mickey. 'Is it better to let evil go unchecked than to sacrifice a little of the good to resist it?'

'And who decides that?' asked Tyrrell. He was swaying slightly as he pulled on his coat, struggling to find the armholes. 'You? Parker? Who decides what is an acceptable level of good to sacrifice? How much evil has to be committed in the name of good before it becomes an evil in itself?'

He patted his pockets, and heard the satisfying jangle of his keys. Mickey hoped that they weren't car keys.

'Go write your book, Mr. Wallace. I won't be reading it. I don't think you'll have anything to tell me that I don't already know. I'll give you one piece of advice for free, though. No matter how bad his friends are, Parker is worse. I'd step lightly when I'm asking about them, and maybe I'd be inclined to leave them out of your story altogether, but Parker is lethal because he believes that he's on a crusade. I hope that you expose him for the wretch he is, but I'd watch my back all the way.'

Tyrell made a gun with his hand, pointed it at Mickey, and let his thumb fall like a hammer on a chamber. Then he walked, a little unsteadily, from the bar, shaking hands with Hector one more time before he left. Mickey put away his notebook and pen, and went to pay the tab.

'You a friend of the Captain's?' asked Hector, as Mickey calculated the tip and added it to the bill by hand for tax purposes.

'No,' said Mickey. 'I don't think I am.'

'The Captain doesn't have many friends,' said Hector, and there was something in his tone. It might almost have been pity. Mickey looked at him with interest.

'What do you mean?'

'I mean that we get cops in here all the time, but he's the only one who drinks alone.'

'He was IAD,' said Mickey. 'Internal Affairs.'

Hector shook his head. 'I know that, but that's not it. He's just—'

Hector searched for the right word.

'He's just a prick,' he concluded, then went back to reading his body building magazine.

17

Mickey wrote up his notes on the Tyrrell interview in his room while the details were still fresh in his mind. The pimp stuff was interesting. He Googled the name Johnny Friday, along with the details that Tyrrell had shared with him, and came up with some contemporary news reports, as well as a longer article that had been written for one of the free papers entitled 'Pimp: The Brutal Life and Bad End of Johnny Friday.' There were two pictures of Friday accompanying the article. The first showed him as he was in life, a spare, rangy, black man with hollow cheeks and eyes that were too large for his face. He had his arms around a pair of young women in lacy underwear, both of whom had their eyes blacked out to preserve their anonymity. Mickey wondered where they were now. According to the main article, young women who became professionally acquainted with Johnny Friday were not destined to lead happy existences.

The second picture had been taken on the mortuary slab, and showed the extent of the injuries that Friday had received in the course of the beating that took his life. Mickey figured that Friday's family must have asked for the photograph to be released; that, or the cops had wanted it done in order to send out a message. Friday wasn't even recognizable as the same man. His face was swollen and bloodied; his jaw, nose, and one of his cheekbones broken; and some of his teeth were sheared off at the gums. He had suffered extensive internal injuries too: one of his lungs had been punctured by a broken rib, and his spleen had ruptured.

Parker's name wasn't mentioned, which was no surprise, but a 'police source' had indicated to the writer that there was a suspect in the killings, although there was not enough evidence as yet to press charges. Mickey calculated the odds in favor of Tyrrell being that source, and decided they were about even. If he was, then it meant that, even a decade ago, he'd had doubts about Parker, and he might have had some justification for them. Mickey hadn't cared much for Tyrrell, but there was no denying that the man who had killed Johnny Friday was dangerous, someone capable of inflicting grave violence, an individual filled with anger and hatred. Mickey tried to balance that with the man he had encountered in Maine, and what he had heard about him from others. He rubbed his still tender belly at the memory of the punch that he had received on Parker's front porch, and the light that had flared briefly in the man's eyes as he had struck the blow. Yet no other blows had followed, and the anger in his face was gone almost as quickly as it had appeared, to be replaced by what Mickey thought was shame and regret. It hadn't mattered to Mickey then – he had been too busy trying not to cough his guts up – but it was clear upon reflection that, if Parker's anger was still not yet fully under his control, then he had learned to rein it in to some degree, although not quickly enough to save Mickey from a bruised belly. But if Tyrrell was right, this man had Johnny Friday's blood on his hands. He was not just a killer, but a murderer, and Mickey wondered how much he had truly changed in the years since Johnny Friday's death.

When he was finished with the Tyrrell material, he opened a paper file on his desk. Inside were more notes: twenty-five or thirty sheets of paper, each covered from top to bottom in Mickey's tiny handwriting, illegible to anyone else thanks to a combination of his personal shorthand and the size of the script. One sheet was headed with the words 'Father/ Mother.' He intended to go out to Pearl River at some point to talk to neighbors, store owners, anyone who might have had contact with Parker's family before the killings, but he had some more homework to do on that first.

He checked his watch. It was after eight. He knew that Jimmy Gallagher, who had partnered Parker's father down in the Ninth Precinct, lived out in Brooklyn. Tyrrell had given him that, along with the name of the investigator from the Rockland County District Attorney's Office who had been present at the interviews with Parker's father following the killings. Tyrrell thought that the latter, ex-NYPD, name of Kozelek, might talk to Wallace, and had initially offered to smooth the way, but that was before their conversation had come to a bad-tempered end. Wallace figured that call wasn't going to be made now, although he wasn't afraid to tap Tyrrell again, once he'd sobered up, if the investigator proved reluctant to speak.

The partner, Gallagher, was another matter. Wallace could tell that Tyrrell hadn't liked Gallagher any more than he'd liked Charlie Parker. He went back to his notes from that afternoon and found the exchange in question.

W: Who were his friends?

T: Parker's?

W: No, his father's.

T: He was a popular guy, well liked down in the Ninth. He probably had a lot of friends.

W: Any in particular?

T: He was partnered with – uh, what was his name now? – Gallagher, that's it. Jimmy Gallagher was his partner down there for years. (Laughs) I always – ah, it doesn't matter.

W: Maybe it does.

T: I always thought he was queer myself.

W: There were rumors?

T: Just that: rumors.

W: Was he interviewed in the course of the investigation into the Pearl River killings?

T: Oh yeah, he was interviewed all right. I saw the transcripts. It was like talking to one of those monkeys. You know the ones: see no evil, speak no evil, hear no evil? Said he knew nothing. Hadn't even seen his old buddy that day.

W: Except?

T: Except that it was Gallagher's birthday when the

killings occurred, and he was down in the Ninth, even though he'd requested, and been given, a day off. Hard to believe that he would have gone to the Ninth on his day off, and his birthday, what's more, and not hooked up with his partner and best friend.

W: So you think that Gallagher went down to meet some people for a birthday drink, and if that was the case, Parker would have been among them?

T: Makes sense, doesn't it? Here's another thing: Parker was on an eight-to-four tour that day. A cop named Eddie Grace covered for Parker so that he could finish his tour early. Why would Parker have been calling in favors unless it was to meet up with Jimmy Gallagher?

W: Did Grace say that was why he covered for Parker?

T: Like everyone else, Grace knew nothing and said nothing. The precinct clerk, DeMartini, saw Parker skip out, but didn't say anything about it. He knew when to turn a blind eye. A waitress in Cal's said Gallagher was with someone on the night of the killings, but she didn't get a good look at the guy, and he didn't stay long. She said it might have been Will Parker, but then the bartender contradicted her, said it was someone else in the bar with Gallagher, a stranger, and the waitress subsequently decided that she'd been mistaken.

W: You think someone put pressure on her to change her story?

T: They closed ranks. It's what cops do. They protect their own, even if it's the wrong thing to do.

Mickey paused at that point in his notes. Tyrrell's face had changed when he spoke about ranks closing, of men being protected. Perhaps it was the IAD investigator in him, a deep-seated hatred of corrupt men and the code of *omerta* that protected them, but Mickey didn't think that was all. He suspected that Tyrrell had been outside the loop even before he joined IAD. He wasn't a likeable man, as Hector had pointed out, and it might have been the case that the 'Rat Squad' had given him the opportunity to punish those whom he despised in the guise of a crusade against corruption. Mickey filed that observation away, and returned to his reading.

T: What I couldn't figure out was, what did it matter if Gallagher was with Parker that night, unless Gallagher knew something about what was going to happen?
W: You're talking about a premeditated killing.

Mickey recalled that Tyrrell had reconsidered at that point.

T: Maybe, or Gallagher knew why Parker ended up killing those two kids and wanted to keep that knowledge to himself. Whatever the reason, I know Jimmy Gallagher lied about what happened that night. I've read the IAD reports. As far as we were concerned, after that, Jimmy Gallagher was a marked man for the rest of his career.

Mickey found Gallagher's name in the phone book. He considered making a call before heading out to Bensonhurst, then decided that he might be better off surprising him. He wasn't sure what he hoped to gain from speaking to Gallagher, but if Tyrrell was right, then there was at least one crack in the story constructed around the events of the day on which the Pearl River killings had taken place. As a reporter, Mickey had learned to become the water in the crack, widening it, weakening the structure itself, until it finally collapsed to reveal the truth. The killings and their aftermath would play an important part in Mickey's book. They'd offer him scope to consult a couple of rent-a-psychologists who'd give him chapter and verse on the impact on a son of his father's involvement in a murder-suicide. Readers ate that stuff up.

He took the subway out to Bensonhurst to save a few bucks and found Gallagher's street. He knocked on the door of the neat little house. After a couple of minutes, a tall man answered the door.

'Mr. Gallagher?'

'That's right.'

Gallagher's lips and teeth were stained red. He'd been drinking wine when Mickey called. That was good, unless he had company. It could mean that his defenses might be down some. Mickey had his wallet in his hand. He removed a card from it and handed it over.

'My name's Michael Wallace. I'm a reporter. I was hoping to talk to you for a few minutes.'

'About what?'

And now it was time for Mickey to massage the

truth a little: a lie in the service of a greater good. He doubted if Tyrrell would have approved.

'I'm putting together a piece about changes in the Ninth Precinct over the years. I know you served down there. I'd like to speak to you about your memories of that time.'

'A lot of cops passed through the Ninth. Why me?'

'Well, when I was looking for people to talk to, I saw that you'd been involved in a lot of community activities over here in Bensonhurst. I thought that social conscience might give you a better insight into the people and the neighborhood of the Ninth.'

Gallagher looked at the card. 'Wallace, huh?'

'That's right.'

He leaned forward and tucked the card carefully into the pocket of Mickey's shirt. It was a curiously intimate gesture.

'You're full of shit,' said Gallagher. 'I know who you are, and I know what you're trying to write. Cops talk. I knew about you from the moment you started sniffing around in things that don't concern you. Take my advice: let this one go. You don't want to go nosing around in these corners. Nobody worth talking to is going to help you, and you may just bring a heap of trouble down on your head in the process.'

Mickey's eyes glittered. They had turned to hard little jewels set into his head. He was getting tired of being warned off.

'I'm a reporter,' he said, even though this was no longer the case. 'The more people tell me not to look into something, the more I want to do it.'

'That doesn't make you a reporter,' said Gallagher. 'It makes you a fool. You're also a liar. I don't much care for that in a man.'

'Really?' said Wallace. 'You've never lied?'

'I didn't say that. I like it as little in myself as I do in you.'

'Good, because I believe that you lied about what happened on the day that Will Parker killed those two teenagers out in Pearl River. I'm going to do my best to find out why. Then I'll be back here, and we'll talk again.'

Gallagher looked weary. Mickey wondered how long he'd been waiting for all of this to come back on him. Probably since the day his partner had turned into a murderer.

'Get off my step, Mr. Wallace. You're spoiling my evening.'

He closed the door in Mickey's face. Mickey stared at it for a moment, then took the business card from his pocket and tucked it into the door frame before heading back to Manhattan.

Inside the house, Jimmy sat at his kitchen table. There was an empty glass beside him, and half a bottle of Syrah, along with the remains of his evening meal. Jimmy liked cooking for himself, even more than he liked cooking for other people. When he cooked for himself he didn't have to fret about the results, about what other people might think of what he'd prepared. He was able to cook to his own satisfaction, and he knew what he enjoyed. He'd been looking forward to a quiet evening with a good bottle of wine and an old noir movie on TCM. Now his sense of calm, which had already been fragile, was shattered. It had been fragile ever since Charlie Parker came to his door. At that moment, Jimmy had felt as though the ground were slowly being eroded from beneath his feet. He had hoped that the past had been laid to rest, however uneasily. Now, the earth was shifting, exposing tattered flesh and old bones.

He had always been troubled by the possibility that, in lying to the investigators, in keeping silent over the decades that followed, he had done the wrong thing. Like a splinter buried deep in the flesh, the knowledge of how he had conspired with others to bury the truth, even the little of it that he knew, had festered inside him. Now the time was fast approaching when the infection would either be purged from his body, or destroy him.

He filled his glass and walked to the hallway. Taking a sip of his wine, he dialed the number for the second time since Parker had visited him. It was answered after five rings. In the background, he heard noises – plates being washed, the laughter of women – as the old man said hello.

'It's Jimmy Gallagher,' he said. 'There's another problem.'

'Go on,' said the voice.

'I've just had a reporter here, name of Wallace, Mickey Wallace. He was asking about . . . that day.'

There was a brief silence. 'We know about him. What did you tell him?'

'Nothing. I stuck to the story, like you told me to, like I've always done. But—'

'Go on.'

'It's coming apart. First Charlie Parker, now this guy.'

'It was always going to come apart. I am only surprised that it has taken so long.'

'What do you want me to do?'

'About the reporter? Nothing. His book will never be published.'

'You seem very certain about that.'

'We have friends. Wallace's contract is about to be cancelled. Without the promise of money for his efforts, he'll lose heart.'

Jimmy wasn't so sure about that. He'd seen the look on Wallace's face. Money might have been part of the impulse behind his investigation, but it wasn't the sole motivation. He was almost like a good cop, Jimmy thought. You didn't pay him to do his job, you paid him *not* to do something else. Wallace wanted the story. He wanted to find out the truth. Like all those who achieve success against the odds, there was a touch of the fanatic to him.

'Have you spoken to Charlie Parker?'

'Not yet.'

'If you wait for him to come to you, you may find that his anger is commensurately greater. Call him. Tell him to come down and talk.'

'And do I also tell him about you?'

'Tell him everything, Mr. Gallagher. You've been faithful to your friend's memory for a quarter of a century. You've protected his son, and us, for a long time. We're grateful to you, but it's time now to expose these hidden truths to the light.'

'Thank you,' said Jimmy.

'No, thank you. Enjoy the rest of your evening.'

The phone was hung up. Jimmy knew that it might be the last time he heard that voice.

And, in truth, he wasn't sorry.

18

The day after my confrontation with Mickey Wallace, I decided to tell Dave Evans that I wanted to take a week off from the Bear. I was determined to put pressure on Jimmy Gallagher, and maybe hit Eddie Grace again. I couldn't do that while commuting back and forth between Portland and New York and relying on having Sundays off.

And something else had emerged. Walter Cole had been unable to turn up anything new about the investigation into the Pearl River killings, except for one curious detail.

'The reports are too clean,' he told me over the phone. 'The whole thing was a whitewash. I spoke to a guy in records. He said the file is so thin, if you turn it sideways it's invisible.'

'That's no surprise. They buried it. There was no percentage in doing anything else.'

'Yeah, well, I still think there was more to it than that. The record was purged. You ever hear of something called Unit Five?'

'Doesn't ring any bells.'

'Ten years ago, all records relating to the Pearl River killings were ring-fenced. Any request for information beyond what was in the files had to go through this Unit Five clearance, which meant contacting the commissioner's office. My guy didn't feel comfortable even talking about it, but anyone who wants to know more than the bare details about what happened at Pearl River has to put in a request to Unit Five.'

But Walter wasn't finished.

'You know what else is covered by the Unit Five order? The deaths of Susan and Jennifer Parker.'

'So what's Unit Five?' I asked.

'I think you are,' said Walter.

I met Dave at Arabica, at the corner of Free and Cross, which, as well as having some of the best coffee in town, now occupied the best space, with art on the walls and light pouring through its big picture windows. The Pixies were playing in the background. All things considered, it was hard to find fault with the place.

Dave wasn't overjoyed at being asked to give me time away from the bar, and I could hardly blame him. He was about to lose two staff, one to maternity and the other to a girlfriend in California. I knew he felt that he was spending too much time doing general bar work and too little time on paperwork and accounts. I had been hired to take some of that burden off him, and instead I was leaving him mired even more deeply than he had been before I arrived.

'I'm trying to run a business here, Charlie,' said Dave. 'You're killing me.'

'We're not real busy, Dave,' I said. 'Gary can take care of the Nappi delivery, and then I'll be back in time for next week's truck. We're overstocked on some of the microbrews anyway, so we can let them run down.'

'What about tomorrow night?'

'Nadine's been asking for extra shifts. Let her take up some of the slack.'

Dave buried his face in his hands.

'I hate you,' he said.

'No, you don't.'

'Yes, I do. Take your week off. If we're still here when you get back, you owe me. You owe me big time.'

That night did nothing to improve Dave's mood. Somebody tried to steal the ornamental bear head from the dining room, and we only spotted that it was missing when the thief was about to drive from the parking lot with the head sticking out of the passenger window. We were hit by cocktail freaks, so that even Gary, who seemed to have a better knowledge of cocktails than most, was forced to resort to the cheat sheet kept behind the bar. Students ordered rounds of cherry bombs and Jäger bombs, and the sickly smell of Red Bull tainted the air. We changed fifteen kegs, three times as many as the average for an evening although still some way off the record of twenty-two.

And there was also sex in the air. There was a woman in her fifties at the far end of the bar who couldn't have been more predatory if she'd had claws and razor teeth, and she was soon joined by two or three others to form a pack. The bartenders called them 'flossies' after a semimythical dental supplies saleswoman who was reputed to have serviced a series of men in the parking lot over the course of a night. Eventually, they attracted a couple of International Players of the World to themselves, macho types whose aftershave fought a battle of the fragrances with the lingering odor of Red Bull. At one point, I considered turning a hose on them all to cool them down, but before the need arose they departed for a darker corner of town.

By the time 1 a.m. arrived, all fifteen staff were exhausted, but nobody wanted to go home just yet. After the beer towers were cleaned and the coolers stocked, we fixed some burgers and fries, and most people had a drink to unwind. We turned off the satellite system that provided music for the bar, and instead put a mellow iPod playlist on shuffle: Sun Kil Moon, Fleet Foxes, the reissue of Dennis Wilson's *Pacific Ocean Blue*. Finally, people started to drift away, and Dave and I checked that everything was off in the kitchen, snuffed the last of the candles, checked the bathrooms to make sure everyone was out, then put the cash in the safe and locked up. We said good-bye in the parking lot, and before we went our separate ways, Dave told me again that he hated me again.

After I had opened the front door of my house, I paused at the threshold and listened. My encounter with Mickey Wallace, and his story about the two figures he had glimpsed, had unsettled me. I had let those ghosts go. They didn't belong here any longer.

Yet, as before, when I had gone through the house after Wallace's departure, I experienced no sense of dread, no true unease. Instead, the house was quiet, and I felt its emptiness. Whatever had been here was now gone.

The message light on my answering machine was flashing. I hit the button, and heard Jimmy Gallagher's voice. He sounded a little drunk, but the message was still clear and simple, and the timing of it preordained.

'Charlie, come on down here,' said Jimmy. 'I'll tell you what you want to know.'

IV

Three may keep a secret, if two of them are dead.

Benjamin Franklin (1706–1790),
Poor Richard's Almanac

19

Jimmy Gallagher must have been watching for me to come, as he answered the door before I even knocked. I imagined him, for a moment, sitting at his window, his face reflected in the gathering dark, his fingers tapping on the sill, anxiously seeking the one whom he was expecting, but as I looked into his eyes I saw that there was no anxiety, no fear or concern. In truth, he appeared more relaxed than I had ever seen him. He was wearing a T-shirt over a pair of paint-stained tan pants, topped off by a Yankees hooded top and an old pair of penny loafers. He looked like a man in his twenties who had suddenly woken up from a nap to find that he had aged forty years while still being forced to wear all the same clothes. I had always believed him to be a man for whom appearance was everything, for I could never recall him without a jacket and a clean, starched shirt, often finished with a tasteful silk tie. Now, all formality had been stripped from him, and I wondered, as the night drew on and I listened to the secrets pour out of him, if those strictures he had placed on his dress had merely been one part of the defenses he had constructed to protect not only himself and his own identity, but the memories and lives of those about whom he cared.

He didn't say anything when he saw me. He just opened the door, nodded once, then turned around and led the way to the kitchen. I closed the door behind me and followed him. A pair of candles burned in the kitchen, one on the windowsill and a second on the table. Beside the second candle stood a bottle of good – maybe very good – red wine, a decanter, and two glasses. Jimmy tenderly touched the neck of the bottle, stroking it as though it were a beloved pet.

'I've been waiting for an excuse to open it,' he said. 'But these days, I don't seem to have too many causes for celebration. Mostly, I go to funerals. You get to my age, that's what you do. I've been to three funerals already this year. They were all cops, and they all died of cancer.' He sighed. 'I don't want to go that way.'

'Eddie Grace is dying of cancer.'

'I heard. I thought about going to see him, but Eddie and me—' He shook his head. 'All we had in common was your old man. When he went, Eddie and me had no reason to talk.'

I recalled what Eddie had said to me just before I left him, about how Jimmy Gallagher had spent his life living a lie. Maybe Eddie had been referring, however obliquely, to Jimmy's homosexuality, but I knew now that there were other lies to be uncovered, even if they were lies of omission. Still, it wasn't for Eddie Grace to judge how any man lived his life, not in the way that he had judged Jimmy. We all presented one face to the world, and kept another hidden.

Nobody could survive otherwise. As Jimmy unburdened himself, and my father's secrets were slowly revealed to me, I came to understand how Will Parker had buckled under the weight of them, and I felt only sadness for him and for the woman he had betrayed.

Jimmy took a corkscrew from a drawer and carefully cut the foil on the bottle before inserting the tip of the corkscrew into the cork. It took only two twists, and then a single pull, for the cork to release with a satisfying, airy pop. He looked at it to make sure that it wasn't dry or decaying, and cast it to the side.

'I used to sniff the corks,' he said, 'but then someone pointed out that it tells you nothing about the quality of the wine. Shame. I liked the ritual of it, until I found out that it made me look like a know-nothing.'

He positioned the candle behind the bottle as he decanted it, so that he could see the sediment approaching the neck.

'No need to let it stand for long,' he said, once he was finished. 'That's just with younger wines. It softens the tannins.'

He poured two glasses, and sat. He held his glass to the candlelight to examine it, lifted it to his nose, sniffed, then swirled the wine around before sniffing again, holding the bowl in his hands to warm it. Finally, he tasted it, moving the wine around in his mouth, savoring the flavors.

'Fantastic,' he said, then raised his glass in a toast. 'To your old man.'

'To my old man,' I echoed. I sipped the wine. It tasted rich and earthy.

'Domaine de la Romanée-Conti, ninety-five,' said Jimmy. 'A pretty good year for burgundy. That's a six hundred dollar bottle of wine we're drinking.'

'What are we celebrating?'

'The end.'

'Of what?'

'Of secrets and lies.'

I put my glass down. 'So where do you want to begin?'

'With the dead baby,' he said. 'With the first dead baby.'

Neither of them had wanted to work the 12 to 8 that week, but that was the way the cookie had crumbled, them was the breaks, or whatever other cliché one might have decided to apply to a situation when there was only one end of the stick to grasp, and it wasn't the fragrant end. That evening, the precinct was holding a party at the Ukrainian National Home over on Second Avenue, which always smelled of borscht and pierogi and barley soup from the restaurant on the first floor, and where the director Sidney Lumet would rehearse his movies before beginning filming, so that, over time, Paul Newman and Katharine Hepburn, Al Pacino and Marlon Brando would all walk up and down the same steps as the cops of the Ninth. The party was to celebrate the fact that three of its officers had been awarded combat crosses that month, the name given to the green bars received by those who had been involved in a shootout. The Ninth was already the Wild West back then: cops were dying.

If it came down to you and the other guy, you shot first and worried about the paperwork later.

New York then wasn't like it was now. In the summer of '64, the racial tensions in the city had come to a head with the killing of fifteen-year-old James Powell in Harlem by an off-duty patrolman. What started out as orderly protests against the killing turned into riots on July 18th, when a crowd gathered at the 123 in Harlem shouting, 'Murderers!' at the cops inside. Jimmy and Will had been sent up as part of the reinforcements, bottles and bricks and garbage-can lids raining down on them, looters helping themselves to food and radios and even weapons from the neighborhood stores. Jimmy could still recall a police captain pleading with the rioters to go home, and hearing someone laugh and call back: 'We are home, white boy!'

After five days of rioting in Harlem and Bed-Stuy, one person was dead, 520 had been arrested, and the writing was on the wall for Mayor Wagner. His days had already been numbered, even before the riots. The annual murder rate had doubled to six hundred a year under his administration, and even before the Powell shooting the city had been reeling from the murder, in her middle-class Queens neighborhood, of a woman named Kitty Genovese who was stabbed in the course of three separate assaults by the same man, Winston Moseley, twelve people witnessing or hearing the murder while it was in progress, most of them declining to intervene in any way beyond calling the cops. It was felt that the city was coming apart, and Wagner bore the brunt of the blame.

None of these concerns about the state of the city came as news to the men of the Ninth. The Ninth was affectionately known as 'the Shithouse' by those who served there, less affectionately so by everyone else. They were a law unto themselves, the men of that precinct, and they guarded their territory well, keeping an eye out not only for the bad guys but for some of the good guys too, like captains looking to kick ass on a slow day. 'Fly in the Shithouse,' someone would call in over the radio, and then everyone would stand a little straighter for as long as was necessary.

Jimmy and Will were ambitious back then, both looking to make sergeant as soon as possible. The competition was tougher than before, since Felicia Spritzer's lawsuit in 1963 that resulted in female officers being allowed to take promotional examinations for the first time, with Spritzer and Gertrude Schimmel making sergeant the following year. Not that Jimmy and Will gave a rat's ass, unlike some of the older guys who had a lot of views on where a woman's place was, none of which included wearing three stripes in one of their precincts. They both had a copy of the patrol guide, thick as a Bible in its blue plastic ring binder, and they carried the guide with them whenever they took a break so that they could test each other's knowledge. In those days, you had to do detective work as a patrol officer for five years before you could make detective, but you wouldn't start bringing in sergeant's money until you made second grade. They didn't want to be investigators anyway. They were street cops. So they decided that they'd both try for the sergeant's exam, even if it meant that they'd have to leave the Ninth, maybe even have to serve in different precincts. It would be tough, but they knew that their friendship would survive it.

Unlike a lot of other cops, who worked as bouncers, keeping the guineas from Brooklyn out of the clubs, or as bodyguards for celebrities, which was boring, they didn't have second jobs. Jimmy was a single man, and Will wanted to spend more time with his wife, not less. There was still a lot of corruption in the force, but it was mostly small-time stuff. In due course, drugs would change everything, and the commissions would come down hard on bent cops. For now, the best that could be hoped for would be the occasional dollar job: escorting the movie theater manager to the night safe with the day's takings, and getting a couple of bucks for drinks left on the back seat in return. Even taking lunch 'on the arm' would soon come to be frowned upon, though most places in the Ninth didn't do it anyway. Cops paid for their own lunches, their own coffee and donuts. The majority ate lunch at the precinct house. It was cheaper, and there weren't too many places to eat in the Ninth anyway, at least none that the cops liked, the ham and cheddar with hot mustard at McSorley's apart, or, in later years, Jack the Ribbers over on 3rd, although eat lunch at Jack the Ribbers and you weren't going to be doing anything more strenuous than rubbing your stomach and groaning for the rest of the day. The guys in the Seventh were lucky, because they had Katz's, but the cops in the Ninth weren't allowed to cross precinct lines just because the bologna was better down the block. The NYPD didn't work that way.

On the night of the first dead baby, Jimmy was working as recorder for the first half of the tour. The recorder took all of the notes and the driver took the wheel. Halfway through, they switched. Jimmy was the better recorder. He had a good eye and a sharp memory. Will had just enough recklessness to make him the better driver. Together, they made a good team.

They were called to a party over on Avenue A, a 10–50, some neighbors complaining about the noise. When they got to the building, a young woman was puking into the gutter while her friend held her hair away from her face and stroked her back. They were so stoned that they barely glanced at the two cops.

Jimmy and Will could hear music coming from the top floor of the walk-up. As a matter of course, they kept their hands on the grips of their guns. There was no way of telling if this was just a regular party that was getting a little out of hand or something more serious. As always in these situations, Jimmy felt his mouth go dry, and his heart began to beat faster. A week earlier, a guy had taken a flight off the top of a tenement in the course of a party that had started off just like this one. He'd almost killed one of the cops who was arriving to investigate, landing just inches from him and spraying him with blood when he hit. Turned out that the flyer had been skimming from some guys with vowels at the ends of their names, Italians who were applying their business acumen to the newly resurgent heroin market, which had been largely dormant since the teens and twenties, the Italians not yet realizing that their time was coming to an end, their dominance soon to be challenged by the blacks and the Colombians.

The apartment door was open, and music blared from a stereo, Jagger singing about some girl. They could see a narrow hallway, leading into a living area, and the air was thick with tobacco and booze and grass. The two officers exchanged a look.

'Call it,' said Will.

They stepped into the hall, Jimmy leading. 'NYPD,' he shouted. 'Everybody stay calm, and stay still.'

Cautiously, Will behind him, Jimmy peered into the living room. There were eight people in various stages of intoxication or drug-induced stupor. Most were sitting or lying on the floor. Some were clearly asleep. A young white woman with purple stripes through her blond hair was stretched out on the couch beneath the window, a cigarette dangling from her hand. When she saw the cops she said: 'Oh shit,' and began to get up.

'Stay where you are,' said Jimmy, motioning with his left hand that she should remain on the couch. Now one or two of the more together partygoers were waking up to the trouble they might be in, and looking scared. While Jimmy kept an eye on the people in the living room, Will checked the rest of the apartment. There was a small bedroom with two beds: one an empty child's cot, the other a double piled with coats. He found a young man, probably nineteen or twenty,

and barely compos mentis, on his knees in the bathroom, trying unsuccessfully to flush an ounce of marijuana down a toilet with a broken cistern. When he frisked him, Will found three twists of heroin in one of the pockets of the kid's jeans.

'What are you, an idiot?' Will asked.

'Huh?' said the kid.

'You're carrying heroin, but you flush the marijuana? You in college?'

'Yeah.'

'Bet you're not studying to be a rocket scientist. You know how much trouble you're in?'

'But, man,' said the kid, staring at the twists, 'that shit is worth money!'

Will almost felt sorry for him, he was so dumb. 'Come on, knucklehead,' he said. He pushed him into the living room and told him to sit on the floor.

'Okay,' said Jimmy. 'The rest of you, against the walls. You got anything I should know about, you tell me now and it'll go easier on you.'

Those who were able to rose and assumed the position against the walls. Will nudged one comatose girl with his foot.

'Come on, sleeping beauty. Nap time's over.'

Eventually, they had all nine standing. Will frisked eight of them, excluding the boy he had searched earlier. Only the girl with the striped hair was carrying: three joints, and a four-ounce bag. She was both drunk and high, but was coming down from the worst of it.

'What are these?' Will asked the girl.

'I don't know,' said the girl. Her voice was slightly

slurred. 'A friend gave them to me to look after for him.'

'That's some story. What's your friend's name? Hans Christian Andersen?'

'Who?'

'Doesn't matter. This your place?'

'Yes.'

'What's your name?'

'Sandra.'

'Sandra what?'

'Sandra Huntingdon.'

'Well, Sandra, you're under arrest for possession with intent to supply.' He cuffed her and read her her rights, then did the same with the boy he had searched earlier. Jimmy took the names of the rest, and told them that they were free to stay or to leave, but if he passed them on the street again he'd bust them for loitering, even if they were running a race at the time. All of them went back to sitting around. They were young and scared, and they were gradually coming to realize how lucky they were not to be in cuffs, like their buddies, but they weren't together enough to head out into the night just yet.

'Okay, time to go,' Will said to the two in cuffs. He began to lead Huntingdon from the apartment, Jimmy behind him with the boy, whose name was Howard Mason, but suddenly something seemed to flare in Huntingdon's brain, cutting through the drug fog.

'My baby,' she said. 'I can't leave my baby!'

'What baby?' asked Will.

'My little girl. She's two. I can't leave her alone.'

'Miss, there's no child in this apartment. I searched it myself.'

But she struggled against him. 'I'm telling you, my baby is here,' she shouted, and he could tell that she wasn't faking or deluded.

One of the group in the living room, a black man in his twenties with a beginner's Afro, said, 'She ain't lyin', man. She do have a baby.'

Jimmy looked at Will. 'You sure you searched the place?'

'It's not Central Park.'

'Hell.' He turned Mason back toward the living room. 'You, sit on the couch and don't move,' he told him. 'Okay, Sandra, you say you have a kid. Let's find her. What's her name?'

'Melanie.'

'Melanie, right. You're sure you didn't ask someone to look after her for the evening?'

'No, she's here.' Huntingdon was crying now. 'I'm not lying.'

'Well, we'll soon find out.'

There weren't very many places to search, but they called the girl's name just the same. The two cops searched behind the couches, in the bathtub, and in the kitchen closets.

It was Will who found her. She was under the pile of coats on the bed. He could tell that the child was dead from the moment that his hand touched her leg.

Jimmy took a sip of wine.

'The kid must have wanted to lie on her mother's

bed,' he said. 'Maybe she crawled under the first coat for warmth, then fell asleep. The other coats were just piled on top of her, and she suffocated under them. I can still remember the sound her mother made when we found her. It came from someplace deep and old. It was like an animal dying. And then she just folded to the floor, her arms still cuffed behind her. She crawled to the bed on her knees and started to burrow under the coats with her head, trying to get close to her little girl. We didn't stop her. We just stood there, watching her.

'She wasn't a bad mother. She worked two jobs, and her aunt looked after her kid while she was at work. Maybe she was doing a little dealing on the side, but the autopsy found that her daughter was healthy and well cared for. Apart from the night of the party, nobody ever had any cause to complain about her. What I'm saying is that it could have happened to anyone. It was a tragedy, that's all. It was nobody's fault.

'Your old man, though, he took it bad. He went on a bender the next day. Back then, your father could drink some. When you knew him, he'd cut all that stuff out, apart from the occasional night out with the boys. But in the old days, he liked a drink. We all did.

'That day was different, though. I'd never seen him drink the way he did after he found Melanie Huntingdon. I think it was because of his own circumstances. He and your mother wanted a child real bad, but it didn't look like it was going to happen for them.

Then he sees this little kid lying dead under a pile of coats, and something breaks inside him. He believed in God. He went to church. He prayed. That night, it must have seemed as if God was mocking him just for the hell of it, forcing a man who had seen his wife miscarry again and again to uncover the body of a dead child. Worse than that, maybe he stopped believing in any kind of God for a time, as if someone had just pulled up a corner of the world and revealed black, empty space behind it. I don't know. Anyway, finding the Huntingdon kid changed him, that's all I can say. After it, he and your mother went through a real rough patch. I think she was going to leave him, or he was going to leave her, I don't recall which. Wouldn't have mattered, I suppose. The end result would still have been the same.'

He put the glass down and let the candlelight play upon the wine, spreading red fractals upon the tabletop like the ghosts of rubies.

'And that was when he met the girl,' he said.

Her name was Caroline Carr, or that was what she said. They had responded to an attempted B and E call at her apartment. It was the smallest apartment they had ever seen, barely large enough to contain a single bed, a closet, and a table and chair. The kitchen area consisted of two gas rings in one corner, and the bathroom was so tiny that it didn't even have a door, just lengths of beaded string for privacy. It was hard to see why anyone might have considered it worth breaking into. One look around told them that the girl didn't have anything worth stealing. If she had, she would have sold it to rent a bigger place.

But the space suited her. She was tiny, just a shade over five feet tall, and thin with it. Her hair was long and dark and very fine, and her skin was translucently pale. It seemed to Jimmy as if she might expire at any minute, but when he looked in her eyes he saw a real strength and ferocity at her core. She might have appeared fragile, but so did spider silk until you tried to break it.

She was frightened, though, of that he was certain. At the time, he put it down to the attempted burglary. Someone had clearly tried to jimmy the lock on the window from the fire escape outside. She had woken to the noise, and had immediately run to the phone in the hallway outside to call the cops. One of her neighbors, an elderly woman named Mrs. Roth, had heard her screaming and offered her safe haven in her apartment until the police came. As it happened, Jimmy and Will had been only a block away when the call from Central came through. Whoever had tried to break in was probably still at the window when the sirens began to sound. They filled out a 61, but there wasn't much more that they could do. The perps were gone, and no harm had been done. Will suggested talking to the landlord about getting a better lock for the window, or maybe a security grill of some kind, but Carr just shook her head.

'I won't be staying here,' she said. 'I'm going to leave.'

'It's the big city,' said Will. 'These things happen.'

'I understand. I have to move, though.'

Her fear was palpable, but it wasn't unreasoning, and it wasn't merely an overreaction to a disturbing, if commonplace, incident. Whatever was frightening her, it was related only in part to the events of that night.

'Your father must have felt it too,' said Jimmy. 'He was quiet as we drove away. We stopped to pick up a couple of coffees, and as we sat drinking them, he said: "What do you suppose that was about?"

'"It's going down as a ten-thirty-one. That's all there is to it."

'"But that woman was scared."

'"She lives alone in a shoebox. Someone tries to break in, she hasn't got too many places to run."

'"No, it's more than that. She didn't tell us everything."

'"What are you now, psychic?"

'Then he turned to me. He didn't say anything. He just stared me down.

'"Okay," I said. "You're right. I felt it too. You want to go back?"

'"No, not now. Maybe later."

'But we never did go back. At least, I didn't. Your father did, though. He went back. He might even have gone back that night, after the tour ended.

'And that was how it began.'

Will told Jimmy that he didn't sleep with Caroline until the third time they met. He claimed that it had never been his intention to get involved with her in that way, but there was something about her, something that made him want to help her and protect her. Jimmy didn't know whether to believe him or not, and he didn't suppose it mattered much one way or another. There had always been a sentimental streak to Will Parker and, as Jimmy liked to say, quoting Oscar Wilde, 'sentimentality is the bank holiday of cynicism.' Will was having problems at home and he was still troubled by the death of Melanie Huntingdon, so maybe he saw the possibility of some kind of escape in the form of Caroline Carr. He helped her to move. He found her a place on the Upper East Side, with more space and better security. He put her in a motel for two nights while he negotiated the rent down on her behalf, then drove into the city one morning instead of taking the train and put all of her belongings, which didn't amount to much, in the back of his car and took her to her new apartment. The affair didn't last longer than six or seven weeks.

During that time, she became pregnant.

I waited. I had finished my wine, but when Jimmy tried to refill my glass I covered it with my hand. I felt light-headed, but it was nothing to do with the wine.

'Pregnant?' I said.

'That's right.' He lifted the wine bottle. 'You mind if I do? It makes all this easier. I've been waiting a long time to get rid of it.'

He filled the glass halfway.

'She had something, that Caroline Carr,' said Jimmy. 'Even I could see that.'

'Even you?' Despite myself, I smiled.

'She wasn't to my taste,' he said, smiling back. 'I hope I don't need to say any more than that.'

I nodded.

'That wasn't all of it, though. Your father was a good-looking man. There were a lot of women out there who'd have been happy to ease him of some of his burdens, no strings attached. He wouldn't have been obliged to buy them more than a drink. Instead, here he was finding a place for this woman and lying to his wife about where he was going so that he could help her move.'

'You think he was infatuated with her?'

'That's what I believed at the start. She was younger than he was, though not by much and, like I said, she had a certain allure. I think it was tied up with the impression of fragility that she gave, even if it was deceptive. So, yeah, sure, I thought it was an infatuation, and maybe it was, at the start. But later, Will told me the rest of it, or as much of it as he wanted to tell me. That was when I started to understand, and that's when I started to worry.'

His brow furrowed, and I could tell that, even now, decades later, he struggled with this part of the story.

'We were in Cal's on the night Will told me that Caroline Carr was convinced she was being hunted. I thought he was joking at first, but he wasn't. Then I started to wonder if the girl had spun him some line of bullshit. You know, damsel in distress, bad men on the horizon: shitty boyfriend, maybe, or psycho ex-husband.

'But that wasn't it. She was convinced that whoever, whatever, was hunting her wasn't human. She talked about two people, a man and a woman. She told your father that they'd started hunting her years before. She'd been running from them ever since.'

'And my father believed her?'

Jimmy laughed. 'Are you kidding me? He might have been a sentimentalist, but he wasn't a fool. He thought she was a wacko. He figured he'd made the biggest mistake of his life. He had visions of her stalking him, arriving at his house decked out in garlic and crucifixes. Your old man might have gone off the rails a little, but he was still capable of driving the train. So, no, he didn't believe her, and I think he started trying to disentangle himself from the whole mess. I guess he also realized that he ought to be with his wife, that leaving her wouldn't solve any of his problems but would just give him a whole new set of them to deal with.

'Then Caroline told him she was pregnant, and his world collapsed around him. They had a long talk on the evening of her visit to the clinic to get checked out. She never even mentioned abortion, and your father, to his credit, never raised it either. It wasn't just because he was Catholic. I think he still recalled that little girl buried under the pile of coats, and his wife's miscarriages. Even if it meant the end of his marriage, and a life of debt, he wasn't going to suggest that the pregnancy should be terminated. And Caroline, you know, she was really calm about the whole thing. Not happy, exactly, but calm, like the pregnancy was a minor medical procedure, a thing that was worrying but necessary.

'Your father, well, he was kind of shocked. He needed some air, so he left her and went to take a walk. He decided, after thirty minutes of his own company, that he wanted to talk to someone, so he stopped at a pay phone across from her apartment and started to call me.

'And that was when he saw them.'

They were standing in a doorway close by a convenience store, hand in hand: a man and a woman, both in their early thirties. The woman had mousy hair that brushed her shoulders, and she wore no makeup. She was slim, and dressed in an old-fashioned black skirt that clung to her legs before flaring slightly at her shins. A matching black jacket hung open over a white blouse that was buttoned to the neck. The man wore a black suit with a white shirt and black tie. His hair was short at the back and long in front, parted on the left and hanging greasily over one eye. Both of them were staring up at the window of Caroline Carr's apartment.

It was their very stillness that drew Will's attention to them. They were like pieces of statuary that had been positioned in the shadows, a temporary art installation on a busy street. Their appearance reminded him of those sects in Pennsylvania, the ones that frowned upon buttons as signs of vanity. In their utter focus on the windows of the apartment, he saw a fanaticism that bordered on the religious.

And then, as Will watched them, they began to move. They crossed the street, the man reaching beneath his jacket as he went, and Will saw the gun appear in his hand.

Will ran. He had his own .38 with him, and he drew it. The couple was halfway across the street when something drew the man's attention. He registered the approaching threat, and turned to face it. The woman continued moving, her attention fixed only on the apartment building before her and the girl who was hiding within, but the man stared straight at Parker, and the policeman felt a slow tightening in his gut, as though someone had just pumped cold water into his system and it was responding with the urge to void itself. Even at this distance, he could tell that the man's eyes were not right. They were at once too dark, like twin voids in the pallor of the gunman's face, and too small, chips of black glass in a borrowed skin pulled too tightly over a larger skull.

The woman looked around, only now becoming aware that her partner was no longer beside her. She opened her mouth to say something, and Parker saw the panic on her face.

The truck hit the gunman from behind, briefly pitching him forward and upward, his feet leaving the ground before he was dragged beneath the front wheels as the driver braked, his body disintegrating beneath the massive weight of the truck, his life ending in a smear of red and black. The force of the impact knocked him out of his shoes. They lay nearby, one upside down, the other on its side. A tendril of blood seeped out toward the shoes from the broken form under the truck, as though the body were trying to reconstitute itself, to build itself once again from the feet up. Somebody screamed.

By the time Will reached the body, the woman had disappeared. He glanced under the truck. The man's head was gone, crushed by the left front wheel of the truck. He showed his shield, and told an ashen-faced man standing nearby to call in the accident. The driver climbed down from his cab and tried to grab hold of Will, but he slipped by him and was only barely aware of the driver falling to the ground behind him. He ran to Caroline's building, but the front door was still locked. He inserted the key and opened the door by touch, his attention fixed on the street, not the keyhole. As the key turned he slipped inside and closed the door hard behind him. When he got to the apartment he stood to one side, trying to control his breathing, and knocked once.

'Caroline?' he called.

There was no reply for a moment, then, softly: 'Yes.'

'You okay, honey?'

'I think so.'

'Open up.'

His eyes searched the shadows. He thought that he could smell a strange perfume on the air. It was sharp and metallic. It took him a few seconds to realize that it was the smell of the dead man's blood. He looked down and saw that it was on his shoes.

She opened the door. He stepped inside. When he tried to reach for her, she moved away.

'I saw them,' she said. 'I saw them coming for me.'

'I know,' he said. 'I saw them too.'

'The one who got hit . . .'

'He's dead.'

She shook her head.

'No.'

'I'm telling you, he's dead. His skull was crushed.'

She was leaning against the wall now. He gripped her shoulders.

'Look at me,' he said. She did as he asked, and he saw hidden knowledge in her eyes.

'He's dead,' he said, for the third time.

She let out a deep breath. Her eyes flicked toward the window.

'Okay,' she said, and he knew that she did not believe him, although he could not understand why. 'What about the woman?'

'Gone.'

'She'll come back.'

'We'll move you.'

'Where?'

'Somewhere safe.'

'This place was supposed to be safe.'

'I was wrong.'

'You didn't believe me.'

He nodded. 'You're right. I didn't. I do now. I don't know how they found you, but I was wrong. Look, did you make any calls? Did you tell anyone – a friend, a relative – where you were?'

Her eyes turned back to him. She looked tired. Not frightened or angry, just weary.

'Who would I call?' she asked. 'I have no one. There's only you.'

And with nowhere else to turn, Will called Jimmy Gallagher, so that while the cops gathered statements, Jimmy was moving Caroline to a motel in Queens, but not before driving around for hours, trying to shake off anyone who might be following them. When he had her safely checked in, he stayed with her in her room until, at last, she fell asleep, then he watched TV until morning came.

While he did so, Will was lying to the cops on the scene. He told the officers that he'd been uptown visiting a friend, and had seen a man crossing the street with a gun in his hand. He had challenged him, and the man had been turning in response, his gun raised, when the truck hit him. None of the other witnesses seemed to recall the woman who had been with him; in fact, the other witnesses couldn't even remember seeing the man cross the street. It was as though, for them, he had materialized in that spot. Even the driver of the truck said that one second the street in front of him was empty, and the next there was a man being pulled under the wheels of his vehicle. The driver was in shock, although there was no question of any blame accruing to him; the lights had been in his favor, and he had been well within the speed limit.

Once he had made his statement, Will waited for a time in a coffee shop, watching the front of the now empty apartment house and the bustle at the spot of the man's death, hoping to see the woman with the washed-out face and the dark eyes, but she did not come. If she was mourning the loss of her partner, she was doing so elsewhere. Finally, he gave up and joined Jimmy and Caroline at the motel, and while Caroline slept, he told Jimmy everything.

'He told me about the pregnancy, the woman, the dead man,' said Jimmy. 'He kept returning to the way the guy had looked, trying to pinpoint what it was about him that was so . . . wrong.'

'And what did he decide?' I asked.

'Another man's clothes,' said Jimmy.

'What does that mean?'

'You ever see somebody wearing a suit that isn't his, or trying to fit his feet into borrowed shoes, ones that are maybe a size too small or too large? Well, that was what was wrong with the dead man, according to your father. It was like he'd borrowed another man's body, but it didn't fit the way that it should. Your old man worried at it like a dog at a bone, and that was the best that he could come up with, weeks later: it was almost as if he felt there was something living inside that guy's body, but it wasn't him. Whatever he had once been, or whoever he had once been, was long gone. This thing had chewed it away.'

He watched me then, waiting for a response. When none came, he said: 'I'm tempted to ask if you think that sounds crazy, but I know too much about you to believe you if you said "yes."'

'You ever get a name on him?' I asked, ignoring what he had just said.

'There wasn't much of the guy left to identify. A sketch artist came up with a pretty good likeness, though, based on your father's description, and we circulated it. Bingo! A woman comes forward, says it looks like her husband, name of Peter Ackerman. He'd run off on her five years before. Met some girl in a bar, and that was it. Thing about it was, the wife said it was completely out of character for her husband. He was an accountant, a by-the-numbers guy. Loved her, loved his kids. He had his routines, and he stuck to them.'

I shrugged. 'He wouldn't be the first man to disappoint his wife in that way.'

'No, I guess not. But we haven't even gotten to the strange stuff. Ackerman had served in Korea, so his prints eventually checked out. The wife gave a detailed description of his appearance though, since his face was gone: he had a Marine tat on his left arm, an appendectomy scar on his abdomen, and a chunk missing from his right calf where a bullet had caught him at the Chosin Reservoir. The body taken from under the truck had all of those markings, and one more. It seemed like he'd picked up another tattoo since he'd deserted his wife and family. Well, not so much a tattoo. More of a brand.'

'A brand?'

'It was burned into his right arm. Hard to describe. I'd never seen anything like it before, but your old man followed it up. He found out what it was.'

'And?'

'It was the symbol of an angel. A fallen angel. "An– " something, was the name. Animal. No, that's not it. Hell, it'll come to me.'

I was treading carefully now. I didn't know how much Jimmy knew of some of the men and women I had encountered in the past, and of how some of them shared strange beliefs, convinced that they were fallen beings, wandering spirits.

Demons.

'This man was marked with an occult symbol?'

'That's right.'

'A fork?' That was a mark I had seen before. The ones who bore it had called themselves 'Believers.'

'What?' Jimmy's eyes narrowed in confusion, then his expression changed and I understood that he knew more about me than I might have wished, and I wondered how. 'No, not a fork. It was different. It didn't seem like anything that had meaning, but everything does, if you look hard enough at it.'

'And the woman?'

Jimmy stood. He went to his wine rack and removed another bottle.

'Oh, she came back,' he said. 'With a vengeance.'

20

The two men kept Caroline Carr on the move, never allowing her to stay in any one place for more than a week. They used motels and short-term rentals. For a time, they put her in a cabin in the woods upstate, close to a small town where a former cop from the Ninth, a cousin of Eddie Grace's, had moved to become chief of police. The cabin was occasionally used to stash witnesses, or those who just needed to be hidden away until a particular situation cooled off, but Caroline hated the quiet and the isolation. It made her more nervous than she had been before, for she was a creature of cities. Out in the country, every sound signaled an approaching threat. After three days in the cabin, her nerves were shredded. She was so frightened that she even called Will at home. Thankfully, his wife wasn't there, but the call shook Will. Their affair had already come to a mutually agreed-upon end, but sometimes he would stand in his yard and wonder just how he had managed to screw everything up so badly. He was constantly tempted to confess all to his wife. He even dreamed that he had done so, and he would wake wondering why she was still sleeping beside him. He felt sure that she must suspect something and was just waiting for the right moment to voice those suspicions. Nothing was ever said, but her silence served only to increase his paranoia.

He was also becoming increasingly aware of the fact that he knew almost nothing about Caroline Carr. She had sketched only the barest details of her life for him: an upbringing in Modesto, California; the death of her mother in a fire; and her growing awareness of the two figures that were now pursuing her. Caroline had managed to stay ahead of them for so long, but she had grown careless, and become tired of running. She had almost begun to welcome the thought that they might find her, until that night when they tried to break into her apartment and her fear of them overcame any misplaced desire she might have had to end the chase. She could not tell Will why they had targeted her, for she said that she did not know. She knew only that they were a threat, and they wanted to end her life. When he asked her why she had not gone to the police, she had laughed at him, and the scorn in her voice had hurt.

'You think I didn't? I went to them after my mother died. I told them that the fire had been started deliberately, but they were looking at a disturbed, grief-stricken girl, and they didn't listen to a word I said. After that, I decided that the best thing to do was to look after myself. What else could I do? Tell people I was being hunted for no reason by a man and woman that nobody had ever seen except me? They'd have locked me up, and then I would have been trapped. I kept everything to myself until I met you. I thought that you were different.'

And Will had held her and told her that he was different, even as he wondered if he was being drawn into a frightened young woman's elaborate fantasy. But then he recalled the man with the gun, and the pale woman with the dead eyes, and he knew that there was some truth in all that Caroline Carr had told him.

He had begun to make informal inquiries about the tattoo on the late Peter Ackerman's arm, and eventually he was referred to a young rabbi by the name of Epstein out in Brooklyn Heights. Over a glass of sweet kosher wine, the rabbi had talked to him of angels, of obscure books that, as far as Will could tell, had been left out of the Bible because they were even stranger than most of the stuff that had been left in, and that was saying something. As they spoke, Will began to realize that the rabbi was interrogating him as much as he was interrogating the rabbi.

'So this is a sect, a cult of some kind, that Peter Ackerman became involved with?' said Will.

'Perhaps,' said the rabbi. Then: 'Why does this man interest you so much?'

'I'm a cop. I was there when he died.'

'No, there's more to this.' The rabbi sat back in his chair and tugged on his short beard. His eyes never left Will's face. Eventually, he seemed to reach a decision. 'May I call you Will?'

Will nodded his assent.

'I am going to tell you something now, Will. If I have guessed right, then I would appreciate it if you would confirm that it is so.'

Will felt that he had no choice but to agree. As he told Jimmy later, he had somehow become involved in an exchange of information.

'This man was not alone,' said Epstein. 'There was a woman with him. She was probably close to his own age. Is that correct?'

'How did you know that?'

Epstein produced a copy of the symbol that had been found on Peter Ackerman's body.

'Because of this. They always hunt in pairs. After all, they are lovers. The male—' He pointed to the Ackerman symbol before slipping another sheet of paper from behind it. '—and the female.'

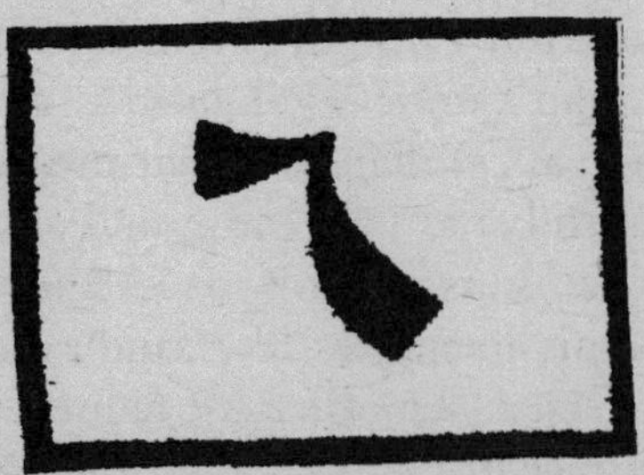

Will examined them both.

'So this woman is part of the same cult?'

'No, Will. I don't believe that this is a cult at all. This is something much worse . . .'

Jimmy pressed his fingertips to his head. He was thinking hard. I left him to it. Epstein: I had met the rabbi on a number of occasions, and had helped him to track down his son's killers, and in all that time he had never told me that he had known my father.

'Their names,' Jimmy said. 'I can't remember their names.'

'What names?'

'The names the rabbi told Will. The man and the woman, they each had names. Like I told you, the man's was "An—" something, but I can't remember the woman's. It's like they've been cut from my memory.'

He was becoming frustrated and distracted.

'It doesn't matter for now,' I said. 'We can come back to it later.'

'They all had names,' said Jimmy. He sounded confused.

'What?'

'It was something else the rabbi told Will. He said that they all had names.' He looked at me with something like despair. 'What does that mean?'

And I remembered my own grandfather in Maine uttering those same words as Alzheimer's began snuffing out his memories like candle flames caught between fingers. 'They all have names, Charlie,' he had said, his face bright with a terrible urgency. 'They all have *names*.' I didn't know what he meant, not then. It was only later, when faced by creatures like Kittim and Brightwell, that I began to learn.

'It means that even the worst of things can be named,' I told Jimmy. 'And it's important to know those names.'

Because with naming came an understanding of the thing.

And with understanding came the possibility of its destruction.

The need to protect Caroline Carr put huge additional pressure on them both, at a time when the city was in turmoil, and the demands upon them as police officers were seemingly unceasing. In January of 1966, the transit workers had gone out on strike, all 34,000 of them, crippling the transport network and wreaking havoc with the city's economy. Eventually, Mayor Lindsay, who had succeeded Wagner in 1966, had buckled, what with the public complaining and Michael Quill, the union leader, taunting him from behind bars as a 'pipsqueak' and 'a boy in short trousers.' By giving in to the transit workers, though, Lindsay – who was a good mayor in so many ways, let no one say otherwise – had opened the floodgates to an ongoing series of municipal strikes that would blight his administration. The anti-draft movement was starting to simmer, a pot that had been threatening to come to the boil ever since 400 activists had picketed the Whitehall Street induction center, a couple of them even burning their draft cards. It was still open season on dissenters, though, because most of the country was behind LBJ, even though US troop strength had escalated from 180,000 to 385,000, US casualties had tripled, and 5,000 US soldiers would be dead by the end of that year alone. It would be another year before public opinion truly began to turn, but for now activists were more concerned with civil rights than Vietnam, even as some were gradually beginning to realize that one fed into the other, that the draft was unfair because most of those being called up by white draft boards were young black men who couldn't use college as an excuse to defer since they had no chance of going to college in the first place. There were so-called 'new bohemians' in the East Village, and marijuana and LSD were becoming the drugs of choice.

And Will Parker and Jimmy Gallagher, both young men themselves, and not unintelligent, put on their uniforms each day and wondered when they would be asked to break the heads of kids their own age, kids with whom, at least in Will's case, they were largely in agreement. Everything was changing. They could smell it in the air.

Meanwhile, Jimmy was wishing that they'd never met Caroline Carr. After she made the call to Will's home, Jimmy had to drive up and take her back to Brooklyn, where she stayed in his mother's house in Gerritsen Beach, close to the Shell Bank Creek. Mrs. Gallagher owned a small, one-story bungalow, with a peaked roof and no yard, that stood on Melba Court, one of the warren of alphabetically ordered streets that had once served as a summer resort for Irish-Americans, until Gerritsen proved so popular that the houses were winterized so that people could live there year-round. Hiding her in Gerritsen gave Jimmy and, occasionally, Will, an excuse to see her, because Jimmy went down to visit his mother at least once every week. In addition, this part of Gerritsen was small and tightly knit. Strangers would stand out, and Mrs. Gallagher had been warned that there were people looking for the girl. It made Jimmy's mother yet more vigilant than she already was; even at her most relaxed, she put the average presidential bodyguard to shame. When neighbors asked about the young woman who was staying with her, Mrs. Gallagher told them that she was a friend of a friend and had recently been bereaved. A terrible shame, what with the poor girl expecting. She gave Caroline a thin gold band that had once belonged to her own mother, and told her to wear it on her ring finger. Her supposed bereavement kept even the worst snoopers at bay, and on the handful of occasions when Caroline joined Mrs. Gallagher for an evening at the Ancient Order of Hibernians on Gerritsen Avenue, she was treated with a gentleness and respect that made her feel both grateful and guilty.

In Gerritsen, Caroline was content: she was close to the sea, and to the residents-only Kiddie Beach. Perhaps she even saw herself playing there on the sand with her own child, spending summer days eating at the concession stand, listening to bands on the stage and watching the big parade on Memorial Day. But if she did imagine such a future for herself and her unborn child, she never spoke of it. It might have been that she did not want to put a hex on her wish by speaking it aloud, or maybe – and this was what Mrs. Gallagher told her son on the phone when he called one day to check on the girl – she saw no future for herself at all.

'She's a nice girl,' said Mrs. Gallagher. 'She's quiet and respectful. She doesn't smoke and she doesn't drink, and that's good. But when I try to talk to her about what she plans to do once the baby is born, she just smiles and changes the subject. And it's not a happy smile, Jimmy. She's sad all the way through. More than that: she's frightened. I hear her crying out in her sleep. For God's sake, Jimmy, why are these people after her? She doesn't look like she could do harm to a fly.'

But Jimmy Gallagher didn't have the answer, and neither did Will Parker. But then, Will had problems of his own.

His wife was pregnant again.

Will watched her bloom as her term drew on. Even though she'd suffered so many miscarriages in the past, she said that this pregnancy felt different. At home, he would catch her humming softly in the chair by the kitchen window, her right hand resting on her belly. She could stay that way for hours, watching clouds scud by and the last leaves slowly spiraling from the trees in the garden as winter began to take hold. It was almost funny, he thought. He'd slept with Caroline Carr three or four times, and she'd become pregnant. Now his wife, after so many miscarriages, had managed to carry their unborn child for seven months. She looked like she was glowing from within. He had never seen her happier, more content within herself. He knew of the guilt that she had experienced after the earlier losses. Her body had betrayed her. It would not do what it was supposed to do. It was not strong enough. Now, at last, she had what she wanted, what they had both wanted for so long.

And he was tormented by it. He was having a second child with another woman, and the knowledge of his betrayal was tearing him apart. Caroline had told him that she wanted nothing from him, except that he keep her safe until the baby was born.

'And after that?'

But, as with Jimmy Gallagher's mother, she declined to answer the question.

'We'll see,' she would say, then turn away.

The child was due to be born one month before his wife was likely to give birth. They would both be his children, yet he knew that he would have to let one go, that if he wanted his marriage to survive – and he did, more than anything else – then he could not be a part of his first child's life. He wasn't even sure that he could offer more than minimal financial support, not on a cop's salary, despite Caroline's protestations that she didn't want his money.

And yet he didn't wish to let this child simply disappear. He was, despite his failings, an honorable man. He had never cheated on his wife before, and he felt his guilt about sleeping with Caroline as an ache so strong that it made him reel. More than ever before, he felt the urge to confess but it was Jimmy Gallagher who dissuaded him one evening after a post-tour beer in Cal's.

'Are you crazy?' Jimmy said. 'Your wife is pregnant. She's carrying the child that you've both wanted for years. After all that's happened, you may not get a second chance like this one. Apart from what the shock might do to her, it'll destroy her and it'll destroy your marriage. You live with what you did. Caroline says that she doesn't want you to be part of her child's life. She doesn't want your money, and she doesn't want your time. Most men in your situation would be happy with that. If you're not, then the loss is the price that you pay for your sins, and for keeping your marriage together. You hear me?'

And Will had agreed, knowing that what Jimmy said was true.

'You have to understand something,' said Jimmy. 'Your old man was decent and loyal and brave, but he was also human. He'd made a mistake, and he was trying to find a way to live with it, to live with it and to do the right thing by all concerned, but that just wasn't possible, and the knowledge of it was ripping him apart.'

One of the candles was sputtering as it neared the end of its life. Jimmy went to replace it, then paused and said: 'You want, I can put the kitchen light on.'

I shook my head, and told him that the candles were fine.

'That's what I thought,' he said. 'Somehow, it doesn't

seem right telling a story like this in a brightly lit room. It's just not that kind of story.'

He lit a new candle, then resumed his seat and continued his tale.

At Epstein's request, a meeting was arranged with Caroline. It took place in the back room of a Jewish bakery in Midwood. Jimmy and Will drove Caroline to the rendezvous under cover of night, the by-now heavily pregnant young woman lying uncomfortably under some coats on the back seat of Jimmy's mother's Eldorado. The two men were not privy to what passed between the rabbi and Caroline, although they were together for over an hour. When they were finished, Epstein spoke with Will and asked him about the arrangements that had been made for Caroline's lying-in. Jimmy had never heard that phrase used before, and was embarrassed when it had to be explained to him. Will gave Epstein the name of the OB-GYN, and the hospital in which Caroline intended to deliver her baby. Epstein told him that alternative arrangements would be made.

Through Epstein's agencies, a place was obtained for Caroline in a small women-only clinic in Gerritsen Beach itself, not far from PS 277 on the other side of the creek from where she was staying. Jimmy had always known that the clinic was there, and that it catered to those for whom money was no great object, but he hadn't been aware of the fact that babies could be delivered behind its doors. Later, he learned that it wasn't usually the case, but an exception had been made at Epstein's request. Jimmy had offered to lend Will money to cover some of the medical costs, and he had accepted on condition that a firm schedule of repayments was agreed upon, with interest.

On the afternoon that Caroline's water broke, both Jimmy and Will were on the 8 to 4 tour, and they drove together to the hospital after Mrs. Gallagher had left a message for Jimmy at the station house asking him to call her as soon as he could. Will, in turn, phoned his wife, intending to tell her that he and Jimmy were helping Jimmy's mother with some stuff, which had a grain of truth embedded in the substance of the lie, but she was not home and the phone rang unanswered.

When they arrived at the clinic, the receptionist said: 'She's in eight, but you can't go in. There's a waiting room down the hall on the left, with coffee and cookies. Which one of you is the father?'

'I am,' said Will. The words sounded strange in his mouth.

'Well, we'll come get you when it's over. The contractions have started, but she won't give birth for a couple of hours. I'll ask the doctor to talk to you, and maybe he can give you a few minutes with her. Off you go.' She made a shooing movement with her hands, a gesture she had presumably demonstrated to thousands of useless men who had insisted on trying to clutter up her wards when they had no business being around.

'Don't worry,' she added, as Will and Jimmy resigned themselves to a long wait, 'she's got company.

Her friend, the older lady, she arrived with her, and her sister went in just a few minutes ago.'

Both men stopped.

'Sister?' said Will.

'Yeah, her sister.' The nurse spotted the look on Will's face, and instantly became defensive. 'She had ID, a driver's license. Same name. Carr.'

But Will and Jimmy were already moving, heading right, not left.

'Hey, I told you, you can't go down there,' shouted the receptionist. When they ignored her, she reached for a phone and called security.

The door to room eight was closed when they reached it, and the corridor was empty. They knocked, but there was no reply. As Jimmy reached for the handle, his mother appeared from around the corner.

'What are you doing?' she said.

Then she saw the guns.

'No! I just went to the bathroom. I—'

The door was locked from the inside. Jimmy stepped back and kicked at it twice before the lock shattered and the door flew open, exposing them to a blast of cool air. Caroline Carr lay on a raised gurney, her head and back supported by pillows. The front of her gown was drenched with red, but she was still alive. The room was cold because the window was open.

'Get a doctor!' said Will, but Jimmy was already shouting for help.

Will went to Caroline and tried to hold her, but she was starting to spasm. He saw the wounds to her stomach and chest. A blade, he thought; someone used a blade on her, and on the child. No, not just someone: the woman, the one who had watched her lover die beneath the wheels of a truck. Caroline's eyes turned to him. Her hand gripped his shirt, staining it with her blood.

And then there were doctors and nurses. He was pulled away from her, forced out of the room, and as the door closed he saw her fall back against the pillows and lie still, and he knew that she was dying.

But the child survived. They cut it from her as she died. The blade had missed its head by a quarter of an inch.

And while they delivered it, Will and Jimmy went hunting for the woman who had killed Caroline Carr.

They heard the sound of the ignition as soon as they exited the clinic, and seconds later a black Buick shot from the lot to their left and prepared to turn on to Gerritsen Avenue. A streetlight caught the face of the woman as she glanced toward them. It was Will who responded first, firing three shots as the woman reacted to their presence, turning left instead of right so that she would not have to cross in front of them. The first shot took out the driver's window, and the second and third hit the door. The Buick sped away as Will fired a fourth time, running behind it as Jimmy raced for their own car. Then, as Will watched, the Buick seemed to wobble on its axles, then began to drift to the right. It struck the curb outside the Lutheran church, then mounted it and came to a rest against the railings of the churchyard.

Will continued running. Now Jimmy was at his side, all thoughts of their own vehicle abandoned when the car had come to a stop. As they drew nearer, the driver's door opened and the woman stumbled out, clearly injured. She glanced back at them, a knife in her hand. Will didn't hesitate. He wanted her dead. He fired again. The bullet struck the hood, but by then the woman was already moving, abandoning the car, her left foot dragging. She dove right onto Bartlett, her pursuers closing the distance rapidly. As they turned the corner, she seemed frozen beneath a streetlight, her head turned, her mouth open. Will aimed, but even injured she was too fast. She stumbled to her right, down a narrow alley called Canton Court.

'We have her,' said Jimmy. 'That's a dead end. There's just the creek down there.'

They paused as they reached Canton, then exchanged a look and nodded. Their weapons held high, they entered the dark space between two cottages that led to the creek.

The woman was standing with her back to the bank, caught in the moonlight. The knife was still held in her hand. Her coat was slightly too long for her, and its sleeves hung over the second knuckles of her fingers, but not so far as to obscure the blade.

'Put it down,' said Jimmy, but he was not talking to her, not yet. While his eyes remained fixed on the woman, he laid the palm of his hand on the warm barrel of Will's revolver, gently forcing it down. 'Don't do it, Will. Just don't.'

The woman twisted the blade, and Jimmy thought that he could still see traces of Caroline Carr's blood upon it.

'It's over,' she said. Her voice was surprisingly soft and sweet, but her eyes were twin shards of obsidian in the pallor of her face.

'That's right,' said Jimmy. 'Now drop the knife.'

'It doesn't matter what you do to me,' said the woman. 'I am beyond your law.'

She dropped the knife, but at the same time her left hand moved, the sleeve of her coat pulling back to reveal the little pistol concealed by its folds.

It was Jimmy who killed her. He hit her twice before she could get a shot off. She remained standing for a second, then tumbled backward into the cold waters of the Shell Bank Creek.

She was never identified. The receptionist at the hospital confirmed that she was the same woman who had claimed to be Caroline Carr's sister. A false Virginia driver's license in the name of Ann Carr was found in her coat pocket, along with a small quantity of cash. Her fingerprints were not on file anywhere, and nobody came forward to identify her even after her picture appeared on news shows and in the papers.

But that came later. For now, there were questions to be asked, and to be answered. More cops came. They flooded the clinic. They sealed off Bartlett. They dealt with reporters, with curious onlookers, with distressed patients and their relatives.

While they did so, a group of people met in a room

at the back of the hospital. They included the hospital director; the doctor and midwife who had been monitoring Caroline Carr; the NYPD's deputy commissioner for legal affairs; and a small, quiet man in his early forties: the rabbi, Epstein. Will Parker and Jimmy Gallagher had been instructed to wait outside, and they sat together on hard plastic chairs, not speaking. Only one person, except for Jimmy, had expressed sorrow to Will at what had occurred. It was the receptionist. She knelt before him while he waited, and took his hand.

'I'm so sorry,' she said. 'We all are.'

He nodded dumbly.

'I don't know if—' she began, then stopped. 'No, I know it won't help, but maybe you might like to see your son?'

She led him to a glass-walled room and pointed out the tiny child who lay sleeping between two others.

'That's him,' she said. 'That's your boy.'

They were called into the meeting room minutes later. Those present were introduced, all except for one man in a suit, who had followed the two cops into the room and was now watching Will carefully. Epstein leaned toward Will and whispered: 'I'm sorry.'

Will did not reply.

It was the deputy commissioner, Frank Mancuso, who formally broke the silence.

'They tell me you're the father,' he said to Will.

'I am.'

'What a mess,' said Mancuso, with feeling. 'We

need to get the story straight, all of us. Are you two listening?'

Will and Jimmy nodded in unison.

'The child died,' said Mancuso.

'What?' said Will.

'The child died. It lived for a couple of hours, but it seems that there was some damage caused by the knife wound to the womb. It died as of—' He checked his watch. '—two minutes ago.'

'What are you talking about?' said Will. 'I just saw him.'

'And now he's dead.'

Will tried to leave, but Epstein grabbed his arm.

'Wait, Mr. Parker. Your child is alive and well, but as of now, only the people in this room know it. He's already being taken away.'

'Where?'

'Somewhere safe.'

'Why? He's my son. I want to know where he is.'

'Think, Mr. Parker,' said Epstein. 'For a moment, just think.'

Will was silent for a time. When he spoke, he said: 'You believe that someone is going to come after the child.'

'We believe that it's a possibility. They can't know that he survived.'

'But they're dead. The man and the woman. I saw them both die.'

Epstein looked away. 'There may be others,' he said, and, even amid his grief and confusion, the cop in Will wondered what Epstein was trying to hide.

'What others? Who are these people?'

'We're trying to find that out,' said Epstein. 'It will take time.'

'Right. And in the meantime, what happens to my son?'

'Eventually, he'll be placed with a family,' said Mancuso. 'That's all you need to know.'

'No', said Will, 'it isn't. He's my son.'

Mancuso bared his teeth. 'You're not listening, Officer Parker. You don't have a son. And if you don't walk away from this, you won't have a career either.'

'You have to let him go,' said Epstein gently. 'If you love him as a son, then you have to let him go.'

Will looked at the unknown man standing by the wall.

'Who are you?' Will asked. 'Where do you fit into all of this?'

The man didn't answer, and he didn't flinch under the glare of Will's anger.

'He's a friend,' said Epstein. 'That's enough for now.'

Mancuso spoke again. 'Are we all singing from the same hymn sheet, Officer? You'd better tell us now. I won't be so good natured if this matter raises its head outside these four walls.'

Will swallowed hard.

'Yes,' he said. 'I understand.'

'Yes, sir,*' said Mancuso.*

'Yes, sir,' repeated Will.

'And you?' Mancuso turned his attention to Jimmy Gallagher.

'I'm with him,' said Jimmy. 'Whatever he says goes.'

Glances were exchanged. It was over.

'Go home,' said Mancuso to Will. 'Go home to your wife.'

And when they passed the glass-walled room again, the cot was already empty, and the receptionist's face was creased with grief as they passed her desk. Already, the cover-up had begun. Without words to convey her sympathy for a man who had, in one night, lost his child, and the mother of his child, she could only shake her head and watch as he disappeared into the night.

When Will at last returned home, Elaine was waiting for him.

'Where have you been?' Her eyes were swollen. He could tell that she had been crying for hours.

'Something came up,' he said. 'A girl died.'

'I don't care!' It was a scream, not a shout. He had never heard her utter such a sound before. Those three words seemed to hold more pain and anguish than he had ever thought could be contained inside the woman he loved. Then she repeated the words, this time forcing each one out, expelling them like phlegm from her mouth.

'I don't care. You weren't here. You weren't here when I needed you.'

He knelt down before her, and took her hands in his.

'What?' he said. 'What is it?'

'I had to go to the clinic today.'

'Why?'

'Something was wrong. I felt it, inside.'

He tightened his grip, but she would not, could not, look up at him.

'Our baby's dead,' she said softly. 'I'm carrying a dead baby.'

He held her then, and waited for her to cry, but she had no more tears left to shed. She simply lay against him, silent and lost in her grief. He could see his reflection in the mirror on the wall behind her, and he closed his eyes so he would not have to look at himself.

Will led his wife to the bedroom, and helped her to get between the sheets. The doctors at the clinic had given her some pills, and he made her take two.

'They wanted to induce it,' she said as the drugs took hold. 'They wanted to take our baby away, but I wouldn't let them. I wanted to keep it for as long as I could.'

He nodded, but he could not speak. His own tears began to fall. His wife reached up and wiped them away with her thumb.

He sat beside her until she fell asleep, then stared at the wall for two hours, her hand in his, until slowly, carefully, he released it and let it fall to the sheets. She stirred slightly, but she did not wake.

He went downstairs, and called the number that Epstein had given him when they first met. A woman answered sleepily, and when he asked for the rabbi, she told him that he was in bed.

'He had a long night,' she explained.

'I know,' he replied. 'I was there. Wake him. Tell him it's Will Parker.'

The woman clearly recognized the name. She put the phone down, and Will heard her walk away. Five minutes passed, and then he heard Epstein's voice.

'Mr. Parker. I should have told you at the hospital: it's not good for us to stay in contact this way.'

'I need to see you.'

'That's not possible. What's done is done. We must let the matter rest.'

'My wife is carrying a dead baby,' said Will. He almost vomited the words out.

'What?'

'You heard me. Our child is dead in the womb. They think the umbilical cord got wound around its throat somehow. It's dead. They told her yesterday. They're going to induce labor and remove it.'

'I'm sorry,' said Epstein.

'I don't want your pity,' said Will. 'I want my son.'

Epstein was silent. 'What you're suggesting isn't—'

Will cut him off.

'Don't tell me that! You make this happen. You go to your friend, Mr. Quiet in his nice suit, and you tell him what I want. Otherwise, I swear I'll make so much noise that your ears will bleed.' Suddenly, the energy began to leach from his body. He wanted to crawl into bed and hold his wife, hold his wife and their dead child. 'Look, you told me that the boy would have to be taken care of. I can take care of him. Hide him with me. Hide him in plain sight. Please.'

Epstein sighed. 'I will talk to our friends,' he said

at last. 'Give me the name of the doctor who is looking after your wife.'

Will did so. The number was in the address book beside the telephone.

'Where is your wife now?'

'She's asleep upstairs. She took some pills.'

'I'll call you in one hour,' said Epstein, and hung up.

One hour and five minutes later, the phone rang. Will, who had been sitting on the floor beside it, picked it up before it had a chance to ring a second time.

'When your wife wakes up, Mr. Parker, you must tell her the truth,' said Epstein. 'Ask her to forgive you, then tell her what you propose.'

Will did not sleep that night. Instead, he mourned for Caroline Carr, and when dawn broke he put his grief for her aside and prepared for what he felt certain would be the death of his marriage.

'He called me that morning,' said Jimmy. 'He told me what he intended to do. He was prepared to gamble everything on the possibility of holding on to the boy: his career, his marriage, the happiness, even the sanity, of his wife.'

He was about to pour some more wine into his glass, then stopped.

'I can't drink any more,' he said. 'The wine looks like blood.' He pushed the bottle and the glass away. 'We're nearly done anyway, for now. I'll finish this part, and then I have to sleep. We can talk again tomorrow. If you want, you can spend the night. There's a guest room.'

I opened my mouth to object, but he raised his hand.

'Believe me, when I've finished tonight, you'll have enough to think about. You'll be grateful that I've stopped.'

He leaned forward, his hands cupped before him. They were trembling.

'So your old man was waiting at your mother's bedside when she woke . . .'

I think, sometimes, of what my father and mother endured that day. I wonder if there was a kind of madness to his actions, spurred on by his fear that he seemed destined to lose two children, one to death and the other to an anonymous existence surrounded by those who were not related by blood to him. He must have known, as he stood above my mother, debating whether to wake her or let her sleep on, delaying the moment of confession, that it would sunder relations with her forever. He was about to inflict twin wounds upon her: the pain of his betrayal, and the perhaps greater agony of learning that he had succeeded in doing with another what she had failed to do for him. She was carrying a dead child in her womb, while her husband had, only hours before, looked upon his own son, born of a dead mother. He loved his wife, and she loved him, and he was now going to hurt her so badly that she would never fully recover.

He did not tell anyone of what transpired between

them, not even Jimmy Gallagher. All I know is that my mother left him for a time and fled to Maine, a precursor to the more permanent flight that would occur after my father's death, and a distant echo of my own actions after my wife and child were taken from me. She was not my birth mother, and I understand now the reasons for the distance there was between us, even unto her death, but we were more similar than either of us could have imagined. She took me north after the Pearl River killings, and her father, my beloved grandfather, became a guiding force in my life, but my mother also assumed a greater role as I grew older. I think, sometimes, that only after my father died did she truly find it in her heart to forgive him, and perhaps to forgive me the circumstances of my birth. Slowly, we drew closer to each other. She taught me the names of trees and plants and birds, for this was her place, this northern state, and although I did not fully appreciate then the knowledge that she was trying to impart, I think I understood the reasons for her wanting to communicate it to me. We were both grieving, but she would not allow me to be lost to it. And so each day we would walk together for a time, regardless of the weather, and sometimes we would talk, and sometimes we would not, but it was enough that we were together, and we were alive. During those years, I became hers, and now, every time I name to myself a tree, or a flower, or a tiny creeping thing, it is a small act of remembrance for her.

* * *

Elaine Parker called her husband after a week had passed, and they spoke for an hour. Will was granted unpaid leave, authorized, to the puzzlement of some at the precinct, by the deputy commissioner for legal affairs, Frank Mancuso. Will went north to join his wife, and when they returned to New York they did so with a child, and a tale of a difficult, premature birth. They named the boy Charlie, after his father's uncle, Charles Edward Parker, who had died at Monte Cassino. The secret friends kept their distance, and it was many years before Will heard from any of them again. And when they did make contact, it was Epstein who was sent, Epstein who told him that the thing they had long feared was upon them once more.

The lovers had returned.

21

Mickey Wallace felt as though the mist had followed him from Maine. Tendrils of it drifted past his face, reacting to each movement of his body like a living thing, slowly assuming new shapes before slipping away altogether, as though the darkness were weaving itself into being around him, enfolding him in its embrace as he stood before the small house on Hobart Street in Bay Ridge.

Bay Ridge was almost a suburb of Brooklyn, a neighborhood unto itself. Originally it had consisted mostly of Norwegians, who lived there when it was known as Yellow Hook in the nineteenth century, and Greeks, with some Irish thrown in, as there always were, but the opening of the Verrazano Narrows Bridge in the 1970s had changed that makeup as people began to move out to Staten Island, and by the early 1990s Bay Ridge was becoming progressively more Middle Eastern. The bridge dominated the southern end of the area, although Mickey had always felt that it looked more real by night than by day. The lights seemed to give it substance; during the day, by contrast, it looked like a painted backdrop, a gray mass too big for the buildings and streets below.

Hobart Street lay between Marine Avenue and Shore Road, where a series of benches overlooked Shore Road Park, a steep, tree-lined slope leading down to the Belt Parkway and the waters of the Narrows. At first glance, Hobart seemed to consist only of apartment buildings, but on one side was a small row of brownstone, one-family homes, each separated from its neighbor by a driveway. Only 1219 bore the marks of abandonment and neglect.

The presence of the mist reminded Mickey of what he had experienced out at Scarborough. Now, once again, he was standing before a house that he believed to be empty. This was not his neighborhood, not even his city, yet he did not feel out of place here. After all, it was a crucial element in the story that he had followed for so long, the story that he was now going to set down in print. He had stood here before over the years. The first time was after Charlie Parker's wife and child had been found, their blood still fresh on the walls and floor. The second time was after Parker had tracked down the Traveling Man, when the reporters had an ending to their story and sought to remind viewers and readers of the beginning. Lights shone upon the walls and windows, and neighbors came onto the street to watch, their proximity to the action a good indication of their willingness to talk about what had happened there. Even those who were not residents at the time had opinions, for ignorance was never an obstacle to a good sound bite.

But that was a long time ago. Mickey wondered how many people even remembered what had taken place behind those walls, then figured that anyone who had lived in this place when the murders were committed, and who continued to live here now, would find it hard to erase the memory of them. In a way, the house challenged them to forget its past. It was the only unoccupied residence on the street, and its exterior spoke eloquently of its emptiness. For those who knew of its history, the simple sight of it, its very otherness, would be enough to evoke memories. For them, there would always be blood on its walls.

Mickey's search of the property records indicated that there had been three different occupants in the years since the killings, and the house was currently owned by the bank that had taken possession of it after the most recent residents had defaulted on their payments. He found it hard to imagine why anyone would want to live in a place that had known such violence. True, the house had probably initially been sold for far less than its market value, and the cleaners employed to scrub every visible trace of the killings from within would have done their job well, but Mickey felt certain that something must have lingered, some trace of the agonies that had been endured there. Physical? Yes. There would be dried blood between the cracks in the floor. He had been told that one of Susan Parker's fingernails had not been recovered from the scene. Initially, it was thought that her killer had taken it as a souvenir, but now it was believed that it had broken as she scraped at the boards and had slipped between them. Despite repeated searches, it had not been found. It was probably still down there somewhere, lying amid dust and wood chips and lost coins.

But it was not the physical aspects that interested Mickey. He had been to many murder sites, and had grown attuned to their atmosphere. There were some places that, had one not known in advance of the killings that had occurred in them, might well have seemed normal and undisturbed. Flowers grew in yards beneath which children had once been buried. A little girl's playroom, painted in bright oranges and yellows, banished all memories of the old woman who had died there, smothered during a botched burglary when this was still her bedroom. Couples made love in rooms where husbands had beaten wives to death and women had stabbed errant lovers while they slept. Such sites were not tainted by the violence to which they had played host.

But there were other gardens and other houses that would never be the same after blood was spilled upon them. People sensed that something was wrong as soon as they set foot on the property. It didn't matter that the house was clean, that the yard was well tended, that the door was freshly painted. Instead, an echo remained, like the slow fading of a final cry, and it triggered an atavistic response. Sometimes the echo was so pronounced that even the demolition of the premises and the construction of a replacement markedly different from its predecessor was not enough to counter the malign influences that remained. Mickey had visited a condo in Long Island built on the site of a house that had burned down with five children and their mother inside, a fire set by the father of two of the children. The old lady who lived down the street told him that, on the night they died, the firemen could hear the children crying for help, but the heat of the flames was too intense, and they were not able to rescue them. The newly built condo had smelled of smoke, Mickey recalled; smoke, and charred meat. Nobody who lived there stayed longer than six months. On the day that he had inspected it, all of the apartments were available for rent.

Perhaps that was why the Parker house still stood. Even to have knocked it down would have made no difference. The blood had seeped through the house and into the soil beneath, and the air was filled with the sound of screams stifled by a gag.

Mickey had never been inside 1219 Hobart. He had seen pictures of the interior, though. He had prints of them in his possession as he stood at the gate. Tyrrell had provided them, dropping them off at Mickey's hotel earlier that day, along with a terse note apologizing for some of the things that he had said in the course of their meeting. Mickey didn't know how he had come by them. He figured that Tyrrell must have retained his own private file on Charlie Parker after he left the department. Mickey was pretty sure that was illegal, but he wasn't about to complain. He'd looked at the photos in his hotel room, and even after all that he'd seen as a reporter, and his own knowledge of the details of the Parker killings, they had still shaken him.

There was so much blood.

Mickey had approached the Realtor appointed by the bank to oversee the most recent sale of the property, and told the woman responsible that he was interested in buying and refurbishing the house. She hadn't mentioned anything about its history when they had spoken on the phone, which was hardly surprising, and she'd jumped at the chance to show him around. Then she'd asked his name and, when he told her, her manner changed.

'I don't think that it would be appropriate for me to show you that property, sir,' she had said.

'May I ask why?'

'I think you know why. I don't believe you're serious about your inquiry.'

'What does that mean?'

'It means that we're aware of who you are, and of what you're doing. I don't think admitting you to the Hobart Street property would be helpful to any future sale.'

Mickey had hung up. He should have known better than to use his real name, but he hadn't expected Parker to obstruct him in that way, assuming it was Parker who had made the call to the Realtor. He remembered Tyrrell's stated belief that someone was protecting Parker. If that was true, then a person or persons as yet unknown might have alerted the Realtor to what Mickey was doing. It didn't matter. He wasn't above bending the law a little to suit his own purposes, and breaking into the old Parker house didn't strike him as a felony, no matter what a judge might say.

He was pretty certain that the house wouldn't have

an alarm. It had been vacant for too long, and he didn't figure that a Realtor would want to be disturbed in the dead of night because an alarm was ringing in an unoccupied property. He checked to make sure that the street was quiet, then made his way up the drive to the gate at the side of the house, a grassless yard beyond. He tried the gate. It didn't move. For a moment he thought it might be locked, but he could see no way that it could be unless it had been welded shut. Simultaneously, he pushed down on the handle and pressed the weight of his body against the gate. He felt it give, the metal of the handle scraping against the concrete pillar, and then it opened. He stepped through and closed it behind him, then turned the corner of the house so that he was hidden from view.

The back door had two locks, but the wood was damp and rotting. He tested it with his fingernails and pieces of it fell to the ground. He took the crowbar from beneath his coat and began working at the wood. Within minutes, he had made a gap big enough to gain access to the top lock. He inserted the crowbar as far as it would go, then pushed sideways and up. There was a cracking sound from inside, and the lock broke. He moved on to the second lock. The frame quickly splintered and the bolt broke through the wood.

Mickey stood on the step and stared into the kitchen. This was where it had happened. This was the place in which Parker – Parker the revenger, Parker the hunter, Parker the executioner – had been born. Before the deaths of his wife and daughter, he had been just another face on the street: a cop, but not a very good one; a father and a husband, and not much good in those roles either; a man who drank some – not enough to qualify as an alcoholic, not yet, but enough that, in years to come, he might find himself starting on the booze a little earlier each day until at last it became a way to begin the day instead of finishing it; a drifter, a being without purpose. Then, on a December night, the creature that became known as the Traveling Man entered this place and took the lives of the woman and child within, while the man who should have protected them sat on a bar stool feeling sorry for himself.

Those deaths had given him purpose. At first it was revenge, but that gave way to something deeper, something more curious. The desire for revenge alone would have destroyed him, eating away at him like a cancer, so that even when he found the release for which he had yearned, the disease would already have colonized his soul, slowly blackening his humanity until, shriveled and rotten, it was lost forever. No, Parker had found a greater purpose. He was a man who could not easily turn away from the suffering of others, for he found its twin deep within himself. He was tormented by empathy. More than that, he had become a magnet for evil, or perhaps it would be truer to say that a shard of evil deep within himself resonated in the presence of a greater foulness, and drew him to it, and it to him.

All of this, born in blood.

Mickey closed the door, flicked on his flashlight,

and walked through the kitchen, looking neither right nor left, taking in nothing of what he saw there. He would conclude his visit in that room, just as the Traveling Man had done. He wanted to follow the killer's trail, to view this house as the killer had viewed it, and as Parker had seen it on the night that he returned home to find what was left of his wife and child.

The Traveling Man had come in through the front door. There was no sign of forced entry. The hallway was now empty. Mickey compared it with the first of the photographs that he had brought with him. He had ordered them carefully, numbering them on the back. The first showed the hallway as it had once been: a bookcase on the right, and a coat rack. On the floor was a mahogany flower stand, and beside it a broken flowerpot and a plant of some kind, its roots exposed. Behind the plant, the first of the stairs leading up to the second floor. Three bedrooms there, one no larger than a storage room, and a single small bathroom. Mickey didn't want to go up there just yet. Jennifer Parker, three years old, had been asleep on the couch in the living room when the killer entered. She had a weak heart, and it spared her the agony of what was to come. Between the time that the killer entered and the final display of the bodies, she had suffered a massive release of epinephrine into her system, resulting in ventricular fibrillation of the heart. In other words, Jennifer Parker had died of fright.

Her mother had not been so lucky. There had been a struggle, probably near the kitchen. She had managed to get away from her attacker, but only momentarily. He had caught up with her in the hall, and had stunned her by banging her face against the wall. Mickey moved on to the next photograph: a smear of blood on the wall to his left. He found what he believed to be the spot, and ran his fingers across it. Then he knelt down and examined the floorboards, trailing his hand along the wood, just as Susan Parker had done as she was dragged back to the kitchen. The hallway had been only partially carpeted, leaving the edges of the boards exposed on either side. It was here, somewhere, that Susan had lost her fingernail.

Was her daughter dead by then, or had the sight of her mother, dazed and bleeding, triggered the attack that led to Jennifer's death? Maybe she had fought to save her mother. Yes, that was probably it, Mickey thought, already piecing together the most favorable narrative, the most gripping version he could find of the story. There had been rope marks on the child's wrists and ankles, indicating that she had been restrained at some point. She woke, realized what was happening, tried to scream, to fight. A blow was struck, knocking her to the ground; just such an injury had been recorded in the autopsy. Once her mother had been subdued, the killer restrained the daughter in turn, but by then the girl was already dying. Mickey glanced into the living room, now furnished only with dust and discarded paper and dead insects. Another photograph, this time of the couch. There was a doll lying on it, half obscured by a blanket.

Mickey moved on, trying to visualize the scene as

Parker had experienced it. Blood on the walls and on the floor; the kitchen door almost closed; the house cold. He took a deep breath, and turned to the final photograph: Susan Parker on a pine chair, her arms tied behind her back, her feet bound separately to the front legs, her head down, her face obscured by her hair, so that the damage to the face and eyes was not visible, not from this angle. Her daughter lay across her mother's thighs. Not so much blood on her. Her throat had been cut, as was her mother's, but by then Jennifer was already dead. Light shone through what seemed at first glance to be a thin cloak laid across Susan Parker's arms, but which Mickey knew to be her own skin, pulled back to complete the macabre *pietà*.

With the image clear in his head, Mickey opened the kitchen door, ready to impose this old vision of hell on the empty room.

Except now the room was not empty. The back door was half open, and there was a figure in the shadows behind it, watching him.

Mickey stumbled back in shock, his hand instinctively raised to his heart.

'Jesus,' he said. 'What—'

The figure moved forward, and was caught by the moonlight.

'Wait a minute,' said Mickey as, unbeknownst to him, the final sands of his life began slipping through his fingers. 'I *know* you . . .'

22

Jimmy had moved on to coffee, enlivened by a glass of brandy. I stuck with coffee alone, but I barely touched it. I tried to pinpoint how I was feeling, but at first there was only a numbness that gradually gave way to a kind of sadness and loneliness. I thought of all that my parents had endured, of my father's lies and betrayal and my mother's pain. For now, my only regret was that they were no longer there for me, that I could not go to them and tell them that I understood, that it was all okay. Had they lived, I wondered when, or if, they would together have told me of the circumstances of my birth, and I recognized that, coming from them, the details would have been more difficult to bear, and my reactions would have been more extreme. Sitting in Jimmy Gallagher's candlelit kitchen, watching his wine-stained lips move, I felt that I was listening to the story of another man's life, one with whom I shared certain qualities but who was, ultimately, distant from me.

With each word that he spoke, Jimmy seemed to relax a little more, but he also appeared to be growing older, although I knew it was only a trick of the light. He had lived to be a repository of secrets; now, as they seeped from him at last, so some of his life force went with them.

He sipped his brandy. 'Like I said, there's not much more to tell.'

Not much more to tell. Only the story of my father's final day, and the blood that he shed, and the reasons why.

Not much more to tell. Only everything.

Jimmy and Will kept their distance from each other after Will and Elaine returned from Maine with their new child, and they spoke to no one else of what they knew. Then, one December night, Jimmy and Will got drunk together at Chumley's and the White Horse, and Will thanked Jimmy for all that he had done, for his loyalty and his friendship and for killing the woman who had taken Caroline's life.

'You think of her?' asked Jimmy.

'Caroline?'

'Yes.'

'Sometimes. More than sometimes.'

'Did you love her?'

'I don't know. If I didn't then, I do now. Does that make any sense?'

'As much as anything does. You ever visit the grave?'

'Just a couple of times since the funeral.'

Jimmy remembered the funeral, in a quiet corner of Bayside Cemetery. Caroline had told Will that she didn't have much time for organized religion. Her folks had been Protestants of some stripe, so they found a minister who said the right things as she and the child were laid in the ground. Will, Jimmy, and the rabbi, Epstein, were the only other people in attendance. Epstein had told them that the male infant had come from one of the hospitals in the city. His mother had been a junkie, and the kid hadn't lived for more than a couple of hours after he was born. The mother didn't care that her child was dead or, if she did, she didn't show it. She would later, Jimmy believed. He couldn't countenance the possibility that a woman, no matter how sick or high she was, could remain untroubled by the death of her child. Elaine's own labor had been discreetly induced while she was in Maine. There had been no formal burial. After she had made the decision to stay with Will, and to protect the child cut from Caroline Carr, Epstein had spoken with her over the phone, and had made her understand how important it was that everyone believed Caroline's child was Elaine's own. She had been given time to mourn her own baby, to cradle the small, dead thing in her arms, and then it was taken from her.

'I'd go more often, but it upsets Elaine,' said Will.

I'll bet it does, thought Jimmy. He didn't know how the marriage had survived and, from the hints Will had dropped, it wasn't entirely certain that it would *survive. Still, Jimmy's respect for Elaine Parker had only grown in the aftermath of what had occurred. He couldn't even begin to imagine what she felt as she looked at her husband, and at the child she was raising as her own. He wondered if she could yet even distinguish hatred from love.*

'I always bring two bunches of flowers,' continued

Will. 'One for Caroline, and one for the kid they buried with her. Epstein said it was important. It had to look like I was mourning both of them, just in case.'

'In case what?'

'In case someone is watching,' said Will.

'They're gone,' said Jimmy. 'You saw them both die.'

'Epstein thinks there might be others. Worse than that . . .'

He stopped talking.

'What could be worse?' asked Jimmy.

'That, somehow, they might come back.'

'What does that mean, "come back"?'

'Doesn't matter. The rabbi's fantasies.'

'Jesus. Fantasies is right.'

Jimmy raised his hand for another round of drinks.

'And the woman, the one I shot? What did they do with her?'

'They burned her body, and scattered the ashes. You know, now I'd like to have taken a minute with her, before she died.'

'So you could have asked her why,' said Jimmy.

'Yes.'

'She wouldn't have told you anything. I could see it in her eyes. And—'

'Go on.'

'It'll sound strange.'

Will laughed. 'After all that we've been through, could anything sound strange?'

'I suppose not.'

'So?'

'She wasn't afraid to die.'

'She was a fanatic. Fanatics are too crazy to be afraid.'

'No, it was more than that. I thought, just before I fired, that she smiled at me, as if it didn't matter if I killed her or not. And that stuff about being "beyond your law." Jesus, she gave me the creeps.'

'She was sure that she'd done what she came to do. As far as she was concerned, Caroline was dead and so was her baby.'

Jimmy frowned. 'Maybe,' he said, but he didn't sound like he believed it, and he wondered at what Epstein had told Will, about how they might come back, but he couldn't figure out what that might mean, and Will wouldn't tell him.

In the years that followed, they rarely discussed the subject. Epstein did not contact either Will or Jimmy, although Will thought that he had sometimes seen the rabbi when Will took his family into the city to shop or to see a movie or a show. Epstein never acknowledged his presence on those occasions, and Will did not approach him, but he had the sense that Epstein, both in person and through others, was keeping an eye on Will, his wife, and, most especially, his son.

Only rarely would Will tell Jimmy of the state of his relationship with his wife. It had never recovered from his betrayal, and he knew that it never would, yet at least they were still together. But there were times when his wife would be distant from him, both emotionally and physically, for weeks on end. She struggled, too, with their son or, as she would throw at Will when her rage and hurt got the upper hand, 'your son.' But, slowly, that began to change, for the boy knew no mother but her. Will thought that the turning point came when Charlie, then eight years old, was struck by a car while learning to ride his new bike around the neighborhood. Elaine was in the yard when it happened, saw the car strike the bike and the boy fly into the air and land hard upon the road. As she ran, she heard him calling for her: not for his father, to whom he seemed naturally to turn for so many things, but for her. His left arm was badly broken – she could see that as soon as she reached him – and there was blood pouring from a wound in his scalp. He was struggling to remain conscious, and something told her that it was important for him to stay with her, that he should not close his eyes. She called his name, over and over, as she took a coat from the driver of the car and, gently, placed it under the boy's head. She was crying, and he saw that she was crying.

'Mommy,' he said. 'Mommy, I'm sorry.'

'No,' she replied, 'I'm sorry. It wasn't your fault. It was never your fault.'

And she stayed with him, kneeling over him, whispering his name, the palm of her hand caressing his face; and she sat beside him in the ambulance; and she sat outside the theater as they operated on him to stitch his scalp and set his arm; and hers was the first face he saw when he came to.

After that, things were better between them.

* * *

'My father told you all this?'

'No,' said Jimmy. 'She told me, after he died. She said you were all that she had left of him, but that wasn't why she loved you. She loved you because you were her child. She was the only mother you knew, and you were the only son she had. She said that she'd sometimes forgotten that, or didn't want to believe it, but as time went by she realized the truth of it.'

He got up to go to the bathroom. I remained seated thinking of my mother in her final days, lying in her hospital bed, so altered by the disease that I hadn't recognized her when I had first entered her room, believing instead that the nurse had made some mistake when she directed me down the corridor. But then she made a small gesture in her sleep, a raising of her right hand, and even in her illness the grace of it was familiar, and in that moment I knew it was her. In the days that followed, as I waited for her to die, she had only a few hours of lucidity. Her voice was almost gone, and it seemed to pain her to speak, so instead I read to her from my college texts: poetry, short stories, snippets from the newspaper that I knew would interest her. Her father had come down from Maine, and we would talk to each other as she dozed between us.

Did she consider, as she felt the darkness clouding her consciousness like ink through water, telling me all that she had withheld from me? I am sure that she did, but I understand now why she did not. I think that she may also have warned my grandfather to say nothing, because she believed that if I knew the truth then I might begin digging.

And if I began digging, I would draw them to me.

When Jimmy returned from the bathroom, I saw that he had splashed water on his face, but he had not dried it properly, and the drops looked like tears.

'On that last night . . .' he began.

They were in Cal's together, Jimmy and Will, celebrating Jimmy's birthday. Some things had changed in the Ninth, but they were still the same in many ways. There were galleries where once there had been dive bars and deserted buildings, and shaky underground movies were being shown in empty storefronts that were now functioning as avant-garde theaters. A lot of the old places were still there, although their time, too, would soon come to an end, some of them with shadows cast over the memories of them. At Second and Fifth, the Binibon was still serving greasy chicken salad, but now people looked at the Binibon and recalled how, in 1981, one of its customers had been Jack Henry Abbott, the writer and ex-con championed by Norman Mailer, who had worked for his release. One night, Abbott got into an argument with a waiter, asked him to step outside, and then stabbed him to death. Jimmy and Will had been among those cleaning up in the aftermath, the two men, like the precinct that they worked, both changed yet still the same, altered in aspect but still in uniform. They had never made sergeant, and they never would. That was the price that they had paid for what had happened on the night Caroline Carr died.

They were still good cops, though, one of the small

cadre of city, transit, and housing officers who did more than the minimum, fighting the general strain of apathy that had infected the force, in part a consequence of a widespread belief that the suits and brass at the Puzzle Palace, as One Police Plaza was known to the rank and file, were out to get them. It wasn't entirely untrue either. Make too many drug busts and you attracted the attention of your superiors for all the wrong reasons. Make too many arrests and, because of the overtime payments required to process them and see them through court, you were accused of taking money from the pockets of other cops. Best to keep your head down until you could cash out at twenty. The result was that there were now fewer and fewer older cops to act as mentors to the new recruits. By virtue of their years on the force, Jimmy and Will practically qualified as village elders. They had become part of the plainclothes Anticrime Unit, a dangerous assignment that involved patrolling high-crime areas waiting for signs that something was about to go off, usually a gun. For the first time, both were talking seriously about cashing out.

Somehow, they had found a quiet corner away from the rest, cut off by a raucous throng of men and women in business suits celebrating an office promotion. After that night, Will Parker would be dead, and Jimmy Gallagher would never set foot in Cal's again. After Will's death, he found that he could not remember the good times he had enjoyed there. They were gone, excised from his memory. Instead there was only Will with a cold one at his elbow, his hand raised to make a point that would remain forever unspoken, his expression changing as he looked over Jimmy's shoulder and saw who had entered the bar. Jimmy had turned around to see what he was looking at, but by then Epstein was beside them, and Jimmy knew that something was very wrong.

'You have to go home,' said Epstein to Will. He was smiling, but his words gave the lie to his smile, and he did not look at Will as he spoke. To a casual observer, he would have appeared only to be examining the bottles behind the bar, choosing his poison before he joined the company. He wore a white raincoat buttoned to the neck, and on his head was a brown hat with a red feather in the band. He had aged greatly since Jimmy had last seen him at Caroline Carr's funeral.

'What's wrong?' asked Will. 'What's happened?'

'Not here,' said Epstein, as he was jostled by Perrson, the big Swede who was the linchpin of the Cabaret Unit. It was a Thursday night, and Cal's was buzzing. Perrson, who stood taller than anyone else in the bar, was handing shots of booze over the heads of those behind him, sometimes baptizing them a little along the way.

'God bless you, my son,' he said as someone protested. He guffawed at his own joke, then recognized Jimmy.

'Hey, it's the birthday boy!'

But Jimmy was already moving past him, following another man, and Perrson thought that it might have been Will Parker, but later, when questioned, he would claim to have been mistaken, or confused about the time. It might have been later when he saw Jimmy, and Will could not have been with him, because Will would have been on his way back to Pearl River by then.

It was cold outside. The three men kept their hands thrust deep into their pockets as they walked away from Cal's, from the precinct house, from familiar faces and speculative glances. They did not stop until they came to the corner of St. Mark's.

'You remember Franklin?' said Epstein. 'He was the director of the Gerritsen Clinic. He retired two years ago.'

Will nodded. He recalled the worried-looking man in the small office, part of a conspiracy of silence that he still did not fully understand.

'He was killed at his home last night. Someone cut him badly to make him talk before he died.'

'Why do you think that it's something to do with us?' said Will.

'A neighbor saw a male and a female leave the house shortly after eleven. They were both young, he said: older teenagers at most. They were driving a red Ford. This morning, the offices of Dr. Anton Bergman in Pearl River were burgled. Dr. Bergman, I believe, looks after the health of your family. A red Ford was seen parked close by. It had out-of-state plates: Alabama. Dr. Bergman and his secretary are still trying to confirm what was removed, but the drug cabinets were intact. Only the patient records were rifled. Your

family's records are among those that are missing. Somehow they've made the connection. We didn't hide our tracks as well as we thought.'

Will looked pale, but still he tried to argue. 'That doesn't make any sense. Who are these kids?'

It took a moment for Epstein to answer. 'They're the same ones who came for Caroline Carr sixteen years ago,' he said.

'No.' It was Jimmy Gallagher. 'Uh-uh. They're dead. One of them got crushed by a truck, and I shot the other. I watched them pull her body from the creek. And even if they had lived, they'd be in their forties or fifties by now. They wouldn't be children.'

Epstein turned on him. 'They're not children! They're—' He composed himself. 'Something is inside each of them, something much older. These things don't die. They can't die. They move from host to host. If the host dies, then they find another. They are reborn, over and over again.'

'You're crazy,' said Jimmy. 'You're out of your mind.'

He turned to his partner for support, but none came. Instead, Will looked frightened.

'Aw Jesus, you don't believe this, do you?' said Jimmy. 'They can't be the same ones. It's just not possible.'

'It doesn't matter,' said Will. 'They're here, whoever they are. Franklin would have told them about how the death of the baby was covered up. I have a boy the same age as the one who was supposed to have died. They made the connection, and the medical records will confirm it. He's right: I have to go home.'

'We'll have people looking for them too,' said Epstein. 'I've made some calls. We're moving as fast as we can, but . . .'

'I'll go with you,' said Jimmy.

'No. Go back to Cal's,' said Will.

'Why?'

Will gripped Jimmy's arms and looked him in the face. 'Because I have to end this,' he said. 'Do you understand? I don't want you to be caught up in it. You have to stay clean. I need you to be clean.' Then he seemed to remember something. 'Your nephew,' he said. 'Marie's boy? He's still with the Orangetown cops, isn't he?'

'Yeah, he's out there. I don't think he's on duty until later, though.'

'Can you call him? Just ask him to go to the house and stay with Elaine and Charlie for a while. Don't tell him why. Just make up some excuse about an old case, maybe an ex-con with a grudge. Will you do that? Will he *do that?'*

'He'll do it,' said Jimmy.

Epstein handed Will a set of car keys.

'Take my car,' he said, pointing to an old Chrysler parked nearby. Will nodded his thanks, then began to stride away, but Epstein reached for his arm, holding him back.

'Don't try to kill them,' said Epstein. 'Not unless you have no other choice.'

Jimmy saw Will nod, but his eyes were far away. Jimmy knew what Will intended to do.

Epstein walked away in the direction of the subway.

Jimmy made the call to his nephew from a phone booth. Afterwards, he went back to Cal's where he drank and made small talk, his mind detached from the actions of his body, his mouth moving of its own volition, and he stayed there until word came that Will Parker had shot two kids up in Pearl River, and he had been found in the locker room of the Ninth, tears streaming down his face, waiting for them to come for him.

And when they asked him why he had driven all the way back to the city, he could tell them only that he wanted to be among his own.

23

He could have gone to his fellow cops, of course, but what would he have told them? That two kids were coming to kill his son; that those two kids could be hosts for other entities, malign spirits who had already killed the boy's mother and had now returned to murder her child? Perhaps he might have concocted a lie, some tale of how they had threatened his family, or he could have fed them the information that a car resembling the one they were driving had been seen close to the director's office after his death, and a young man and a young woman had been glimpsed leaving his house on the night that he was killed. All of that might well have been enough to hold them, assuming they were found, but he didn't want them merely to be held: he wanted them gone forever.

The rabbi's warning against killing them had not gone unheeded. Instead, it had broken something inside him. He had thought that he could cope with anything – murder, loss, a child suffocated beneath a pile of coats – but now he was no longer certain that this was true. He did not want to believe what the rabbi had told him, because to do so would be to throw aside all of the certainties he felt about the world. He could accept that somebody, some agency as yet unknown, wanted his son dead. It was an appalling purpose, and one that he could not understand, but he could deal with it as long as its agents were human. After all, there was no proof that what the rabbi believed was actually true. The man and woman who had been hunting Caroline were dead. He had watched them both die, and had gazed upon their bodies after death.

But they were different then, weren't they? The dead are always different: smaller, somehow, and shrunken in upon themselves. Their faces change, and their bodies collapse. Over the years, he had become convinced of the existence of a human soul, if only because of the absence he witnessed in the bodies of the deceased. Something departed at the moment of death, altering the remains, and the evidence of its leaving was visible in the appearance of the dead.

And yet, and yet . . .

He thought back to the woman. She had been less damaged than the man in the course of her dying. The wheels of the truck had left him beyond identification, but she was physically intact apart from the holes that Jimmy's bullets had made in her, and they had caught her in the upper body. Looking upon her face after she was pulled from the water, Will had been astonished at the change in her. It was hard to believe that this was the same woman. The cruelty that had animated her features was gone but, more than that, her looks were softer, as though her bones had been blunted, the sharp edges removed from her cheeks and her nose and her chin. The imperfect mask that had covered her face for so long, one that was based on her own appearance yet subtly altered, had fallen away, disintegrating in the cold waters of the creek. He had looked at Jimmy and seen the same reaction. Unlike him, though, Jimmy had spoken it aloud.

'It doesn't even look like her,' he had said. 'I see the wounds, but it's not her . . .'

The crime scene guys had looked at him in puzzlement, but had said nothing. They knew that different cops responded in different ways to their involvement in fatal shootings. It was not their place to comment.

Oh yes, something had left her as she died, but Will did not believe, or did not want to believe, that it had come back again.

So while Jimmy Gallagher's nephew guarded Will's son, he drove around Pearl River, pausing at intersections to peer along the cross streets, shining his flashlight on dark cars in parking lots, slowing down to stare at young couples, daring them to look back at him, for he felt sure that he would be able to identify the ones who had come for his son by the look in their eyes.

Perhaps he had always been fated to find them. In the hours that followed, he wondered if they had been waiting for him, knowing that he would come yet certain that he would not be able to act against them. They were strangers to him, and even if the rabbi had warned him of their true nature, who could ever truly believe such a thing?

And something would come for Epstein too, in time. It was not their purpose. It would be left to another. The rabbi could wait . . .

And so they had not moved as his flashlight found them on the patch of waste ground not far from his home. They had seen the other man, big, red-headed, arrive at the house, and they had glimpsed the pistol in his hand. Now that they knew where the boy was, and had learned for certain the truth about his parentage, they were anxious to move against him, to finish the task they had been assigned so long before. But if they were to rush it and make a mistake, then he would be lost to them again. The red-headed man was armed, and they did not want to die, neither one nor both. They had already been separated for too long, and they loved each other. This time, the struggle to reunite had been shorter than before, but the separation had still been painful for them. The boy had been traced by another, the one called Kittim, who had whispered foul things in his ear, and the boy had known them to be true. He had traveled north, and in time, aided by Kittim, he had found the girl. Now they burned for each other, rejoicing in their physicality. Once the boy was dead, they could disappear and be together forever. They just had to be careful. They did not want to take any chances.

And here was the boy's father approaching; they recognized him immediately. Curious, the girl thought: the last time she had seen him was at the moment of her death. Now here he was, older and grayer, tired and weak. She smiled to herself, then leaned over and gripped the boy's hand. He turned to look at her, and she saw an eternity of longing in his eyes.

'I love you,' she whispered.

'And I love you.'

Will got out of the car. He had a gun in his hand, held close to his right thigh. He shone his flashlight on them. The boy raised his hand to shield his eyes.

'Hey, man,' he said. 'What's the deal with the light?'

Will thought that the boy looked vaguely familiar. He was from somewhere in Rockland County, of that Will was certain, although he was a recent arrival. He seemed to recall something about juvie stuff, maybe from visiting down at Orangetown with the local cops.

'Keep your hands where I can see them, both of you.'

They did as they were told, the boy resting his palms upon the wheel, the girl placing her painted fingernails upon the dashboard.

'License and registration,' said Will.

'Hey, you a cop?' said the boy. He had a lazy drawl, and he grinned as he spoke, letting Parker know that this was all a charade, a farce. 'Maybe you need to show me some ID first.'

'Shut up. License and registration.'

'Behind the visor.'

'Reach up slowly with your left hand.'

The boy shrugged but did as he was told, holding the license for the cop to see once he had retrieved it.

'Alabama. You're a long way from home.'

'I've always been a long way from home.'

'How old are you?'

'Sixteen,' he said. 'And then some . . .'

Will stared at him, and he saw the darkness in the boy's eyes.

'What are you doing here?'

'Sitting. Taking time out with my best girl.'

The girl giggled, but it wasn't a pretty sound. Parker thought that it sounded like something bubbling in a pot on an old stove, something that would scour you if it touched your skin.

Parker stepped back.

'Get out of the car.'

'Why? We ain't done nothing wrong.' The tone of the boy's voice changed, and Parker heard the adult in him come through. 'Besides, you still ain't shown us no ID. You might not be a cop at all. You could be a thief, or a rapist. We ain't moving until I see a badge.'

The boy watched as the flashlight wavered for a moment, and knew that the cop was uncertain now. He had his suspicions, but they weren't enough to act on, and the boy was enjoying taunting him, although not as much as he would enjoy leaving him with the knowledge that he had been unable to save his son from death.

But it was the girl who spoke, and doomed them.

'So, what you gonna do, Officer Parker?' she said, giggling.

There was a moment of silence.

'How do you know my name?'

The girl was no longer giggling. The boy licked his lips. Maybe the situation could yet be rescued.

'I guess someone pointed you out to us. Lot of cops around here. Guy was naming them off to me.'

'What guy?'

'Someone we met. People are friendly to strangers in this town. That's how we know who you are.'

He licked his lips again.

'And I know what you are,' said Parker.

The boy stared at him, and he changed. He had an adolescent's inner rage, an inability to control himself in adult situations. Now, as the cop challenged him, the old thing inside him was revealed for an instant, a thing of ash and fire and charred flesh, a thing of transcendent beauty and untrammeled ugliness.

'Fuck you, and your child,' said the boy. 'You have no idea what we are.'

He turned his left wrist slightly, and the symbol on his arm was revealed to Will by the flashlight's beam.

And in that instant, what was fractured inside Will Parker came apart forever, and he knew that he could take no more. The first shot killed the boy, entering just above his right eye and exiting through the back of his head, burying itself in the rear seat amid blood and hair and brain matter. There was no need for a second, but Will fired one anyway. The girl opened her mouth and screamed. She leaned over and cradled the ruined head of her lover, then gazed at the one who had taken him from her again.

'We'll come back,' she whispered. 'We'll keep coming back until it's done.'

Will said nothing. He simply lowered the gun and shot her once in the chest.

When she was gone, he went back to his car and placed his gun on the hood. There were lights coming on in nearby porches and hallways, and he saw a man standing in his yard, looking over at the two cars. He tasted salt on his lips, and thought that he had been crying, but then the pain came and he realized that he had bitten his tongue.

In a daze, he got back in the car and began to drive. As he passed the man in the yard, he saw recognition brighten the witness's face, but he didn't care. He didn't even know where he was going until the lights of the city appeared before him, and then he understood.

He was going home.

They questioned him for most of that night, once they got him back to Orangetown. They told him that he was in trouble, having left the scene of a shooting, and in response he gave them the least elaborate lie that he could concoct: he had seen the car on waste ground as he was heading home, having been alerted to its presence by someone who had recognized him at an intersection, but whose name he did not know. The car had flashed its lights, and he thought that the horn might have sounded. He stopped to check that everything was okay. The boy had taunted him, pretending to reach for something inside his jacket: a weapon, perhaps. Will had warned him, and then had fired, killing the boy and the girl. After he had gone over the story for the third time, Kozelek, the investigator from the Rockland County DA's office, had requested a moment alone with him, and the other cops, both IAD and local, had consented. When they were gone, Kozelek stopped the tape and lit a cigarette. He didn't offer one to Will.

'You weren't driving your own car,' said Kozelek.

'No, I borrowed a friend's.'

'What friend?'

'Just a friend. He's not involved. I wasn't feeling so good. I wanted to get home as quickly as possible.'

'So this friend gives you his car.'

'He didn't need it. I was going to drop it back off in the city tomorrow.'

'Where is it now?'

'What does it matter?'

'It was used in the course of a shooting.'

'I don't remember. I don't remember much after the shooting. I just drove. I wanted to get away from it.'

'You were traumatized. Is that what you're saying?'

'That must have been it. I never shot anybody before.'

'There was no gun,' said Kozelek. 'We looked. They were unarmed, both of them.'

'I didn't say that they were armed. I said that I thought the boy might *have been armed.'*

Kozelek drew on his cigarette and examined the man seated opposite him through the smoke. He had appeared detached from the whole process from the moment they had taken him in for questioning. It could have been shock. The IAD detectives had arrived from the city with copies of Will Parker's service record. As he had just said, he had never killed anyone before, either officially or, from what Kozelek could ascertain, unofficially. (He had been with the NYPD himself for twenty years, and he had no illusions about such matters.) His responsibility for the shootings of the two young people would be difficult for him to accept. But that wasn't how Kozelek read the situation: it wasn't so much that Will Parker was in shock, but that he seemed to want the whole thing to be over and done with, like a condemned man who seeks only to be taken straight from the courtroom to his place of execution. Even his description of events, which Kozelek believed to be a lie, was halfhearted in its absence of truth. Parker didn't care if they believed him or not. They wanted a story, and he had given them a story. If they wanted to pick holes in it, they could go right ahead and do it. He didn't care.

That was it, thought Kozelek. The man didn't care. His reputation and career were on the line. He had blood on his hands. When the circumstances of the killings began to emerge, the press would be baying for his *blood, and there would be those within the department who might be prepared to throw Will Parker to the dogs as a sacrifice, a way of showing that the department wouldn't tolerate killers on the force. Already, Kozelek knew, that discussion was taking place, as men with reputations to protect balanced the advisability of weathering the storm and standing by their officer against the possibility that to do so might further tarnish the reputation of a department that was already unloved and still reeling from a series of corruption investigations.*

'You say that you didn't know these kids?' said Kozelek. The question had been asked more than once already in that room, but Kozelek had caught a flicker of uncertainty in Parker's face each time he had denied any knowledge of them, and he saw it again now.

'The boy looked familiar, but I don't think I'd ever met him.'

'His name was Joe Dryden. Native of Birmingham, Alabama. Arrived here a couple of months ago. He already had a record: nickel-and-dime stuff, mostly, but he was on his way to greater things.'

'Like I said, I didn't know him personally.'

'And the girl?'

'Never saw her before.'

'Missy Gaines. Came from a nice family in Jersey. Her parents reported her missing a week ago. Any idea how she might have come to be with Dryden in Pearl River?'

'You asked me these questions already. I told you: I don't know.'

'Who visited your house yesterday evening?'

'I don't know. I wasn't there.'

'We have a witness who says he saw a man enter your house last night. He stayed for some time. The witness seems to be under the impression that the man had a gun in his hand.'

'Like I said, I don't know what you're talking about, but your witness must be mistaken.'

'I think the witness is reliable.'

'Why didn't he call the cops?'

'Because your wife answered the door and allowed the man to enter. It appears that she knew him.'

Will shrugged. 'I don't know anything about it.'

Kozelek took a final drag on his cigarette, then stubbed it out in the cracked ashtray.

'Why'd you turn off the tape?' asked Will.

'Because IAD doesn't know about the armed man,' said Kozelek. 'I was hoping you might tell me why you thought they were sufficiently at risk that you needed to protect them, and how that might connect to the two kids you shot.'

But Will didn't answer and Kozelek, realizing that the situation was unlikely to change, gave up for the time being.

'If IAD does find out, they'll question your wife. You need to get your story straight. Jesus, why couldn't you just have thrown down a gun? A gun in the car, and all of this would be unnecessary.'

'Because I don't have a throwdown,' said Will, and for the first time he showed some real animation. 'I'm not that kind of cop.'

'Well,' said Kozelek, 'I have news for you: there are two dead kids in a car, both of them unarmed. So, as of now, you are *that kind of cop . . .'*

24

We were coming to the end.

'I picked your father up from the Orangetown PD before noon,' said Jimmy. 'There were reporters outside, so they put a cop who'd just come off duty in the backseat of an unmarked sedan with a coat over his head, and then they drove him out in an explosion of flashbulbs while I waited at the back of the station house for your father. We drove to a place called Creeley's in Orangetown. It's not there anymore. There's a gas station where it used to be. Back then, it was the kind of bar that did a good burger, kept the lights low, and nobody asked anybody anything beyond "Another one?" or "You want fries with that?" I used to go there with my nephew and my sister sometimes. We don't talk so much anymore, my sister and me. She lives out in Chicago now. She thought I put my nephew at risk by asking him to do what he did for you and your mother, but we'd been growing apart from each other long before that.'

I didn't interrupt him. He was circling the awfulness of what was to come, like a dog fearful of taking tainted meat from a stranger's hand.

'As it happened, there was nobody in the place

when we got there, apart from the bartender. I knew him, and he knew me. I guess he might have recognized your father too, but if he did, he didn't say anything either way. We had coffee, we talked.'

'What did he say?'

Jimmy shrugged, as if it were a matter of no consequence. 'He said what Epstein had said: they were the same people. They looked different, but he saw it in their eyes, and the girl's words and the marking on the boy just confirmed it. That threat of returning. I think of it all the time.'

He seemed to shiver slightly, still water brushed by a cold breeze.

'And then, just before he fired the first shot, he said he could have sworn that their faces changed.'

'Changed?'

'Yeah, changed, just like the woman I killed at Gerritsen Beach, I guess. Best he could explain it, he said it was like a pair of masks that they wore became transparent for an instant, and he saw the things behind them. That was when he pulled the trigger on the boy. He couldn't even remember killing the girl. He knew that he'd done it; he just couldn't recall how it had happened.

'After an hour, he asked me to drive him back home, but when we left Creeley's there were two IAD guys waiting for us. They told me that they'd take Will to the house. They said they were worried about reporters, but I think they just wanted a few more minutes alone with him in the hope that I might have convinced him to come clean. I mean, they knew what he had told them didn't add up. They were just having trouble finding the cracks in his version. I don't think he said anything more, though. Later, after he died, they tried to sweat me, but I didn't tell them anything either. After that, I was pretty much done as a cop. I served out my time at the Ninth, just so I could claim my full benefits and pension.

'So that was the last time I saw Will, as the IAD guys were taking him away. He thanked me for all that I'd done, and he shook my hand. I should have known what was coming then, but I wasn't looking out for it. We had never shaken hands before, not since the first day we met at the academy. It just wasn't a thing for us. I watched him go, and then I came back here. The call came through before I'd even had a chance to take off my shoes. It was my nephew who told me. The thing of it was, if you'd asked me then if I was surprised, I'd have said "no." Twenty-four hours earlier, I'd have told you it could never happen, Will Parker eating his gun, but, looking back, when we were sitting in Creeley's I could tell that he wasn't the same man. He looked old, and beaten. I don't think he could believe what he had seen, and what he had done. It was just too much for him.

'The funeral was a strange one. I don't know what you remember of it, but there were people who should have been there but weren't. The commissioner didn't show, and that wasn't a surprise, not for what was being tagged as a murder-suicide. But there were others – brass, mainly, suits from the Puzzle Palace – who stayed away when usually they'd have made an appearance. There was a bad smell around what happened, and they knew it. The papers were all over them, and they didn't like it. In a way, and you'll forgive me for saying it, your old man dying was the best thing that could have happened for them. If an inquiry had vindicated him, the press would have hauled them over the fires of hell for it. If the shootings were found to be unjustified, then there would have been a court case, and the cops on the street, and the union, they'd all have been spitting nails. When Will killed himself, they got to bury the whole mess along with him. The investigation into what happened was always set to be inconclusive once he was gone. The only people who knew the truth of what took place on that patch of waste ground were all dead.

'Will got an inspector's funeral, though, the whole deal. The band played, and there were white gloves and black ribbons, and a folded flag for your mother. Because of the way he went, his benefits were in doubt. You may not know this, but an inspector from Police Plaza, a guy named Jack Stepp, he had a quiet word with your mother as she was walking back to the funeral car. Stepp was the commissioner's fixer, the guy who cleaned up behind the scenes. He told her that she'd be taken care of, and she was. They paid the benefits under the table. Somebody made sure that she was done right by, that you were both looked after.

'Epstein contacted me after the funeral. He didn't attend. I think it was too high profile for him, and he's not a high-profile guy. He came here, to this house, and he sat in the chair that you're sitting in now, and he asked me what I knew about the killings, and I told him the same thing that I've told you, all of it. Then he went away, and I never saw him again. I didn't even speak to him until you came along asking questions, and then Wallace turned up after you, and I felt that I had to inform Epstein. Wallace I wasn't worried about so much: there are ways that these things can be handled, and I figured he could be frightened off if the need arose. But you: I knew you'd keep coming back, that once you'd gotten it into your head to go nosing around in the dirt then you wouldn't stop until you came up with bones. Epstein told me that his people were already working on stopping Wallace, and that I should tell you what I knew.'

He sat back in his chair, spent.

'So now you know everything.'

'And you kept it hidden all this time?'

'I didn't even discuss it with your mother and, to tell you the truth, I was kind of glad when she said she was taking you up to Maine. It made me feel like I didn't have to be responsible for you. It made me feel like I could pretend to forget everything.'

'Would you ever have told me if I hadn't come asking?'

'No. What good would it have done?' Then he seemed to reconsider. 'Look, I don't know,' he said. 'I've read about you, and I've heard the stories about the people you've found, and the men and women you've killed. All those cases have been touched by something strange. Maybe, in the last couple of years, I've thought that you should be told so that—'

He was struggling to find the right words.

'So that what?'

He settled upon them, although not happily. 'So that you'd be ready for them when they came again,' he said.

25

The call came through to my cell phone shortly before midnight. Jimmy had gone to make up the bed in the spare room, and I was seated at the kitchen table, still trying to come to terms with what he had told me. The ground beneath my feet no longer seemed solid, and I did not trust myself to stand and remain upright. Perhaps I should have doubted Jimmy's story, or at least remained skeptical of some of the details until I could investigate them further for myself, but I did not. I knew in my heart that all he had told me was true.

I checked the caller ID before I answered, but I did not recognize the number.

'Hello?'

'Mr. Parker? Charlie Parker?'

'Yes.'

'This is Detective Doug Santos over at the Six-Eight. Sir, I was wondering where you happen to be right now?'

The Six-Eight covered Bay Ridge, where I had once lived with my family. Cops from that precinct, as well as Walter Cole, had been the first on the scene on the night that Susan and Jennifer died.

'Why?' I asked. 'What's going on?'

'Please, just answer the question.'

'I'm in Brooklyn. Bensonhurst.'

His tone changed. Where at first he had merely been brusque and efficient, there was now a greater urgency to his words. I didn't know how it had happened, but in the space of a couple of seconds I sensed that I had become a potential suspect.

'Can you give me an address? I'd like to talk to you.'

'What's this about, Detective? It's late, and I've had a long day.'

'I'd prefer to speak to you in person. That address?'

'Hold on.'

Jimmy had just come back from the bathroom. He raised an eyebrow in inquiry as I covered the phone with my hand.

'It's a cop from the Six-Eight. He wants to talk to me. Is it okay with you if I meet him here? I'm getting a vibe from him that tells me I might be in need of an alibi.'

'Sure,' said Jimmy 'You get a name?'

'Santos.'

Jimmy shook his head. 'Don't know him. It's late, but, if you want, I can make some calls, find out what's happening.'

I gave Santos the address. He told me that he'd be there within the hour. Meanwhile, Jimmy had begun to call his own contacts, although Walter Cole remained an option if he came up short. He also disposed of the empty wine bottle while he made the first call, which turned out to be enough for him to find out something. When he hung up the phone, he was shaken.

'There's been a killing,' he said.

'Where?'

'You won't like it. 1219 Hobart. There's a dead man in the kitchen of your old house. You may have mixed feelings when you hear who it is. It's Mickey Wallace.'

Santos arrived half an hour later. He was tall and dark, and probably not much more than thirty years of age. He had the hungry look of someone who intended to ascend the career ladder as fast as humanly possible, and wouldn't be troubled by stomping on fingers on the way up. He looked disappointed when it emerged that I had an alibi for the entire evening, and a cop alibi at that. Still, he accepted a cup of coffee and, if he wasn't exactly friendly, he thawed enough not to hold the fact that I was no longer a viable suspect against me.

'You knew this guy?' he asked.

'He was planning to write a book about me.'

'And how did you feel about that?'

'Not so good. I tried to discourage him.'

'You mind if I ask how?' If Santos had been endowed with antennae, they'd have started twitching. I might not have killed Wallace myself, but I could have found someone else to do it for me.

'I told him that I wouldn't cooperate. I made sure that nobody else I was close to would cooperate with him either.'

'Looks like he didn't take the hint.' Santos sipped his coffee. He seemed pleasantly surprised at the taste. 'It's good coffee,' he said to Jimmy.

'Blue Mountain,' said Jimmy. 'Only the best.'

'You say you worked the Ninth?' said Santos.

'That's right.'

Santos turned his attention back to me. 'Your father worked the Ninth too, didn't he?'

I almost admired Santos's ability to come up to speed so quickly. Unless he'd been keeping tabs before now, someone must have read the salient details of my file over the phone to him as he'd driven to Bensonhurst.

'Right again,' I said.

'Catching up on old times?'

'Is that relevant to the case at hand?'

'I don't know. Is it?'

'Look, detective,' I said, 'I wanted Wallace to stop nosing around in my life, but I didn't want him dead. And if I was going to have him killed, I wouldn't have had it done in the room where my wife and daughter died, and I'd have made sure that I was far away when it happened.'

Santos nodded. 'Guess you're right. I know who you are. Whatever else people say about you, you're not dumb.'

'Nice to hear,' I said.

'Ain't it, though?' He sighed. 'I talked to some people before I came here. They said it wasn't your style.'

'They tell you what was my style?'

'They told me I didn't want to know, and I trusted them on it, but they confirmed that it wasn't what was done to Mickey Wallace.'

I waited.

'He was tortured with a blade,' said Santos. 'It wasn't sophisticated, but it was effective. My guess is that someone wanted him to talk. Once he'd told what he knew, his throat was cut.'

'Nobody heard anything?'

'No.'

'How was he found?'

'Patrol saw that the side gate to the house was open. The uniform went around back, saw a light in the kitchen: a small flashlight, probably Wallace's, but we'll have it checked for prints just in case.'

'So what next?'

'You free?'

'Right now?'

'No, later this week, for a date. The hell do you think?'

'I'm done here,' I said. I wasn't, of course. Had there been no other distractions, I would have stayed with Jimmy in the hope of squeezing every last detail out of him early the next morning, once I'd had a chance to absorb all that I had been told. I might have made him go through everything again, just to be certain that there was nothing he had omitted, but Jimmy was tired. He was a man who had spent an evening confessing not only his own sins, but the sins of others. He needed to sleep.

I knew what Santos was about to ask, and I knew that I would have to say yes, no matter how much it pained me.

'I'd like you to take a look at the house,' said Santos. 'The body's gone, but there's something I want you to see.'

'What?'

'Just take a look, okay?'

I agreed. I told Jimmy that I would probably return to speak to him over the next few days, and he said that he would be there. I should have thanked him, but I did not. He had held too much back for too long. As we left, he stood on the porch and watched us go. He raised a hand in farewell, but I did not respond.

I had not been back at Hobart Street for years, not since I had removed the last of my family's possessions from the house, sorting them into those that I would keep and those I would discard. I think that it was one of the hardest tasks I've ever performed, that service for the dead. With each item that I put aside – a dress, a hat, a doll, a toy – it seemed that I was betraying their memory. I should have kept it all, for these were things that they had touched and held, and something of them resided in these familiar objects, now rendered strange by loss. It took me three days. Even now, I can recall sitting for an hour on the edge of our bed with Susan's hairbrush in my hand, stroking the hairs that had tangled on its bristles. Was this too to be discarded, or should I keep it along with the lipstick that had molded itself to the shape of her, the blusher that retained the imprint of her finger upon it, the unwashed wineglass marked by her hands and her mouth? What was to be kept, and what was to be forgotten? In the end, perhaps I kept too much; that, or not enough. Too much to truly let go, and too little to lose myself entirely in their memory.

'You okay?' asked Santos as we stood at the gate.

'No,' I said. I saw TV cameras, and flashes exploded in my eyes, leaving red spots in their wake. I saw patrol cars, and men in uniform. And I was back in another time, my knee bruised and my trousers torn, my head in my hands and the image of the dead frozen on my retina.

'You want a minute?'

More flash-guns, closer now. I heard my name being called, but I did not react.

'No,' I said again, and I followed Santos to the back of the house.

It was the blood that did it. Blood on the kitchen floor, and blood on the walls. I could not enter the kitchen. Instead, I gazed upon it from outside until I felt my stomach begin to churn and sweat broke out on my face. I leaned against the cool woodwork of the house and closed my eyes until the nausea passed.

'Did you see it?' asked Santos.

'Yes,' I said.

The symbol had been drawn in Wallace's blood. His body had already been removed, but the position in which he was found had been marked. The symbol had been created just above where Wallace's head had rested. Nearby, the contents of a plastic folder had been scattered across the floor. I saw the photographs, and knew why Wallace had been here. He wanted to relive the killings, and their discovery.

'Do you know what that symbol means?' asked Santos.

'I've never seen it before.'

'Me neither, but I'm guessing that whoever did this signed his handiwork. We've searched the rest of the house. It's clean. Looks like it all happened in the kitchen.'

I turned to look at him. He was young. He probably didn't even understand the import of his own words. And yet I could not forgive him his crassness.

'We're finished here,' I said.

I walked away from him, and straight into another barrage of flashes, of camera lights and shouted questions. I froze for a moment as I realized that I had no way of leaving this place. I had come with Santos. I had no car of my own. I saw someone standing under a tree, a familiar figure: a big, tall man with short silver hair shorn in a military cut. In my confusion, it took me a moment to place him.

Tyrrell.

Tyrrell was here, a man who, even after I left the force, had made it clear to me that he believed I should be behind bars. Now he was striding toward me, outside the place where Mickey Wallace had been killed. Wallace had hinted that some people had been willing to talk to him, and I knew then that Tyrrell had been one of them. Some of the reporters saw him coming, and one of them, a guy named McGarry who'd been on the police beat for so long that his skin had a blue tinge, called Tyrrell's name. It was clear from the way the older man was moving that some kind of confrontation was about to occur, and it would take place in the glare of cameras and the red lights of handheld recording devices. That was how Tyrrell would want it.

'You sonofabitch,' he shouted. 'This is your fault.'

The bright, steady light of a TV camera was shining upon Tyrrell. He'd been drinking, but he was not intoxicated. I prepared to face him, and then a hand gripped my arm, and Jimmy Gallagher's voice said, 'Come on. Let's get you out of here.' Exhausted though he was, he had followed me here, and I was grateful to him for it. I saw the frustration in Tyrrell's face as he watched his quarry escape, denied his moment in front of the media, and then the more together reporters were turning to him for a comment, and he began to spill his bile.

Santos watched Parker depart, and saw Tyrrell begin talking to the reporters. Santos didn't know why Tyrrell was blaming Parker for what had happened, but he knew now that there was bad blood between the two men. He would talk to Tyrrell, in time. He turned away, and watched a man in a nicely cut dark suit who had slipped past the cordon and seemed to be staring intently at the receding lights of Jimmy Gallagher's car. Santos moved toward him.

'Sir, you have to step back behind the line.'

The man flipped the wallet in his palm to reveal a badge and a Maine State Police ID, but he didn't look at Santos, who felt his hackles rise as a consequence.

'Detective Hansen,' said Santos. 'Can I help you with something?'

Only when the car had turned onto Marine Avenue and was gone from sight did Hansen respond to Santos. His eyes, like his hair and his suit, were very dark.

'I don't think so,' he said, and walked away.

That night I slept in Jimmy Gallagher's house, in a clean bed in an otherwise unfurnished room, and in my dreams I saw a dark figure bent over Mickey Wallace, whispering and cutting, in the house on Hobart Street, and behind them, as in one film playing over another, each depicting the same setting from a similar angle but at different moments in time, I saw another man hunched over my wife, speaking softly to her as he cut her, the body of my dead child on the floor nearby waiting to be violated in turn. And then they were gone and there was only Wallace in the darkness, the blood bubbling from the wound in his throat, his body trembling. He was dying, alone and afraid, in a strange place . . .

A woman appeared in the doorway of the kitchen. She wore a summer dress, and a little girl stood beside her, gripping the thin material of her mother's clothing with her right hand. They walked to where Wallace lay, and the woman knelt beside him and stroked his face, and the child took his hand, and together they calmed him until his eyes closed and he left this world forever.

26

The girl's body had been wrapped in plastic sheeting, then weighted with a rock and dumped in a pond. It was discovered when a cow slipped into the water and one of its legs became tangled on the rope securing the plastic. As the cow, a Horned Hereford of no small value, was hauled from the pond, the body came with it.

Almost as soon as it was found, the locals in the small southern Idaho town of Goose Creek knew who it was. Her name was Melody McReady, and she had disappeared two years earlier. Her boyfriend, Wade Pearce, had been questioned in connection with her disappearance and, although the police had subsequently ruled him out as a suspect, he had killed himself one month after Melanie went missing, or so the official version went. He had shot himself in the head, even though he didn't appear to own a gun. Then again, people said, there was no understanding the nature of grief – or guilt, for there were those who felt that, regardless of anything the cops might have said, Wade Pearce had been responsible for whatever happened to Melody McReady, although such suspicions owed more to a general dislike of the Pearce family than to any real evidence of wrongdoing on Wade's part. Still, even those who believed Wade was innocent weren't too sorry when he shot himself, because Wade was a vicious jerk, just like the rest of the men in his family. Melody McReady had ended up with him because her own family was almost as screwed up as his was. Everybody knew that it would end in tears. They just hadn't expected bloodshed too, and a body eventually dragged from still waters on the leg of a cow.

DNA tests were conducted on the remains to confirm the identity of the young woman, and to find any possible traces left by whoever had killed her and dumped her in old Sidey's pond, although the investigators were skeptical of anything useful being revealed. Too much time had gone by, and the body had not been sealed in the plastic, so the fish and the elements had had their way with her.

To their surprise, then, one usable print was recovered from the plastic. It was submitted to AFIS, the FBI's fingerprint identification system. The detectives investigating the discovery of the body then sat back to wait. AFIS was overburdened by submissions from law enforcement agencies, and it could take weeks or months for a check to be conducted, depending upon the urgency of the case and the extent of the AFIS workload. As it happened, the print was checked within two weeks, but no match was found. Along with the print had come a photograph of a mark that had been found carved on a rock by the pond, a photograph that eventually found its way to Unit Five of the agency's National Security Division, the arm of the FBI responsible for collecting intelligence and carrying out counterintelligence actions related to national security and international terrorism.

Unit Five of the NSD was nothing more than a secure computer terminal in the New York field office at Federal Plaza. Its recent NSD designation, and the new title of Unit Five that came with it, were both flags of convenience, approved by the Office of the General Counsel in order to ensure that cooperation from law enforcement was swift and unconditional. Unit Five was responsible for all inquiries linked, however peripherally, to the investigation into the actions of the killer known as the Traveling Man, the individual responsible for the deaths of a number of men and women at the end of the 1990s, among them Susan and Jennifer Parker, wife and daughter of Charlie Parker. Unit Five had, over time, also absorbed earlier information on the death of a man named Peter Ackerman in New York in the late sixties, the shooting of an unidentified woman at Gerritsen Beach some months later, and the Pearl River killings involving William Parker, information that had been assembled by an ASAC, an assistant special agent in charge of the New York field office, and subsequently passed on to one of his successors. In addition, its files contained all known material on the cases with which Charlie Parker had been involved since he became a PI.

Other agencies, including the NYPD, were aware of Unit Five designations, but ultimately only two people had full access to the unit's records: the special agent in charge of the New York field office, Edgar Ross, and his assistant, Brad. It was this assistant who, twenty minutes after the initial referral, knocked on his boss's door with four sheets of paper in his hands.

'You're not going to like this,' he said.

Ross looked up as Brad closed the door behind him.

'I never like anything that you tell me. You never bring good news. You never even bring coffee. What have you got?'

Brad seemed reluctant to hand over the papers, like a child concerned about submitting flawed homework to his teacher.

'Fingerprint request submitted to AFIS, taken from a body dump in Idaho. Local girl, Melody McReady. She disappeared two years ago. Body was found in a pond, wrapped in plastic. The print came from the plastic.'

'And we got a match?'

'No, but there was something else: a photograph. That started ringing bells.'

'Why?'

Brad looked uneasy. Despite the fact that he had been with his boss for almost five years now, everything to do with Unit Five troubled him greatly. He'd read details of some of the other cases that had been automatically flagged for the unit's attention. Without exception, every one of them gave him the creeps. Similarly without exception, every one of them seemed to involve, peripherally or directly, the man named Charlie Parker.

'The prints didn't match, but the symbol did. It's been found on two earlier bodies. The first was the corpse of an unknown woman fished from the Shell Bank Creek in Brooklyn over forty years ago, after she was shot by a cop. She was never identified. The second match comes from the body of a teenage girl killed in a car at Pearl River about twenty-six years ago. Her name was Missy Gaines: a runaway from Jersey.'

Ross closed his eyes and waited for Brad to continue.

'Gaines was shot by Charlie Parker's father. The other woman was killed by his father's partner sixteen years earlier.'

Now, reluctantly, he proffered the papers. Ross examined the symbol on the first sheet from the McReady body dump and compared it to the symbol from the earlier killings.

'Aw, hell,' he said.

Brad reddened, even though he knew that he was not to blame for what was to come. 'It gets worse. Look at the second sheet. This was found hacked into a tree near the body of a kid called Bobby Faraday.'

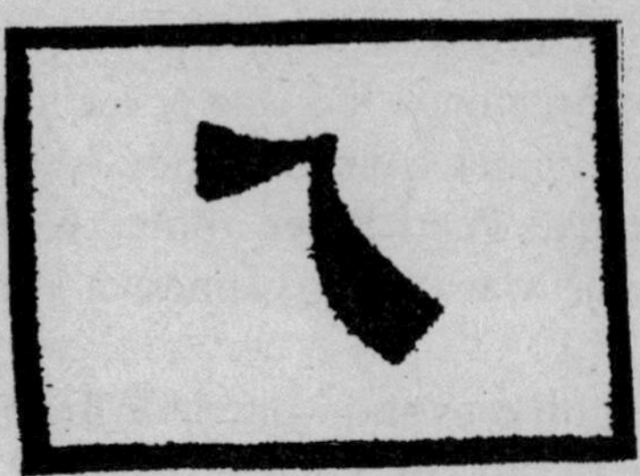

This time Ross swore more forcefully.

'The third one was cut into the wood beside the back door of the Faraday house. It was assumed that they'd killed themselves, but the chief, a guy named Dashut, didn't seem so sure. Took them five days to find it.'

'And we're only getting it now?'

'State police never passed it on. They're kind of territorial out there. Eventually, Dashut just got tired of the lack of progress and went over their heads.'

'Get me every piece of paper you can find on the McReady girl and the Faradays.'

'Already on their way,' said Brad. 'They should be here within the hour.'

'Go wait for them.'

Brad did as he was told.

Ross put the papers beside a set of photographs that had been on his desk since earlier that morning. They came from the previous night's crime scene at Hobart Street, and showed the symbol that had been drawn on the wall of the kitchen with Mickey Wallace's blood.

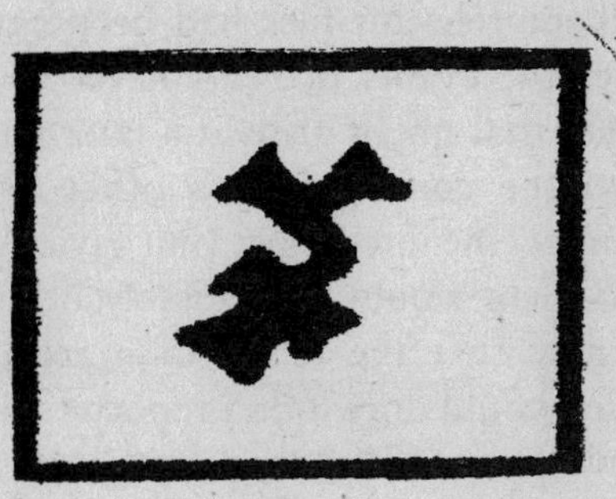

Ross had been informed of the murder within an hour of the discovery of Wallace's body, and had asked for evidence photos and copies of all documentation relating to the case to be made available to him by nine the following morning. As soon as he saw the symbol, Ross began covering the trail. Calls were made to One Police Plaza, and the symbol was scrubbed from the kitchen wall. All those who had been present at the scene were contacted and warned that the symbol was crucial to the case, and any mention of it outside the immediate investigative team would result in disciplinary action and, ultimately, dismissal without recourse to appeal. Additional locks were placed on all police files relating to the Pearl River killings, the shooting in Gerritsen Beach, and the accidental death of Peter Ackerman at the intersection of 78th and 1st nine months before. The lock prevented those files from being accessed without the express permission of both SAC Ross and the NYPD's Deputy Commissioners of Operations and Intelligence, even though all the relevant files had been carefully 'sterilized' after the events in Pearl River to ensure that any matches that might arise at a later date would be referred to the commissioner's office and, when it subsequently came into being, Unit Five. Any inquiries relating to them would immediately be red-flagged.

Ross knew that the death of a reporter, even a former one, would draw other reporters like flies, and the circumstances of Wallace's death, killed in a house where two high profile murders had been committed a decade earlier, would attract further attention. It was important to keep a lid on the investigation, but it couldn't be too tight or the more excitable reporters would start to sense a cover-up. Therefore, it was decided, in conjunction with One Police Plaza, that a suitably sympathetic 'face' would be presented to the media, and a series of carefully controlled unofficial briefings would disseminate enough information to keep the media at bay without actually divulging anything that might be considered dangerous to the conduct of the investigation.

Ross traced his fingers over the picture of the symbol on the wall, then retrieved copies of four different photos from the various files on his desk. Soon, its surface was covered with variations on the same images: symbols burned into flesh, cut into wood, and carved on stone.

Ross turned his chair to the window and looked out over the city. As he did so, he dialed a number using a secure line. A woman answered.

'Let me speak to the rabbi, please,' said Ross.

Within seconds, Epstein was on the line.

'It's Ross.'

'I was expecting your call.'

'You've heard, then?'

'I received a call last night to alert me.'

'Do you know where Parker is?'

'Mr. Gallagher gave him a bed for the night.'

'Is that common knowledge?'

'Not to the media. Mr. Gallagher had the foresight to remove his license plate when he realized that he might be forced to conduct a rescue.'

Ross was relieved. He knew that, in the absence of a New York lead, reporters had already attempted to track Parker through the bar in Maine in which he was working. A call to the field office in Portland requesting a drive-by at the Parker house had revealed two cars and a TV van parked outside, and the owner of the Great Lost Bear had told an agent that he'd been forced to put a 'No Reporters' sign on his door. To ensure that his request was complied with, he'd hired two large men in hastily made 'No Reporters' T-shirts to man the doors. According to the agent in question, those men had been waiting to start work when he'd visited the bar. They were, he said, without question two of the widest individuals he had ever seen in his life.

'And now?' asked Ross.

'Parker left the Gallagher house this morning,' said Epstein. 'I have no idea where he is.'

'Have you spoken to Gallagher?'

'He says that he doesn't know where Parker has gone, but he confirmed that Parker now knows everything.'

'Then he's going to come looking for you.'

'I'm prepared for that.'

'I have some material I'm sending over to you. You might find it interesting.'

'What kind of material?'

'The symbol that was found on the dead women at Shell Bank Creek and Pearl River? I've got three more versions of it in front of me, one from two years ago, the others from earlier this year. There were apparent killings involved in each case.'

'She's leaving signs, markers for the Other.'

'And now we've got her opposite number leaving his name in blood at Charlie Parker's old house, so he's doing the same.'

'Keep me informed, please.'

'I will.'

They exchanged farewells, and hung up. Ross

summoned Brad back into his presence and told him to put a trace on Parker's cell phone, and two men on Rabbi Epstein.

'I want to know where Parker is before the end of the day,' he said.

'Do you want him brought in?'

'No, just make sure nothing happens to him,' said Ross.

'A little late for that, isn't it, sir?' said Brad.

'Get the hell out of here,' said Ross, but he thought: from the mouths of babes . . .

27

I made the call to Epstein from a pay phone on Second Avenue outside an Indian restaurant that was offering an all-you-can-eat buffet that nobody wanted to eat, so in an effort to drum up business a sad-faced man in a bright polyester shirt had been posted at the door to hand out flyers that nobody wanted to read. It was raining, and the flyers hung damply from his hand.

'I've been expecting your call,' said Epstein.

'For a long time, from what I hear,' I replied.

'I take it that you'd like to meet.'

'You take it right.'

'Come to the usual place. Make it late. Nine o'clock. I look forward to seeing you again.'

Then he hung up.

I was staying in an apartment at 20th and 2nd, just above a locksmith's store. It extended over two decent-size rooms, with a separate kitchen that had never been used, and a bathroom that was just wide enough to accommodate a full rotation of the human body, as long as the body in question kept his arms at his sides. There was a bed, a couch, and a couple of easy chairs, and a TV with a DVD player but no cable. There was no phone, which was why I'd called Epstein from a pay phone. Even then, I'd stayed on the line for only the minimum time required to arrange our meeting. I had already taken the precaution of removing the battery from my cell phone, and had bought a temporary replacement from a drugstore.

I picked up some pastries from the bakery next door, then went back to the apartment. The landlord was sitting on a chair to the right of the living room window. He was cleaning a SIG pistol, which was not what landlords usually did in their tenants' apartments, unless the landlord in question happened to be Louis.

'So?' he said.

'I'm meeting him tonight.'

'You want company?'

'A second shadow wouldn't hurt.'

'Is that a racist remark?'

'I don't know. You do minstrel songs?'

'Nope, but I brought you a gun.' He reached into a leather bag and tossed a small pistol on the couch.

I removed the gun from its holster. It was about seven inches long, and weighed less than two pounds.

'Kimber Ultra Ten Two,' said Louis. 'Ten-shot box magazine. Rear corner of the butt is sharp, so watch it.'

I put the gun back in its holster and handed it to him.

'You're kidding,' he said.

'No, I'm not. I want my license to carry back. I get

caught with an unregistered firearm, and I'm done. They'll flay me alive, then toss what's left in the sea.'

Angel appeared from the kitchen. He had a pot of coffee in one hand.

'You think whoever killed Wallace tortured him to find out his taste in music?' he said. 'He was cut so that he'd tell what he'd learned about you.'

'We don't know that for sure.'

'Yeah, like we don't know evolution for sure, or climate change, or gravity. He was killed in your old house, while investigating you, and then someone signed off on it in blood. Pretty soon, that someone is going to try to do to you what was done to Wallace.'

'That's why Louis is going to stick with me tonight.'

'Yeah,' said Louis, ''cause if I get caught with a gun, then it's okay. Black man always slides on gun charges.'

'I heard that,' said Angel. 'I think it's a self-defense thing: brother-on-brother crime.'

He took the bag of pastries, tore it open, and laid it on the small, scarred coffee table. Then he poured me a cup of coffee, and took a seat beside Louis as I told them everything that I had learned from Jimmy Gallagher.

The Orensanz Center had not changed since last I had visited it some years earlier. It still dominated its section of Norfolk Street, between East Houston and Stanton, a neo-gothic structure designed by Alexander Seltzer in the nineteenth century for the arriving German Jews, his vision inspired by the great cathedral of

Cologne and the tenets of German romanticism. Then it was known as the Anshei Cheshed, the 'People of Kindness,' before that congregation merged with the Temple Emanuel, coinciding with the migration of the German Jews from Kleine Deutschland in Lower Manhattan to the Upper East Side. Their place was taken by Jews from eastern and southern Europe, and the neighborhood became a densely populated warren thronged by those who were still struggling to cope with this new world both socially and linguistically. Anshei Chesed became Anshei Slonim, after a town in Poland, and thus it remained until the 1960s, when the building began to fall into disrepair, only to be rescued by the sculptor Angel Orensanz and converted into a cultural and educational center.

I did not know what the Rabbi Epstein's connection to the Orensanz Center was. Whatever status he enjoyed, it was unofficial yet powerful. I had seen some of the secrets that the center hid below its beautiful interior, and Epstein was the keeper of them.

When I entered, there was only an old man sweeping the floor. He had been there when last I visited, and he had been sweeping then too. I guessed that he was always there: cleaning, polishing, watching. He looked at me and nodded in recognition.

'The rabbi is not here,' he said, instinctively understanding that there could be no other reason for my presence in this place.

'I called him,' I said. 'He's expecting me. He'll be here.'

'The rabbi is not here,' he repeated with a shrug.

I took a seat. There didn't seem to be any point in prolonging the argument. The old man sighed, and went back to his sweeping.

Half an hour passed, then an hour. There was no sign of Epstein. When at last I stood to leave, the old man was seated at the door, his broom standing upright between his knees like a banner held aloft by some ancient, forgotten retainer.

'I told you,' he said.

'Yeah, you did.'

'You should listen better.'

'I get that a lot.'

He shook his head sorrowfully. 'The rabbi,' he said, 'he does not come here so much now.'

'Why?'

'He has fallen out of favor, I think. Or perhaps it is too dangerous for him now, for all of us. It is a shame. The rabbi is a good man, a wise man, but some say that what he does is not fit for this, this *Bet Shalom*.'

He must have noticed my puzzlement. 'A house of peace,' he explained. 'Not *Sheol*. Not here.'

'*Sheol?*'

'Hell,' he said. 'Not here. No longer here.'

And he tapped his foot meaningfully on the floor, indicating the hidden places beneath. When last I had visited the Orensanz Center, Epstein had shown me a cell beneath the basement of the building. In it, he had secured a thing that called itself Kittim, a demon that wished to be a man, or a man who believed himself to be a demon. Now, if what the old man was saying was true, Kittim was gone from this place, banished along with Epstein, his captor.

'Thank you,' I said.

'*Bevakashah*,' he replied. '*Betakh ba-Adonai va'asei-tov.*'

I left him there, and stepped outside into the cold spring sunlight. I had come here for nothing, it seemed. Epstein was no longer comfortable being at the Orensanz Center, or the center was no longer willing to countenance his presence. I looked around, half expecting to see him waiting nearby, but there was no sign of him. Something had happened: he was not coming. I tried to pick out Louis, but there was no trace of him either. Still, I knew he was close. I walked down the steps and headed toward Stanton. After a minute, I felt someone begin to fall into step beside me. I looked to my left and saw a young Jewish man wearing a skullcap and a loose fitting leather jacket. He kept his right hand in his jacket pocket. I thought I could discern the gunsight of a small pistol digging into the material. Behind me, another young man was shadowing my footsteps. They both looked strong and fast.

'You took your time in there,' said the man to my left. He had the slightest hint of an accent. 'Who knew you had such patience?'

'I've been working on it,' I said.

'It was much needed, I hear.'

'Well, I'm still working on it, so maybe you'd like to tell me where we're going.'

'We thought you might like to eat.'

He steered me on to Stanton. Between a deli that didn't appear to have bought fresh stock since the previous summer, judging by the number of dead insects scattered among the bottles and jars in the window, and a tailor who seemed to regard silk and cotton as passing fads that would ultimately bow down before artificial fibers, was a small kosher diner. It was dimly lit, with four tables inside, the wood dark and scarred by decades of hot coffee cups and burning cigarettes. A sign on the glass in Hebrew and English announced that it was closed.

Only one table was occupied. Epstein sat in a chair facing the door, his back to the wall. He was wearing a black suit with a white shirt and a black tie. A dark overcoat dangled from a hook behind his head, topped by a narrow-brimmed black hat, as though their occupant were not sitting below them but had recently dematerialized, leaving only his clothing as evidence of his previous existence.

One of the young men grabbed a chair and carried it outside, then took a seat with his back to the window. His companion, the one who had spoken to me on the street, sat inside but on the opposite side of the door. He did not look back at us.

There was a woman behind the counter. She was probably in her early forties, but in the shadows of the little diner she could have passed for a decade younger. Her hair was very dark, and when I passed her I could see no trace of gray in it. She was also beautiful, and smelled faintly of cinnamon and cloves. She nodded at me, but she did not smile.

I took the seat across from Epstein but turned so that I also had a wall against my back, and could see the door.

'You could have told me that you were *persona non grata* at the Orensanz Center,' I said.

'I could, but it would not have been true,' said Epstein. 'A decision was made, one that was entirely mutual. Too many people pass through its doors. It was not fair, or wise, to put them at risk. I am sorry to have kept you waiting, but there was a purpose: we were watching the streets.'

'And did you find anything?'

Epstein's eyes twinkled. 'No, but had we ventured further into the shadows then something, or someone, might have found us. I suspected that you would not come alone. Was I right?'

'Louis is nearby.'

'The enigmatic Louis. It is good to have such friends, but bad to have such need of them.'

The woman brought food to our table: *baba ghanoush* with small pieces of pitta bread; *burekas*; and chicken cooked with vinegar, olives, raisins, and garlic, with some couscous on the side. Epstein gestured to the food, but I did not eat.

'What?' he said.

'About the Orensanz Center. I don't think I believe that you're on such good terms after all.'

'Really?'

'You don't have a congregation. You don't teach. You travel everywhere with at least one gunman. Today you have two. And there was something you said to me, a long time ago. We were talking, and you used the term "Jesus Christ." None of that strikes me as very orthodox. I can't help but feel that you might have earned a little disapproval.'

'Orthodox?' He laughed. 'No, I am a most *un*orthodox Jew, but still a Jew. You're a Catholic, Mr. Parker—'

'A bad Catholic,' I corrected.

'I'm not in a position to make such judgments. Still, I am aware that there are degrees of Catholicism. I fear that there are many more degrees of Judaism. Mine is cloudier than most, and sometimes I wonder if I have spent too long divorced from my own people. I find myself using terms that I have no business using, slips of the tongue that embarrass me, and worse, or entertaining doubts that do not entertain me. So, perhaps it would be true to say that I left Orensanz before I was asked to leave. Would that make you more comfortable?' He gestured once again at the food. 'Now eat. It's good. And our hostess will be offended if you do not taste what she has prepared.'

I hadn't arranged the meeting with Epstein to play semantic games, or to sample the local cuisine, but he had a way of manipulating conversations to his own satisfaction, and I had been at a disadvantage from the moment I traveled here to meet him. Yet there had been no choice. I could not imagine Epstein, or his minders, permitting an alternative arrangement.

So I ate. I inquired politely after Epstein's health

and that of his family. He asked about Sam and Rachel, but he did not pry further into our domestic arrangements. I suspected he was well aware that Rachel and I were no longer together. In fact, I now believed that there was little about my life of which Epstein was not aware, and it had always been that way, right from the moment my father approached him about the mark on the man who died beneath the wheels of a truck, and whose partner had subsequently killed my birth mother.

When we were done, baklava was brought to the table. I was offered coffee, and accepted. I added a little milk to it, brought to me in a sealed container, and Epstein sighed.

'Such a luxury,' he said. 'To be able to enjoy a coffee with milk so soon after one's meal.'

'You'll have to forgive my ignorance . . .'

'One of the laws of *kashrut*,' said Epstein. 'One is prohibited from eating dairy products within six hours of consuming meat. Exodus: "Thou shalt not seethe a kid in his mother's milk." You see: I am more orthodox than you might think.'

The woman hovered nearby, waiting. I thanked her for her kindness, and for the food. Despite myself, I had eaten more than I had intended. This time, she did smile, but she did not speak. Epstein made a small gesture with his left hand, and she retreated.

'She's a deaf mute,' said Epstein, when her back was turned. 'She reads lips, but she will not read ours.'

I glanced at the woman. Her face was turned from

us, and she was examining a newspaper, her head bent.

Now that the time had arrived to confront him, I felt something of my anger at him fade. He had kept so much hidden for so long, just as Jimmy Gallagher had done, but there were reasons for it.

'I know that you've been asking questions,' he said. 'And I know that you have received some answers.'

When I spoke, I thought that I sounded like a petulant teenager.

'You should have told me when we first met.'

'Why? Because you believe now that you had a right to know?'

'I had a father, and two mothers. They all died for me.'

'And that was precisely why you could not be told,' said Epstein. 'What would you have done? You were still an angry, violent man when we met: grief-stricken, bent on revenge. You could not be trusted. There are some who would say that you still cannot be trusted. And remember, Mr. Parker: I had lost my son when first we met. My concerns were for him, not for you. Pain and grief are not your exclusive preserves.

'But, still, you are right. You should have been told before now, but perhaps you chose the time that was right for you. You decided when to begin asking the questions that led you here. Most have been answered for you. I will do my best to deal with the rest.'

Now that the time had come, I was not sure where to start.

'What do you know of Caroline Carr?'

'Next to nothing,' he said. 'She came from what is now a suburb of Hartford, Connecticut. Her father died when she was six, and her mother when she was nineteen. There are no surviving relatives. If she had been bred to be anonymous, one could not have asked for more.'

'But she wasn't anonymous. Someone came looking for her.'

'So it seems. Her mother died in a house fire. Subsequent investigations revealed that it might have been started deliberately.'

'Might have been?'

'A cigarette smoldering at the bottom of a trash can, with papers piled on top of it, and a gas stove that was not turned off fully. It could have been an accident, except neither Caroline nor her mother smoked.'

'A visitor?'

'There were no visitors that night, according to Caroline. Her mother sometimes entertained gentlemen, but on the night that she died only she and Caroline were asleep in the house. Her mother drank. She was asleep on the couch when the fire broke out, and was probably dead before the flames reached her. Caroline escaped by climbing out of an upstairs window. When we met, she told me that she saw two people watching the house from the woods while it burned: a man and a woman. They were holding hands. But by that time someone had raised the alarm, and there were neighbors rushing to help her, and the fire trucks were on their way. Her main concern was for her mother, but the first floor had already been engulfed. When she thought again about the man and the woman, they were gone.

'She told me that she believed the couple in the woods had started the fire, but when she tried to tell the police of what she had seen they dismissed the sighting as irrelevant, or as the imaginings of a grief-stricken young woman. But Caroline saw them again, shortly after her mother's funeral, and became convinced that they intended to do to her what they had done to her mother; or that, in fact, she might have been the target all along.'

'Why would she think that?'

'A sense she had. The way they looked at her, the way she *felt* when they looked at her. Call it a survival instinct. Whatever the reason for it, she left town after her mother's funeral, intending to find work in Boston. There, someone tried to push her under a T train. She felt a hand on her back, and teetered on the edge of the platform before a young woman pulled her to safety. When she looked around, she saw a man and a woman moving toward the exit. The woman glanced back at her, and Caroline said she recognized her from Hartford. The second time she saw them was at South Station, as she boarded a train to New York. She thought that they were watching her from the platform, but they didn't follow her.'

'Who were they?'

'We did not know then, and we still do not know for sure now. Oh, we know the name of the man who died beneath the wheels of a truck, and of the boy and girl your father killed at Pearl River, but those names ultimately proved useless. The confirmation of their identities did nothing to explain how they came to be hunting Caroline Carr, or you.'

'My father believed that Missy Gaines and the woman who killed my mother were the same person,' I said. 'By extension, he must have believed that Peter Ackerman and the boy who died with Missy Gaines were also the same. How is that possible?'

'We have both witnessed strange things in the years since we first met,' Epstein replied. 'Who knows what we should believe, and what we should discount? Nevertheless, let us look at the most logical, or plausible, explanation first: over a period of more than forty years, someone has repeatedly dispatched a pair of killers, a man and a woman, on a series of assassinations aimed at you, or those close to you, including the woman who was your birth mother. When one couple died, another eventually replaced them. These killers were distinguished by marks on their arms, one for the man and another for the woman, just here.' He indicated a point halfway between his wrist and his elbow on his left forearm. 'There is no reason that we can find for why a succession of couples have been chosen to do this.

'The investigations into Missy Gaines, Joseph Dryden, and Peter Ackerman revealed that all led entirely normal existences for most of their lives. Ackerman was a family man, Missy Gaines a model teenager, Dryden already a tearaway, but no worse than many others. Then, at some point, their behavior changed. They cut themselves off from family and friends. They found a member of the opposite sex previously unknown to them, formed a bond, and went hunting, apparently first for Caroline Carr, and then, in the cases of Gaines and Dryden, for you. So that is the logical explanation: disparate couples, linked only by their intent to do harm to you and your family, either of their own volition or acting on the will of another.'

'But you don't believe the logical explanation.'

'No, I do not.'

Epstein reached behind him and rummaged in the pocket of his overcoat, emerging with a piece of photocopied paper that he unfolded on the table. It was a copy of a scientific article, and it showed an insect in flight: a wasp.

'So, what do you know of wasps, Mr. Parker?'

'They sting.'

'True. Some, the largest group in *Hymenoptera*, are also parasitic. They target host insects – caterpillars, spiders – either by laying eggs externally that attack the host from outside, or by inserting eggs *into* the host body. Eventually, the larvae emerge and consume the host. Such behavior is relatively common in nature, and not just among wasps. The ichneumon fly, for example, uses spiders and aphids to host its young. When it injects its eggs, it also injects a toxin that paralyzes the host. The young then consume the host from the inside out, starting with the organs least necessary for survival, such as fat and entrails, in order to keep the host alive for as long as possible before finally progressing to the essential organs. Eventually, all that is left behind is an empty shell. The manner of consumption does display a certain instinctive understanding that a live host is better than a dead one, but otherwise it's all rather primitive, if undeniably nasty.'

He leaned forward, tapping the picture of the wasp.

'Now, there is a variety of orb spider known as *Plesiometa argyra*, found in Costa Rica. It too is preyed upon by a wasp, but in an interesting way. The wasp attacks the spider, temporarily paralyzing it while it lays its eggs in the tip of the spider's abdomen. Then it leaves, and the spider's ability to move is restored. It continues to function as it has always done, building its webs, trapping insects, even as the wasp larvae cling to its abdomen and feed on its juices through small punctures. This continues for perhaps two weeks, and then something very odd occurs: the spider's behavior changes. Somehow, by means unknown, the larvae, using chemical secretions, compel the spider to alter its web construction. Instead of a round web, the spider builds a smaller, reinforced platform. Once that is complete, the larvae kill their host and cocoon themselves in the new web, safe from wind, rain, and predatory ants, and the next stage of their development begins.'

He relaxed slightly. 'Suppose we were to substitute wandering spirits for wasps, and humans for spiders, then, perhaps, we might begin to have some understanding of how seemingly ordinary men and women could, at some point, change utterly, slowly dying inside while remaining unchanged without. An interesting theory, don't you think?'

'Interesting enough to get a man banned from the local cultural center.'

'Or committed, if he were unwise enough to speak such thoughts too loudly, but this is not the first time that you have heard of such things: spirits flitting from body to body, and people who apparently live beyond their allotted span, slowly rotting yet never dying. Is that not right?'

And I thought of Kittim, trapped in his cell, retreating into himself like an insect hibernating even as his body withered; and of a creature named Brightwell glimpsed in a centuries-old painting, in a photograph from the Second World War and, finally, in this time as he hunted for a being like himself, human in form but not in nature. Yes, I knew of what Epstein was speaking.

'The difference between a spider and a human, though, is the matter of consciousness, of awareness,' said Epstein. 'Since we must assume that the spider has no awareness of its own identity as a spider, then, the pain of its own consumption aside, it has no understanding of what is happening to it as its behavior alters and, ultimately, it begins to die. But a human being *would* become aware of the changes in its physiology or, more correctly, its psychology, its behavior. It would be troubling, at the very least. The host might even consult a doctor, or a psychiatrist. Tests could be carried out. An effort would be made to discover the source of the imbalance.'

'But we're not talking about parasitic flies, or wasps.'

'No, we're talking about something that cannot be seen, but is consuming the host just as surely as the wasp larvae consume the spider, except in this case it is the identity that is being taken over, the *self*. And something in us would slowly become aware of this *other*, this thing preying upon us, and we would fight back at the darkness as it began to consume us.'

I thought for a moment.

'You used the word "apparently" earlier,' I said, 'as in "apparently" they were targeting my birth mother. Why "apparently"?'

'Well, if Caroline Carr was their primary target, why then did they return sixteen years later only to die at Pearl River? The answer, it would seem, is that they were not trying to kill Caroline Carr, but the child she was carrying.'

'Again: why?'

'I don't know, except that you are a threat to them, and you have always been a threat. Perhaps even they do not know for certain the nature of the threat that you pose, but they sense it and they react to it, and their purpose is to extinguish it. They were trying to kill you, Mr. Parker, and they probably believed that they had succeeded, for a time, until they found out that they were wrong, and you had been hidden from them, so they were forced to return and rectify their mistake.'

'And failed a second time.'

'And failed,' echoed Epstein. 'But in the years since then you have begun to draw attention to yourself. You have encountered men and women who share something of their nature, if not their purpose, and it may be that whoever, or whatever, dispatched these things has begun to notice you. It's not hard to draw the necessary conclusion, which is—'

'That they'll return to try again,' I finished.

'Not "will return,"' said Epstein. 'They *have* returned.'

And from beneath the description of the wasp and its actions he withdrew a photograph. It showed the kitchen at Hobart Street, and the symbol that had been painted in blood upon its wall.

'This is also the mark that was found on the body of Peter Ackerman, and on the boy, Dryden, killed by your father at Pearl River,' he said.

Then he added more photographs. 'This is the mark

that was found on the bodies of Missy Gaines and your birth mother's killer. It has since been found at three more crime scenes, one of them old, two of them recent.'

'How recent?'

'Weeks.'

'But unconnected to me.'

'Yes, it would appear so.'

'What are they doing?'

'Leaving signs. For each other and, perhaps, in the case of Hobart Street, for you.'

He smiled, and there was pity in that smile.

'You see, something has returned, and it wants you to know it.'

V

For the dead travel fast.

Bram Stoker (1847–1912),
Dracula (after Burger's 'Lenore')

28

The drunks were out in force. A hockey game had been played that night, and the bar was a magnet for fans because one of the owners, Ken Harbaruk, had enjoyed brief spells with both the Toronto Maple Leafs and the Bruins before a motorcycle accident put an end to his career. He used to say that it was the best thing that could have happened to him, under the circumstances. He was good, but he wasn't good enough. Eventually, he knew, he would have found himself in the minors, playing for nickels and trying to pick up women who were easily impressed in bars a lot like the one he now owned. Instead, he'd been compensated well for his injuries, and had plowed the money into a half-share in a bar that seemed destined to guarantee him the kind of comfortable retirement that would have been denied him had he been able to continue playing. In addition, had he wished, he could still have picked up women who were easily impressed, or so he told himself, but more usually he found himself thinking about his quiet apartment and his soft bed as the long nights in the bar drew to a close. He had a comfortable yet casual relationship with a lawyer who was a well-preserved fifty-one.

They each had homes of their own, and they alternated overnight stays from weekend to weekend, although he sometimes wished for something a little more defined. He would have liked for her to move in with him, but he knew that wasn't what she wanted. She valued her independence. At first, he thought that she was keeping him at a remove in order to ascertain how serious he was about her. Now, after three years, he realized he was being kept at a distance because that was exactly how she wanted it, and if he desired something more then he would have to look elsewhere. He figured he was too old to look for someone else, and he should be thankful for what he had. He was, he felt, reasonably lucky, and reasonably content.

Yet, on nights like this, when the Bruins were playing and the bar was filled with men and women who were too young to remember him, or old enough to recall how inconsequential his career had been, Harbaruk experienced a nagging sense of regret at the path his life had taken which he hid by being even louder and more boisterous than usual.

'But them's the breaks,' he had told Emily Kindler after he'd interviewed her for the waitress job. In fact, she'd hardly been required to say a word. All she had to do was listen and nod occasionally as he retold the story of his life, altering her expression as required to look sympathetic, interested, angry, or happy, according to the dictates of the plot. She believed that she knew his type: genial; smarter than he appeared to be, but with no illusions about his intelligence; the kind of guy who might fantasize about making a pass at her but would never act upon it, and would feel guilty for even thinking such a thing. He told her about the lawyer, and mentioned the fact that he had been married way back, but it hadn't worked out. If he was surprised by how much he was willing to share with her, then she was not. She had found that men wanted to tell her things. They exposed their inner selves to her, and she did not know why.

'Never was able to talk much to women,' Harbaruk told her, as the interview drew to a close. 'Might not seem that way now, but it's true.'

The girl was unusual, he thought. She looked like she could do with a little fattening up, and her arms were so thin that he was pretty sure he could encircle the widest point of her biceps with one hand, but she was undeniably pretty, and what he had first taken for fragility, to the extent that he had almost dismissed the possibility of hiring her as soon as he set eyes on her, was revealing itself to be something more complex and ineffable. There was strength there. Maybe not physical, although he was starting to believe that she was not as weak as she looked, because one thing Ken Harbaruk had always been good at was judging the strength of an opponent, but an inner steeliness. Harbaruk sensed that the girl had been through some hard times, but they hadn't broken her.

'Well, you talked okay to me,' she said.

She smiled. She wanted the job.

Harbaruk shook his head, knowing that he was

being played, but he still found that he was blushing slightly. He felt the heat rise in his cheeks.

'It's nice of you to say,' he replied. 'It's just a shame that everything in life can't be handled with an interview over a soda.'

He stood, and extended his hand. She took it, and they shook.

'You seem like a good kid. Talk to Shelley over there. She's the bar manager. She'll fix you up with some shifts and we'll see how you get along.'

She thanked him, and that was how she came to be waitressing in Ken Harbaruk's Sports Bar and Restaurant – Local Home of the NHL, as the sign above the door announced in big black-on-white letters. Beside it, a neon hockey player shot a puck then raised his hands in the air in triumph. The hockey player was dressed in red and white, a nod to Ken's Polish ancestry. He was always being asked if he was related to Nick Harbaruk, who had enjoyed a career spanning sixteen years, from 1961 to 1977, including four seasons with the Pittsburgh Penguins in the 1970s. He wasn't, but it didn't bother him to be asked. He was proud of his fellow Poles who had succeeded on the ice: Nick, Pete Stemkowski, John Miszuk, Eddie Leier among the old-timers, and Czerkawski, Oliwa, and Sidorkiewicz among the new boys. There were photographs of them on the wall below one of the TVs, part of a little shrine dedicated to Poland.

The shrine was close to where the girl was now picking up glasses and taking last orders. It had been a long night, and she had earned every lousy dollar in tips. Her shirt smelled of spilled beer and fried food, and the soles of her feet were aching. She just wanted to finish up, go home, and sleep. She had a day off tomorrow, the first day since she had arrived here that would not involve working at either the coffee shop, or the bar, or both. She intended to sleep late, and do her laundry. Chad, the young man who had been circling her, had asked her out on a date, and she had tentatively agreed to go to a movie with him, even though her thoughts were still filled with memories of Bobby Faraday and what had befallen him. Still, she was lonely, and she figured a movie couldn't hurt too much.

Ken killed the post-match commentary in an effort to move folks more quickly along, and replaced it with the news. The girl liked the fact that life didn't begin and end with sports for Ken. He read some, and he knew about what was going on in the world. He had opinions on politics, history, art. According to Shelley, he had too many damn opinions, and he was too willing to share them with others. Shelley was in her fifties, and married to an amiable slob who thought that the sun rose when Shelley awoke and that nightfall was the world's way of mourning the fact that soon it would be deprived of the sound of Shelley's voice while she slept. He was already seated at the bar, sipping a light beer as he waited to drive her home. Shelley was fair and worked hard, but as a consequence she didn't like to see any of her 'girls' working less hard than she did. She worked three nights behind the bar, sometimes overlapping with Ken if there was a game on. The girl had so far worked for her five times, and after the first night she had been grateful for the comparative peace of the third night when Ken had taken charge and everything had been a little more relaxed, if also a little less efficient and a little less profitable.

There were only two men left in her section, and they had reached that point of near intoxication where, had the bar not been about to close, she would have been obliged to cut them off. She could tell that they were about to progress from melancholy to mean, and she would be relieved when they were gone. Now, as she cleared away the glasses and empty chicken wing baskets from the table to their right, she felt a pair of taps on her back.

'Hey,' said one of the men. 'Hey, honey. Hit us again.'

She ignored him. She didn't like men touching her like that.

The other one giggled, and sang a snatch of a Britney lyric.

'Hey.'

The tap was harder this time. She turned.

'We're closing,' she said.

'No, you ain't.' He ostentatiously examined his watch. 'We got another five minutes yet. You can see us right for two more beers.'

'I'm sorry, guys. I can't serve you any more.'

Above their heads, the news story on the TV changed. She glanced at it. There were reporters and police cars. Photographs were superimposed upon the scene: a man, a woman, and a child. She wondered what had happened to them. She tried to figure out if it was someplace local, then saw NYPD on the side of one of the cars and knew that it was not. Still, it couldn't be anything good, not if they were showing photographs. That woman and the little girl were either missing or dead, maybe the man too.

'What do you mean you can't give us no more?'

It was the smaller yet more belligerent of the drunks. He wore a Patriots shirt smeared with ketchup and wing juice, and his eyes were glazed behind his cheap spectacles. He was in his mid-thirties, and there was no sign of a wedding ring. A sour smell rose from him. It had been there right from the moment he arrived. At first, she had thought it was because he didn't wash, but now she suspected that it was a substance he secreted, a contaminant from within that mingled with his sweat.

'Let it go, Ronnie,' said his friend, who was taller and fatter and also far drunker than his buddy. 'I got to hit the head.' He stumbled by her, mumbling an apology. He wore a black T-shirt with a white arrow that pointed toward his groin.

The picture on the screen changed again. She looked up. Another man, different from the first, was caught in the glare of the lights. He looked confused, as though he'd wandered out of his house expecting to find quiet, not chaos.

Wait, she thought. Wait. I know you. I *know* you. It was an old memory, one that she couldn't quite place. She felt something stir inside her. There was a buzzing in her head. She tried to shake it away, but it grew louder. Her mouth filled with saliva, and there was a growing pain between her eyes, as though a pin were being inserted into her skull through the bridge of her nose. Her fingertips began to itch.

'Look at me when I'm talking to you,' said Ronnie, but she ignored him. She was experiencing flashes of memory, scenes from a series of old movies playing in her head, except in each one she was the star.

Killing Melody McReady in a pond in Idaho, holding her head beneath the water as her back bucked and the last bubbles of air broke the surface . . .

Telling Wade Pearce to close his eyes and open his mouth, promising him something nice, a big surprise, and then jamming the gun between his teeth and pulling the trigger, because she had been wrong about him. She thought he might have been the one – what one? – *but he was not, and he had begun asking questions about Melody, his girlfriend, and she had smelt the suspicion upon him . . .*

Bobby Faraday, kneeling in the dirt before her, weeping, pleading with her to come back to him, as she walked behind him, took the rope from his saddle bag, and slipped the cord lightly around his neck. Bobby wouldn't leave her alone. He wouldn't stop talking. He was weak. He had already tried to kiss her, to hold her, but his touch repelled her now because she knew that he wasn't the one for her. She had to stop him from talking, from trying to act upon his desires. So the rope tightened and Bobby – strong, lean Bobby – struggled against her, but she was strong, so strong, stronger than anyone could have imagined . . .

A hand on a stove, and the soft hiss as the gas began to seep out, just as it had seeped out decades before in a house owned by a woman named Jackie Carr; the girl waiting for the Faradays to die, one window open just enough so that she could take breaths of night air. And then noise from the bedroom, a body tumbling to the floor: Kathy Faraday, almost overcome by fumes, trying to crawl to the kitchen to turn off the gas, her husband already dead beside her. The girl had been forced to sit on Kathy's back, her mouth covered to protect her from the fumes, until she was sure that the woman was no more . . .

Leaving signs; carving a name – her name, her real name – in places where others might find it. No, not others: the Other, the One she loved, and who loved her in return.

And dying: dying as the bullets ripped into her and she tumbled into cold water; dying while the Other bled upon her, as she slumped forward in the car seat and her head came to rest upon his lap. Dying, over and over again, yet always returning . . .

A hand tugged on her arm. 'You fucking bitch, I said—'

But Emily wasn't listening. These were not her memories. They belonged to another, one who was not her yet was in her, and at last she understood that the threat from which she had been fleeing for so long, the shadow that had haunted her life, had not been an external force, an outside agency. It had been inside her all along, waiting for its moment to emerge.

Emily raised her hands to her head, pressing her fists into the sides of her skull. She closed her eyes tightly and ground her teeth as she struggled against the gathering clouds, trying in vain to save herself, to hold on to her identity, but it was too late. The transformation was occurring. She was no longer the girl she had once believed herself to be, and soon she would cease to be forever. She had a vision of a young woman drowning, just as Melody McReady had drowned, fighting against the coming oblivion, and she was both that woman and the one who was holding her down, forcing her beneath the water. The dying girl broke the water for the last time and looked up, and in her eyes was reflected a being both old and terrible, a black, sexless thing with dark wings that unfurled from its back, blocking out all light, a creature that was so ugly it was almost beautiful, or so beautiful that it had no place in this world.

It.

And Emily died beneath its hand, drowning in black water, lost forever. She had always been lost, right from the moment of her birth when this strange, wandering spirit had chosen her body for its abode, hiding in the shadows of her consciousness, waiting for the truth of itself to be revealed.

Now the thing that she had become looked down at the little man who was holding on to her arm. She could no longer understand what he was saying. His words were merely white noise in her ear. It didn't matter.

Nothing that he said mattered. She smelled him, and sensed the foulness inside him that had forced the stench from his pores. A serial abuser of women. A man filled with hatred and strange, violent appetites.

Yet she did not judge him, just as she would no more have judged a spider for consuming a fly, or a dog for gnawing on its bone. It was in his nature, and she found its echo in her own.

His grip tightened. Spittle flew from his mouth, but she saw only the movements of his lips. He started to rise, then paused. He seemed to realize that something had changed, that what he thought was familiar had suddenly become desperately alien. She freed her arm and moved in closer to him. She placed the palms of her hands on his face, then leaned in to kiss him, her open mouth closing on his, ignoring the bitterness of him, the stink of his breath, his decaying teeth and yellowed gums. He struggled against her for a moment, but she was too strong for him. She breathed into him, her eyes fixed on his, and she showed him what would become of him when he died.

Shelley did not see her go, nor Harbaruk, nor any of the others who had worked alongside her. Had their memories of that night been played back for them, displayed on a screen so that they could see all that had passed before their eyes, the girl's departure would have appeared as a grayish mass moving through the bar, an excised form loosely resembling a human being.

The big man in the arrow T-shirt returned from the

men's room. His friend was sitting where he had left him, staring vacantly at the wall, his back to the bar.

'Time to go, Ronnie,' he said. He patted Ronnie on the back, but the smaller man did not move.

'Hey, Ronnie.' He stepped in front of him, and stopped speaking. Even in his drunken state, he knew that his friend was broken beyond salvation.

Ronnie was weeping tears of blood and water, and his mouth was moving, forming the same words over and over. Every capillary had burst in his eyes, and the whites had turned entirely red, twin black suns set against their skies. He was whispering, but his friend could still hear what he was saying.

'I'm sorry,' said Ronnie. 'I'm sorry, I'm sorry, I'm sorry, I'm sorry . . .'

29

The woman, at a signal from Epstein, had brought more coffee, once again black for him, and a little milk for mine. Between us lay the two symbols.

'What do they mean?' I asked.

'They are letters of the Enochian, or Adamical, alphabet, supposedly communicated to the English magician John Dee and his associates over a period of decades during the sixteenth century.'

'Communicated?'

'Through occult workings, although it may be a constructed language. Whatever its origins, this first is the Enochian letter "Und," the equivalent of our letter "A." In this case, it represents a name: Anmael.'

Jimmy Gallagher, struggling to remember: 'Animal – no that's not it . . .'

'And what is Anmael?'

'Anmael is a demon, one of the Grigori, or the "Sons of God,"' said Epstein. 'The Grigori are also known as "Watchers," or "the ones who never sleep." According to elements of the apocrypha, and the Book of Enoch in particular, they are gigantic beings who, in one version, precipitated the great Fall of the angels through the sin of lust.'

He held up two hands before him, but kept the thumb of his right hand tucked into the palm.

'Nine orders of angels,' he said. 'All sexless, and above reproach.' He moved his thumb, adding it to the rest. 'The tenth is the Grigori, of a different essence from the rest, in form and sexual appetite similar to man, and it is this order that fell. In Genesis, it is the Grigori who lusted after flesh and "took themselves wives" from among the children of men. Such theories have always been a matter of some dispute. The great rabbi Simeon ben Yohai, blessed be his name, forbade his disciples to speak of such matters, but I, as you can see, have no such qualms.

'So, Anmael was one of the Grigori. He, in turn, is linked to Semjaza, one of the leaders of the order. Some say that the angel Semjaza repented of its actions but that, I suspect, had more to do with a desire in the early church for a figure of repentance than anything else.

'Now we have twin angels, Anmael and Semjaza, but here Christian and Jewish views diverge. In Christian orthodoxy, derived in part from Jewish sources, angels are traditionally viewed as sexless, or, in the case of the higher orders, exclusively male. The later Jewish view, by contrast, allows the possibility of male and female angels. The bibliographer Hayyim Azulal wrote in his *Milbar Kedemot* of 1792 that "the angels are called women, as it is written in Zechariah verse nine, Then lifted I up mine eyes, and looked, and behold, there came out two women." The *Yalkut Hadash* says: "Of angels we can speak both in masculine and in feminine: the angels of a superior degree are called men, and the angels of an inferior degree are called women." At the very least, then, Judaism has a more fluid concept of the sexuality of such beings.

'The body of Ackerman, and the boy killed by your father at Pearl River, both bore the Enochian "A," or "Und," burned into their flesh. The women, by contrast, were marked with the letter "Uam," or "S," for Semjaza.'

He paused for a moment, and seemed to consider something. 'I have often thought,' he resumed, 'that the children of men must have been a grave disappointment to such beings. It was our flesh and our bodies that they desired, yet our minds, and our lifespans, must have been like those of insects by comparison. But what if two angels, one male, one female, could inhabit the bodies of a man and a woman, and enjoy their union as equals? And as those bodies wear out, they move on, finding others to inhabit, and then begin to seek each other once again. Sometimes it may take years. It may even be that, on occasion, they fail to come together, and the search continues in another body, but they never stop looking, for they cannot be content without each other. Anmael and Semjaza: soul mates, if one could speak in such a way of beings without a soul; or lovers, of beings who cannot love.

'And the price they pay for their union is, I believe, to do the bidding of another: in this case, that bidding is to bring an end to your existence.'

'Another?'

'A controlling consciousness. It may be that some of those whom you have encountered in the past – Pudd,

Brightwell, our friend Kittim, perhaps even the Traveling Man, among those whose human nature is not in dispute, for did the Traveling Man not reference the Book of Enoch? – also did its bidding, but without even knowing it. Think of the human body: some of its processes are involuntary. The heart beats, the liver purifies, the kidneys process. The brain does not have to tell them to perform these tasks, but they serve the function of sustaining the body. But to lift up a book, to drive a car, to fire a gun in order to end a life, these are not involuntary functions. So, perhaps, there will be some who perform services for another without being aware of it, simply because their own acts of evil fulfill a larger purpose. There will be others, though, who are specifically charged with certain tasks, and hence their awareness will ultimately be greater.'

'And what is this controlling consciousness?'

'That we don't yet know.'

'"We,"' I said. 'I take it you're not talking about you and me.'

'Not entirely.'

'The Collector spoke of my "secret friends." Do you qualify?'

'I would be honored to think so.'

'And there are others.'

'Yes, although some might not be so willing to wear the mantle of friendship in the general sense of the word,' said Epstein, choosing his words with consummate diplomacy.

'No cards at Christmas.'

'No cards at any time.'

'And you won't tell me who they are?'

'For now, it's better that you don't know.'

'Are you afraid that I'm going to make unwanted calls?'

'No, but if you don't know their names then you can't reveal their identities to others.'

'Like Anmael, if he chose to take his blade to me.'

'You're not alone in this matter, Mr. Parker. Granted, you are an unusual man, and I have not yet figured out why you have always been such an object of hatred and, dare I say it, attraction for such foul things, but I have other people to think of too.'

'Is that what Unit Five is: code for what you call my secret friends?'

For a moment, Epstein seemed taken aback, but recovered himself.

'Unit Five is just a name.'

'For what?'

'Initially, for the investigation into the Traveling Man. Since then, its remit has broadened somewhat, I believe. You are part of that remit.'

Rain began to fall. I looked over my shoulder and saw it darken the sidewalk and fall from the dark red awning over the doorway.

'So what do I do?'

'About what?'

'About Anmael, or whoever thinks he's Anmael.'

'He's waiting.'

'For?'

'For his other half to join him. He must believe that

she is close, otherwise he wouldn't have revealed himself. She, in turn, is leaving traces for him, perhaps even without realizing it. When she comes, they'll make their move. It won't be long, not if Anmael was prepared to kill Wallace and mark the wall with his name. He senses her approach, and it will not be long before they are drawn together. We could hide you away, I suppose, but that would be merely to delay the inevitable. To amuse themselves, and to draw you out, they might hurt those close to you.'

'So what would you do, in my shoes?'

'I would choose the ground upon which to fight. You have your allies: Angel and the one who is, presumably, still lurking outside. I can spare a couple of young men who will maintain a discreet distance from you yet keep you in sight. Tether yourself lightly in the place of your choosing, and we will trap them when they come.'

Epstein stood. Our meeting was over.

'I have one more question,' I said.

What might have been irritation flitted across Epstein's face, but he crushed it and assumed once more his habitual expression of benign amusement.

'Ask it.'

'Elaine Parker's child, the one who died: was it a boy or a girl?'

'It was a girl. I believe she named it Sarah. It was taken from her and buried secretly. I do not know where. It was best that nobody knew.'

Sarah: my half sister, buried anonymously in an infants' cemetery in order to protect me.

'But I may have a final problem for you to consider in turn,' said Epstein. 'How did they find Caroline Carr? On two occasions, your father and Jimmy Gallagher hid her well: once uptown, before Ackerman died beneath the wheels of a truck, and then during her pregnancy. Still, the man and the woman managed to track her down. Then someone found out that Will Parker had lied about the circumstances of his son's birth, and they came back to try again.'

'It could have been one of your people,' I said. 'Jimmy told me about the meeting at the clinic. One of them could have let it slip, either deliberately or inadvertently.'

'No, they did not,' said Epstein, and he spoke with such conviction that I did not contradict him. 'And even were I to doubt them, which I do not, none of them was made aware of the nature of the threat to Caroline Carr until she died. All they knew was that she was a young woman in trouble, and in need of protection. It is possible that the secret of your parentage might have leaked out. We removed the details of Elaine Parker's dead child from her medical records, and she severed all contact with the hospital and the obstetrician concerned with monitoring the early stages of her pregnancy. Their files were subsequently purged. Your blood group was a problem, but that should have been a confidential matter between your family and their doctor, and he appears to have been above reproach in all respects. And then we warned your father to always be vigilant, and he rarely failed to heed our warnings.'

'Right up to the night that he fired his gun at Pearl River,' I said.

'Yes, until then.'

'You shouldn't have let him go back there alone.'

'I didn't know what he was going to do,' said Epstein. 'I wanted them taken alive. That way, we could have contained them, and ended this thing.'

He put on his hat and coat and prepared to slip by me.

'Remember what I said. I believe that someone who knew your father betrayed him. It may be that you are at risk of betrayal too. I commit you to the care of your colleague.'

And he and his bodyguards departed, leaving me with the dark haired mute who smiled sadly before she began to extinguish the lights.

A bell rang somewhere in the back of the diner, causing a red bulb to flash above the counter for the woman to see. She put a finger to her lips, telling me that I should remain quiet, then disappeared behind a curtain. Seconds later, she gestured with a finger, asking me to join her.

A small video screen revealed a figure standing in the bay behind the store. It was Louis. I indicated to her that I knew him, and it was okay to let him in. She opened the door.

'There's a car out front,' said Louis. 'Looks like it followed Epstein here. Two men inside wearing suits. Figure feds more than cops.'

'They could have taken me while I was talking to Epstein.'

'Maybe they don't want to take you. Maybe they just want to find out where you're staying.'

'My landlord wouldn't like that.'

'Which is why your landlord is standing here, freezing his ass off.'

I thanked the woman and joined Louis. She closed the door behind us.

'Doesn't say much,' said Louis.

'She's a deaf mute.'

'That would explain it. Good-looking woman, though, if you like the quiet type.'

'You ever think of taking sensitivity training?' I said.

'You think it would help?'

'Probably not.'

'Well, there you go.'

At the end of the street, Louis paused and glanced back at the next corner. A cab appeared. He hailed it, and we pulled away with no signs of pursuit. The cab driver seemed more concerned with his Bluetooth conversation than with us, but to be certain, we switched cabs before we returned to the safety of the apartment.

30

Wrongly, Jimmy Gallagher had never believed himself to be good at keeping secrets. It wasn't in his nature. He was garrulous. He liked to drink, to tell stories. When he drank, his tongue ran away with itself and his filters disintegrated. He would say things and wonder where they came from, as though he were standing outside himself and watching a stranger speak. But he knew the importance of keeping quiet about the origins of Will Parker's son, and even in his cups there were parts of his own life that had remained concealed. Still, he had kept his distance from the boy and his mother after Will killed himself. Better to stay away from them, he felt, than risk saying something in front of the boy that might cause him to suspect, or offend his mother by speaking of things that were better left hidden in cluttered, careworn hearts. And despite his many flaws, in all the years since Elaine Parker had left for Maine with her son he had never once spoken of what he knew.

But he had always suspected that Charlie Parker would come looking for him. It was in his nature to question, to seek out truths. He was a hunter, and there was a tenacity to him that would ultimately,

Jimmy believed, cost him his life. Sometime in the future, he would overstep the mark and look into matters that were best left unexamined, and something would reach out and destroy him. Jimmy was certain of it. Perhaps the nature of his own identity, and the secret of his parentage, might well prove to be that mistake.

He sipped the last of his wine and toyed with the glass, causing candle-cast patterns to flicker upon the walls. There was still a half bottle left beside the sink. A week ago, he would have finished it off and maybe opened another one for good measure, but not now. Some of the urge to drink more than he should had fallen away. He understood that it was to do with the clearing of his conscience. He had told Charlie Parker all that he knew, and now he was absolved.

And yet he also felt that, in confessing, some connection between them had been severed. It was not a bond of trust, exactly, for he and Charlie had never been close, and never would be. He had sensed that, from an early age, the boy had been uneasy around him. But then Jimmy had never really figured out how to relate to kids. His sister was more than fifteen years older than he was, and he had grown up feeling like an only child. Then, too, his parents had been old when he was born. Old. He chuckled. What had they been: thirty-eight, thirty-nine? Still, there had always been a lack of understanding between his parents and their son, even though he had loved them both dearly, and the chasm between them had only widened as he had grown older. They had never discussed his sexuality, although he had always understood that his mother, and perhaps his father too, realized that their son was never going to marry any of the girls who occasionally accompanied him to dance halls or to the movies.

And while he himself recognized his urges, he had never acted upon them. It was partly out of fear, he thought. He did not want his fellow officers to know that he was gay. They were his family, his true family. He did not want to do anything to alienate them. Now, in retirement, he remained a virgin. Funny, but he found it hard to equate that word with a man who was in his late sixties. It was a description that should be applied to young men and women on the brink of new experiences, not older ones. Oh, he was still energetic, and he still sometimes thought that it might be – nice? interesting? – to start a relationship, but that was the problem: he wasn't sure where to start. He wasn't some blushing bride waiting to be deflowered. He was a man with a certain knowledge of life, both good and bad. It was too late, he thought, to surrender himself now to someone with a greater degree of experience in matters of sex and love.

He carefully vacuum-sealed the bottle of red wine and placed it in the refrigerator. It was a hint that he'd picked up from the local liquor store, and it worked fine as long as he remembered to let the wine warm up for a time before he began drinking it again the next day. He turned off the lights, double locked the front and back doors, and went to bed.

* * *

He managed to incorporate the noise into his dream at first, the way he sometimes did when the alarm went off and he was so deep in sleep that bells began ringing in his dreams in turn. In the dream, a wineglass fell from the table and shattered on the floor. It wasn't his wineglass, though, and it wasn't quite his kitchen, although it resembled it. It was now bigger, the dark corners stretching away into infinity. The tiles on the floor were the tiles from the house in which he had grown up, and his mother was nearby. He could hear her singing, even though he could not see her.

He woke. There was silence for a time, then the faintest disturbance: a sliver of glass caught underfoot, scraping against a tile. He climbed silently from his bed and opened his bedside cabinet. The .38 lay on the shelf, cleaned and loaded. He padded across the room in his underwear, and the boards did not creak beneath his feet. He knew this place intimately, every crack and join of it. Even though it was an old house, he could move through it without making a sound.

He stood at the top of the stairs and waited. All was silent again, but still he sensed the presence of another. The darkness became oppressive to him, and suddenly he was frightened. He debated calling out a warning, and by doing so cause whoever was below to flee, but he knew that if he did so his voice would tremble and he would reveal his fear. Better to keep going. He had a gun. He was an ex-cop. If he was forced to shoot, then his own people would look after him. Screw the other guy.

He made his way down the stairs. The kitchen door

was open. A single shard of glass shone in the moonlight. Jimmy's hand was shaking, and he tried to still it by assuming a double-handed grip on the gun. There were only two rooms on the lower level: the living room and the kitchen, linked by a pair of interconnecting doors. He could see that those doors were still closed. He swallowed, and thought that he could taste some of that evening's wine in his mouth. It had gone sour, like vinegar.

His bare feet felt cold, and he realized that the basement door was open. That was how the intruder had entered, and maybe that was how he had left after the wineglass broke. Jimmy winced. He knew that was wishful thinking. Someone was there. He could feel him. The living room was closest. He should search it first, so that whoever was there could not come from behind him when he searched the kitchen.

He glanced through the crack in the door. The drapes were not drawn, but the streetlight outside was broken and only a thin stream of moonlight filtered through the drapes, so it was hard to make out anything at all. He stepped inside quickly, and immediately knew that he had made a mistake. The shadows altered, and then the door struck him hard, knocking him off balance. As he tried to adjust the position of his gun and fire, there was a burning at his wrists. Skin was opened, tendons severed. The gun fell to the floor, blood from his wounds sprinkling on it. Something hit him once on the crown of the head, then again, and as he lost consciousness he thought that he glimpsed a long, flat blade.

* * *

When he came to he was lying on his belly in the kitchen, his hands tied behind his back, his feet bound and drawn up to his buttocks, then linked to the ropes on his hands so that he could not move. He felt cold air on his bare skin, but not as badly as before. The basement door had been closed again, and now only a slight draft came from the gap between the kitchen door and the floor. The tiles were freezing, though. He felt weak. His hands and face were slick with blood, and his head ached. He tried to cry for help until a blade touched his cheek. The figure beside him had been so quiet and still that he had not even sensed its presence until it moved.

'No,' said a man's voice, one that he did not recognize.

'What do you want?'

'To talk.'

'Talk about what?'

'Charlie Parker. His father. His mother.'

Jimmy's movement had caused the blood to flow once again from the wound on his head. It trickled into his eyes, stinging them.

'Talk to him yourself, you want to know anything. I haven't seen Charlie Parker in years, not since—'

An apple was forced into his mouth, pushed in so hard and so far that he could not expel it or even sever it by biting down on it. He stared at his attacker's face, and thought that he had never seen eyes so dark and so merciless. A piece of broken wineglass was held before his eyes. Jimmy's gaze drifted from it to the symbol that seemed to be burned into the skin of the man's forearm, then back to the glass again. He had seen that mark before, and he knew now what he was facing.

Animal. Amale.

Anmael.

'You're lying. I'm going to show you what happens to faggot cops who tell lies.'

With one hand, Anmael gripped the back of Jimmy's neck, holding his head down, while the other hand pushed the broken stem of the wineglass into the skin between his shoulder blades.

Against the apple, Jimmy began to scream.

31

Jimmy Gallagher was discovered by Esmerelda, the El Salvadorean woman who came to his house twice every week to clean. When the police arrived, they found her weeping, but otherwise calm. It turned out that she'd seen a lot of dead men back home, and her capacity for shock was limited. Nevertheless, she could not stop crying for Jimmy, who had always been gentle and kind and funny with her, and had paid her more than was necessary, with a bonus at Christmas.

It was Louis who told me. He came to the apartment shortly after 9 a.m. The story had already made the news shows on radio and TV, although the victim's name had not been confirmed, but it hadn't taken Louis long to find out that it was Jimmy Gallagher. I didn't say anything for a time. I couldn't. Jimmy had kept his secrets out of love for my father and mother and, I believe, out of a misplaced concern for me. Of all my father's friends, it was Jimmy who had been the most loyal to him.

I contacted Santos, the detective who had taken me to Hobart Street on the night that Mickey Wallace's body had been discovered.

'It was bad,' he replied. 'Someone took his time in

killing him. I tried to call you, but your phone was out of service.'

He told me that Jimmy's body had been brought to the Brooklyn office of the chief medical examiner at Kings County Hospital on Clarkson Avenue, and I offered to meet him there.

Santos was smoking a cigarette outside when the cab pulled up to the mortuary.

'You're a hard man to find,' he said. 'You lose your cell phone?'

'Something like that.'

'We need to talk when this is done.'

He tossed the butt, and I followed him inside. He and a second detective named Travis stood at either side of the body while the attendant pulled back the sheet. I was beside Santos. He was watching the attendant. Travis was watching me.

Jimmy had been cleaned up, but there were multiple cuts to his face and upper body. One of the incisions to his left cheek was so deep that I could see his teeth through the wound.

'Turn him over,' Travis said.

'You want to help me?' said the attendant. 'He's a heavy guy.'

Travis was wearing blue plastic gloves, as was Santos. I was bare-handed. I watched as all three of them shifted Jimmy's body, turning him first on his side and then onto his chest.

The word 'FAG' had been carved into Jimmy's back. Some of the cuts were more jagged than the rest, but all were deep. There must have been a lot of blood, and a lot of pain.

'What was used?'

It was Santos who replied. 'The stem of a broken wineglass for the letters, and a blade of some kind for the rest. We didn't find the weapon, but there were unusual wounds to the skull.'

Gently, he moved Jimmy's head, then parted the hair at the crown of his head to reveal a pair of overlapping, square-shaped contusions to the scalp. Santos made his right hand into a fist and brought it down twice through the air.

'I'm guessing a big knife of some kind, maybe a machete or something similar. We figure the killer hit Jimmy a couple of times with the hilt to knock him out, then tied him up and went to work with the sharp edge. There were apples beside his head, with bite marks in them. That was why nobody heard him screaming.'

He did not speak casually, or with a hint of callousness. Instead, he looked tired and sad. This was an ex-cop, and one who was remembered fondly by many. The details of the killing, the word cut into his back, would have circulated by now. The sadness and anger at his death would be tempered slightly by the circumstances. A fag killing: that was how some would speak of it. Who knew that Jimmy Gallagher was queer? they would ask. After all, they'd been drunk alongside him. They'd shared comments with him about passing women. Hell, he'd even dated some. And all that time, he was hiding the truth. And some would say that they had suspected all along, and wonder what he had done to bring this upon himself. There would be whispers: he made an advance to the wrong guy; he touched a kid . . .

Ah, a kid.

'Are you treating this as a hate crime?' I asked.

Travis shrugged and spoke for the first time. 'It might come down to that. Either way, we have to ask questions that Jimmy wouldn't have wanted asked. We'll need to find out if there were lovers, or casual flings, or if he was into anything extreme.'

'There won't be any lovers,' I said.

'You seem pretty sure of that.'

'I am. Jimmy was always kind of ashamed, and always frightened.'

'Of what?'

'Of someone finding out. Of his friends knowing. They were all cops, and old school. I don't think he trusted most of them to stand by him. He thought they'd laugh, or turn their backs on him. He didn't want to be a joke. He preferred being alone to that.'

'Well, if it's not down to his lifestyle, then what is it?'

I thought for a moment.

'Apples,' I said.

'What?' said Travis.

'You said you found apples – more than one – beside him?'

'Three. Maybe the killer thought that Jimmy might bite through after a while.'

'Or maybe he stopped after each letter.'

'Why?'

'To ask questions.'

'About what?'

It was Santos who answered. 'About him,' he said, pointing at me. 'He thinks this is connected to the Wallace thing.'

'Don't you?'

'Wallace didn't have "fag" cut into his flesh,' said Santos, but I could tell that he was playing devil's advocate.

'They were both tortured to make them talk,' I said.

'And you knew them both,' said Santos. 'Why don't you tell us again what you're doing down here?'

'I'm trying to find out why my father killed two teenagers in a car in 1982,' I said.

'And did Jimmy Gallagher have the answer?'

I didn't reply. I just shook my head.

'What do you think he told his killer?' asked Travis.

I looked at the wounds that had been inflicted on him. I would have talked. It's a myth that men can stand up to torture. Eventually, everybody breaks.

'Whatever he could to make it stop,' I said. 'How did he die?'

'He choked. A wine bottle was forced into his mouth, neck first. That's going to hang weight on the hate crime side. It was, whatchacallit, phallic, or that's how it will play.'

It was vindictive, humiliating. An honorable man had been left, naked and bound, with a brand upon his back that would mark him among his fellow cops, casting shadows upon the memory of the individual they had known. I believed then that it wasn't about what Jimmy Gallagher knew or did not know. He had been punished for remaining silent, and nothing that he could have said would have spared him from what was to come.

Santos nodded at the attendant. Together, they moved Jimmy onto his back and covered his face once again, then restored him to his place among the numbered dead. The door was closed on him, and we left.

Outside, Santos lit another cigarette. He offered one to Travis, who accepted.

'You know,' he said, 'if you're right, and this isn't a hate deal, then he died because of you. What are you keeping back from us?'

What did it matter now? It was all coming to a close.

'Go back and look at the files on the Pearl River killings,' I said. 'The boy who died had a mark on his forearm. It looked like it had been burned into the skin. That mark is the same one that was found on the wall at Hobart Street, drawn in Wallace's blood. My guess is that, somewhere in Jimmy's house, you'll find a similar mark.'

Travis and Santos exchanged a look.

'Where was it?' I said.

'On his chest,' said Santos. 'Written in blood. We've been warned to keep quiet about it. I guess I'm telling you because . . .' He thought about it. 'Well, I don't know why I'm telling you.'

'So what was all that about in there? You don't

believe this was a hate crime. You know this is connected to Wallace's death.'

'We just wanted to hear your side of the story first,' said Travis. 'It's called "detecting." We ask you questions, you don't answer them, we get frustrated. I hear it's an established pattern with you.'

'We know what the symbol means,' said Santos, ignoring Travis. 'We found a guy at the Institute of Advanced Theology who explained it for us.'

'It's the Enochian "A,"' I said.

'How long have you known?'

'Not long. I didn't know when you showed it to me.'

'What are we looking at?' asked Travis, calming down some now that he realized that neither Santos nor I was going to be drawn by his baiting. 'A cult? Ritual killings?'

'And what's the connection to you, beyond the fact that you knew both of the victims?' asked Santos.

'I don't know,' I said. 'That's what I'm trying to find out.'

'Why not just torture you?' said Travis. 'I mean, I could understand the impulse.'

I ignored him.

'There's a man named Asa Durand. He lives out in Pearl River.' I gave them the address. 'He says a guy was casing his property a while back, and asking about what happened there. Asa Durand lives in the house where I lived before my father killed himself. Might be worth sending out a sketch artist to test Durand's memory.'

Santos took a long drag on his cigarette, and expelled some of the smoke in my direction.

'Those things will kill you,' I said.

'I was you, I'd worry about my own mortality,' said Santos. 'I assume that you're lying low, but turn your damn cell phone back on. Don't make us haul you in and lock you up for your own protection.'

'We're letting him walk?' asked Travis incredulously.

'I think he's told us all that he's going to for now,' said Santos. 'Isn't that right, Mr. Parker? And it's more than we could get from our own people.'

'Unit Five,' I said.

Santos looked surprised. 'You know what it is?'

'Do you?'

'Some kind of security clearance that a regular wage earner like me doesn't have, I guess.'

'That's about the size of it. I don't know much more about it than you do.'

'Somehow, I don't believe that's true, but I suppose that all we can do now is wait, because my guess is that your name is on the same list that Jimmy Gallagher and Mickey Wallace were on. When whoever killed them gets around to you, either someone will be tagging your toe, or theirs. Come on, we'll give you a ride to the subway. The sooner you're out of Brooklyn, the happier I'll be.'

They dropped me at the subway station.

'Be seeing you,' said Santos.

'Dead or alive,' said Travis.

I watched them drive away. They hadn't spoken to me in the car, and I hadn't cared. I was too busy thinking about the word that had been carved into Jimmy Gallagher's back. How had his killer come to the conclusion that Jimmy was gay? He had kept his secrets close all his life; his own, and those of others. I only became aware of his sexuality from things my mother said after my father's death, when I was a little older and a little more mature, and she had assured me that few of Jimmy's colleagues had known about it. In fact, she said, only two people knew for certain that Jimmy was gay.

One of them was my father.

The other was Eddie Grace.

32

Amanda Grace answered the door. Her hair was loosely tied with a red band, and her face bore no trace of cosmetics. She was wearing a pair of sweatpants and an old shirt, and she was bathed in perspiration. In her right hand she held a kitchen plunger.

'Great,' she said, when she saw me. 'Just great.'

'I take it this isn't a good time.'

'You could have called ahead first. I might even have had time to put the plunger away.'

'I'd like to talk to your father again.'

She stepped back, inviting me inside.

'He was real tired after your last visit,' she said. 'Is it important?'

'I think it is.'

'It's about Jimmy Gallagher, isn't it?'

'In a way.'

I followed her into the kitchen. There was a pungent smell coming from the sink, and I could see dirty water that wasn't draining.

'Something's backed up down there,' she said. She handed over the plunger. I slipped off my jacket and went to work on the sink, while she rested a hip against the sideboard and regarded me.

'What's going on, Charlie?'

'What do you mean?'

'We watch the news. We saw what happened at your old home, and we heard about Jimmy. They're connected, aren't they?'

I could feel the water starting to move. I stepped back and watched it disappear down the sink.

'Did your father have anything to say about it?'

'He seemed sad about Jimmy. They used to be friends.'

'Any idea why they fell out?'

She looked away. 'I don't think my father liked the way Jimmy lived his life.'

'Is that what he told you?'

'No, I guessed it for myself. You still haven't answered my question. What's going on?'

I turned to her, and held her gaze until she looked away.

'Damn you,' she said.

'Like I told you, I'd appreciate a few minutes with Eddie.'

She wiped a hand across her brow, her frustration palpable. 'He's awake, but he's still in bed. It'll take him a while to get dressed.'

'There's no need to go to that trouble. I can talk to him in his room. It won't take long.'

She still seemed to be debating the wisdom of allowing me to see him. I could sense her unease.

'You're different today,' she said.

'From?'

'From the last time you were here. I don't think I like it.'

'I need to talk to him, Amanda. Then I'll be gone, and it won't matter if you ever liked me.'

She nodded. 'Upstairs. Second door on the right. Knock before you go in.'

My tapping on Eddie Grace's door was answered by a hoarse croak. The drapes were closed in the room, and it stank of illness and decay. Eddie Grace's head was supported by a pair of large white pillows. He wore blue-striped pajamas, and the dim light somehow accentuated the pallor of his skin, so that he seemed almost to glow where he lay. I closed the door behind me and looked down on him.

'You came back,' he said. There was a hint of what might have been a smile on his face, but there was no joy to it. Instead, it was a knowing, unpleasant thing, an expression of malevolence. 'I figured you would.'

'Why?'

He didn't even try to lie.

'Because they're coming for you, and you're scared.'

'Do you know what was done to Jimmy?'

'I can guess.'

'He was carved up. He was tortured and then killed, all because he kept his secrets, all because he was a friend to my father and to me.'

'He should have picked his friends more carefully.'

'I guess so. You were his friend.'

Eddie laughed softly. It sounded like air being forced from a corpse, and smelled just as bad. It brought on a fit of coughing, and he gestured for the covered plastic cup on the bedside locker, the kind that little children used with a raised, perforated lip from which to drink. I held it for him as he sucked from it. One of his hands touched mine, and I was surprised by how cold it was.

'I *was* his friend,' said Eddie. 'Then he had to tell your father and me about himself, and after that I cut him loose. He was a faggot, barely a man. He disgusted me.'

'So you cut him off?'

'I'd have cut his balls off if I could. I'd have told everyone what he was. He shouldn't have been allowed to wear that uniform.'

'So why didn't you?' I asked.

'Because they didn't want me to.'

'Who didn't?'

'Anmael, and Semjaza, although that wasn't what they called themselves, not the first time they came to me. I never found out the woman's name. She never said much. The man was called Peter, but later I found out his true name. He did most of the talking.'

'How did they find you?'

'I had weaknesses. Not like Jimmy's. I had a man's weaknesses. I liked them young.'

He smiled again. His lips were cracked, and his remaining teeth were rotting in their gums.

'Girls, not boys,' he continued. 'Never boys. They found out. That's what they do: they find your weaknesses, and they use them against you. A carrot and a stick: they threatened to expose me, but if I helped them, then they'd help me in turn. They came to me after your father started seeing Caroline Carr. I didn't know what they were, not then, but I learned.' His eyes flickered, and for a moment he looked frightened. 'Oh, I learned. I told them about the Carr woman. I knew about her: I was partnered with your father one day, after he met her, and I saw them together.

'Anmael wanted to know where she was. I didn't ask why. I found out where Will had stashed her on the Upper East Side. Then Anmael died, and the woman disappeared. They kept moving Caroline Carr around after that, your father and Jimmy, but they did it quietly. I told Semjaza to follow Jimmy, because your father trusted him more than anyone else. I thought that they just wanted to follow her, maybe steal the child. I was as surprised as anyone when they killed her.'

It was strange, but I believed him. He had no reason to lie, not now, and he was not seeking absolution. He spoke of it as if it were an event that he had witnessed, but in which he had played no direct part.

'When Will came back from Maine with a baby boy, I was suspicious. I knew all about his wife's medical history, about the problems she'd had conceiving, and carrying, a child. It was all too neat. But by then I'd fallen out with Jimmy. I was still on good terms with your old man, or I thought I was, but something changed between us. I suppose Jimmy must have spoken to him, and he chose Jimmy over me. I didn't care. Fuck him. Fuck 'em both.

'I heard nothing for maybe fifteen years. I didn't expect anything else. After all, they were dead, Anmael and the woman, and I'd found ways to keep myself satisfied without them.

'Then a boy and a girl showed up at my place. They sat outside in a car, watching the house. I was bowling, and my wife called me, told me she was worried. I came home, and I swear I knew it was them. I knew before they even showed me the marks on their arms, before they started talking about things that must have happened before they were born, conversations that I'd had with Anmael and the woman before they died. I mean, it was them, in another form. I didn't doubt it. I could see it in their eyes. I told them what I believed about the boy Will and his wife were raising, but they already seemed to have their own suspicions. That was what had brought them back. They knew that the boy was still alive, that *you* were still alive.

'So I helped them again, and still you wouldn't die.'

His eyes closed. I thought he might have drifted off to sleep, but then he spoke, his eyes still shut.

'I cried when your old man killed himself,' he said. 'I liked him, even if he did cut me loose. Why couldn't you just have died back in that clinic? If you had, then it would all have ended there and then. You just won't die.'

His eyes opened again.

'But this time it's different. They're not kids hunting you, and they've learned from their mistakes. That's the thing about them: they *remember*. Each time, they've come a little bit closer to succeeding, but it's urgent now. They want you dead.'

'Why?'

He stared at me, his eyebrows raised. He looked amused. 'I don't think they know,' he said. 'You might as well ask why a white blood cell attacks an infection. It's what it's programmed to do: to fight a threat, and neutralize it. Not mine, though. Mine are screwed.'

'Where are they?'

'I've only seen him. The other, the woman, she wasn't there. He was waiting for her, willing her to come to him. That's the way they are. They live for each other.'

'Who is he? What's he calling himself?'

'I don't know. He didn't say.'

'He came here?'

'No, it was while I was still in the hospital, but not so long ago. He brought me candy. It was like meeting an old friend.'

'Did you feed Jimmy to him?'

'No, I didn't have to. They knew all about Jimmy from way back.'

'Because of you.'

'What does it matter now?'

'It mattered to Jimmy. Do you know how much he suffered before he died?'

Eddie waved a hand in a gesture of dismissal, but he would not meet my eyes.

'Describe him to me.'

He indicated once again that he needed water, and I gave it to him. His voice had grown hoarser and hoarser as he spoke. Now it was barely a whisper.

'No,' he said. 'I won't tell you. And, anyway, do you really think any of this will help you? I wouldn't tell you anything if I thought it would. I don't care about you, or about what happened to Jimmy. I'm almost done with this life. I've been promised my reward for what I've done.'

He lifted his head from the pillow, as though to confide some great secret. 'Their master is good and kind,' he said, almost to himself, then sank back on the bed, exhausted. His breathing grew shallower, and he drifted off to sleep.

Amanda was waiting for me at the bottom of the stairs. Her lips were set so firmly that there were wrinkles around her mouth.

'Did you get what you wanted from him?'

'Yes. Confirmation.'

'He's an old man. Whatever he did in the past, he's paid more than enough for it in suffering.'

'You know, Amanda, I don't believe that's true.'

Her face flushed red.

'Get out of here. The best thing you ever did was leave this town.'

And that much, at least, was true.

33

The woman who was now Emily Kindler in name only arrived at the Port Authority Bus Terminal two days after Jimmy Gallagher was killed. After leaving the bar, she had spent an entire day alone in her little apartment, ignoring the ringing of the telephone, her date with Chad now forgotten, Chad himself reduced to nothing more than a fleeting memory from another life. Once, the doorbell rang downstairs, but she did not answer it. Instead, she reconstructed past lives, and thought about the man whom she had seen on the TV screen in the bar, and she knew that when she found him, then so too would she find her beloved.

Using a poker, she carefully burnt her flesh. She knew the exact place upon which to work, for she could almost see the pattern hiding beneath her skin. When she was done, she bore the old mark.

In time, she left for the city.

At the bus station, it took her almost an hour of looking lost before she was approached. While she was freshening up for the third time in the women's restroom, a young woman not much older than she was approached her and asked if she was okay. The woman's name was Carole Coemer, but everyone called her Cassie. She was blond and pretty and clean, and looked nineteen even though she was actually twenty-seven. Her job was to scout the bus station for new female arrivals, particularly those who looked lost or alone, and befriend them. She would tell them that she was new in town herself, and offer to buy them a cup of coffee, or something to eat. Cassie always carried a backpack, even though it was filled with newspapers topped off with a pair of jeans and some underwear and T-shirts, just in case she had to open it to convince the more skeptical of the waifs and strays.

If they didn't have somewhere to stay, or if nobody was really expecting them in town, she would propose that they spend the night with a friend of Cassie's and then try to find somewhere more long term the next day. Cassie's friend was called Earle Yiu, and he maintained a number of cheap apartments across the city, but the principal one was on Thirty-eighth and Ninth, above a grimy bar called the Yellow Pearl, which was also owned by Earle Yiu. This was a little joke on Earle's part, as he was part Japanese and 'Yellow Pearl' wasn't a million miles removed from 'Yellow Peril.' Earle was very good at assessing the vulnerabilities of young women, although not quite as good as Cassie Coemer who, even Earle had to admit, was a predator of the first degree.

So Cassie would take the girl – or girls, if her day had been particularly productive – to meet Earle, and Earle would welcome them, and arrange to have food delivered or, if he was in the mood, he sometimes cooked for the girls himself. It would usually be something simple and tasty, like teriyaki with rice. Beers would be offered, and a little pot, maybe even something stronger. Then Earle, if he thought the new arrival was suitable and sufficiently vulnerable, would offer to let her and Cassie stay in the apartment for a couple of days, telling them to take it easy, that he knew someone who might be looking for waitresses. The next day, Cassie would drift away, isolating the new arrival.

After two or three days, Earle's disposition would alter. He would arrive early in the morning, or late at night, and wake the girl. He would demand payment for his hospitality, and when the girl couldn't pay – and they could never pay enough to satisfy Earle – he would make his move. Most ended up turning tricks, once Earle and his buddies had broken them in first, if that was necessary, usually in one of Earle's other apartments. Particularly promising candidates would be sold off elsewhere, or escorted to other cities and towns where new blood was scarce. The most unfortunate simply disappeared off the face of the earth, for Earle knew men (and some women) with very particular needs.

Earle was careful in how he used Cassie. He didn't want her to draw any attention to herself, or to become overly familiar to the Port Authority cops at the bus station or the Amtrak stations. Often he would let months go by without putting her into the field, contenting himself with the plentiful supply of Chinese and Korean women who were easily available to him, and harder for the authorities to track once they became part of his operation, but there was always a need for Caucasians and Negroes too, and Earle liked to provide a little variety.

And so it was that Cassie approached Emily and asked if she was okay, then said: 'You new in town?'

Emily stared at her, and Cassie squirmed. For a moment, she was sure that she'd made a mistake. This girl looked young but, like Cassie's, her looks were deceptive, and she was older than she at first appeared. The problem for Cassie was that, for an instant, she experienced a kind of atavistic rush, a sense that this girl was not just old, but very old. It was there in her eyes, which were very, very dark, and in a musty odor that seemed to hang about her. Cassie was ready to back away, cutting her losses, when the girl's demeanor subtly changed. She smiled, and Cassie was captivated by her. She stared deep into the girl's eyes and felt that she had never seen anyone quite so beautiful. Earle would be pleased with this one, and Cassie's reward would be commensurately greater as a consequence.

'Yes,' said Emily. 'I'm new. Very new. I'm looking for a place to stay. Do you think you can help me?'

'Sure, I can help you,' said Cassie. I'd love to, she thought. I'd do anything for you, anything. 'What's your name?'

The girl thought about the question. 'Emily,' she said, at last.

Cassie knew that it was a lie, but it didn't matter

to her. Earle would give her a new name anyway, if she worked out.

'I'm Cassie.'

'Well, Cassie,' said Emily, 'I guess I'm following you.'

Together, the girls walked to Earle Yiu's apartment. Earle wasn't there, which surprised Cassie, but she had a key and a prepared story about how she'd been there earlier in the day, and how Earle had given her a key and told her to come back because the apartment was being cleaned. Emily just smiled, and all was right in Cassie's world.

When they were inside the apartment, Cassie offered to show Emily around. There wasn't much to show, as the apartment was very small, consisting only of one modestly sized area that doubled as living room and kitchen, and a pair of tiny bedrooms, each barely large enough for a single mattress.

'And this is the bathroom,' said Cassie, opening the door on to a room that was so small the sink and toilet almost overlapped from opposite walls, with a shower stall that was little bigger than an upright coffin.

Emily gripped Cassie by the hair and struck her face hard against the edge of the sink. She did it again and again until Cassie was dead, then left her lying against the wall before closing the bathroom door carefully behind her. She took a seat on the old, foul-smelling couch in the living area and turned on the TV, flicking through the channels until she found the local news. She turned up the volume when the anchorman returned to the story of Jimmy Gallagher's killing. Despite the best efforts of the cops and the FBI, someone had been speaking out of turn. A reporter came on-screen, and spoke of a possible connection between the death of Gallagher and the killing of one Mickey Wallace at Hobart Street. Emily knelt down and touched the screen with her fingertips. She was still in that position when Earle Yiu entered. He was in his forties, carrying a little extra weight that he hid with well-cut suits.

'Who are you?' he asked.

Emily smiled at him. 'I'm a friend of Cassie's,' she said.

Earle smiled in return. 'Well, any friend of Cassie's is a friend of mine,' he said. 'Where is she?'

'In the bathroom.'

Instinctively, Earle glanced in the direction of the bathroom, which was just to his left. His brow furrowed. There was a dark, spreading stain on the carpet where it met the door.

'Cassie?'

He knocked once.

'Cassie, you in there?'

He tried the handle, and the door opened. He was still taking in the sight of Cassie Coemer's ruined face when a kitchen knife entered his back and pierced his heart.

When she was sure that Earle Yiu was dead, Emily searched him and found a .22 with a taped butt and nearly 700 dollars in cash. She took Yiu's cell phone and made a call. When she ended it, she knew where Jimmy Gallagher was to be buried, and when.

There were strong locks on the apartment door, as much to prevent anyone from leaving as from entering without permission. Emily secured them all, then turned off the television and sat, still and silent, upon the couch as day became night and night, at last, gave way to morning.

34

Choose your ground: that was what Epstein had told me. Choose the place where you will confront them. I could have run. I could have hidden myself away, and hoped that they would not find me, but they had always found me before. I could have chosen to return to Maine and face them there, but how could I have slept, fearing at any time that they might come for me? How could I have worked at the Bear, knowing that my presence there might put others at risk?

So I spoke to Epstein, and I talked with Angel and Louis, and I chose the ground upon which I would fight.

I would draw them to me, and we would end it at last.

They gave Jimmy the inspector's funeral: the full NYPD works, even better than what they had given my father. Six white-gloved patrolmen carried his flag-draped coffin on their shoulders from St. Dominic's Roman Catholic Church, their shields masked by black ribbons. As the coffin passed by, cops old and new, some in street uniform, some in dress blues, others in the old-man coats and hats of retirement, saluted as one. Nobody smiled, nobody spoke. All were quiet.

A couple of years before, a Westchester DA had been seen laughing and chatting with a state senator while the body of a slain cop was being carried from a church in the Bronx, until a cop told her to shut up. She had done so, instantly, but the slight had not been forgotten. There was a way these things were done, and you screwed with it at your peril.

Jimmy was buried at Holy Cross Cemetery on Tilden, in a plot alongside his mother and father. His older sister was his closest surviving relative. She was divorced, so she stood by the graveside with her three children, one of them Jimmy's nephew Francis who had come to our home on the night of the Pearl River killings, and she wept for the brother she had not seen in five years. The Emerald Society Pipes and Drums played 'Steal Away,' and nobody spoke ill of him, even though the news of what had been carved into his body had by then leaked out. Some might whisper later (and let them whisper: such men were worth little) but not now, not on that day. Today he would be remembered as a cop, and a well-liked one.

And I was there too, in plain sight, because I knew they would be watching in the hope that I might appear. I mingled. I spoke with those whom I recognized. After the burial, I went to a bar named Donaghy's with men who had served alongside Jimmy and my father, and we exchanged stories about both men, and they told me things about Will Parker that made me love him even more, because they had loved him in turn. All the time, I stayed close to groups. I didn't even go to the restroom alone, and I watched what I was drinking, even though I gave the impression that I was matching the others beer for beer, shot for shot. It was easy enough to disguise, for they were more concerned with one another than with me, even though I was welcome in their company. One of them, a former sergeant named Griesdorf, did ask me about the rumored connection between Mickey Wallace's death and what had happened to Jimmy, and for a time there was an awkward silence until a red-faced cop with dyed-black hair said: 'Jesus, Stevie, this isn't the time or the place! Let's drink to remember, then drink to forget.'

And the moment passed.

I spotted the girl shortly after 5 p.m. She was slim and pretty, with long black hair. In the dim light of Donaghy's, she looked younger than she was, and the bartender might have been forced to card her had she asked for a beer. I had seen her at the cemetery, laying flowers on a grave not far from where Jimmy was being buried. I had seen her again walking down Tilden after the funeral, but so were many other people, and I had noticed her more because of her looks than because of any suspicion I might have had of her. Now here she was in Donaghy's, nibbling at a salad, a book on the bar before her, a mirror facing her so that she could see all that was happening behind her. A couple of times, I thought I saw her glancing at me. It might have been nothing, but then she smiled at me when I caught her looking. It was a come-on, or the appearance of one. Her eyes were very dark.

Griesdorf had spotted her too.

'Girl likes you, Charlie,' he said. 'Go on. We're old

men. We need to live vicariously through the young. We'll look after your coat. Hell, you must be dying under there. Take it off, son.'

I stood, and swayed. 'No, I'm done,' I said. 'I wouldn't be good for much anyway.' I shook hands with them all and dropped fifty bucks on the table. 'A round of the best,' I said, 'for my old man, and for Jimmy.'

There was a cheer, and as I left them I staggered. Griesdorf reached out a hand to help me.

'You okay there?'

'I didn't eat much today,' I said. 'Dumb of me. Think you could get the bartender to call me a cab?'

'Sure. Where do you want to go?'

'Bay Ridge,' I said. 'Hobart Street.'

Griesdorf looked at me oddly. 'You sure about that?'

'Yeah, I'm sure.' I handed him the fifty dollars. 'Order those whiskeys while you're there.'

'You want one for the road?'

'No, thanks. If I have one more, I'll be *lying* on the road.'

He took the money. I leaned back against a pillar and watched him go. I saw him call over the bartender, and could hear a little of what passed between them from where I stood. There was no music playing in Donaghy's, and the after-work crowd had not yet begun to arrive. If I could hear what was being said at the bar, so could anyone else.

The cab arrived ten minutes later. By then, the girl was gone.

* * *

The cab dropped me outside my former home. The cab driver looked at the fluttering crime scene tape and asked if I wanted him to wait. He looked relieved when I said no.

There were no cops watching the house. Under ordinary circumstances, there would have been at least one officer on duty to secure the scene, but these were not ordinary circumstances.

I walked around to the side of the house. The gate to the back yard had been draped loosely with a chain and some tape, but the chain lacked a lock: it was there purely for show. The kitchen door, though, had been secured with a new lock and hasp, but it was the work of a moment to open it with the little electric rake that Angel had given me. It sounded very loud in the stillness of the late evening, and as I entered the house I saw a light go on somewhere nearby. I closed the door and waited until the light was extinguished and the darkness grew deeper.

I flicked on my little Maglite, its beam hooded with masking tape so that it would not attract attention if someone happened to look at the back of the house. Anmael's mark had been removed from the wall, probably in case reporters or the terminally curious took it upon themselves to take surreptitious photographs of the kitchen. The position in which Mickey Wallace had been found was still marked, and the cheap linoleum was stained with his dried blood. My beam picked up the kitchen cabinets, more modern than those that had been in the house when I lived there, yet also cheaper and flimsier, and the gas stove, now disconnected. There was no other furniture, apart from a single wooden chair, painted a sickly green, that stood against the far wall. Three people had died in this room. Nobody would ever live here again. The best thing for everyone would be to tear the house down and start afresh, but in the current climate that was unlikely to happen. And so it would fall further and further into decay, and children would dare one another to run into the yard and taunt its ghosts at Halloween.

But sometimes it is not places that are haunted, but people. I knew then why they had returned, those remnants of my wife and daughter. I think I had understood from the moment that Wallace's body was discovered here, and I sensed that he might not have been alone and uncomforted in his final moments, that whatever he had seen, or thought he had seen, while prowling around my property at Scarborough had come to him here in a different form. There was a sense of expectation about the house as I passed through the kitchen, and when I touched the handle on the door my fingertips tingled, as though a small electrical charge had just run through them.

The front door had been taped from the outside, but only the door lock and the security dead bolt held it closed from the inside. I opened them both and left the door slightly ajar. There was no wind, so it stayed as it was. I climbed the stairs and wandered through the empty rooms, a ghost among ghosts, and wherever I stopped I re-created our home in my mind, adding beds and closets, mirrors and pictures, transforming it from what it now was to what it once had been.

There was the shadow of a dressing table against the wall of the bedroom that Susan and I had once shared, and I brought it back, filling its surface with bottles and cosmetics, and a hairbrush with blond strands still caught in its bristles. Our bed returned, two pillows hard against the wall, an imprint of a woman's back upon them, as though Susan had only just absented herself. A book lay with its cover exposed on the bedsheet: lectures by the poet e.e. cummings. It was Susan's comfort book, cummings's descriptions of his life and work interspersed with a selection of poems, only some of them written by the poet himself. I could almost smell her perfume on the air.

Across the hallway was another, smaller bedroom, and as I watched, the vibrancy of its colors was restored, the dull, scarred walls becoming a clean vista of yellow and cream, like a summer meadow ringed with white flowers. The walls were covered mostly with hand-drawn pictures, although there was one large painting of a circus above the small single bed, and another smaller painting of a girl with a dog that was bigger than she was. The girl's arms were curled around the dog's neck, her face buried in its fur, and the dog stared out from the frame as if daring anyone to interfere with its charge. The bright blue sheets on the bed were pulled back, and I could see the outline of a small body against the mattress, and the dent in the pillow where, until seemingly only moments before, a child's head had rested. The carpet beneath my feet was a deep blue.

This was my home on the night that Susan and

Jennifer died, restored to me now as I felt them return, as they all drew closer, the dead and the living.

I heard a sound from downstairs and stepped into the hallway. The light in our bedroom flickered and then went out. Something shifted inside. I did not stop to see what it was, but I thought I saw, in the shadows, a figure moving, and a hint of scent came to me. I stopped at the top of the stairs, and I heard a sound from behind me, as of small, bare feet running across carpeted floors, a child moving from her room to be with her mother, but it might simply have been the boards settling beneath my feet, or a rat disturbed from its lair beneath the floor.

I descended.

At the bottom of the stairs, a poinsettia stood upon a small mahogany table, sheltered from drafts by the coat rack. It was the only houseplant that Susan had been able to keep alive, and she was immensely proud of it, checking it daily and being careful to keep it watered just enough so as not to drown it. On the night that they had died, it had been knocked from its stand, and the first thing that I saw when I entered the house was its roots lying amid scattered earth. Now it was as it had always been, cared for and loved. I reached out for it and my fingers passed through its leaves.

There was a man standing in the kitchen, close to the back door. As I watched, he moved forward a step and the moonlight filtering through the window caught his face.

Hansen. His hands were hidden in the pockets of his overcoat.

'You're a long way from home, detective,' I said.

'And you couldn't stay away from yours,' he replied. 'Must have changed a lot since then.'

'No,' I said. 'It hasn't changed at all.'

He looked puzzled.

'You're a strange man. I never understood you.'

'Well, I know now why you never liked me.'

But even as I said the words, I felt that something was wrong. This wasn't how it was supposed to be. Hansen didn't belong here.

A puzzled look came across his face, as if he had just realized the same thing. His body stretched, as if from a twinge at his back. He opened his mouth and a trickle of blood spilled from one corner. He coughed wetly, and more blood came, a cloud of it that sprayed the wall as he was pushed forward, collapsing to his knees. His right hand fumbled at his pocket as he tried to withdraw his gun, but his strength failed him and he fell flat on his stomach, his eyes half closed, his breathing growing shallower and shallower.

The man who had attacked him stepped over his body. He was in his mid twenties: twenty-six years old, to be exact about it. I knew, because I had hired him. I had worked alongside him in the Great Lost Bear. I had seen his kindness to customers, witnessed his easy way with the line chefs and the waitstaff.

And for all that time, he had kept his true nature hidden.

'Hello, Gary,' I said. 'Or do you prefer your other name?'

Gary Maser held the sharpened machete in one hand. In the other was a gun.

'It doesn't matter,' he said. 'They're just names. I've had more of them than you could imagine.'

'You're deluded,' I said. 'Somebody has been whispering lies to you. You're a nobody. You cut up Jimmy, and you killed Mickey Wallace in that kitchen back there, but that doesn't make you special. You're barely human, but that doesn't mean you're an angel.'

'Believe that if you like,' he said. 'It's of no consequence.'

But my words sounded hollow to me. I had chosen this place in which to confront what had been hunting me, transforming it in my mind to what it once was, but something in Gary Maser seemed to sense that, and respond to it. For an instant, I saw what my father had seen on that night in Pearl River before he pulled the trigger. I saw what had concealed itself within Maser, eating away at him until, at last, there was nothing left of him but an empty shell. His face became a mask, transparent and temporary: behind it, a dark mass moved, old and withered and filled with rage. Shadows curled around it like black smoke, polluting the room, fouling the moonlight, and I knew in my heart that more than my life was at risk here. Whatever torments Maser might inflict upon me in this house, they would be nothing compared with what was to come when my life was ended.

He took another step forward. Even in the moonlight, I could see that his eyes were blacker than I remembered, pupil and iris forming what appeared to be a single dark mass.

'Why me?' I asked. 'What have I done?'

'It is not only what you have done, but what you may do.'

'And what is that? How can you know what's to come?'

'We sensed the threat that you pose. *He* sensed it.'

'Who? Who sent you?'

Maser shook his head. 'No more,' he said, and then, almost tenderly, 'Time to stop running. Close your eyes, and I will bring all of your grief to an end.'

I tried to laugh. 'I'm touched by your concern.' I needed time. We all needed time. 'You've been patient,' I said. 'How long have you worked with me? Five months?'

'I was waiting,' he said.

'For what?'

He smiled, and his face changed. There was a radiance to it that had not been there before.

'For her.'

I turned slowly as I felt a draft at my back. In the now fully open doorway stood the dark-haired woman from the bar. Like Gary's, her eyes now seemed entirely black. She too held a gun, a .22. The shadows that formed around her were like dark wings against the night.

'So long,' she whispered, but her eyes were fixed on the man across from her, not on me. 'So very long . . .'

I understood then that they had come to this place separately, drawn by me and the promise of seeing each other again, but this was the first time they had met, the first time, if Epstein was to be believed, since my father had pulled the trigger on them at a patch of waste ground in Pearl River.

But suddenly the woman broke from her reverie and spun. The gun barked softly twice as she fired into the darkness. Maser, startled, seemed uncertain of what to do, and I knew then that he wanted me to die slowly. He wanted to use his blade on me. But as I moved, he fired the gun, and I felt the ferocious impact as the bullet hit my chest. I stumbled back, striking the door as I fell, and it struck the woman in the back but did not close. A second bullet hit me, and this time there was a searing pain at my neck. I raised my left hand to the wound, and blood pumped through my fingers.

I staggered up the stairs, but Maser's attention was no longer focused on me. There were voices at the back of the house, and he had turned to face the threat. I heard the front door slam shut and the woman screamed something as I reached the top of the stairs and threw myself flat on the floor as more shots came, carving a path through the dusty air above my head. My vision was blurring, and now that I was lying down I found myself unable to rise again. I crawled along the floor, using my right hand like a claw, pushing myself with my feet, my left hand still trying to stem the flow of blood from my neck. I drifted from past to present, so that at times I was moving along a carpeted hallway through clean, brightly lit rooms, and at others there were only bare boards and dust and decay.

There were footsteps coming up the stairs. I heard

firing from the kitchen below, but there was no gunfire in response. It was as though Maser were shooting at shadows.

I slipped into our old bedroom and managed to get to my feet using the wall as support, then stumbled through the ghost of a bed and slumped in a corner.

Bed. No bed.

The sound of water dripping from a faucet. No sound.

The woman appeared in the doorway. Her face was clearly visible in the light from the window behind me. She looked troubled.

'What are you doing?' she said.

I tried to answer, but I could not.

Bed. No bed. Water. Footsteps, but the woman had not moved.

She looked around, and I knew that she was seeing what I was seeing: worlds upon worlds.

'It won't save you,' she said. 'Nothing will.'

She advanced. As she did so, she ejected the spent clip and prepared to insert another, then stopped. She looked down to her left.

Bed. No bed. Water.

A little girl was beside her, and then another figure emerged from the shadows behind her: a woman with blond hair, her face now visible for the first time since I had found her in the kitchen, and where once there had been only blood and bone, there was now the wife I had loved as she was before the blade had finished its work upon her.

Light. No light.

An empty hallway. A hallway empty no longer.

'No,' whispered the dark-haired woman. She slammed the full clip home and tried to fire at me, but she seemed to be struggling to maintain her aim, as though she were being hampered by figures I could only half glimpse. A bullet struck the wall two feet to my left. I could barely keep my eyes open as I reached into my pocket and felt my palm close around the compact device. I withdrew it and pointed it at the woman as she wrenched her own weapon free at last, striking out with her left hand to repel what was behind her.

Bed. No bed. A woman falling. Susan. A little girl at Semjaza's side, tugging at her pants leg, clawing at her belly.

And Semjaza herself as she truly was, a thing hunched and dark, pink-skulled and winged: ugliness with a terrible remnant of beauty.

I raised my weapon. It looked like a flashlight to her.

'You can't kill me,' she said. 'Not with that.'

She smiled and raised her gun.

'Don't. Want. To,' I said, and fired.

The little Taser C2 couldn't miss from that range. The barbed electrodes caught her in the chest and she went down jerking as fifty thousand volts shot through her, the gun falling from her hand, her body twisting on the floor.

Bed. No bed.

Woman.

Wife.

Daughter.

Darkness.

35

I remember voices. I can recall the Kevlar vest being pulled from me, and someone pressing a gauze pad against the wound in my neck. I saw Semjaza struggling against her captors, and thought that I recognized one of the young men who had been with Epstein when we met earlier in the week. Someone asked me if I was okay. I showed them the blood on my hand, but did not speak.

'It didn't hit any arteries, or else you'd be dead by now,' said the same voice. 'It tore a hell of a furrow, but you'll live.'

They offered me a stretcher, but I refused. I wanted to stay on my feet. If I lay down, I was sure that I would lose consciousness again. As they helped me downstairs, I saw Epstein himself, kneeling beside the fallen Hansen as a pair of medics worked on him.

And I saw Maser, his arms behind his back, four Taser electrodes dangling from his body, Angel standing above him and Louis beside him. Epstein rose as I was brought down, and came to me. He touched my face with his hand, but said nothing.

'We need to get him to a hospital,' said one of the

men who was holding me up. There were sirens in the distance.

Epstein nodded, looked past me to the top of the stairs, then said, 'Just one moment. He'll want to see this.'

Two more men brought the woman down. Her hands were bound behind her with plastic restraints, and her legs were tied at the ankles. She was so light that they had lifted her off her feet, although she continued to try to fight them. While she did so, her lips moved and she whispered what sounded like an incantation. As she drew closer, I heard it clearly. What she said was:

'Dominus meus bonus et benignitas est.'

When they reached the bottom of the stairs, someone else took her legs, so that she was stretched horizontally between her captors. She looked to her right and saw Maser, but before she could speak, Epstein stepped between them.

'Foul,' he said as he gazed down upon her. She spit at him, and the sputum stained his coat. Epstein moved to one side, so that she could see Maser once again. He tried to rise, but Louis walked over to where he sat and placed a foot against his throat, forcing his head back against the wall.

'Go on, look at each other,' said Epstein. 'It will be the last time you ever meet.'

And as Semjaza realized what was about to happen, she began to scream the word 'No!' over and over, until Epstein forced a gag into her mouth as she was laid on a stretcher and secured. A blanket was placed over her, and she was carried from the house into a waiting ambulance that sped away without sirens or lights. I looked at Maser, and I saw desolation in his eyes. His lips moved, and I heard him whispering something repeatedly. I couldn't catch what he was saying, but I was sure that they were the same words spoken by his lover.

Dominus meus bonus et benignitas est.

Then one of Epstein's men appeared and jammed a hypodermic needle into Maser's neck, and within seconds his chin slumped to his chest, and his eyes closed.

'It's done,' said Epstein.

'Done,' I said, and at last I let them lay me down, and the light faded from my eyes.

Three days later, I met Epstein once again in the little diner. The deaf mute woman served us the same meal as before, then disappeared into the rear of the place and left us alone. Only then did we talk in earnest. We spoke of the events of that night, and of all that had transpired in the days preceding it, including my conversation with Eddie Grace.

'There is nothing that can be done about him,' said Epstein. 'Even if it could be proved that he had been involved, he would die before they could even get him out of the house.'

A cover story had been invented for the events at Hobart Street. Hansen was a hero. While shadowing me as part of an ongoing investigation, he had encountered an armed man who had attacked him with a blade. Although seriously injured, Hansen managed to fatally wound in turn his as-yet-unidentified assailant, who died on the way to the hospital. The blade was the same one that had been used to kill Mickey Wallace and Jimmy Gallagher. Blood traces on the hilt matched theirs. A photograph of the man in question had appeared in the newspapers as part of the police investigation. It bore no resemblance to Gary Maser. It bore no resemblance to any person, living or dead.

No mention was made of the woman. I didn't ask what had become of her, or her lover. I didn't want to know, but I could guess. They had been hidden away somewhere deep and dark, far from each other, and there they would rot.

'Hansen was one of us,' said Epstein. 'He'd been keeping tabs on you ever since you left Maine. He shouldn't have entered the house. I don't know why he did. Perhaps he saw Maser and decided to try to intercept him before he got to you. He's being kept in a medically induced coma for now. It's unlikely that he'll ever be able to return to his duties.'

'My secret friends,' I said, remembering the words that the Collector had spoken to me. 'I never figured Hansen for one of them. I must be lonelier than I thought.'

Epstein sipped his water. 'He was, perhaps, overzealous in ensuring that your activities were restricted. The decision to rescind your licenses was not his, but he was willing to enforce any decisions that were made. It was felt that you were drawing too much attention, and that you needed to be protected from yourself.'

'It helped that he didn't like me anyway.'

Epstein shrugged. 'He believed in the law. That was why we chose him.'

'And there are others?'

'Yes.'

'How many?'

'Not enough.'

'And now?'

'We wait. You'll get your investigator's license back, and your firearms permit will be restored to you. If we can't protect you from yourself, then I suppose that we have to give you the ability simply to protect yourself. There may be a price, though.'

'There always is.'

'An occasional favor, nothing more. You're good at what you do. The way will be smoothed with state police, local law enforcement, in the event that your involvement might prove useful. Consider yourself an adviser, an occasional consultant on certain matters.'

'And who is going to smooth the way? You, or another of my "friends"?'

I heard the door open behind me. I turned. SAC Ross entered, but he did not remove his coat, or join us at the table. Instead, he simply leaned against the counter of the deli, his hands entwined before him, and looked at me like a social worker forced to engage with a repeat offender of whom he is starting to despair.

'You've got to be kidding,' I said. 'Him?' Ross and I had history.

'Him,' said Epstein.

'Unit Five.'

'Unit Five.'

'With friends like that . . .'

'. . . one needs enemies to match,' finished Epstein.

Ross nodded. 'This doesn't mean that I'm your go-to guy every time you mislay your keys,' he said. 'You need to keep your distance.'

'That won't be hard.'

Epstein raised a placatory hand. 'Gentlemen, please.'

'I have another question,' I said.

'Absolutely,' said Epstein. 'Go ahead.'

'That woman was whispering something as she was carried away. Before I went out cold, I thought I saw Maser saying the same thing. It sounded like Latin.'

'*Dominus meus bonus et benignitas est*,' said Epstein. 'My master is good and kind.'

'Eddie Grace used almost those same words,' I said, 'except he said them in English. What does it mean? Some kind of prayer?'

'That, and perhaps more,' said Epstein. 'It's a play on words. A name has recurred over the course of many years. It's appeared in documents, records. At first we thought it was a coincidence, or a code of some kind, but now we believe that it's something else.'

'Like what?'

'We think that it's the name of the Entity, the controlling force,' said Epstein. '"My master is good and kind." "Good" and "kind." That's what they call the one whom they serve. They call him "Goodkind."'

'Mister Goodkind.'

* * *

It would be a long time before I learned of what passed between Ross and Epstein once I was gone, and only the silent woman kept them company in the dim light of the diner.

'Are you sure it's wise to let him roam?' asked Ross, as Epstein struggled to find the sleeve of his coat.

'We are not letting him roam,' replied Epstein. 'He's a tethered goat, even if he doesn't realize it. We simply have to wait, and see what comes to feed.'

'Goodkind?' asked Ross.

'Eventually, perhaps, if he truly exists,' said Epstein, finding at last his sleeve. 'Or if our friend lives long enough . . .'

I left New York that evening after performing one more service for the dead, this one long delayed. Beneath a simple marker in the corner of Bayside Cemetery, I laid flowers on the grave of a young woman and an unknown child, the final resting place of Caroline Carr.

My mother.

EPILOGUE

My heart asks for peace—
Day after day flies by, and every hour takes away
A little piece of life; but you and I, we two,
We contemplate living . . .

Aleksandr Pushkin (1799–1837), 'It's time, my friend, it's time'

I spent the rest of the week alone. I saw no one. I spoke to no one. I lived with my thoughts, and in the silence I tried to come to terms with all that I had learned.

On Friday night, I went to the Bear. Dave Evans was working the bar. I had already told him by phone that I was done with the job, and he had taken it well. I guess he knew that it would only be a matter of time. I had already received unofficial confirmation that my PI's license would be restored to me within days, just as Epstein had told me, and all objections to my license to carry had been withdrawn.

But that night, it was clear that Dave was swamped. The main bar area was jammed, so it was standing room only. I stepped aside to let Sarah pass by with a tray of beer orders in one hand, a stack of food orders in the other. She looked frazzled, which was unusual, but then I noticed that everybody else who was working did too.

'Gary Maser gave me twenty-four hours' notice, then left,' said Dave, as he juggled mixing a brandy Alexander with keeping an eye on three pints that were pouring simultaneously. 'Pity. I liked him. I figured he might stay on. Any idea what happened there?'

'None,' I said.

'Well, you hired him.'

'My mistake.'

'What the hell. It wasn't fatal.' He gestured at the dressing on my neck. 'Although that looks like it could have been. I guess I shouldn't ask.'

'You could ask, but I'd have to lie to you.'

One of the taps began to splutter and froth.

'Damn it all,' said Dave. He looked at me. 'Do a favor for an old friend?'

'I'm on it,' I said. I went in back and changed the keg. While I was there, two more ran down, so I changed those too. When I came back out, Dave was taking care of the service bar, which dealt with orders from the restaurant, and there were at least ten people waiting for drinks, and only one bartender to deal with them.

So, for one more night, I slipped back into my old role. I didn't mind. I knew now that I would be returning to what I did best, so I enjoyed working one last time for Dave, and quickly fell into all the old routines. Customers came in, and I remembered them by their orders even if I couldn't recall their names: Tanqueray Guy; Margarita Girl; five guys in their thirties who came in every Friday and always ordered five of the same beer, never once experimenting with some of the more exotic brews, so that their arrival was always known as the Charge of the Coors Light Brigade. The Fulci brothers arrived with Jackie

Garner in tow, and Dave contrived to look pleased to see them. He owed them for keeping reporters away from the bar after Mickey Wallace died, even if he suspected that their presence had scared off regular customers too. Now, though, they were sitting in a corner, eating burgers and knocking back Belfast Bay Lobster Red like men who were about to be returned to prison the next day, an experience with which the Fulcis were not unfamiliar.

And so the evening passed.

Eddie Grace woke to the sound of a match being struck in the darkness of his bedroom. The drugs had dulled the pain some, but they had also dulled his senses, so that he struggled for a moment to figure out what time it was, and why he was awake. He thought that he might have dreamed the sound. After all, nobody in the house smoked.

Then a cigarette flared red and a figure shifted in the easy chair to his left; he caught a glimpse of a man's face. He looked thin and unhealthy, his hair slicked back from his head, his fingernails long and, it seemed, nicotine tinged with yellow. His clothes were dark. Even in his own stinking sickbed, Eddie could smell the dankness of him.

'What are you doing here?' said Eddie. 'Who are you?'

The man leaned forward. In his hand he was holding an old police whistle on a silver chain. It had belonged to Eddie's father, and had been passed on to him when the old man retired.

'I like this,' said the stranger, dangling the whistle by its chain. 'I think I'll add it to my collection.'

Eddie's right hand sought the alarm that summoned Amanda to him. It would ring in her bedroom, and she or Mike would come. His finger pressed down on the button, but he heard nothing.

'I took the trouble of disconnecting that,' said the man. 'You won't be needing it anymore.'

'I asked what you were doing here,' Eddie croaked. He was frightened now. It was the only appropriate response in the face of this man's presence. Everything about him was wrong. Everything.

'I'm here to punish you for your sins.'

'For my sins?'

'For betraying your friend. For putting his son at risk. For the death of Caroline Carr. For the girls that you hurt. I'm here to make you pay for all of them. You have been judged, and found wanting.'

Eddie laughed hollowly. 'Fuck you,' he said. 'Look at me. I'm dying. Every day I'm in pain. What can you do to me that hasn't been done already?'

And suddenly the whistle was replaced by a sliver of sharp metal as the man rose and leaned over Eddie, and Eddie thought that he saw other figures crowding behind him, men with hollow eyes and dark mouths who were both there and not there.

'Oh,' whispered the Collector, 'I'm sure I can think of something . . .'

By midnight, the bar was almost empty. The weather report had promised more snow after midnight, and most people had opted to leave early rather than risk driving in a blizzard. Jackie and the Fulcis still sat, bottles racked up before them, but the rest of the customers in the restaurant area were already standing and putting on their coats. Two men at the far end of the bar called for their check, wished me good night, and then departed, leaving only one other drinker at the counter. She had been with a group of Portland cops earlier in the evening, but when they had gone she had stayed, taking a book from her bag and reading it quietly. Nobody bothered her. Although she was small and dark and pretty, she gave off a vibe, and even the International Players of the World kept their distance from her. Still, she looked familiar to me from somewhere. It took me a moment or two, and then I had it. She glanced up and saw me staring at her.

'It's okay,' she said. 'I'm leaving.'

'You don't have to,' I replied. 'The staff usually stay on for a drink, maybe something to eat, on Friday nights. You're not in anybody's way.'

I indicated the glass of red wine at her right hand. There was only a single mouthful left.

'Fill that up for you?' I asked. 'It's on the house.'

'Isn't that illegal after hours?'

'You going to report me, Officer Macy?'

Her nose wrinkled. 'You know who I am?'

'Read about you in the papers, and I've seen you around some. You were involved in that business out on Sanctuary.'

'As were you.'

'Only at the edges.' I reached out a hand. 'My friends call me Charlie.'

'Mine call me Sharon.'

We shook hands.

'Shaving cut?' she asked, pointing at my neck.

'I have an unsteady hand,' I said.

'Bad news for a bartender.'

'That's why I quit. Tonight's a favor for an old friend.'

'What will you do instead?'

'What I used to do. They took away my license for a time. Soon, I'll have it back.'

'Evildoers beware,' she said. There was a smile on her face, but her eyes were serious.

'Something like that.'

I replaced her glass with a clean one, and filled it with the best California we had in the house.

'Will you join me?' she said, and when she spoke those words they seemed to promise, at some point in the future, more than a drink in a dimly lit bar.

'Sure,' I said. 'It would be a pleasure.'

ACKNOWLEDGMENTS

I am immensely grateful to a number of people who gave generously of their time, and their knowledge, when it came to the research for this book. In particular, I would like to thank Peter English, formerly of the Ninth Precinct in New York, who brought its streets to life for me, and without whom this book would be much poorer. Dave Evans and all the staff at The Great Lost Bear (www.greatlostbear.com), the best bar in Portland, Maine, were immensely hospitable, and willing to give a job to a detective who was down on his luck. My thanks also to Joe Long, Seth Kavanagh, Christina Guglielmetti, Clair Lamb (www.answer-girl.net), Mark Hall, and Jane and Shane Phalen, all of whom helped me to mask my ignorance at various stages in the writing. Any mistakes are my own, and I apologize for them.

Books and articles that proved useful include *New York: An Illustrated History* by Ric Burns and James Sanders, with Lisa Ades (Alfred A. Knopf, 1999); *The Columbia Guide to America in the 1960s* by David Farber and Beth Bailey (Columbia University Press, 2001); *The Sixties: Years of Hope, Days of Rage* by Todd Gitlin (Bantam, 1993); *The Movement and the*

Sixties: Protest in America from Queensboro to Wounded Knee by Terry H. Anderson (Oxford University Press, 1995); *The Neighborhoods of Brooklyn*, John B. Manbeck, Consulting Editor (Yale University Press, 1998); and 'Spider manipulation by a wasp larva' (*Nature*, Vol. 406, 20 July, 2000).

Thank you to Sue Fletcher, my editor at Hodder & Stoughton in London, and the staff at Hodder; to Emily Bestler, my editor at Atria in New York, and everyone at Atria and Simon and Schuster; to my agent, Darley Anderson, and his wonderful team; and to Madeira James (www.xuni.com) and Jayne Doherty, who look after my Web site but whose kindness and support go far beyond that. I would be lost without you all.

Finally, much love to Jennie, Cameron, and Alistair, who have to put up with all the behind-the-scenes stuff.

JOHN CONNOLLY ON THE PARKER NOVELS:

'Since about the second book I've thought of the Parker novels as a sequence rather than a series, in that each book develops themes, ideas and plots from the preceding books.'

Although each novel is self-contained, and can be enjoyed as a compelling thriller, collectively the Parker novels form a rich and involving epic sequence in which characters reappear and clues laid down in earlier stories are solved in later ones. Here is a précis of key events in each of the Charlie Parker novels.

Former NYPD Charlie Parker first appears in **Every Dead Thing** on a quest for the killer of his wife and daughter. He is a man consumed by violence, guilt and the desire for revenge. When his ex-partner asks him to track down a missing girl, Parker embarks on a grim odyssey through the bowels of organised crime; to cellars of torture and death; and to a unique serial killer, an artist who uses the human body as his canvas: The Travelling Man. By the end of the novel, Parker realises he is at the beginning of another dark journey – to avenge the voiceless victims of crime: the poor, women and children. It is a journey on which his dead wife and child will be constant ghostly companions.

In **Dark Hollow,** Parker returns to the wintry Maine landscape where he grew up and becomes embroiled in another murder hunt. The chief suspect is Billy Purdue, the ex-husband of the dead woman, and Parker is not the only one on his trail. Aided by his friends, hitmen Angel and Louis (first encountered in **Every Dead Thing**), Parker must go back thirty years into his own grandfather's troubled past and into the violent origins of a mythical killer, the monster Caleb Kyle. Parker's personal life seems to take an upward turn in the attractive form of psychologist Rachel Wolfe.

Parker's empathy with the powerless victims of crime is growing ever stronger. It makes him a natural choice to investigate the death of Grace Peltier in **The Killing Kind** – a death that appears to be a suicide. The discovery of a mass grave – the final resting place of a religious community that had disappeared forty years earlier – convinces Parker that there is a link between Grace and these deaths: a shadowy organisation called The Fellowship. His investigation draws him into increasingly violent confrontations with the Fellowship's enforcer, the demonic arachnophile, Mr Pudd. Genial killers Angel and Louis join Parker again as he descends into a honeycomb world populated by dark angels and lost souls.

Parker's relationship with Rachel reaches a new level in **The White Road**, but he is still driven to solve the most challenging of cases. A black youth faces the death penalty for rape and murder; his victim, the daughter of one of the wealthiest men in South Carolina. It is a case with its roots in old evil, and old evil is Charlie Parker's speciality. But this turns out not to be an investigation, but rather a descent into the abyss, a confrontation with dark forces that threaten all Parker holds dear.

Evil men from his past unite to exact a terrible revenge on the private detective. Seemingly unconnected events turn out to be part of a complex and intricate pattern.

The Killing Kind and **The White Road** effectively form two halves of a single, larger narrative and are probably best read in order.

In 'The Reflecting Eye', a long novella featured in the **Nocturnes** collection, Parker becomes involved in a curious investigation into a former killer's abandoned house, and learns that someone, or something, seems be using its empty rooms as a base from which to hunt for victims. This novella introduces us for the first time to the character known as the Collector, an individual who will come to play an important, and sinister, role in the books that follow, most particularly in **The Unquiet** and **The Lovers**.

The Black Angel is not an object; it is not a myth. The Black Angel lives. And it is a prize sought for centuries by evil men. Not that Charlie Parker's latest case starts this way; it starts with the disappearance of a young woman in New York. Her abductors believe that no one will come looking for her, but they are wrong. For Alice is 'blood' to Parker's sidekick, the assassin Louis, and Louis will tear apart anyone who attempts to stop him finding her.

The hunt turns into an epic quest that will take Parker and his team to an ornate church of bones in Eastern Europe and a cataclysmic battle between good and evil. It marks a dawning realisation in Parker that there is another dimension to his crusade, a dangerous dimension that Rachel finds herself increasingly unable to live with.

The Unquiet begins with a missing man, a once respected psychiatrist who went absent following revelations about harm done to children in his care. His daughter believes him dead, but is not allowed to come to terms with her father's legacy. For someone is asking questions about Daniel Clay: the revenger Merrick, a father and a killer obsessed with discovering the truth about his own daughter's disappearance. Living apart from Rachel and their child, Charlie Parker is hired to make Merrick go away, but finds strange bonds with the revenger, who has drawn from the shadows pale wraiths drifting through the ranks of the unquiet dead. At the end of the novel comes a tantalising reference to Parker's own parentage that will inform events in **The Lovers.**

But first Angel and Louis take centre stage in **The Reapers,** where the elite killers themselves become targets. A wealthy recluse sends them north to a town that no longer exists on a map. A town ruled by a man with very personal reasons for wanting Louis' blood spilt. There they find themselves trapped, isolated and at the mercy of a killer feared above all others: the assassin of assassins, Bliss. Thanks to Parker, help is on its way. But can Angel and Louis stay alive long enough for it to reach them?

The bloody events in **The Unquiet** result in Parker losing his PI licence, so he returns to Maine and takes a job in a Portland bar while the fuss dies down. But **The Lovers** shows Parker engaged on his most personal case yet: an investigation into his own origins and the circumstances surrounding the death of his father. When he was a boy, Parker's father, himself a cop, killed a pair of teenagers then took his own life. His actions were never explained. Parker's quest for that explanation reveals lies, secrets and betrayal. Haunting it – as they have done all his life – are two figures in the shadows, an unidentified man and woman with one purpose: to bring an end to Parker's existence.

Look out for the next instalment, **The Whisperers,** to be published in May 2010.